THE
HAUNTED
MESA

Also available in Large Print
by Louis L'Amour:

Bowdrie's Law
Jubal Sackett
Passin' Through
Ride the River
Riding for the Brand
Dutchman's Flat
The Walking Drum

THE HAUNTED MESA

LOUIS L'AMOUR

G.K. HALL & CO.
Boston, Massachusetts
1988

Published in Large Print by arrangement with
Bantam Books, Inc.

Maps by Alan McKnight.

G.K. Hall Large Print Book Series.

Set in 16 pt Plantin.

Library of Congress Cataloging in Publication Data

L'Amour, Louis, 1908–
    The haunted mesa.

    (G.K.Hall large print book series)
    1. Large type books.   I. Title.
[PS3523.A446H3   1988]   813'.52   87-25143
ISBN 0-8161-4362-5   (lg. print)
ISBN 0-8161-4363-3 (pbk. : lg. print)

To Gilbert and Charlotte Wenger

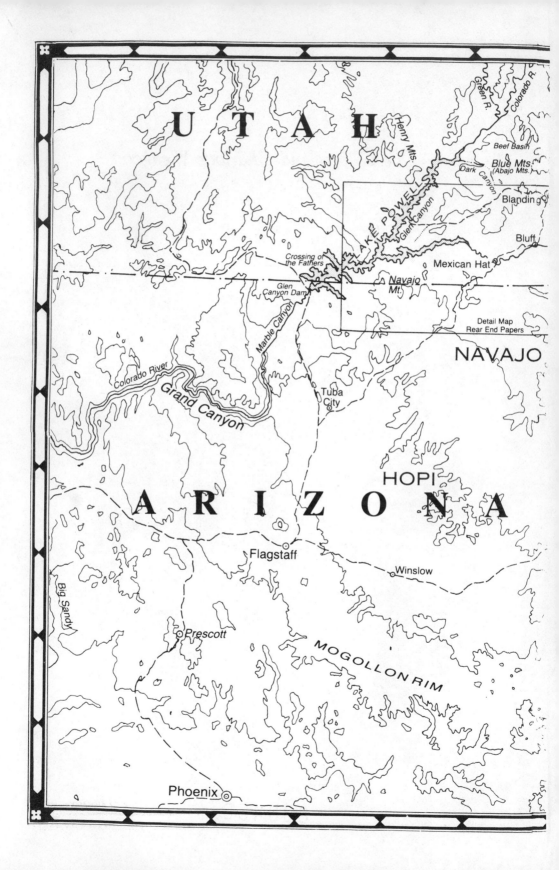

La Sal
Mts.

COLORADO

Monticello

Dove
Creek

Silverton

SAN JUAN MOUNTAINS

La Plata Mts.

Rio Grande

ovenweep

Parrott City

Vallecito R.

Tamarron

Durango

Ute
Mt.

Mesa
Verde

Eagle's
Nest

UTE

San Juan River

anyon
Chelly

Chaco
Canyon

ZUNI   N E W

Santa Fe

M E X I C O

FOUR CORNERS
SOUTHWESTERN U.S.
Contour interval 3000 feet
Scale of Miles

| 0 | 10 | 20 | 30 | 40 | 50 | 60 |

Rio Grande

Plains of
St. Augustine

Bat Cave

APACHE

Rio Grande

Alan McKnight

I

IT WAS NIGHT, and he was alone upon the desert. It had been over an hour since he had seen another car, a Navajo family in a pickup.

He shivered. What was the matter with him? Ever since leaving the highway he had felt a growing uneasiness. Had he not traveled hundreds of lonely roads before this? Or was it that old memory, haunting him still?

Yet why should that be so? It was only a story told by an old man at a lunch counter, and he had heard many such stories and spent a good part of his life proving them to be illusions, fabrications, or misunderstood phenomena. Why had that one story clung to his memory? Was it the old man himself?

He drove slowly, watching for the turnoff he had been warned would be hard to find. The road was a mere trail among low sandhills, with the dark outlines of square-edged mesas looming gainst the sky.

Of course, Erik Hokart's letter was a part of it. That letter had come from a badly frightened man,

1

and no man he had ever known was more cool, concise, and self-sufficient than Erik Hokart.

There was no sound but that of the car itself, nothing to see but that narrow avenue of light carved by the headlights through a tunnel of darkness.

He leaned forward, peering into the night, trying to see the turnoff in time. On impulse he pulled over and stopped, shutting off the motor and the lights.

He sat very still in the darkness, listening. Listening for what?

With the lights out, the desert was gray tufted with black spots of desert growth. Here and there loomed tall columns, and one rocky mass shaped like a pipe organ.

It was absolutely still. How rarely, he thought, can modern man experience a total silence! Yet the desert had it to offer, as well as the high mountains.

Opening the car door he stepped out into the chill night air, but he did not close the door behind him. The sound would have seemed like an obscenity in this all-pervading stillness. A step away from the car, he stood listening.

What he hoped to hear was the approaching sound of Erik's four-wheel-drive vehicle. No doubt he was still too far away. Somewhere in the canyon ahead, Erik had suggested.

To the westward lay a long mesa, stark and black against the sky. That would be the one Erik had mentioned in his letter. It was also the one he himself remembered. Almost ten miles long and some two thousand feet high, the last three hundred to five hundred feet sheer rock. Had he ever mentioned to Erik his knowledge of that mesa?

As he turned back to the car, something flared at the corner of his eye. Turning quickly, startled, he stared at the flare on the mesa's dark rim.

For a space of what must have been thirty seconds it flared, changed color slightly, then vanished.

He stared at the end of the mesa where the light had appeared. A campfire was unlikely at that height, and in that location.

A crashed plane? He had heard no sound of motors, no explosion, seen nothing except that odd flare.

Puzzled and more than a little disturbed, he got back into his car, and a half mile further he found the turnoff for which he was watching. He turned down a sandy slope and drove along the bottom of a dry wash. From here on, he had been advised, it would be rough going, even for a four-wheel drive, but he had a shovel in the back of the car and some steel mesh he could unroll ahead if necessary. Many desert roads followed washes but he had never liked them. This was not the season for flash floods and the skies were clear, but flash floods had a way of happening when least expected. Long ago, when only a teenager, he had watched a man lose all he had in just such a flood.

The man had given him a lift, and it was raining hard in the mountains. They had reached a wash and he warned the driver it was not safe. The man had merely smiled tolerantly and started across the wide wash. Unhappily, about two thirds of the way across, they stuck in the sand. Working to free the car, they almost missed hearing the roar of the oncoming waters.

A strange coolness touched their faces, and startled, they looked up. A wall of water, no less than eight feet high with great logs riding its crest, was sweeping around a bend of the narrower canyon.

The rush of water struck the canyon wall at the bend, throwing spray fifty feet into the air. For one frozen instant they stared, and then they ran.

The rushing wall of water was a good two hundred yards off, and they were less than thirty yards from the nearest bank. They beat the flood by half a step.

Turning, they looked back at the wash, running bank-full. He remembered the shocked and empty look on the man's face.

He had said, "This will run off in half an hour or less, but you'd better forget your car. There will be nothing left but twisted metal with sand all through the engine block."

"All I had was in that car," the man replied.

That had been a long time ago but he had saved his battered valise, although it contained only two worn pairs of blue jeans, some shirts, socks, and underwear. In those days he had always carried his razor and his comb in his pocket.

The wash down which he now drove showed evidence of more than one such flood. Brush and debris were piled against rocks and trees, some of it quite recent. In this country you worried when there were clouds over the mountains; in the Kunluns bordering Tibet on the north, you worried when the skies were clear, for on such days in that clear, thin air the hot sun melted the snows high in the mountains, and flash floods roared down the canyons when there was not a cloud in the sky.

Leaning forward, he peered at the mesa rim, but all was dark. The track he followed now split into several and he chose the one most followed. He swung wide around a big old cottonwood, a sure sign of ground water, and drove down the narrow alley of light, then to the crest of a low sandy hill. Getting out, he stood beside the car and listened into the night.

Irritably, he reflected that Erik could at least have met him halfway. He was tired and in no mood to prowl through this lonely country in the night.

Erik had suggested they meet on the Canyon road—which was so indefinite as to be totally unlike Erik. He himself had suggested they meet at Jacob's Monument, a monolith of stone they both knew and unlike any formation close by.

"No!" Erik had said. "Not there! Especially not there!"

That was during their last telephone conversation, at least a month ago, when they had first talked of his coming for a visit. Three weeks later had come the letter, hastily scrawled, a desperate plea for help.

He glanced around uneasily, then backed up against the car. It was a lonely, eerie place. . . . No sooner had the thought come than he brushed it aside. Odd, how that old story had stuck in his mind, always lurking in the shadows of his memory, demanding to be recognized yet repeatedly brushed aside.

The trouble was, the story would not be dismissed, and no doubt a good part of his career since then had been influenced by it. Yet when he had first discussed this country with Erik he had not mentioned the story. Erik knew the country only from having flown over it in passing from New York or Chicago to Los Angeles, and he was not the sort of man to listen to such a tale with anything but impatience.

Mike Raglan had been nineteen when he first heard the story, and only two weeks later he had seen No Man's Mesa for the first time.

He had been employed in the old Katherine Mine near the Colorado River when the decision was made to cease operations for a while. Four of them had been sitting on the station at the 300 level discussing what to do next. They were eating their lunches with small appetite, as they would now be out of work and jobs were scarce. He had commented that he did not know where he would go.

"Why not ride along with me?" Jack had suggested. "I've some claims up on the Vallecito and

I must do the assessment work. There are mines around Durango and at Silverton and you might find a job." With nothing better in sight, Mike Raglan agreed.

Jack was a machineman and had been running a stoper on the same shift with him for several months. He was a congenial, easygoing man of sixty or more with memories of the great days at Goldfield, Tonopah, Randsburg, and Cripple Creek. He had grown up in the Four Corners area and his grandmother had been a Paiute. He spoke the language well.

They had driven to Flagstaff and then to Tuba City. Farther along somewhere they had turned into an old trail for Navajo Mountain.

There were few places Jack hesitated to go with his old car. Its high center enabled it to straddle rocks that would have disabled a later model. He carried a kit of tools, a spare fanbelt, and odds and ends of nuts, bolts, and baling wire, as well as an axe, shovel, and saw. There were always a couple of five-gallon cans of gasoline, one of water, and a roll of steel mesh used in crossing deep sand. There was literally no place he would not go when traveling or prospecting.

They had been eating supper in a greasy spoon restaurant in Flagstaff when they met the old cowboy. He was an acquaintance of Jack's from years past.

"Know this country," he said to Mike. "When I was your age I cowboyed all over. Rode for the Hashknife an' the French outfit. Then I taken to huntin' for the Lost Adams gold. Found color here an' there, made a livin'. Punched cows around Winslow and down on the Big Sandy. Then I come back to this country an' prospectin' again."

He peered at Mike. "You're young. Years ahead of you. You prospectin'?"

"I'm rustling a job. Jack an' me worked together down Arizona way."

"Remind me of m'self when I was your age. Full o' dreams o' what I'd do if I struck it rich. Well, I never got rich but I did make a good livin'. Found me a good woman, too. Still got her. Got enough to last our years." He sized Mike up. "You got nerve, boy? You easy skeered?"

"About the same as most."

"He's got sand," Jack interrupted. "Seen him in action. He's a scrapper and a damn good one." Jack got up. "I'm turnin' in, Mike. We'll pull out at daybreak."

"I'll finish my coffee," Mike said.

The old man filled the cups, then leaned back in the booth and looked at Mike. "Boy, I'm eighty-eight m' last birthday. I can ride as good as ever but I can't climb. Don't want to, anyways. Like I said, we got enough put by, me an' my woman. We lost a boy. Never had no others.

"Never told my story to anybody. Never felt no call to, an' didn't want to be called a liar. Folks always figured I'd struck me a pocket, an' I surely did." He chuckled. "Only it weren't raw gold but ree-fined gold. Pure! I found some all right an'

8

there's aplenty where it came from if'n you aren't skeered of ha'nts and the like.

"Eighty-eight, that's what I am, an' my woman's almost as old. No way you figure it do I have much time left. I never told my own boy. I was skeered for him. Never told nobody until now an' I'm fair itchin' to get it off my chest before I go.

"But I'm warnin' you, boy—git you some gold an' git out. Don't try to stay, an' once out, for God's sake don't try to go back!

"They never knowed what I found. They hunted me, but believe me, nobody's goin' to trail this here coon across no desert. *Nobody!*

"They never knowed who it was got through an' I fought shy of that country ever since. I tell you, boy, there's things about this world nobody knows. That there desert now, them mountains around Navajo an' east of there?

"That's wild country, boy! *Wild!* There's places yonder you see one time an' they never look the same again. There's canyons no man has seen the end of, nor ever will, either, unless they get through to the Other Side."

"The other side?"

"That's what I said, boy. The Other Side. Folks are forever sayin' there's two sides to everythin'.

"Well, why should there be only two sides? Why not three sides or even four? I don't know nothin'. I don't even claim to know, only I stumbled onto somethin' mighty strange out yonder. I figured on it some an' I spent some months just a-watchin' an' layin' low. I ain't claimin' I know how it works, but I know *when!* I don't know what causes it, or how such things can be, but it worked one time for me. Trouble is, they *knew!* Somehow, they *knew.* Only by the time they got there I was gone, an' I stayed gone!"

He took a swallow of coffee, wiped the back of his hand across his mustache, and said, "I'm goin' to give you a map. It's on canvas an' I made it my ownself. Only part of it was copied from a gold plate on a wall. That part I know nothin' about. I copied it, figurin' it was the key to somethin', I don't know what."

"You found pure gold? Was it high-grade? Jewelry rock?"

"It was ree-fined gold, boy. Discs, like. Size of a saucer. An' there was cups, dishes, an' the like o' that, besides."

Mike Raglan remembered the evening. He liked the story but he was a skeptic. The West was filled with stories of buried treasure and lost mines, treasures whose value increased as prices inflated. Years ago the treasures had been worth thirty or sixty thousand dollars, but all figures had become astronomical, so the value of hidden treasures had inflated as well. Thirty million was a popular figure nowadays.

If even half the stories were true, a large part of the population must have been engaged in burying treasure and losing mines. Outlaws were popularly supposed to have buried their loot when most of them couldn't spend it fast enough. Most of them spent their loot on wine, women, and song, al-

10

though there's not much record that they wasted much time singing.

"I've got a map. . . ."

Here it was, the pitch. The map of the hidden gold would be sold only to him, for X number of dollars. Well, he'd heard that pitch before and still had his first map to buy.

"How much?"

"Ain't for sale. Not for any price. I aim to *give* it to you, son, but I'll warn you. I'm givin' you grief. Least you do as I did. Study it, learn it well, then make your move an' get out. There's no other way."

The old man was silent as he refilled the cups. "I got to warn you about that country, boy. I been there twenty, thirty times, maybe. Just when you think you know it, somehow it's all twisted all bally-which-way. You stand where you stood before but *nothin'* looks the same.

"Nothin' even *feels* the same. Did you ever wake up in the night an' find everythin' out of kilter? The door seems in the wrong place? Everythin' switched around? Well, that country can be that way, only it doesn't stay that way for minutes—it's like that for *hours!*"

He paused, staring out into the night's darkness. "You listen to me, boy. You do like I done. When that country seems all catty-corner-wise, you stay where you're at. Don't you *move!* Don't let nobody get you down into that crazy, twisted-up country!

"Three, maybe four times in thirty years I seen

11

it. Each time I had sense to stay right where I was.

"I had me an ol' burro them days. Canny beast! Follered it over mesa an' canyon for nigh thirty years. It was that ol' burro learned me. With green grass an' water right down the slope, that ol' burro wouldn't take a step! I pushed him one time, tol' him not to be such a damn fool, but he jus' laid back his ears an' wouldn't move!"

He reached into an inside pocket and brought out a piece of canvas, opening it on the table. "There she be. This here is Navajo Mountain. Nobody's goin' to miss that. Biggest thing around, an settin' right in the middle of some of the roughest country you ever did see. Canyons so deep you have to look twice to see the bottom. You look as far as you can see, then you start from there an' look again.

"That squiggly line? That's the San Juan River. Empties into the Colorado. Most of the time she flows in the bottom of a canyon. There's a trail leads from Navajo goin' east. Mighty rough."

"That's the way we're headed."

"Keep goin', son. Just don't stop. You keep a-goin'."

II

THE OLD COWBOY put his finger on a mesa, carefully drawn on the canvas map. "That's the place to fight shy of. You're gettin' into cliff-dweller

12

country but you won't find any up there. Them old Injuns was *smart!* They wanted no part of that place!

"But it ain't just that one spot. There's forty or fifty square miles of country it's best to leave alone. Not to say I was never there. I got in there a time or two. There was an old Injun, a fine old man. Knowed him for years before he said anything to me about that there place.

"He said there was a 'way,' whatever that meant, but all those who knew how to use it were gone. It was a clan secret an' the clan died out. Or was killed off by somebody who wanted the 'way' kept secret."

He pushed the canvas toward Mike Raglan. "Stick this inside your shirt an' never let anybody know you got it. There's those would kill to get their hands on it, and it would serve them right. That's why I never told nobody until now.

"I'm an old man, boy. I seen the sun set over that red rock country many's the time. I seen men go into that country who never came back. I've knowed others who come back stark ravin' mad, memory gone an' their wits along with it.

"There's another world over there somewheres. At least there's a way to get to it. Like them Spanish men in their iron suits. They *seen* the Seven Cities of Cibola. They *really* seen 'em! They weren't lookin' at any pueblos with the sun on 'em. They just happened to see through the veil. Somehow it was open then and they seen right through and never got over what they seen!

13

"They are there, boy! I seen 'em, too! But there's evil over there, evil like you an' me can't even imagine. It was that ancient evil that drove the cliff dwellers into this world, comin' through, as they said it, a hole in the ground.

"In their kivas, their ceremonial centers, there's what they call a *sipapu*. It's a hole in the floor that symbolizes how they escaped from the evil. But that evil is still over there, son, an' don't you forget it!"

That had been a long time ago, and Mike Raglan had told the story to no one, not even to Erik Hokart. Yet he had warned Erik about the country. He had advised him to forget it, to choose any other place, but Hokart would not listen.

Later, on that same early trip, he had mentioned the mesa to Jack. "No Man's Mesa," the old miner said. "We camp near there tomorrow night, if we're lucky." He shook his head. "There's not much in the way of roads—some trails and wagon routes the Navajos use. I been through there a-horseback but never with a car. You may have to walk ahead an' scout a route, roll rocks out of the way and such. It's mighty rough country."

"Know anything about that mesa?"

Jack was a long time in replying. Finally he shrugged. "Just a big chunk of rock, talus slopes, sheer rock around the rim. Kind of out-of-the-way and nobody pays it much mind."

Indicating one of Jack's Paiute friends, Mike

suggested: "Ask him if he knows anything about it."

Jack waved a hand, his manner just a little too casual. "Nothing to ask, and don't look for it on a map. Chances are they'll have it in the wrong place, even in the wrong state."

"I am curious."

"Ask a Hopi then. They've been here forever. My advice is to forget it."

"I want to climb it. See what's on top."

"You're crazy, Mike. Let well enough alone."

Climb it he had, but that was another story and too long ago. He had covered a lot of country since then, had grown older and, he hoped, wiser.

He got back in the car and locked the doors, then leaned his head back. He was tired, really tired. Where the devil was Erik? All he wanted now was a quiet meal and his bed at Tamarron. No, he would settle for the bed. He could eat tomorrow.

He sat up, started the car, and drove slowly, carefully along the road toward the San Juan. The long mesa from which he had seen the flare towered over him now, dark and threatening. The northern tip of the mesa loomed against the sky like the prow of a giant ship.

Peering ahead he could see the gleam of water. That would be the San Juan River, or water backed up by Glen Canyon Dam. He had not been in this country since the dam was built. He started to get out of the car, then paused, taking time to thread his belt through the holster loop and buckle up

15

again. He wore the holster on his left side, situated for a cross-draw or a left-hand draw if necessary.

Often he climbed into high, relatively inaccessible places and habitually carried the gun as a protection against an inadvertent meeting with a bear or mountain lion. The chance of such an encounter was slight, but after one near brush with a lion he had gone prepared. He had no desire to kill anything nor did he have any desire to be a chance victim. The gun had a reassuring feel. He stepped down from the car and closed the door softly behind him.

With the sound there was a scurry of movement off in the dark, a rattle of pebbles, then silence. His hand on his gun, he waited.

He was not the sort to shoot at any sound, nor at anything he could not identify, but the movement disturbed him. It might have been a coyote but his impression was of something larger.

For a long time he waited. It was unlike Erik Hokart, who was meticulous about keeping appointments. He paced the road near the car. It was cold, as desert nights were apt to be. He put his hand on the door handle. Suddenly, from the edge of the mesa towering above him, there was a brilliant flare. Only a momentary flash, yet for that instant it shed a white radiance all around, and then, just as suddenly, it was gone.

In the utter darkness that followed, the desert seemed to scurry with life. He glimpsed vaguely a rush of naked figures, and something smashed hard into the side of his car. He turned sharply and for an instant stared into the wide, expression-less eyes of a naked creature. It seemed not to see him at all, but scrambled around his car and ran off into the night, leaving behind a heavy fetid odor as of something dead.

Then the creatures—or men, or whatever they were—vanished into the night and he was alone. Only the odor lingered.

There were far-off retreating sounds, then silence. He shuddered, then got quickly into his car and closed the door, locking it.

It had happened so suddenly there had been no chance for fear. Shaken, he turned the car about and drove back to Tamarron, where he was staying.

The drive was long and day was breaking before he drew up in front of the lodge. Leaving the motor running, he went to the desk for his mail before driving on to the condominium. There was a handful of letters and a small packet wrapped in brown paper and tied with string. It bore no stamps and no postmark.

He recognized the handwriting and turned back to the desk clerk. "When did this come? Were you here when it was delivered?"

"It was about ten o'clock last night. I asked if she wanted me to inquire whether you were in or not, but she shook her head. She just put the package on the counter, looked at me strangely, then turned away. When she got to the door she turned and looked around—not just at me, at everything."

"You seem to have paid attention."

She flushed. "Well . . . she was strange, some-how."

"Strange?"

"She was very beautiful, exotic-looking. Like nobody around here. I thought at first she was an Indian, but not like any I ever knew. But it was the way she *looked* at me, but not really at *me*, at my face, my hair, my clothes."

"Why not? You're an attractive girl."

"It wasn't that. She looked at me like she had never seen anyone or anything that looked like me. I mean that, seriously."

Once at the condominium he tossed the packet on the bed, and his .357 magnum alongside it. The important thing now was rest. The long flight from New York, the resulting jet lag, and the long drives at night had him ready for collapse.

He was getting into bed when the telephone rang.

"Mr. Raglan?" It was the girl at the desk. "I thought you had better know. There was a man in here just now asking for that package you picked up. He said he was to deliver it to you."

"What did you tell him?"

"That you had picked it up, of course. Then he asked where the girl was who delivered it." She paused. "Mr. Raglan, you will think me a fool, but he frightened me. I have no idea why, but something about him frightened me."

"What about the girl?"

"He . . . I didn't like him, Mr. Raglan, and I

18

am afraid I lied. I told him I saw no girl, that it was a man who brought it."

"And . . . ?"

"You should have seen his face! It was livid! A *man?* He yelled it, Mr. Raglan, and then he rushed outside and got into a van."

"Thank you for telling me."

"I hope I didn't do anything wrong."

"You couldn't have handled it better. Thank you."

For a moment he stood by the bar, thinking. Maybe he had lived too long with doubts and suspicions, but at this point he had no idea what was going on or how Erik was involved, if at all. Until he knew more he must move with caution. Erik was, he gathered, in serious trouble, but what kind of trouble? And over what? What kind of trouble could a man get into in the desert, miles from anyone?

Opening the packet he discovered what he had half-expected to discover, Erik Hokart's daybook. Erik had long kept a record of his work when a step-by-step record of an experiment might be very important indeed. Tossing the book to the bed, he took up a copy of an Eric Ambler mystery he had finished reading and rewrapped it with the same paper and string, leaving it in plain sight at the end of the bar.

A few minutes later he was in bed with the daybook under his pillow and his .357 close to his hand.

A light snow was falling at the time he dropped

off to sleep. It was his last memory for several hours.

When the years have accustomed a man to danger there are some feelings that remain with him; one is a subconscious awareness. Exhausted as he was, a surreptitious stirring awakened him. *Somebody or something was in the room!*

Ever so slightly he lifted his head. A broad-shouldered man, his back toward Mike, had just moved up to the bar and picked up the brown-wrapped package. The man turned toward the window.

With the .357 in his hand Mike said, "I can't imagine why a man would risk his freedom to steal a book he could buy on any newsstand for a couple of dollars."

"Book?"

"Erik Hokart and I have exchanged books for years. If he reads one he likes he sends it to me and I do the same with him. But if you want it that bad, please take it."

"Book?"

"Get out! If you come here again I'll kill you. I don't like thieves."

The man ducked through the slit where the curtain joined and through the glass doors, which stood open. Mike heard the sound as the man dropped to the ground—no great drop for an active man.

Walking to the window Mike drew it shut and locked it, watching the man crossing toward the

20

highway. Headlights came on and a white van moved off toward Durango.

Taking the daybook and his gun, he went into the bathroom and showered and shaved. As he shaved he thought about Erik. That the man believed himself in serious trouble was obvious from his letter. Even from his first message it had been clear that something was wrong, and Erik was not given to sudden notions or apprehensions.

Erik's telephone call had been brief and to the point. "I need," he said, "somebody with your particular interests, somebody with your brand of thinking. I will cheerfully pay all expenses and for your time."

"It's impossible right now, Erik. I've started something that must be finished."

Erik had been silent, then had said, "Come as soon as you can, all right? I don't want to talk to anybody else about this."

"What is it? What's wrong?"

Again that hesitation. Was he speaking from a public phone? Were there others around, perhaps listening? "Tell you when you get here. You'd think I was off my rocker." He hesitated again. "At least, anybody else would."

They had said their goodbyes and then Erik had said, quickly. "Mike? Please! I'm desperate!"

Mike remembered how he had hung up, startled, staring at the phone. That was so unlike Erik Hokart. The man must truly be in trouble, but at that time he had not connected it to his own knowledge of the country. Somehow the two ideas

21

had not come together in his mind. Had he realized . . .

Then he got the letter. The writing was erratic,
totally unlike Erik's.

> For God's sake, come at once!
> I need you, Mike, if ever I needed anyone. If
> it's money, I'll pay, but come! And be careful.
> Trust no one. No one at all.
> Meet me on the Canyon road, you know the
> one. If I am not there, for God's sake, find me!
> If anyone can handle this it will be you. I am
> sending the record as far as it goes. Get us out
> of this, Mike, and I'll be forever indebted.

III

US? WAS SOMEONE with him then? Mike had worried about that plural more than once since the
letter arrived, and during his flight west. None of
it made sense. Erik had always been a loner, attractive to women but seemingly not attracted by
them.

Mike Raglan turned the idea over in his mind
while dressing. Then he made coffee and seated
himself at a table where he could see both the
glass doors and the front entrance. He put the
.357 on the table in front of him.

He was not expecting trouble, yet they had gone
so far as to force an entry to his condo in the
night. What might follow he did not know.

22

He opened the daybook, and using his thumb as a marker he sat back, curiously reluctant to delve into its contents. Men had taken the country too much for granted. The obvious dangers and benefits tended to obscure much else, and most people had thought of the West in terms of fur, buffalo, gold, silver, cowboys, Indians, and cattle, rarely looking beyond the surface.

The Indians the white man met were no more the original inhabitants of the country than were the Normans and Saxons the original inhabitants of England. Other peoples had come and gone before, leaving only their shadows upon the land. Yet some had gone into limbo leaving not only physical artifacts but spiritual ones as well. Often, encroaching tribes borrowed from those who preceded them, accepting their values as a way of maintaining harmony with the natural world.

There were ancient mysteries, old gods who retired into the canyons to await new believers who would bring them to life once more.

Who has walked the empty canyons or the lonely land above the timber and not felt himself watched? Watched by what ghost from a nameless past? From out of what pit of horror and fear?

The Indian had always known he was not alone. He knew there were *others*, things that observed. When a man looked quickly up, was it a movement he saw or only his imagination?

The terms we use for what is considered supernatural are woefully inadequate. Beyond such terms as *ghost, specter, poltergeist, angel, devil,* or *spirit,* might there not be something more our purposeful blindness has prevented us from understanding?

We accept the fact that there may be other worlds out in space, but might there not be other worlds *here?* Other worlds, in other dimensions, coexistent with this?

If there are other worlds parallel to ours, are all the doors closed? Or does one, here or there, stand ajar?

Each year our knowledge progresses, each year we push back the curtain of ignorance, but there remains so much to learn. Our theories are only dancing shadows against a hard wall of reality.

How few answers do we possess! How many phenomena are ignored because they do not fall into accepted categories!

Ours is a world that has developed along materialistic, mechanistic lines, but might there not be other ways? Might there not be dozens of other ways, unknown and unguessed because of the one we found that worked?

Mike Raglan refilled his cup and put the daybook on the table. He did not know the answers. He had seen things and heard things that made him wonder. In a lifetime devoted to exposing fraud and deception, investigating haunted houses, mediums, and cult religions, he had come upon a few things that left him uneasy.

That man now? The one he had found in his condo, stealing his book. Who was he? Why did he want the daybook? Did he want it for himself or was he sent by someone to find it?

Why Mike had the impression, he did not know, but he did believe the man was sent by others. He had obviously come to secure the daybook, and he might return.

He agreed with the girl at the desk that there was something about him, some aura of strangeness. Yet he also had the look of a professional, a man who knew his job and how to go about it.

Mike took up the book. It was an ordinary loose-leaf notebook with ruled pages, and Erik had written with a brush pen. The writing was thick, black, easily read.

Landed on mesa top. It is certainly different, as we perceived from the air. The top a rough oval, absolutely flat and tufted with short bunches of vegetation. Soil deep but seems to have been badly leached. Along one side an edging of crags, yet the rocks themselves are smooth. The mesa falls off steeply on that side. On the other sides it also falls steeply away. Oddly enough, seems to have been purposely ringed with slabs of rock. Most unusual. My impression, which may be mistaken, is that the mesa top may have been cultivated in the far-distant past.

Found three walls almost intact. Roofed them with plywood sheet. Will do nicely for sleeping and a construction shanty while building. A table for blueprints, a corner for tools, one room for camping under cover.

View tremendous! San Juan River lies below.

Across the river a huge mesa rears its head. Must be nearly ten miles long, talus slope, and last three to five hundred feet are sheer rock. That must be the one called No Man's Mesa, probably for good reasons.

Sunday. Relaxed today, scouted around, worked on the walls of my shelter. Remarkably well built. Mortar treated with substance to make it set harder. It is different from other cliff houses or pueblos, but styles vary and the builders were learning as they worked.

The house I plan to build, doing most of the work myself, will consist of ten rooms, and a patio, all from native stone and built into the rocks that back up the mesa at that point. The building may require a year or more. This is a dream house, the site chosen because it is one of the most remote in the country.

Monday. Awakened by fierce growling. Chief on his feet, teeth bared, every hair bristling, growling deep in his chest. Chief is unusually large, weighing 160 pounds. The Tibetan mastiffs have been guard dogs for thousands of years, known to fight bears, tigers, or wild yak, to attack anything invading their premises.

It was the middle of the night. I spoke sharply but he continued to growl. Rising up from the army cot that was my bed, I saw a faint reddish glow emanating from the adjoining room. For a moment I feared the place was afire but the color was wrong. Catching up my pistol I stepped into the next room, prepared

26

for I know not what. I stopped, astonished. The red glow was coming from my blueprint!

There, drawn into my plans with a glowing red line was another room! A round room, resembling a kiva of the cliff dwellers!

Mike Raglan put down the book and stared out at the snow. The tracks of his recent visitor were still clearly marked in the snow between his condo and the highway, so that at least was no dream.

His coffee was cold. He walked to the sink and emptied his cup, then ran it full of hot water to heat the cup again. He liked his coffee hot and a warm cup kept it so longer. He refilled the cup with coffee and went back to his seat.

No wonder Erik had sent for him! The trouble was that, for the time being at least, Mike Raglan had had enough of puzzles and mysteries. What he wanted now was peace and quiet, time to think, to study, to consider some of the things he had learned, or thought he had learned.

He had been orphaned at twelve, when his parents drove into a filling station during a holdup and were shot dead without any awareness of what was happening. The next two years he had lived on a ranch, helping with the work, riding, and hunting. The family then broke up in a divorce and for a year he worked as an assistant to a carnival magician working the county fairs. Following that, he ran a shooting gallery at an amusement park. He had become a better than average shot while working on the ranch but at the shooting gallery he perfected his skills.

When the season closed he spent several months out of work. He was often hungry, and the few jobs he could find were hard labor.

When spring came again he returned to the carnival, operating the shooting gallery on his own. Twice, when the magician was too far gone in his cups, Mike had carried on with his show. The magician was a Lebanese and from him Mike picked up a smattering of Arabic. At sixteen he was doing a man's work and accepting a man's responsibilities. He gave his age as twenty-four.

Knowing the show offered no future, he made a point of making local contacts wherever they went. The result was a job that paid little more than room and board with a small-town daily paper and job printer. For the next seven months he swept floors, answered the telephone, delivered orders, and did whatever needed doing. In the meantime, he read.

He haunted the public library, helped out occasionally in a secondhand bookstore, trying to get some of the education he had missed. By the end of the third month he was writing occasional pieces for the paper and selling a few ads. By the end of the fifth month he received a small raise.

His social life was almost nonexistent. He talked to waitresses in cafés where he ate, with his boss or the tramp printer who worked the presses.

His first contact away from work was with a former missionary who had become a professor of

Bible studies at a local college. The professor had lived in Damascus and spoke Arabic, so they often spoke the language, enabling him to become fluent. Several times he attended his friend's classes, picking up a bit of Bible knowledge as well as learning of the Holy Lands.

He began dating a local girl but her parents disapproved. Who was he, after all, but a drifter with no future? Smoothly but effectually her parents broke it off; at the time he was heartbroken, with a feeling he had been treated unjustly.

He moved on, worked in lumber woods, managed to sell an article on carnival life, and another on deer to a wildlife journal. Again he went to work for a small-town daily, and when the editor-operator became ill, ran the paper for him until his recovery was complete. His career underwent a sudden change when the editor returned.

A few days before, a man had arrived in town who professed to communicate with the dead. Before their eyes he received messages from long-dead relatives of the townspeople, including advice for the lovelorn as well as suggestions on how to invest their money.

Melburn called him into the office. "Mike? Didn't you work with a magic show once?"

"Yeah."

"Have you been hearing about this medium who just came to town? Could he be faking it?"

"He is a fake. He's using one of the oldest routines in the world. We used it in carnivals to read hidden messages."

29

"I want you to expose him, Mike. Then do a story about it. He's been telling old Mrs. McKenna that he has a communication from her dead husband on how she should invest her savings."

"You want me to attend a seance?"

"Yes, I do. Get the goods on him, do a story on it, and we can syndicate the story."

He had exposed the charlatan and, after the story's syndication, followed it with an article on a haunted house. Unwittingly, he had found his career.

A national magazine hired him to do a series on haunted houses; another followed on famous magicians. A visit to Haiti and the resulting book on voodoo brought him a best seller. After that he began a series of trips to far-out, mysterious places. In the Sahara he visited the tomb of Tin Hinan, followed by the Caves of the Thousand Buddhas, then to Socotra, the Enchanter's Island. He had spent most of a year in Tibet.

In the space of a year he became an international celebrity. He dug into history to uncover strange events, studied phenomena ignored by science, and although an acknowledged skeptic, he closed his mind to nothing. Quick to detect fraud, he had also come to realize there was a residue of something, something not quite explainable by any method he knew. At least not by present knowledge.

Time and again he had found himself skirting something shadowy, something that lacked substance yet seemed to be there. Many times he found it necessary to pursue other angles of approach, and it was upon one of these problems that he first met Erik Hokart.

Hokart was an inventor, a specialist in some areas of electronics. Far more than most research scientists Hokart was keenly aware of the commercial possibilities of some of their discoveries. The result was that he had gone into business and made millions, promptly retiring to enjoy what he had.

It was Erik who had guided Mike Raglan through some of the labyrinths of mathematics and physics. Often they discussed Erik's obsession with the canyon country of Utah and Arizona, and a place in which to build.

The final choice had been Erik's own. Had Mike known, he would have strongly advised Erik Hokart to choose another place, yet what reasons could he have given?

Mike Raglan looked again across the snow where the mysterious white van had stood waiting.

Another occupant? Or simply an empty van? Was there one man or two? Or more?

Uneasily, he considered what little he knew. Erik was in trouble. Erik had contrived, somehow, to have this daybook delivered to him.

This man or these men knew of its delivery and tried to recover it. Hence, it was evidence, important evidence of what had happened or was happening to Erik.

After all, there need be nothing supernatural.

31

Erik Hokart was a very wealthy man. Kidnapping was not impossible, nor was revenge.

What he might have done Mike could not guess, although he doubted anything really serious, but in obtaining wealth one often made enemies, if only through jealousy.

Was that element of strangeness all imagination? If so, the girl at the desk had felt it, too.

And what of the other girl? The beautiful girl who delivered the package? Who was she? What had become of her?

Mike reached over and picked up the daybook. . . .

IV

WHEN MIKE RAGLAN first picked up the daybook it had opened almost automatically at the spot where he began to read, so there had been no reason to examine it in detail. Now he opened at the very first page.

The first half-dozen pages were notations having to do with the construction Erik was planning. Materials to be ordered, speculations on dimensions of rooms and what their views would encompass.

Obviously he had carried the book in his pocket for just that purpose, and it had been convenient when he had more to relate.

Turning the pages, Mike went on to where his reading had stopped, and he began again.

When I awakened, the happenings of the night seemed like a dream, yet when I checked the blueprint the red glow was gone but the line I had drawn with the compass remained. Or at least, I had thought of drawing that line. Oddly enough, the circular room made architectural sense and fitted perfectly with what I had previously drawn. I went outside to check the location.

Had I dreamed it all? Was it a species of nightmare? Had there actually been such a glowing line? Had I further doubts, Chief would have dispelled them, for he kept sniffing about, whining a little, starting at the slightest sound. The Tibetan mastiff, let me add, has a much better nose than his English counterpart, and this dog had been given me, on his return from Tibet, by Mike Raglan. He was already a half-grown dog.

He seemed not to like what he smelled, but when he followed the trail outside and along the mesa, he lost it.

I went to the area where the circular room would be if built. Certainly, no leveling would be required, for the earth was utterly flat. Seeing what appeared to be a flat stone I stooped to pick it up and toss it out of the way. The stone refused to budge. Digging near it I discovered it was not simply a loose stone but part of a wall. I dug further and the wall showed a slight curving.

Wednesday. For two days I have been digging, throwing dirt like one gone mad. I must get Mike out here. He won't believe this. Actually, I am not digging, merely excavating, for all this earth is fill. I have seen ruins half-filled with debris, but this is nothing of the kind. This was done purposefully with an intent to preserve.

I am a fool, but a frightened fool. Mike might make sense of this. I cannot. Once I began digging I worked like one obsessed. Each time I abandoned the dig something drove me back to the hole again. Chief has been pacing the rim of the kiva, for that is what it is, pacing and growling or whining. That he is worried is obvious but he refuses to descend into the hole with me.

Mike put the daybook down. His coffee had grown cold again. He emptied the cup and refilled it. Erik had made an interesting discovery and it should be reported to a competent archaeologist for study. It might very well be important, for most of the known kivas had been found in a state of at least partial ruin.

Erik had never, so far as Mike could recall, shown more than a casual interest in the Indians of the Southwest. Naturally, he would have seen some of the publications, available in the area, on the cliff dwellers. Possibly he had read some that would make him familiar with Anasazi architecture.

The glowing red line on the blueprint? Did somebody or some*thing* want that kiva excavated? If so, why? And who?

That mesa where Erik had chosen to build was remote, and in a rarely visited area.

Mike walked to the window and stared out at the snow. The footprints were there, a sharp reminder that he dealt with reality.

Where was Erik? Why had he not kept their appointment? Why had Erik chosen such a remote place? Had he been kept from that appointment? Was he dead? Injured? A prisoner?

That was preposterous. Yet, was it? After all, a man had forced entry into his condo to steal this very book, and might well try it again when he realized, as by now he must, that he had been tricked.

Irritated and worried, Mike Raglan took up the book once more.

If their intent was to preserve that piece of the ruin intact they had succeeded. The question is, if all other ruins were abandoned to time and the elements, why preserve this one? Was it a shrine? Something so special it must be preserved at all costs?

Not only are the walls intact but the plaster as well, and the plaster is covered with symbols. The plaster is intact except at one point where there is evidence of water-staining.

Thursday. A restless, uneasy night! Chief apparently awake all night, growling during most of it although he would not leave my side. Several times I believed I heard stirrings outside and once I was almost sure that somebody peered in at me.

I awoke with a headache and a bad taste in my mouth. Starting a small fire in my stove I made coffee, then walked outside. Like a fool I forgot to look for tracks until both the dog and I had moved about enough to destroy any that might have been left. Looking at the kiva again I realized this one had no sipapu.

The sipapu, as I understand it, is a hole in the floor of the kiva symbolizing that opening through which the Anasazi emerged into this world. The sipapus I have seen range from the size of a teacup to twice that.

On the contrary, there is in this kiva, which must represent a cultural aberration, a blank window or niche in the wall similar to the *mihrab* in a mosque. In uncovering this niche the earth before it had fallen away and the concave wall of the niche seemed composed of some soft-looking gray substance which I felt a curious reluctance to touch, so did not.

Returning from my hurried look at the kiva, I noticed something I had overlooked. My drafting pencil was gone, but in its place was an exquisite little jar, not over three inches tall!

Putting down the daybook, Mike finished his coffee. He had better get back out there and find Erik. Even as the thought came, his instinct told

36

him to leave it alone. It was Erik's problem, not his. Erik was the one who had chosen to move into the area and build a home there, though Mike had advised against it.

"My conscience is clear," he said aloud.

Even as he spoke the words he recognized their untruth. Erik had called for help, had called out to him, and Erik was not inclined to ask anyone for anything. If Mike did not help, who else was there? And who even knew Erik Hokart needed help? How many even knew he was out there?

After all, was Mike Raglan not the man who delved into magic and the supernatural? Was he not the skeptic? The man who took nothing for granted?

As for being a skeptic, he was so only up to a point. A half-dozen times he had touched upon something from which he shied away. The truth was, he liked his world and had no desire to venture into any other. Yet there could be a logical explanation for what was happening out there, even for those strange flares from atop the mesa.

And those creatures he had glimpsed in the night? What were they? Perhaps some naked Indians. Perhaps he had stumbled upon some Penitentes. He knew the name but little more about them except that they observed some mysterious rites of their own.

Those flares now? Were the creatures responding to them? Had they been some sort of signal?

Uneasily, he began getting his gear together. A small survival kit which he always carried, a hunting knife, an extra box of .357 cartridges. On second thought, he added another box. What was he going to do, fight a war? He filled a canteen, gathered some odds and ends of emergency food, still unsure of what he planned to do.

Although Erik had suggested meeting him on the Canyon road, the mesa where Erik was building was north of the river and there was no way of getting from one to the other without crossing the bridge at Mexican Hat. He would come in from the north and visit Erik's place first.

And after that? He shied from the question. By that time he would surely have found Erik or some communication from him.

He took up the daybook again.

Later. Desperately, I have tried to resume work on my plans, trying to keep my thoughts away from the odd circumstances, but my thoughts refuse to concern themselves with the mundane problems of construction.

Suddenly Chief began barking furiously, and seizing a club, I dashed outside. My appearance seemed to lend him courage, and leaping into the kiva he charged toward the blind window, only it had changed. The back of the niche was now a thick oily-looking cloud, which did not enter the kiva, but remained in the window frame.

Chief charged the window, barking furiously. I yelled at him to come back, and when he did obey I dropped into the kiva to collar him.

38

Assuming I was with him he leaped through the window, and his barking faded into the distance.

Chief was gone! But gone where? The window was on the cliff's edge and leaping through he must have fallen several hundred feet to the rocks below.

Yet he had not fallen. I had distinctly heard him barking away into the distance, obviously chasing something, or somebody.

For a long moment I stood riveted to the spot, "Frozen" might have been a better term, for I was cold, utterly cold. Turning, I climbed clumsily from the kiva, skinning my knee in the process.

Stumbling, I went back into my camp in the ruin and sat down on my cot. I wiped my hand over my face. Despite the coolness of the morning I was wet with sweat.

Sanity. I must cling to sanity. Reason, logic, common sense.

Something had happened I could not explain. Naturally, I had heard of mysterious disappearances. There had been the case of the man crossing an open field in full view of several people and vanishing before their eyes. There was also the story of a man who had gone to a spring for water. His tracks were plainly visible in the fresh-fallen snow but they ended abruptly, short of the spring. The bucket was there, lying on its side. The man was gone. Faintly, his voice was heard, calling for help. Gradually

39

the voice weakened and after a while was heard no more.

It was a long time before I could shake off the fear that gnawed at my guts. I realized now that I had never been truly afraid before. Had it not been for Chief, I would have abandoned the place at once, never to return or even to repeat the story. Yet Chief was a good and faithful beast and he would not have ventured into the kiva or through the window had he not believed I was with him.

All right, I would begin there. Something had happened which I did not understand, yet we deal with forces every day which most of us do not fully comprehend. How many of us who turn the dial of a radio or television can explain the principles of either?

My dog had vanished. If he had gone through that window he had gone into something or somewhere. I must recover my dog. If it meant going into that somewhere, then it must be done.

He had leaped through and I had heard him barking. Hence, the process of passing through had not changed him. He could still bark and he retained the incentive to bark, so whatever he passed through had not altered him physically, nor had his mental attitude been changed.

My pencil had been taken but a gift left in exchange. Hence, whatever was on the other side of the window could reason, had ethical standards of a sort, and might be reached by some means of communication. I then took the first sensible, logical step. I went back to the kiva and called my dog.

Nothing happened. Could sound reach beyond the barrier? Suppose I went through? Could I get back?

Returning to my drawing board I sat down, and using a notepad, I tried to reason it through. Common sense warned me to sit tight. If Chief could return, he would. It might be a day or it might be two. The "window" was obviously an opening to something, perhaps another dimension, perhaps a world coexistent with our own.

Did I believe that? I had not sufficient information to make a decision, but what other explanation was there? I knew the idea had been around for thousands of years, and certain speculations in contemporary physics seemed to allow for the possibility, at least. And that opening obviously led to somewhere.

Moreover, whoever had drawn that red line on my blueprint had obviously wanted such an opening.

Why? And why had it been so carefully closed up in the beginning? Had there been something over there they feared? Or an attempt to keep our two worlds separate?

The Hopi Indians, I understood, believe this to be the Fourth World. The Third World, which they left to come into this through a "hole in the ground," had been evil.

What evil? Was it a thing? A being? Some

tangible force? Or was it a state or condition? I knew too little of their beliefs to venture an opinion, but knew they had some affinity with what the Navajo called the Anasazi, the Ancient Ones.

Did some monstrous thing lurk beyond that window? Had the kiva been filled in to keep it out?

V

WHO DREW THE red line on my plans? Obviously, somebody on this side, somebody who wanted a way back.

The taking of my pencil seemed more the act of a child, or someone desperately in need of a way to communicate.

Was there not another opening? After all, how did the person who drew the red line get over here?

But all this was mad! Mad! What I needed was somebody like Mike Raglan who was familiar with the literature on this sort of thing.

Monday. Much has happened. I awakened the other morning to find my drafting pencil returned with the point worn down to where it could no longer be used.

For a moment or two I was puzzled. Then it hit me: Suppose whoever took the pencil did not know how to sharpen one? On a hunch I sharpened the pencil, then stood it erect in the dime-store sharpener and left it, along with a couple of extra pencils.

In the morning they were gone, and so was an old sweater, a cardigan. It had been hung over a camp chair nearby. For a moment I was irritated. Old as it was, I liked that cardigan. It was cashmere and warm.

This morning, to my surprise, I found my old sweater returned, and beside it, folded neatly, was another sweater. This was entirely new, a dark brown across the shoulders bleeding to a lighter, then still another lighter shade.

To my surprise the sweater fitted to perfection. Where the brand name had been in the collar of my sweater there was a sunflower worked in gold thread!

Wednesday. Cleaned last of the earth from the kiva. Now I must study the paintings. I have deliberately avoided them until they could be examined in their entirety.

Thursday. Awakened to find a sunflower on my desk! If I am haunted it is by gentle creatures, indeed!

This afternoon, suddenly, there was Chief! He stood looking at me and only when I called his name did he approach me, but once he was close and got my smell in his nostrils he was excited as a puppy. Tucked behind his collar was a sunflower!

To say that I was startled would understate the case, for Chief was a one-man dog to such a degree that nobody could touch him but me. If

I was present to admonish him he would some-times permit liberties from a vet, but only some-times. Yet somebody had obviously placed that sunflower where it was.

Nonetheless, I am uneasy. I am half-inclined to give up my project and return to the normal and everyday. Not for more than a week have I enjoyed a decent night's sleep

All morning I struggled to recall what I had heard about other dimensions, parallel worlds and their possibilities. I could remember noth-ing definite and began to realize how such spe-cialization as mine could be sadly limiting.

Mike Raglan put down the daybook and walked again to the window. Erik Hokart was not a man given to wild flights of imagination. He was an acknowledged authority in several aspects of elec-tronics, as well as having considerable business acumen. His foresight and his patents had earned him a considerable fortune, all based upon simple logic.

He was not the sort of man to overlook much of anything, and not likely to be tricked. The nearest town was, Mike believed, not closer than eighty or ninety miles, and nobody lived in the vicinity. South of the river there were a couple of trading posts, and some scattered Navajos, but they were a people who minded their own affairs.

So what was happening? Hokart evidently had begun to believe in the existence of a parallel world of some sort, and whatever was going on was important enough to someone to send a goon after Hokart's daybook.

Where was Erik? Who was the girl who delivered the book? And who was the man who came to retrieve it? What of the kiva?

"I'd better get out there," Mike Raglan said, speaking aloud. "I'd better get right to the spot. If Erik is not there . . ."

He spread out a map of the Four Corners area and studied possible routes. Getting to where Hokart was constructing his home was not easy. It was remote country, and although the roads were generally good most of them were unsurfaced. There was no road leading right to Hokart's place, which was one of the attractions for him. He enjoyed being alone.

Erik had, Mike knew, planned on coming and going by helicopter, at least during the construction phases. What materials he would need would be delivered by the same means.

He remembered Erik's discovery of the mesa. He had been flying low over the area when he saw that flat-topped mesa, different from any around it. The top gave the appearance of having once been cultivated, but long ago. The position, the view in all directions, the isolation of it had immediately seized his attention. From that moment Erik Hokart had thought of no other place. "I can use the native rock," he had said. "There's plenty of good building material around the base of the cliff."

Time was no object and he had resolved to build it himself, as he wished.

Erik had always been one to do things his own way, but this time he had run into something totally unfamiliar, something for which he was not prepared.

Uneasily, Mike ran over the events in his mind. Erik had no friends who were inclined to practical jokes, nor was there anyplace close around where anybody could stay unless willing to camp out under rigorous conditions.

Slowly, thinking all the while, Mike Raglan began putting his gear together. To what he had already assembled he added binoculars. Yet he found himself curiously reluctant to leave Tamarron, knowing that once he returned to the area of Hokart's house he was committed.

For nearly twenty years he had been investigating mysteries, exposing frauds, venturing into little-known areas of thought, yet this time he felt he was walking on the brink of something to be feared. This was truly the unknown.

Yet why should he feel that way? What evidence did he have?

Sitting down, he wrote a careful outline of what had transpired and what he was about to do. If anything happened to him there must be a record, some evidence he could leave behind. He had a feeling he was going off the deep end. He would leave his notes with the daybook, and leave them in a safe place.

He took up the daybook again.

Was I afraid? Nothing fearsome had happened, yet I was dealing with the unknown, with a whole new set of principles and ideas of which I knew nothing.

I tried to think of it as a hoax, yet I could not. I remembered Mike saying that when dealing with what people called the supernatural, some background in legerdemain was essential. A scientist searches for truth and is not skilled in trickery or deception.

Many things that might seem miraculous can be duplicated by any working magician, as the marvelous is his professional occupation. Those who wish to find miracles are easily imposed upon, for they come with a mind prepared for belief.

Saturday. Again a restless night. There were vague stirrings in the darkness and Chief lay close beside me, occasionally growling, sometimes whining. After awakening in the morning I lay still for some time, thinking. Suddenly, my mind was made up. I was getting out. I would leave today. I would take my personal gear, leave the rest, and simply get out of here.

Knowing Chief, Mike was worried. He was a proud, fierce dog, afraid of nothing, yet now he was acting in ways totally unlike himself. Ordinarily, Chief would have charged anything that came near, be it man, bear, wolf, or whatever. If he was not doing so there was something of which he was afraid, something that disturbed the dog's deepest instincts.

Suppose Erik was right and he had discovered a way to another dimension? Obviously, the dog had passed through and returned unharmed in any physical way, so a man might do the same thing— a man or a woman.

Who was leaving the sunflower insignia? The actual flowers? Who had taken the pencils, and for what reason?

Tomorrow, Mike decided. He would go tomorrow. He would set out bright and early, leaving the daybook and his notes in some secure place. Best of all, he thought, he could mail it to an old friend formerly with the FBI, to be acted upon in case of Mike's disappearance.

He loaded his four-wheel-drive car with a sleeping bag, some trail rations, extra water, and the extra ammunition he'd brought along.

Then he sat down and stared out the window, seeing nothing, not even the snow or the magnificent cliffs that bordered the highway. He saw only himself and what lay ahead. The truth of the matter was, he realized, he did not want to go. Was he losing his zest for adventure? His curiosity about the unknown? Or was he afraid of finding something that would upset his easy world?

From childhood we have learned to adjust ourselves to three dimensions; it is a world we understand, and in which we are at home. New ideas keep invading our complacency, and slowly, steadily, our world has broadened and grown more complex. Once, a man had only to adjust to his small village or town, the people around him, and the street on which he lived. He had to adjust to the power, the king, the lord of the manor—whoever it was who controlled his world. Within these limits he was comfortable.

Soldiers and sailors returned with stories of the far places, of lands different from our own, and slowly the world grew wider. Most of what men heard they only half believed. Then the world began to broaden swiftly. From slow-moving sailing craft to transatlantic steamers and then to flying, men crossed new boundaries.

World War II had taken young Americans to the far corners of the earth, and suddenly farm boys from Kansas or Vermont were talking easily of Burma, Guadalcanal, and Morocco. They were at home in places their fathers could not have found on a world map, and with the end of the war, suddenly, planes were flying everywhere.

People who a few years before might have spent a rare winter in Florida were now doing business in Saudi Arabia, Yemen, and Oman. Children were growing up who used computers as easily as their fathers had used a fountain pen. Drastic changes were taking place, and the speed of invention and discovery had increased manyfold.

Now we had put a man on the moon, had sent spacecraft to check on the outermost planets— spacecraft that now had gone on into infinite space beyond the solar system. And Einstein and the quantum theory were injecting strange new possibilities into our narrow world.

The man who sat before a television set with a can of beer to watch a football game rarely realized that the world was exploding around him. The convenient horizons were disappearing, and the jobs at which he worked were being eliminated by progress. Changes that had once needed centuries were now happening almost overnight, and the jobs available were calling for greater expertise. The common laborer who had been with us forever was finding himself on skid row with no place to go, and no possibilities of work.

A few things remained constant. The earth under his feet, the sky overhead, the road down which he could drive. For centuries there had been tales of other worlds, and people had read them or listened to them or watched them on *The Twilight Zone*, interested and amused but never taking them very seriously.

It was always an amusing subject for casual conversation among friends, and offered room for speculation. Occasionally there had been stories of mysterious disappearances, usually explained away with bored amusement by some scientist with too much else on his mind.

To deal with the expanding world around us was quite enough. Mike Raglan found no place in his thinking for yet another dimension, for a world here, right alongside our own. He was not mentally prepared to deal with it. He could understand the possibilities without knowing any more about the physics of it than the average man who can't explain how his television set works.

Mike Raglan did not want there to be another dimension. He did not need one. He was having trouble enough dealing with the three he had. Yet he remembered primitive people with whom he had dealt who accepted such ideas, who did not even think of them as a cause for wonder. Often their language could cope with such ideas with no adjustments whatsoever, and the same was true of their thinking.

What of the Australian aborigines and their "dream time"?

Mike picked up the daybook. Reluctantly, hesitantly, he turned the pages to where he had stopped reading.

Immediately, I gathered what was important to me. My plans, notebooks, and the few books I'd brought along for reading. A half-dozen books I would leave, for one day I might return, briefly at least.

It is not easy to see a dream die, and this home upon the mesa was a dream I'd had since boyhood. Suddenly, reluctant to go, I glanced around.

And there she stood.

VI

MY FIRST IMPRESSION was that she did not look like a girl who would leave a sunflower on a man's table, nor put one behind a dog's collar.

My second impression, simultaneous with the first, was that she was the most beautiful woman I had ever seen.

She stood just outside my door in the sunlight. Her hair was very black, parted in the middle and done in two knots on the back of her head. Her skin was the color of old ivory, her eyes very large and dark.

The next thing of which I was aware was Chief. He was growling, but uncertainly, as if confused. At once I realized this could not be the person Chief had permitted to touch him.

She motioned, indicating I should follow, so I stepped to the door and watched her walk to the kiva. With a walk like that she had no need to beckon.

Yet I hesitated. Chief was holding back, pressing against my leg as if to prevent my going. There was something here he distrusted, and rightly so. She paused at the kiva's edge to look back. When she saw me still standing in the ruin's door, she beckoned again. I shook my head. For an instant I thought I glimpsed a flicker of irritation on her face, but it might have been my imagination.

Beautiful she certainly was, yet "striking" might have been a better description. However, there was about her a subtle sense of evil, of foreboding. Despite her beauty, every sense in me warned me I should shrink from her, that I should draw back, that here was evil.

Her clothing seemed to be of the same material as the cardigan left me by the girl of the sunflowers, but of finer thread, figured with an Indian motif, but much more sophisticated than any American Indian garment I had seen. She wore turquoise jewelry of the finest quality.

"You have fear? Of me?"

Her voice was low, a lovely sound, holding a little of invitation, a little taunting.

Unwittingly, not knowing what to say, I said the wrong thing.

"I must wait. I have builders coming to work on my house." My gesture took in the area.

"No!" Her tone was strident. "There must be no one! No one, do you comprehend?"

"I am sorry. This land is mine. I shall build a home here."

"What do you say? The land is yours? All land belongs—" She broke off suddenly. "Come!" Her tone was imperious. "I show you!"

"I cannot," I repeated.

From her manner I gathered she was not accustomed to refusal, but in this situation she was obviously uncertain how to deal with it. "Now! Come, or you will be sent for. You will bring the wrath upon you."

A moment she hesitated. Then she descended into the kiva and disappeared.

Instantly I had the impression that I should get away, as far, far away as possible, and as quickly as it could be done.

Ten minutes later, this book tucked into my pocket, I was hurrying down the trail. My four-wheel-drive vehicle was waiting at the end of the road not far away, a rarely used trail. I had almost reached it when somebody hissed at me from a clump of rocks and juniper.

Turning sharply, I faced a slender, lovely girl with a sunflower in her hair.

"No! They wait for you! You must not go!"

"What do they want from me?"

"They wish nobody here! They take you. They get from you all. Then they kill."

"Who are you?"

"I am Kawasi. I am runaway. They find me, they kill."

"But you speak English?'

"I speak small. Old man tell me words."

"But she spoke English, too. The other one."

"They have four hands people who speak. No more."

"Four hands?"

She held up her hands, closed her fingers, then opened them. Four hands, twenty people.

"We go now. I show." Turning quickly, she went down through the rocks, rounding a boulder into an ancient path, steep and narrow, that led down to the river. In the shadow of the cliff, she hesitated. "You must cross river or wait until darkness and float down to great lake."

"What will you do?"

"I go back—if I can. It is not always. Only through kiva is always, that not possible for me."

"You come through at another place?"

"It is a sometime place. Only sometime." She gestured. "Long time past my people live all about here. Bad times come. Much dry. Wild, wander-about people come. They fight us. Take our corn. Some people walk-away, some go back to old place, where we come from before. Much evil there."

"But you are not evil."

"I am not. She is. She has very high place. We fear. You fear, too. You sleep with her, you dic. She is Poison Woman."

"Are you Indian?"

"What is Indian? I do not know 'Indian.' "

"Your people lived here? Where?"

"Nobody live here. Special to gods. Priests come to plant witch plants on this mesa. My folk live far away. Big cave, many house. On other side we have big house, many rooms. Here all fall to pieces, I think."

Cliff dwellers? They could have been. The Hopi had a legend they had come into this world through a hole in the ground. Might it have been from another dimension? From what some called a parallel world?

"And your people now?"

"Over there. Many are gone. They are slaves or dead. It is evil, over there."

"You spoke of the woman who came for me as a 'Poison Woman.' What did you mean?"

"From childhood they fed on poisons. Not enough to kill, but enough to make free of poison. They special to the gods. Their flesh is soaked with a poison from secret herbs. They do not die, but any man who lies with them dies. When a man has an enemy he sends a Poison Woman to him."

Until it grew dark we hid among the rocks and juniper, and although searchers came close they did not find us. Then we worked our way east by old trails, scarcely seen in the night.

Friday. I have returned. I have escaped them for the moment. I have hidden what was possible, and a map as well.

Mike, if you get this, for God's sake, help us!

Kawasi urged me to cross the river but I was sure we could escape them without that. We were more than twenty miles from a paved road and I wanted one more attempt at my Jeep. Under cover of darkness we got close. Nobody seemed near. Leaping into the Jeep, I thrust my key into the ignition and the Jeep roared into life. There was a shout, a rush from the darkness, but the car leaped forward. I struck a man across the face and we were away. A mile down the road we turned into another track.

Town, when we reached it, was more than sixty miles away and safe, or so I believed. We ate in a small restaurant, almost at closing time. Kawasi asked many questions about the café, cars, buses. I explained about ordering meals, buying tickets and clothing. Taking money from my pocket, I gave her a hundred dollars and some change. "If anything happens to me, get my book to Mike Raglan at Tamarron."

"It is not possible. They are here."

A shadow flickered by the window. I went to the cash register. A stout, baldheaded man in an apron came to take my money. I paid him. "Friend, I am Erik Hokart. I am building southwest of here and I need a gun. Have you got one?"

He just looked at me. "Mister, I got a gun. Ever'body hereabouts has one, but I wouldn't lend my gun to anybody."

Turning, I looked outside. My Jeep stood waiting. Nobody was near. If we . . .

Kawasi was gone!

VII

FOR A MOMENT I stood perfectly still, my hands flat upon the counter, my back to the window. Had Kawasi escaped somehow without being seen? Or had they taken her through a back door?

"Sir," I said quietly, "keep your gun but let me warn you that if they come in, you had better use it. They may decide they want no witnesses.

"My name is Erik Hokart, as I have told you. Please remember it when inquiries are made. If the law does not investigate, I have a friend who will. His name is Mike Raglan."

"Look here, Mister, I don't know what kind of trouble you're in but I'll call the police, and—"

"From the kitchen, then. If you pick up that telephone they will kill you."

"Who's 'they'?" He peered past me. "I don't even see nobody."

"I'll run for my Jeep. You'd better get out of here, too."

Mike Raglan put down the daybook and swore, softly and bitterly. He glanced again at the book, frowning.

The daybook had been written for Erik himself, until he evidently got the idea it would be the easiest way to communicate to Mike what had taken place.

Quickly, Mike checked his haversack and his gun, and slipped his boot-knife into place. As he stopped in the doorway, he took care to check the position of his car. Several other vehicles were parked nearby but all seemed empty, and there were no cars he did not recognize. He went to his car, got in, and promptly locked the doors after checking behind the seat. Then he backed out and headed for the highway.

He paused at the security gate. "If anybody

asks for me, you don't know whether I am in or not," he told the guard.

Several times he checked his rearview mirror but saw no evidence he was followed. Hours later he pulled into the small Utah town, looking for the café he remembered from previous visits.

It was gone! On the site were a few blackened timbers and still-rising wisps of smoke. Up the street was another café that had been closed on his last trip due to a slackening of business during the off-season. It was open now. With another careful look around he parked the car where he could watch it and went inside.

Three Navajos sat at the counter drinking coffee, and a truck driver was finishing a meal. His rig stood outside, close to the pickups belonging to the Navajos. There was a girl sitting alone in a back booth.

He dropped into a seat not far from her. When the waitress came for his order, he commented, "Looks like you had a fire up the street."

"I'll say! It put my girlfriend out of her job! She was waiting tables on the morning shift—then the fire and she's out of work."

He ordered ham and eggs. "Anybody hurt?"

"Jerry. He owned the place. He's in the hospital now, if you can call it that. The cook managed to get him out with their clothes afire. The cook was burned a little, but Jerry . . . he's in a bad way.

"They say he was hurt somehow other than the burns, but nobody knows much about it."

"How'd it start?"

"Who knows? The cook swears it started up front."

She went to turn in his order and he glanced at the girl in the booth. She was just sitting there with a cup of coffee in front of her. He looked again. She was very attractive, but subdued somehow.

The waitress returned with his coffee. "You should have seen that fire! Like an explosion, almost, only there wasn't any explosion, just a sort of *poof*. The whole building was gone in less time than it takes to tell it."

"What's Jerry say about it?"

"Him? He can't talk. The cook says there were at least two customers the last time he looked up front, and he looked because he was getting ready to close up. There was a girl, and this man who asked Jerry for a gun—"

"A gun?"

"The cook heard him, and stopped what he was doing to listen. Fine-looking man, he said, looked like a businessman, but a mighty scared one. Jerry turned him down, of course. Nobody but a damned fool loans a gun to a stranger—or, for that matter, to a friend."

"What then?"

"All of a sudden this girl is in the kitchen. The cook started to ask her what she thought she was doing, but she ran out the back door.

"The cook heard the front door close and headed up front, and that was when it happened. There was that sudden *poof* and Jerry was knocked right into his arms and then the whole place was in flames. He dragged Jerry outside."

"What happened to the man who wanted the gun?"

The waitress shrugged. "Ran off, I guess. His car is still here, keys in the ignition. The chief of police impounded it. He's got it over at the station."

"And the girl?"

The waitress's voice lowered, but she cast a meaningful glance at the girl in the back booth. "Nobody knows, but *she's* been around all morning. Looks like she's watching for somebody."

Mike glanced at the girl and their eyes met. He looked away. "That man who asked for the gun? Did he say anything else?"

"Just something about him building down in the desert, but we all knew that." She went for his breakfast and returned. "This is a big country, Mister, but there aren't that many people, and everybody usually knows what's going on and where.

"He's bought gas here in town, groceries, and sometimes he eats here. I've seen him around, and he's good-looking. Started all the girls wondering if he's single. But he minds his own affairs and bothers nobody. His name is Hokart."

"Where can I find the chief?"

"He's down to Mexican Hat on business but should be in later today."

"Any strangers in town?"

61

"No, except for her. There's not a lot of traffic through here in the winter. In the summer we get tourists, but not like over in Durango. We don't have the narrow-gauge train and we're off the main route, but we do get tourists." She looked at him. "Did you know Erik Hokart?"

He hesitated a moment. "He's a friend of mine. That's why I'm here."

She brought the coffeepot and refilled his cup. The Navajos had gone; so had the truck driver. She looked at Mike. "You aren't from around here?"

"I spent some time in this country, years back. In fact, I told Hokart a good deal about it before he decided to come out. He was from back east, but he had fallen in love with this country. He planned to make his home here."

She left to get on with her work. Mike glanced over at the girl, then took his plate and his coffee and crossed to her booth. "Kawasi?" he asked.

The momentary fear left her eyes. "You are Mike Raglan?" She spoke the name in two distinct syllables.

He sat down. "Do you speak English?"

"Small. Old man tell me."

"What happened to Erik?"

"They have him. They take him."

"Did they burn the restaurant? How?"

"I do not know. It is . . . a thing . . . like . . ." She touched the edge of the saucer. Lifting his cup, she took the saucer by the edge and made a backhand move as if to throw it. "They . . ." She

62

gestured again. "It is fire then, big fire, very quick."

"These things they throw? They are big?"

"Small. Smaller as"—she indicated the top of the cup—"so."

"They burn?"

"They break, then burn."

"Have the police talked to you yet?"

"No."

"Kawasi, I know nothing of your land, wherever it is. I know nothing of your people. I have read what Erik wrote, but I must know who your enemies are, where they have taken Erik, and what they will do to him. I must also know how to get where Erik is."

Suddenly, Mike thought of her. "Have you eaten? Do you have any money?"

"I eat nothing. To sleep I give money."

He motioned to the waitress and ordered for her. When the woman was gone, Kawasi said, "How to get back I do not know. I am far from place I hear of."

"Could you find the place if I took you back there?"

"I do not know. I look."

For several minutes he waited while she ate. What the hell was happening? What kind of a mess was this? Certainly, from Erik's notes and the burned café, he understood that these people, whoever they were, were dangerous. They were not playing games. But who were they? What were they?

"Tell me what you can. I know nothing."

"Long ago"—Kawasi made a sweeping gesture—"my people live all about here. They cut trees to build house or for burn. They plant corn and squash. No rain comes. Year after year, no enough rain. Fierce people come. They kill our people, steal grain. Soon they camp nearby to steal whatever. We are not many. Some go away.

"Long time before, we come to this place from another. We come from a place turning evil. We come to escape evil. Some wish to return. Two go back, and they say all is green there, plenty of rain, and only a few people there, so we go back.

"It was against old beliefs, but our people feared hunger and the fierce enemies coming down from the North, so some went back.

"But the evil was still there. It had not gone. Our people had closed the top of their heads and could no longer hear the Voices."

"Where is this place you went back to?" Mike waited, half afraid of what he knew he would hear.

"It is on Other Side. I do not know what to say, what words. It is like this, only . . . only *different.*"

"You said they went back. How did they go?"

"There are places, openings sometimes, never always. Places where can go through to Other Side. The old man who tells me your words, he got through but never get back. He was young man then. He was what he say a 'cow-boy'? They come to look for him. Somehow they know he is

64

on Other Side. He very . . . he keeps away from them. Somehow . . . they do not find him. I think he kills one man, but he finds ways to hide."

"He is there yet?"

"Still there. Some of my people know. They help him. But he very how you say? Strong? He know how to hide. Now I do not think they look any more. Maybe. I do not know."

"What do you call him?"

"He is Johnny. Only Johnny."

"Your people were the cliff dwellers? The old ones the Navajo call the Anasazi?"

"Yes."

Mike glanced out the window. The street looked the same as always. A truck was parked across the way, its driver coming toward the café. His own Jeep was in plain sight. Two local men stood across the street talking. All seemed to be as usual.

What was he to do? If they had taken Erik back, wherever "back" was, then he was gone, perhaps gone forever.

"What will they do with Erik?"

"Many questions. When no more answers, they kill. They hate much and they fear. They rule all, yet they live in fear. They fear to lose their power, they fear we who do not agree will get strength from Other Side. They fear ideas from your side. Any who get through they kill."

"Then some do get through?"

She shook her head. "Not often. In my memory only two, I think. Or maybe they did not tell us all. Long ago there was a boy, a young man who got through. I do not know what happened. Long, long before that, there were two men who hunt gold. They were tortured, killed, then left on Other Side."

"What do they know about us? The people on this side?"

"Much. Sometimes they send men to steal. To kill. You have things to listen, things to speak long distances. This they want."

And Erik was a specialist in the field. What he did not know, nobody knew. If they discovered this they might keep him alive.

"What about the kiva?"

"It is mystery place. Long ago story say it is secret way to pass through. The kiva is sacred place, but evil men close it up. Now they want open."

She sipped her coffee. "I think they make house now. I think they want always place, an all time open place to go and come."

Mike watched the street, trying to bring his thoughts into focus. What was going on here? Was this real? Or some elaborate hoax? He knew nothing about physics but he knew such things were said to be possible, that parallel worlds could exist. At least, some believed they could. He had seen things in Central Asia and Tibet . . . could there be a connection? He doubted it.

Erik's cry for help must be heeded. Whatever else might or might not be true, he was in trouble, and he had called on Mike for help.

66

"Over there? After your people went back from here, what happened?"

She shook her head. "I know little. For a time they lived as always, then change. It was my ancestor who began it.

"He was very young boy when, by himself, he built a larger dam to save water. He grew fine crops. He found new ways to do things. He created devices—what you call machines—to do things. The evil ones decided he was bewitched and killed him.

"They could not kill his thoughts. Those who killed him began to use his magic. They built stronger walls and larger houses and they built other dams. Then they made laws to say who can have water and when. People accepted the laws because they were good and they kept away much trouble. But the ones who said yes or no on water soon made other laws which were not good. So some of us left them and went to a new place to live as we always had.

"They came against us because we did not obey. Some they killed and some they took as slaves, but then we found a place where my ancestor had worked when building things, and we found some other things he had made and some he had begun to make. We used those things to fight them and they left us alone. Johnny helped. He said my ancestor was another Davinch."

"Da Vinci? Leonardo da Vinci was an artist who invented many things."

"I think so."

"You have come over to this side. Have you done this often?"

"It is not permitted. Somehow they know. I do not know how, but instantly they know. If one comes through he is seized. They do not rest until he is taken."

"What about those who rule? Do they go over?"

"They say no, yet sometimes do. Or once they did and then a great water covered the place and for long time they could not until Erik opened the kiva."

"But there are other ways? He who drew the line on Erik's blueprints must have come some other way."

"There are sometime ways. I do not understand but sometimes there are openings. That is how I am here."

"The great water was probably what we call Lake Powell. We built a dam to stop the water of the Colorado and drowned most of what was Glen Canyon."

They were both silent. His eyes sought the street. Suppose they came now? What would he do?

"I must help him," he said.

"You cannot. They have him."

"Where will they take him?"

"It is a bad place, a place of fear. It is an old place, a place that was there before we entered into the Fourth World, your world. I have not been there but he who was my mother's father knew it."

She looked at him with sudden realization.

"Now it is you they must take. They must have you. They wish none to know their world exists and now you do."

"And you also."

She shrugged a shoulder. "They know of me. I am hated. I am wanted most of all. I am head of family now, of clan. They look to me. I am descend from He Who Had Magic, the old one who made many things. I must go back."

"There's the kiva."

"No. That is their way. They will watch and they are very near to it."

"But you came!"

"My way is not sure, very dangerous, but there is a way that is open, most times open. They do not know it. We do not. Only the Saqua know."

"The Saqua? The hairy ones?"

"You know of them? They are not people, but they know things others do not. They come to hunt or to take sheep to eat."

"Sheep? From the Indians?"

"They take sheep. I do not know whose sheep."

He finished his coffee. "We had better get away from here and do some planning."

Raglan started to rise but a hand dropped on his shoulder. He glanced up.

The man was stocky, strongly built. He wore a badge. "Mind? I've a few questions for the lady. For you, too, for that matter."

He turned and called to the waitress. "Marie? Another cup of coffee."

He glanced from one to the other. "I'm Gallagher. I'll ask the questions."

─────────── **VIII** ───────────

HE GLANCED AT Mike Raglan, then at the girl. "What's your name, ma'am?"

"Kawasi."

"You from around here?"

"I am . . . tour-ist." She spoke calmly, without hesitation or fear.

"You're an Indian?"

"Long ago my people live near here. I have come to see where it was."

He turned to Raglan. "You two old friends?"

"We've just met. I recognized her from the description of a mutual friend—Erik Hokart."

"Hokart? Is he the one who plans to build somewhere down the river? Some kind of scientist, isn't he?"

"That's his reputation, but he's a successful businessman as well. The two do not always go together. Yes, he loves this part of the country and planned to build a home there. He made a fortune in electronics and can afford to live wherever he wishes."

Gallagher took his coffee from the waitress and sipped it, then turned his attention to Kawasi. "Were you in the restaurant when it burned?"

"No, but I was in it just a moment before. When I saw those men I was frightened. I ran."

70

"What men?"

"I do not know them. There were two, perhaps another. I am not sure. Mr. Hokart was afraid and went to the counter to ask the man for a gun. The man would not give it."

"He was right. What did Hokart do then?"

"I do not know. I am gone."

"Where'd you go?"

"I hide. Then for room for sleep."

Gallagher turned to Mike. "What do you know about Hokart? Was he on anything? Narcotics?"

"Not him. He was far too sensible a man. He didn't need any crutches. He was a sober, almost too serious a man, something of a loner because he did his best thinking when alone. What he really wanted was a place away from the telephone. You know, when a man attains great success, people are forever coming to him with ideas and he did not need ideas from anyone else.

"He wanted a place where he could sit and think. I would not actually call him a scientist. He was an inventor of sorts but he had the ability to make things work. Many of his friends were doing pure research, but Erik had a way of sensing the practical value of things. He knew how to turn their work into money."

"Anybody want to kill him?"

"Nobody I know. He had no relatives. No heirs. Most of his friends had every reason to keep him alive."

If Gallagher knew anything, he appeared to have no intention of revealing it. From his questions he seemed to Mike to be feeling his way, searching for some explanation of what had happened.

"Ma'am, you said you were afraid of those men. Why?"

"I am in the desert with Mr. Hokart. He very . . . very anxious. We get into car and those men jump from behind rocks, but we drove away. Then they come to the restaurant."

"Where's Hokart now?"

"We were just wondering about that," Raglan said. "They must have taken him."

"Kidnapped?"

"Something of the kind. From what I have heard, no bodies were found in the fire, so he must have escaped that. You have his car, I believe."

Gallagher sipped his coffee, mulling it over. He was a shrewd, intelligent man and Mike hoped he was accepting the story, which was about as much of the truth as he knew, not referring to speculations. Gallagher glanced at Raglan suddenly. "What's your business?"

"I'm a writer, mostly about the far-out and far-away. I've known Erik for several years and he wanted my advice."

"On what?"

"This country, particularly. I used to live around here, wandering the back country."

"What country?"

"Dark Canyon, Fable Canyon, Beef Basin, the Sweet Alice Hills, Woodenshoe—you name it."

Grudgingly, Gallagher nodded. "Sounds like you

72

know something about it." He took a swallow of coffee. "Know anybody who'd want to kidnap Hokart?"

"No." Raglan hesitated. Then he said, "Officer, Hokart and I have exchanged books from time to time, mostly paperbacks. One was left for me at Tamarron where I am staying. A short time later a man broke into my condo and tried to steal it."

"Steal a book? What the hell for?"

"You've got me. He took it thinking it was something else, I suspect."

In as few words as possible, Raglan explained about the warning from the girl at the desk, then awakening in his bed with the man standing at the bar.

"Lucky he didn't kill you," Gallagher said.

Raglan smiled. "I think I could have persuaded him not to," he said mildly.

Gallagher looked at him again. "You got a description?"

"About five nine or ten, judging by his height against the bar, dark hair and eyes, swarthy skin. Very broad-shouldered. My feeling was that he was a very tough, dangerous man."

"What makes you think so?"

"He was under control. Not the least nervous. He took in the situation at a glance. He saw I wasn't going to try to stop him and knew an attempt to kill me would stir up more trouble than it was worth. My feeling was that he was a professional, knew what he was doing at every step, and was not to be stampeded. He just turned and went out."

"And then?"

"I went to the window and watched him cross the snow to the highway. He got into a white van. It pulled away toward Durango."

"You called him a professional. What did you mean?"

"Just what I said. I've known such men in a dozen countries. He was a CIA, FBI, KGB type. He knew exactly what he was doing and didn't plan to do any more or any less."

"What did he weigh?"

"About my weight. One-ninety, I'd say, but to most people he would look fifteen pounds lighter. Moved like a cat. He was nobody to play games with."

"This Hokart—he ever work for the government? Secret stuff?"

"Not lately—at least not that I know of. He's done something of the sort in the past."

Nobody spoke for several minutes. The officer impressed him, so Raglan decided to take a chance. If he told the man what he believed he might be considered off his rocker, but he wanted to prepare Gallagher for what he might encounter. This was no time to let such a man go it blind.

"I take it you've been around here for some time."

"Most of my adult years. Why?"

Again Mike hesitated. "This used to be considered kind of spooky country. I don't mean right

74

here, but off there toward the river. When Hokart asked me to come out, I had the impression that whatever was worrying him was from around there.

"You may believe I'm nuts but I think we're walking on the thin edge of something. I wouldn't want a lot of people down there, disturbing things. If you decide to go down there, take somebody who can keep his mouth shut and somebody who knows this country."

Gallagher sat back and stared at Mike. Then he half-turned. "Marie? Bring me a cheeseburger. On rye. And bring us some more coffee."

He glanced out of the window, following Raglan's eyes. "You expecting somebody?"

"Yes, and no. Nor was I last night when that man came into my condo. I am watching for a white van."

"There's been one around. I've seen one twice in the past couple of days." Gallagher glanced back. "What made Hokart decide to build down there? Of all places?"

"He'd flown over this country going and coming, and fell in love with the beauty of it. He decided he wanted a home atop a mesa, some place where he could sit and think. He planned to build it himself, out of native rock. He was handy with tools, and he was in no hurry."

"That's the last place in the world I'd choose."

Their eyes were on Gallagher, waiting. "Used to be some Paiutes lived down there. All gone now. Nobody seems to know where. There were a couple of mining ventures, too, but they didn't last long." He looked directly at Raglan. "Kind of creepy, they said."

Gallagher nursed his cup in both hands. He was studying Raglan. "I'm beginning to place you now. You're a writer, you say. Are you the Raglan who debunks mysteries? Haunted houses and the like?"

"Yes, but let's just say that I investigate mysteries. I'm not debunking anything, really. Just looking for the truth."

"That why Hokart got you out here?"

"Yes."

"I guess you've seen a lot of odd things. I heard about you being in Haiti, Tibet, and down there in the jungle country of Peru."

"I've been around, and yes, I've seen some strange things, and I've a hunch, Gallagher, that you know something of what we're up against."

The man did not reply for several minutes. "No," he said slowly, "I don't. That country down there isn't in my bailiwick and I stay out of it. Most of us do, and that goes for the Indians, too. They don't like it much."

His cheeseburger came, and when he had taken a bite, chewed, and swallowed, he looked at Raglan again. "But that man you were talking about was no ghost. And that fire—"

"Kawasi said one of the men threw some discs and when they broke, there was flame."

Gallagher looked over at her. "How big were the discs?"

She indicated the top of his coffee cup. "That big, maybe a little larger."

"Gallagher, at the risk of you thinking me crazy, I want to leave a thought with you. The Hopis say, and apparently the Anasazi believed it, that this is the Fourth World."

"Everybody around here knows that story."

"And that they left the Third World because it was evil."

"That's the story. What's on your mind?"

"Suppose when the drought came, and the warring Indians from the North, that some of them went back into that Third World, where it was evil? Suppose some of them knew how to go back and forth?"

Gallagher did not look at Raglan. He looked out of the window and chewed on his cheeseburger. "You're asking me to believe quite a lot," he said thoughtfully. "But what about the van?"

"They'd have to have a working base over here. A place to keep the van and whatever else they need. They would want a useful place that wasn't too obvious."

He was silent again. People were coming into the restaurant and from time to time somebody spoke, glancing curiously at Raglan and Kawasi.

"If I suggested such a thing they'd say I had a screw loose. Not that a lot of people around here don't believe in Navajo witchcraft." Gallagher glanced at Raglan again. "What about you? Are you going to be around?"

"Hokart has disappeared. I am going to look for him. I may get my tail in a crack."

"You're likely to, if what you say is true. I'll see if I can locate that van."

"Gallagher? If you find it you'd better have a man or two as a backup. I mean it. They will play for keeps, and if what I'm thinking is right they can escape beyond your jurisdiction."

Gallagher finished his cheeseburger. "Sometimes my jurisdiction is what I want it to be."

He looked at Kawasi. "Where will you be?"

"With me," Mike said, "when it's possible. To-night she will be in the motel next door. If your people could keep an eye on it . . ."

"We can and we will. I've got some good boys here."

He touched the napkin to his mouth. "That Third World now . . . ?"

"I may have to go there."

Gallagher took a long look at Raglan. "You really believe all this? I mean—well, I've talked to the Indians, and once in a while one of them, when he's alone and not with any of the others, he'll come up with some mighty strange tales. But still . . ." He shook his head.

"At this moment Gallagher, I've no other way to go. I have some evidence which I cannot share with you now. It does not belong to me. I believe it is either solid evidence or an example of a weird kind of insanity. In any case, you had a restaurant destroyed in a flash fire. That's evidence. Erik Hokart has vanished, and that's a fact. We may find him and we may not.

"Erik had some weird experiences. He has told

me of them. He has met at least one very beautiful woman from the Other Side—"

"Are you kidding?"

"I am serious. And a warning, Officer. If you meet her, leave her alone or you will die."

"She is a Poison Woman," Kawasi said. "I believe there are six now."

"A Poison Woman?"

"The story seems to be that such women are impregnated with poison to which they are immune, but which will kill any man who touches them. Sexually, I mean. I've heard such stories in the Middle East and India."

"Kind of takes the fun out of things, doesn't it?" Gallagher glanced at Kawasi. "Do you believe that?"

"I do."

He shook his head. "Well, you've got her convinced, anyway."

"I told him," Kawasi said. "I warned him as I warn you. She belongs to The Hand."

"The 'Hand'?"

"He who rules is called The Hand."

Gallagher stared at her. "I don't know what to believe. I started out buying part of this, anyway, but now . . . well, I don't know."

"It is true," Kawasi said.

"You believe in this Third World?" Gallagher asked skeptically. "You really believe in it?"

She was very cool, and very beautiful. "I believe in it. I have to believe in it. I have lived there all my life until now."

IX

GALLAGHER STARED AT her for a moment. Then his attention shifted to Raglan. "I'd better deal with something I'm fitted for.

"That man, now? The one who came into your condo? You got anything more than his height and weight? And that he was a 'professional'—whatever that means?"

"You're a professional, Gallagher, in your way. He was a professional, too. As to description: He had a scar, maybe two inches long, on his right jawbone. His ears were flat and close-set, not much in the way of lobes. His hairline was low—if it wasn't a hairpiece, and I doubt it was. His skin color was a little darker than Kawasi's and his eyes were smaller—a strong-boned, rather hard face, fleshy over the cheekbones."

"You're pretty good," Gallagher said. He made some notes, then glanced up at Raglan. "If you figure on going out to that mesa where Hokart was building, be careful. When you turn off the highway you'll be on your own."

He turned to Kawasi. "I'm not buyin' what you say, meaning no disrespect. It's pretty far-out, you've got to admit that, but let's suppose what you say is true. What's it like over there?"

"Like here, but different. The sun is . . . is not the same. It is like sun shining through mist.

80

There are many green fields, many meadows, all watered by ditches."

Gallagher got up. "You going down there? To where Hokart was building?"

"I think so."

"Where else?"

"I'll be there, here, at Tamarron, or en route, but I'm not looking for trouble. I do want to find him and get him out of any trouble he might be in."

"Be careful." Gallagher started away. "Poison Woman? Boy, that's a new one!"

"Very old, actually. The story was that if a king wanted to get rid of a rival he just made him a present of such a girl. After that, no trouble."

Gallagher shrugged. "Well, if you got to go . . ."

When he was gone, Kawasi looked at Mike. "Who he is?"

"The law. He's an officer. Investigates crimes, things like the fire. Don't underrate him. I think he's a very smart, very cagey young man."

"He is good?"

"I think so. And capable."

"He did not believe me."

Raglan waved his hand around. "None of them would, not entirely. Don't tell anybody anything. They would think you lied. Just tell them your folks used to live around here, that you are part Indian."

"I am all what you call 'Indian,' I think."

They were silent, and Mike Raglan watched the

81

street. If "they" had gone so far as to come into his condo in the night and to set fire to the café to destroy Erik and Kawasi, they would not hesitate to eliminate him. Dared he take her with him? But where could he leave her? The police had other duties, but this was a small town and they would not miss very much, if anything.

"I must go back to the mesa. I must be sure Erik is not there."

"I go with you."

"This cowboy you know? The old man?"

"Johnny?"

"How did he get over to . . . to the 'Other Side'? The kiva was not open then?"

"There are sometime ways. It is a thing . . . I do not understand. Sometimes open, sometimes closed. It has no what you call . . . pattern? He tell me he chasing wild cow. What he speaks is 'maverick.' It run away, he chase it, go ver' fast down hillside with his rope swinging. The cow disappear, and then he charge after. . . . He is on Other Side. It just happen, and he cannot find the way back. Maybe it is closed. I do not know. He does not know. He never find way back."

"What happened then?"

"They know someone come. They come look. He hide. They no find." She raised her eyes to Raglan's. "The land much wild where he is. Wild cow, sometime wild horse. He was young cowboy then. He old cowboy now. They never find him to live."

"He killed some of them?"

82

"I think maybe. He does not say, but I hear talk that men look for him, men die. Now nobody look. He has been there long time and nothing happen bad for them, so they no longer care. I think."

"Do you know where he is?"

"Oh, yes! He friendly to us. He *is* friendly to us."

They were silent again and he considered the situation. He had an idea that Gallagher was doing the logical thing. He would be looking for the white van. It was the one bit of hard evidence he had, and it was something tangible that Gallagher himself had seen.

Certainly, if "they" were to operate on this side they must have a base, a place to sleep, to keep the van when it was not in use—a place not too far from their way back, if they had to go back.

He was dealing with something of which he knew nothing at all, nor did he know with whom he was dealing. For all he knew, some of them had been living under cover on this side for years. There might even be one of them in this very restaurant. It would be a logical listening post. If they had a base on this side it might have been established many years ago. He would have to be very, very careful.

Where did they get the van, for example? And it must have a license. The driver must have a driver's license. That implied a connection.

Did they have more than one vehicle?

"Kawasi? Would you recognize one of the people from the Other Side if you saw one? I mean, there may be many over here."

"I think . . . maybe. I do not be sure. I think sometimes I know."

He got up. "Let's go." At the cash register he paid his check, and she watched carefully.

Outside the restaurant he stopped, looking around. The street was empty. A pickup drove by, with two Navajos in front. He crossed the street to his car, glancing back as he opened the door. Nobody seemed to pay any attention.

Most of these people were Mormons and they knew each other. That might help Gallagher.

He drove to the nearest gas station and filled his tank. Thoughtfully, he watched the filling-station attendant. Another good place for a listening post; but the boy was paying no attention.

As they turned into the road, Raglan saw a car parked alongside the highway a good mile ahead. It was Gallagher's car. As he neared it a hand reached out, flagging him down.

Gallagher was alone. "You got a gun?"

Raglan hesitated briefly. "Yes. I always carry one when I go into the mountains."

"Keep it handy."

Raglan mentioned his speculation about the possibilities of a longstanding base, and Gallagher nodded. "I been thinking the same thing. Been running people through my mind, wondering who and where."

He sat silent, staring down the road. Then he glanced over at Raglan. "Kinda spooky," he said.

"I can't deal with it. Not yet, anyway." He paused again. "I've been reading an article about you." He held up the magazine. "You're used to this sort of thing."

"You never get used to it," Raglan said. "The frauds are easy. Almost any halfway decent magician can beat them at their own game. Most of the tricks they use were old-hat fifty years ago. People believe because they wish to believe and they don't want the frauds exposed.

"If someone expects miracles they will see miracles."

"I got some ideas." Gallagher looked at Raglan. "Better keep this under your hat. No use to get a lot of talk started."

Raglan started his car and moved down the road. The turnoff was miles ahead and very easily missed. He would have to watch closely.

Kawasi was quiet, resting her eyes, almost asleep. Mike did not feel like talking nor did she, it seemed. He was trying to remember the map Erik had sent him. It was a far different route from the one he had taken down the Canyon road, which was far away to the south. He was well over an hour from town when he turned off the highway and took the dim desert trail. When he had driven a short distance the road dipped into a hollow and he stopped the car.

Kawasi's eyes opened. "What is it?"

He was getting out of the car. "I want to look at the road. See if there are tracks."

He walked to the road ahead, pausing by the

front bumper to study the trail. After a moment he walked on ahead, keeping alongside the trail, not wishing to smudge the tracks.

There were tire-prints from two different vehicles. The tracks were several days old, with the paw-prints of a porcupine and several ground squirrels and some snake tracks crossing them. He walked several hundred feet, studying the tracks. The first car had been driven very fast by someone who obviously knew the road—probably Erik Hokart. He had been followed by another car, certainly not the white van. Yet there were no returning tracks, so where was Erik now? Where had they taken him?

Kawasi was sitting up, watching him. "They did not come back this way," he told her.

She shrugged. "They have other ways, not sure ways, but they exist."

Where was Erik? If they had a hideout, a base on this side, had they taken him there? He suggested it to Kawasi.

"I think maybe," she said, "but not long. The Hand would wish to have him to be questioned."

"And then killed?"

"Perhaps, but I do not think so. He is scientist? I think The Hand keep him, work him. He has . . . how do you say? He has things for listening. Big ears."

She paused. "He listen to what people speak to each other. All the time listen."

From where Mike stood he could see the highway, if such it could be called. It was a lonely road along which maybe two or three cars an hour traveled. He saw nothing now. He turned, sweeping the country with his eyes. Of course there were many places a watcher could be and remain hidden.

He got into the car and started down the road. He should have a rifle or, better still, a shotgun, a sawed-off shotgun for easy handling.

After a few miles the trail branched and he took the easternmost branch. The desert growth increased as they drew nearer to some rugged ridges of bare rock. He glanced at Kawasi. "Are you frightened?"

"Yes. They bad people. They want me very much. They very much afraid of people over here. No discipline, they say."

"Have many been over here?"

"Oh, no! It is impossible! Almost impossible. For a long time, nobody. Sometimes an accident. If someone come from here he is tracked down and killed. At once."

"And Johnny? The cowboy?"

"They try. He too wise. He leave no tracks. He hide very well. Several places for hide. Finally they decide he not important."

"And you?"

"I am rebel. I think too much. I ask questions. I am threat, so I escape to hills where others wait." She paused while Raglan negotiated a sharp turn and a dip through a wash. "There is bad dry time. Nothing grow. The plants make no seeds. Some die, many sick. They send a man for seeds, but some will not grow." She looked at Raglan. "Is not same as here—some plants grow, some not. We do not know why. It is decide there must be a permanent way. You say *permanent?* It is always way we need. Much seed."

She paused again, looking out over the desert. "What you call broccoli? It will not grow over there. It is try often. Tried often.

"Your corn is different, much bigger. But your seed does not grow well over there. It is puzzle."

Raglan drew up behind a juniper to study the road ahead and the country around. Something was bothering him, and he had known such feelings before. Something was wrong, and he was feeling increasingly uneasy, yet he could see nothing out of the ordinary.

He had been listening with only half his attention. Some seeds that would not grow? Broccoli, among others. But wasn't broccoli a developed plant? He knew too little about such things.

He was foolish to have come out here so late in the day. He should have waited, as he had planned to do, until morning, when he would have a full day of sunshine in which to look about.

But he had to find Erik, and if Erik was lying injured on the mesa, he must be found and helped. Above all, the key to this must be at its point of origin. At least, that was where he must begin.

Nothing moved on the desert. He started on, tooling the car around a bend in the trail and down a steep incline. Momentarily he took his right hand from the wheel to touch his .357 magnum. It was reassuring.

"When you cross over," he asked, "is there any physical reaction? I mean, does it affect your body? Or your mind?"

"A little. Sometimes the head spins. What is it you say—'dizzy'? I think so. And"—she put her hand on her stomach—"one is sickish, feeling bad down there. Some never get over. Sometimes it is hours, sometimes days."

She put her hand on his arm. "Mr. Raglan? There is somebody out there. I know it. I feel it."

He stopped the car again. It was not very hot now, but there seemed to be heat waves dancing. Slowly, he let his eyes search out the terrain before him.

Nothing . . . ? Nothing he could see, but he knew what she meant. He could feel it, too.

"Over there"—she pointed—"is where Erik leaves his car. You can get no closer."

He let the car roll forward. The place was too open, too exposed. There were low hills around, much growth such as would be found in any semidesert area. Here and there were boulders, rocks, and a few ridges.

She touched his arm again. "Mr. Raglan? I fear."

"Call me Mike," he said.

X

FOR AN INSTANT after he switched off the ignition he felt a wave of almost panic. The sound of the motor had been somehow reassuring, and now in the utter silence he felt cut off, isolated.

The car was security; it was escape, a way back to the normal, the usual, the everyday.

What was he doing here, anyway? Why was he not back at Tamarron, going down to the San Juan Room for breakfast in a normal, sensible, attractive world? What was he doing out here at the end of everything?

Shadows were appearing now, shadows among the rocks, among the scattered juniper and the brush. A faint wind stirred. He swallowed, checked his gun again, and took a flashlight from the glove compartment. "We won't be long," he said, and hoped he was right. "We will just walk over and see if Erik is around."

He stepped down from the car and closed the door. The sound was loud in the stillness. She sat very quietly, staring ahead. He walked around the car and opened her door. She took his hand and stepped down.

She looked at him. "I fear," she said. "Something is wrong. There is something—"

"We won't be long," he said again, wondering why he had been such a fool as to bring her.

Yet she knew the way and he did not. "Let's

90

go," he said, and she started off, looking quickly around. He felt in his pocket to be sure he had taken the keys from the ignition. He had them. Turning, he checked the position of the car. He was a fool. He should have turned it around for a quick getaway. He had always done that when in wild country. Why had he not done so now?

Was it because he was not coming back? That was absurd. Of course he was coming back, and within the hour.

Kawasi walked quickly, surely. He followed, keeping his eyes busy, straining his ears for the slightest sound.

What was wrong with him? He had been in the desert before. He had been in many deserts—the Sahara, the Takla Makan, the Kalahari—and all of them had their mysteries. His thoughts returned to the Takla Makan and the smoky fires of camel dung and movements in the night.

He had been close to something there, not only in the desert but in the Kunlun Mountains, which bordered that desert on the south. He had been close to something disturbing, something with which he had been unwilling to cope. Was not this the same sort of situation?

There was no more than a suggestion of a path. When they neared the end of the mesa on which they walked, he could see that other one ahead of him, and beyond, a small box canyon. He turned left, weaving his way among rocks and wild shrubs. Pausing to catch his breath he found Kawasi close behind him. The car was now far away, barely discernible among the rocks. For a moment he had an overwhelming urge to turn back. What was he getting into, anyway?

"If Erik is not there . . ." he began.

"He will not be," Kawasi said. "He is on the Other Side. They have him."

Something within him cringed. He did not like to think of that "Other Side," nor to believe in it. He knew now that he did not wish to cope with unreality, and that was how he thought of it. Of course, he reminded himself, if it did exist it was simply another phase of reality. He had dealt most of his life with the eerie, the impossible, the strange. These had been his daily fare, but they had been, for the greater part, simply illusion, fraud, and legerdemain. People were gullible because they wished to believe. His role had been to see the reality, to expose the chicanery.

So far, all he had encountered except for some experiences in Sinkiang and Tibet, had been easily exposed by someone skilled in illusion.

Pausing, she pointed. "It is right over there, beyond the rocks."

She indicated a low mound of red rock. "Erik planned to build there, using the standing rock for walls."

"And the kiva?"

"It is close by."

They started on and his hand touched his pistol butt. It was a comforting feeling, but would a bullet work against these . . . what? These creatures?

What *was* he thinking? Kawasi was one of them, or said she was.

What if it was some kind of an elaborate swindle? After all, Erik was a wealthy man. He had money, lots of it. Suppose all this was some kind of a plan to get money from him?

If so, Kawasi must be a part of it, and this he did not wish to believe. Yet better men had been deceived by seemingly nice women before this. But if it was not a fraud, was Kawasi normal? Was she *human?*

What were they like, those creatures from the Other Side? Did Kawasi truly exist? Or was she merely a phantom, something from beyond the veil, from that world of evil the old Indians had fled?

What was the Other Side? That question shadowed Mike's every thought, every decision. He had heard of parallel worlds, of other dimensions. Strange disappearances had been a part of his life. And there had been many such. The case of the *Iron Mountain,* for example, a riverboat with a crew and fifty-five passengers that steamed around a bend in the Mississippi into oblivion. Or at least that was the story.

Its barges were found adrift, but there had been no wreckage, no sound of an explosion. The story had been well known along the river in 1872 and since, but of course, the Mississippi had given birth to many legends.

There was no path, no trail as such, yet Kawasi walked quickly among the rocks until suddenly they were there. He stopped, struck by the strange appearance of the mesa top. It gave the appearance of having been a field, badly leached, but nonetheless a field.

Mesas with any amount of soil on top were few. More often than not, in this part of the country, mesas were almost flat rock with occasional patches of earth supporting a meager growth of brush and occasional small trees, usually juniper.

The ruined walls were close by, covered by a sheet of plywood weighted down with rocks to make a temporary shelter. Inside he found Erik's sleeping bag, an air cushion, a small gas stove, and a few dishes. There was also a small portable ice chest and a food box, closed tight.

He glanced around the workroom where, on a wide and long table, were spread the plans for the house Erik had projected. Glancing out the window he could see the space between the rocks Erik planned to utilize. If the natural rock floor were smoothed just a little, it would be quite level. Two major walls would be solid rock, both flat on the inner side. Actually, he would have only two walls to build, unless he decided to add more rooms— something easily done. The view was magnificent.

Across the river, and downriver just a little, was the great mesa where he had seen the flare of light. He paused, frowning. With all that had happened since, he had forgotten the incident. Was there a connection? Might that have been the instant that Erik vanished?

Looking around for Kawasi, he saw her standing, staring off at the mesa.

"What is it?" He spoke softly, moving toward her.

She did not turn toward him, but said, "That place! It looks like . . ."

"Like what?"

She shook her head. "It cannot be." She looked toward the West. "If it was . . . over there . . ." She shook her head again. "It cannot be."

He looked around again. "Erik is not here, that's obvious. I guess we'd better go back."

"No! Please! You must not! We must not! Not tonight!"

"What's wrong? Why not tonight?"

"It would be dangerous. They . . . they are worse at night. They would see us but we could not see them. It is better if we stay here."

He did not want to stay. He wanted to get away, to get back to a town, to people—anywhere but here. Nor did he relish the drive back over those winding desert trails where it was easy enough to miss a turn by daylight, let alone at night.

It was an eerie, lonely place. The drop down to the river must be almost sheer, and several hundred feet. The mesa was a peninsula of rock pointing downstream, almost due west, and surrounded by deep gorges except at the place where they had approached it.

"All right," he agreed reluctantly, "but as you can see, the accommodations aren't much."

He went back into the ruin. A glance into the portable refrigerator showed cheese and some cold cuts, a few cold drinks. There was a case of cold drinks, a mixed lot, sitting nearby. He went outside and looked around for fuel. He wanted a fire; he wanted very much to have a fire.

Nearby there was a stack of roots, broken branches, and the trunks of a few lightning-blasted trees—nothing large but good fuel. He needed only a few minutes to build a fire. Kawasi walked to it and put out her hands to it, gratefully. "It is cold," she said.

Stars were appearing now, and only the tops of mesas, ridges, and the distant Navajo Mountain were catching the last glow of light.

"I'll make some coffee," he said.

Erik had planned well. There were supplies enough to last for some time. Did he bring them all himself? Or did someone come to him? By helicopter, perhaps? That would certainly be the easiest way, and there was plenty of room for landing.

He took out his gun and checked it. Kawasi watched him, then asked, "It is a weapon?"

"A gun," he said, "a pistol. Did Erik have one, do you know?"

"I do not know. I think possible. I think maybe. It is different, more flat."

"An automatic, I expect. I wonder if they found it?" He glanced at her. "Would they search him? Go through his pockets?"

"I think yes. I do not know, but . . ."

More than likely they would. How much did they know of guns? Or did they have some of their own? Or some similar weapon? Or, if they could come back and forth, might they not have brought weapons from this side?

The last light was disappearing, so he added fuel to the fire, causing it to blaze up. Instinctively, he looked toward the long mesa where he had seen the flare. It was dark and ominous.

Closer, just across the river, was another mesa. He recognized its shape, remembering there had been some mining there at one time, but unsuccessful mining, if he remembered correctly.

He found some bread in the food chest and made sandwiches from the cold cuts. When the coffee was ready, they sat down in the opening of the ruin.

He thought, suddenly, of the kiva. It would be on his left. Or was it to the right? He tried to remember what Erik had said.

He turned to Kawasi. "I am afraid," she said.

"You need not be. We will manage."

"But if they come?"

He shrugged. "Stay behind me. Let me handle it."

"But you do not know. They have means to . . . to make you helpless. And they are evil, evil!"

He added fuel to the fire and handed her a plate with a sandwich and then a cup of coffee. He sipped his own, and it tasted good. The air was cold, and the coffee warmed him.

His eyes were busy, his every sense alert. He bit

into his sandwich, glad of the silence, realizing that every slightest sound could be heard. He glanced at Kawasi. She was beautiful. Really, truly beautiful in a very quiet unassuming way.

"Over there," he suggested, "you live in a house?"

" 'House'?" She puzzled over the word. "It is a cave where I live. Where the old ones lived. You see, we must hide. They look for us. Always they look."

"How do they live?"

"What you call this?" She indicated the walls. "It is room?"

"It was once. Yes, I'd call it a room."

"Over there, in the other place, many rooms are together, many people live. Each family have rooms but all in one place."

"Like an apartment building? Or a pueblo?"

"Yes! Pueblo! It is a word I know. I hear it spoken, although the word is not ours. There are many pueblo, some very fine."

He stood up, cup in hand, and let his eyes reach beyond the firelight, out into the darkness, seeking, watching.

"How large is your country?" he asked. "How much land?"

She shook her head. "I do not know. I think no one knows. Those who work know where they work. They know where are park places. To go far from where we sleep or work is not allowed."

She paused. "Sometimes I believe even they do

not know, those who command us. I think they know little more than we."

She paused. "Once it was not so. When my people ruled—"

"Your people?"

"Yes. My great-grandfather was . . . was what you call He Who Rules. There was sudden attack. He was kill. Others took control, and we escape. Now my people live in far hills where nobody comes. Or nobody did come until Erik. Then all is change."

Slowly, the story took shape. Evidently her family had ruled for many years, and then there had been a palace revolution. The evil ones took control, or the ones she implied were evil. Her family and a few others had escaped to the lonely canyons where nobody came, and lived as the Old Ones had lived.

"The ones the Navajo called the Anasazi?"

"Yes, I—" She caught her breath, and something moved out in the darkness.

Mike Raglan stood very still. His gun was in his holster but he was wishing it was in his hand.

There was something out there, something very close, something coming nearer, and nearer. . . .

XI

THE FACE OF Kawasi was very pale. She moved closer to him.

The sky was clear, blue with early night, and

already a few bright stars shone. Downriver and across loomed the long dark bulk of the great mesa.

"It's all right, Kawasi." He spoke quietly. "No need to be afraid."

Something moved out there beyond the firelight, something drawing closer. His hand went to his gun. Suddenly it was there, looming across the fire at the very edge of the light.

It was a dog, a very large dog. It was Chief.

He sighed in relief. "Chief?" He spoke quietly. "Come, Chief!"

The mastiff remained where he was, testing the air with his nose, watchful and wary.

"It's all right, Chief. Don't you remember me?"

The big dog came forward another step, then another. "Come on, Chief. It's all right. Where's Erik, Chief? Where's your master?"

The dog drew nearer, then came around the fire, and Mike put out a hand. "You remember me, Chief? We're old friends. We came out of Tibet together, you and I. We walked down the mountains and we camped in the desert."

With sudden realization the big dog leaped up, yelping with excitement. "Easy! Easy, boy! You're too big for that now! You'd knock a man down!"

Kawasi had drawn back in amazement while he ruffled the hair around Chief's neck and talked to him. "Where'd you leave Erik, Chief? We've got to find him, Chief."

The big dog was beside himself with joy. "Settle down now, boy, and I'll find you something to

100

eat. Seems to me I saw a case of dog food back here." He went over to a box under the drafting table and got out two cans of dog food and emptied them into the dog's dish. Chief wasted no time but went to eating as if starved.

Kawasi stared at him. "It is a beast? You speak like to person."

Mike chuckled. "You've asked a good question, Kawasi. To me, Chief has always been a person. We met each other when he was a tiny puppy in Tibet, up in the Chang-Tang. He was given to me by an old friend there, and I gave him to Erik when he was coming out here. I thought he might need him. He's been with Erik a while now but I guess at heart we both still felt he was my dog."

He looked up at her, apologetically. "I was traveling a lot and had no place to keep a dog. This fellow is used to big, open country. He needs room to move."

Chief had emptied his dish and Mike filled it with water. The big dog drank greedily.

"You like beasts?" She was puzzled. "Why is this?"

He glanced at her. "You do not have dogs over there?"

"It is not permitted." Kawasi said. "But even if it was"—she shook her head—"we would not think of keeping a beast." She puckered her brow. "Why is this? Why you like him?"

"He's my friend," Mike replied. "The dog was the first animal domesticated by man, and they've been companions these thousands of years. I expect the first dogs were captured wolf puppies that were raised for food, and they became such good companions the people decided not to eat them. Men and dogs began hunting together and that settled it, I guess."

"We do not keep beasts except for food and for skins," she said primly.

"You miss a lot," he said. "Of course, there are people among us who do not keep dogs for pets." He paused. "I think it is more a custom among Europeans and Americans than others, with the exception of some nomadic peoples."

" 'Nomadic'? I do not know what it is."

"People who wander from place to place, often driving cattle or sheep to fresh grazing lands. Do you not have people of that kind?"

She frowned again. "I do not know. There is great desert. I do not believe anybody goes past it, ever. There are miles of plantings, although not so much as long ago. All is controlled by the Lords of Shibalba."

"Shibalba?"

"It is the name of where I live."

"The Maya have a legend of an underground place where live the enemies of men. It is called Xibalba."

"It is the same, I think."

He added fuel to the fire, and a few sparks flew up. "Once when we talked you said you saw something familiar in the mesa over there? Do you remember?"

She looked over her shoulder, then shifted position so the mesa was no longer behind her. "It is like a place I know on the Other Side. It cannot be, yet . . ."

"You think it is the same?"

"It cannot be, and yet I think . . . it is like, but different somehow. I do not like it," she added. "I do not even like to think about it."

Chief lay close to them, his head on his paws. Mike looked out across the mesa, his eyes straying beyond to the silver of the river. The stars were very bright, the night dark. Somewhere, far off, a coyote howled. Chief lifted his big head, listening.

Kawasi was silent, staring into the fire. Mike slowly began arranging his thoughts, trying to face his problem and decide what was necessary. There was no use in going it blind. He must have a plan, but one he could adjust to circumstances.

Of what he was facing he had no idea, beyond hostile people in a world of which he knew nothing. A dozen times in the past he had come upon accounts of mysterious disappearances or appearances for which there was no logical explanation. Ships, planes, even a whole Chinese Army had vanished without logical explanation. But what was logical? Only that which men knew, and they know so little.

Erik was gone.

A thin film of dust lay over the worktable and the blueprints. The sleeping bag was rolled up tight, something one did in desert country for fear of snakes, spiders, or scorpions taking refuge in one's bed. They were not the best of sleeping companions.

He unrolled the bag. "You can sleep in it. I'll make out with Erik's parka."

He brought fuel closer to the fire, then walked out away from the ruin. The mesa top was thick with powdery soil and only a sparse growth of weeds. The night was cool; the stars seemed very close. All was still, and he knew the nearest habitation was at least an hour's drive, unless there was some Navajo hogan south of the river, which was deep and offered no crossing nearer than Mexican Hat.

The night reminded him of Sinkiang, the Kunluns, and the Pamirs. This was a ghostly, haunted land. Men had lived here and died here, but others had vanished—into what? He knew the feeling from the Kunluns, those mountains that border Tibet on the north, virtually unknown to climbers or travelers, offering few passes, yet one of the mightiest mountain ranges on earth. Only a few local people knew those mountains, and there were areas into which even they did not venture.

He listened into the night, thinking of tomorrow when he would examine the kiva.

There was no sound. The big dog walked out to stand beside him, testing the wind with his nose. Deep in his chest he growled. Mike dropped a hand to the dog's head. "Watch 'em, boy!" he said softly. "You watch 'em now!"

How he wished the dog might tell him what he knew, what he smelled. Yet the growl warned him they were not alone. There was somebody, some *thing* out there.

He walked back, picking up more fuel for the fire. Kawasi was in the sleeping bag, and her even breathing told him she was probably asleep. He touched the butt of his pistol again.

What was it like over there? Would his pistol even *work?* Suppose it would not? Suppose the passing of the veil wrought some unexpected change in him? In his personality? His comprehension? His awareness?

Kawasi seemed all right, and there had certainly been nothing physically wrong with the man who had come into his condo at Tamarron.

If he did go over, what could he do? He knew nothing of the place, nothing of its customs or its people except that they were different from here, no doubt different from any place he had visited.

The Hopi and some other Indians believed this was the Fourth World. Of the two first worlds they professed to remember little or nothing, but because the Third World had become evil, they had fled through a hole in the ground into this world. That was one of the legends.

Another story said the Hopi had crossed the sea to get here, but the disparity did not bother him. The world of the story has no boundaries, and no barrier can keep a story from traveling, although it may take on local color.

He was not surprised that the Hopi had several stories of their origin. Often a man of one tribe would bring home to his lodge a woman of another, and when she bore children she would relate to them the stories she had heard as a child, and so stories from one tribe became the stories of another.

Mike Raglan squatted beside the fire. He had to think this thing through, weigh the problems, and choose a course of action.

Erik Hokart was gone, and Erik was depending on him for help.

Apparently Erik was a prisoner, but was he actually in what they had been thinking of as the Other Side, or was he held somewhere here? The idea of a kidnapping still seemed reasonable. It was all very well to talk of a parallel world, whatever that meant, but he was a rational human being who believed in dealing with the here and the now. He had trouble enough dealing with one world without thinking of another.

Whoever they were who had Erik had shown themselves willing and capable of using force. The ruins of the burned-out café were proof enough of that, and the man who had gotten into his condo was another.

He poked sticks into the coals of the fire, which was dying down. Suppose it was a simple kidnapping? Their next step would be a note demanding ransom, but who would receive such a note? Erik had no relatives, or none Mike had ever heard of. Not many people knew that he, Mike Raglan, was a friend of Erik's. If he knew of no one to whom a ransom note might be sent, how could the kidnappers know?

A foreign government could be ruled out. Erik had not done any government work for some time and it was doubtful if anyone had known of that. With the speed of change in such areas, whatever Erik had done would now be out of date and no longer important.

Revenge? But for what? Erik was not a man who made enemies. Always a gentleman, a quiet, hardworking man who never paraded his skills or his wealth, he was a man who did not attract animosity.

Nonetheless, he was gone. He was not here on the mesa. His car had been abandoned in town. His possessions were here, even his shaving kit.

Mike poked at the fire, shying from the problem he must face. Fantastic as the story seemed to be, Erik was missing, and wherever he was he was depending on Mike Raglan to help him, to save *them*. He had written in the plural, so there had to be somebody with him.

Kawasi might have the answer. She might be able to tell him who the other person was, if it was not Kawasi herself.

He looked away from his fire, listening. Had he heard something? Chief was sleeping, or seeming to sleep. Earlier he had growled, so there had been something out there.

A coyote? A mountain lion? Or some other person? Or *thing?*

Mike was glad he had talked to Gallagher. There was no nonsense about the man but he did have imagination. How much of the story he accepted was open to question, but at least he had listened.

The burned-out café was very much his business, and he had seen the white van. Whatever base they had might have been established for years, and those who lived there might be known in the community. Gallagher was working on the case, and he would keep hunting for an answer, no matter where it came from.

The night was very still. The stars were bright. A soft wind moved across the mesa, stirring the stiff leaves, rustling them. Mike listened for any unnatural sound, any whisper that did not belong to the usual night.

Old stories of haunted houses and mysterious happenings came to mind. Suppose there was truth to some of them? Suppose some of the stories of witches and ghosts had derived from visits across the veil?

Some of his Indian friends accepted things as true that a white man would doubt, but the white man judged from limited knowledge and might be too quick to scoff. He hunched his shoulders under Erik's parka. The night was cold, as desert nights are apt to be. He stared into the outer darkness but could see nothing.

The world over there was evil. In what way? *Evil* was a word with many meanings. Evil was to some a sin against God. To others it was a sin against society. What had been the evil from which the Anasazi fled into this Fourth World? A social evil? He doubted it. Men did not flee from a social evil. They passed laws, or they ignored such evils; yet this evil had caused them to flee, to abandon the world in which they lived, leaving all behind.

What was the evil from which they fled? What was so fearsome, so terrible, that they would leave all behind?

What was the evil some had been willing to accept by returning?

That was a question he must ask Kawasi.

Mike Raglan got to his feet. He added fuel to the fire. He peered into the darkness.

Why could he not sleep? What was it out there that lurked, waiting? Why did it not close in, attack him? Was the evil that lay over on the Other Side a physical thing? Was it something that might attack, that could attack? Or was it some more subtle evil?

He glanced toward Kawasi. She slept, soundly. He walked toward her, looking all around. The ancient wall was close behind her, solid as the day it was built.

He sank down beside her and looked at his watch. It was scarcely midnight and he had been believing it was almost morning.

The flames danced weirdly; shadows shifted and changed. The butt of the gun under his hand was cool. He eased it in the holster for quicker use.

Chief's head was up. Mike looked where the dog was peering into the night. He started to rise.

A hand touched his.

"Don't!" It was Kawasi. "Do not go out there! Not now, no matter what happens!"

XII

HE HESITATED, A little irritated. What was there to fear?

"They come to the fire," Kawasi whispered. "They watch the fire."

For several minutes, neither spoke. Raglan listened, touching his tongue to dry lips. What "they" were he had no idea, but he remembered the creatures who responded to the flash of light or fire from the top of the mesa. Were these the same?

He heard a vague rustling, a stirring, then silence. Should he put out the fire? It would not be easy to do without exposing himself more than he wished and he did not like the idea of being left in the dark.

He started to move and her hand touched his arm. "They must not see you," she whispered. "Be still, and they will go away as the fire dies down."

He wished it were morning, still hours away. He liked to deal with trouble in the clear light. The creatures he had seen seemed manlike, and he did not want to kill anything. In any event, a killing could lead to many questions and much trouble. If there was an investigation, and there certainly would be, how could he explain his situation? Who would believe such a story?

Hunched in the shadows beyond the fire, they waited. Kawasi sat very close, her arm warm against his. She, at least, was real. Or was she? What *was* real?

The fire died to red coals and a few thin tendrils of flame. His leg was cramped and he changed position carefully, trying to peer beyond the fire and into the night. He could see the dark rim of the rocks, and beyond it the sky where the night told its beads with stars.

No shadows, no movement. "I think they've gone," he whispered.

"Wait!" She put a restraining hand on his arm.

He relaxed slowly. Tired of the long waiting, he felt his eyes close. He opened them, shaking his head to clear it of sleep. He must get some rest. He'd had very little since leaving the East, as his first night's rest at the condo had been interrupted.

He was leaning against the cot, his head against the edge of the bedroll. His eyes closed.

Footsteps awakened him, and it was broad daylight. He started to get up, then stopped.

Kawasi was gone!

Gone where? He got up hurriedly, then stopped abruptly. Gallagher was standing outside the door, looking in at him.

Mike Raglan looked quickly around. Kawasi was gone—gone as though she had never been. At least she was not here. He looked around again, then stepped outside.

Gallagher was staring at him. "What's the matter? What's wrong?"

"She's gone. Kawasi is gone."

He looked down the length of the mesa. Sunlight was touching the rocks in the distance and Navajo Mountain was aglow with a reflection of the rising sun. The rocks over toward where Rainbow Bridge stood were a brilliant rust-red.

"What d'you mean, gone?"

"She was here, right beside me when I fell asleep. We were waiting for the fire to die down." He paused, realizing how foolish his words must sound. "There was something out there, some *things*. She said they were attracted by the fire."

Gallagher's hands were on his hips. "You say she's gone. Gone where?" Gallagher's eyes were cool. "I drove out here to ask her some questions, a lot of questions. Now you say she's gone."

He made a sweeping gesture. "Gone *where?* Where is there to go? Your car is over there, just where you left it. I didn't see anybody when I drove over, and I started before daylight. I am going to ask you again, Raglan. Where is she?"

"I'm telling the truth. She was right here beside me. We were both listening to whatever was out there, and I was dead tired. I caught myself nodding a couple of times and tried to stay awake. I guess I fell asleep."

Gallagher looked around. "You say something was out here?"

"Just beyond where you're standing, I'd guess. We heard a rustling, a sound of movement. I saw nothing and I don't believe she did. Whatever it was, she said they were drawn by the fire and would go away when it died down."

"She's a witness, Raglan. An important witness. I need to talk to her. She was last seen with you, heading out this way. She couldn't just vanish."

"No?"

"Don't start that again. I don't buy it." He paused a moment. "I found your white van, or at least *a* white van."

Raglan waited, his eyes sweeping the mesa. There had to be footprints in that dust. If there had been movement, there had to be signs of movement. "And . . . ?"

"Paiutes. Been here for years. Nothing unusual about them at all—just folks."

"Are you sure?"

"Not much of a place. Been standing there for years. They run a few sheep, keep a pony or two. Lots of Indians don't feel right unless they have some horses. Even if they don't ride them, they want them."

"You found the van?"

"Sure. Right there in the garage alongside the house."

"Garage?"

"Sheet-metal building. Kind of a workshop or something. I guess they make their own repairs."

"You talked to them?"

"Sure. There were three of them there. Old

man and woman and a young buck, maybe twenty-five or so."

Mike Raglan felt let down. He had thought if they found the van there might be a lead. "You know these people?"

"No, I don't know them. I talked to Weston about them—he's their nearest neighbor. He's known the old folks for years. Seems their people used to live close around here but they pulled out and went away, years back. Weston says the old folks never bother anybody. He picks up junk, stuff along the highway. Old tires, anything thrown out or abandoned. The old man does. Sells stuff occasionally."

Gallagher walked past him into the ruin. He glanced at the blueprints, then into the next room at the cot, the bedroll.

Raglan walked out on the mesa. There was a confusion of tracks, blurred, nothing definite. Somebody had been here. He said as much.

"You could have made those tracks," Gallagher said, "just gathering wood. Or Hokart could have. There hasn't been any rain or high winds to wipe them out. They might have been there for weeks."

"There'd be dust sifted over them." Raglan walked away several steps. "Gallagher? Take a look at this. Do you think I have feet like that?"

"This" was a large, distinct print of a bare foot, a very large foot.

Gallagher looked at it and was silent. Suddenly he squatted down on his haunches. "I'll be

114

damned!" he whispered. Then he pointed. "Will you look at that?"

At the end of each toe—and they were well-defined—there was the mark of a claw. Or of a long untrimmed toenail. But sharper, like a claw.

Gallagher stood up and looked around. For a long moment he looked all about and then he said, "She's gone. Do you reckon those things got her?"

Mike Raglan had been shying away from the idea. "No," he said, "I don't know how they could have gotten her without a struggle. She was deathly afraid of them and would never have gone into the dark where they were, and they would have had to go over me to get her."

"Then where is she?"

Reluctantly, he said. "I think she went away, after they had gone. I think she went because she wanted to, or had to, but of her own volition."

Gallagher looked at him. "Went where? I told you I was on the road, and I saw nobody. She wouldn't just wander off into the desert and fall into a canyon, would she?"

"Maybe she went back where she came from. To the Other Side."

Gallagher stuck his thumbs in his belt. "You on that kick again? I've been thinking about that. It's nonsense. Pure unadulterated nonsense! I don't buy it." He paused. "You're in trouble, Raglan. Maybe what you should do is get on the wire and get yourself a good lawyer. We've got two disappearances here, one of them a wealthy man, an-

115

other a beautiful girl. The only connecting link is you."

"And the kiva."

"There's a lot of kivas." He glanced around, then said, "Let's have a look."

Erik had staked out his rooms, indicating the projected floor plan of the house. Two of the rooms—the large living room and the study—were to have walls of native rock which needed only a little smoothing and shaping. The floor as well would be of natural rock.

Gallagher paused, studying the strings and stakes that marked the layout of the rooms. "Quite a place. You say he was going to build this himself?"

"That was the idea. I suspect he might have called somebody in to do the plumbing and the wiring."

"Away out here," Gallagher commented, "he wasn't going to have many visitors."

"He didn't want them. Erik had an apartment in New York, beautiful place, but he wasn't social. He had a few friends, mostly people he met in a business way. He wanted time to think, to be away from the telephone."

Gallagher looked around again. "Everywhere he looked," he said, "he'd have a view. It would be something to wake up to, I'll give him that." He paused again. "He have any family? Any heirs?"

"Nobody I know of, but there must have been somebody. He wasn't a talkative person. Not about personal affairs."

"Where was he from?"

"I've no idea. He was an American, I am sure of that, and I believe his ancestry was Swiss, but I can't be sure. Like I said, he didn't talk."

"A kind of a mystery man?"

"I never thought of him that way. He never seemed to be mysterious—just a quiet sort who minded his own affairs and made a mint of money doing it."

Gallagher glanced toward where the kiva lay but made no move toward it. "Odd," he said, "you being the one he sent for when he was in trouble, yet you know nothing about him."

Raglan shrugged, disturbed in spite of himself. "He thought he was calling an expert. When your plumbing goes haywire you call a plumber. If you aren't feeling well, you call a doctor. Something strange was happening, so he called me."

"Makes sense," Gallagher agreed. "This place here"—he waved a hand—"beautiful place, all right, but what about water?"

"What?"

"Where was he going to get water for the house? Of course, if money was no object . . ."

"It wasn't."

"Look," Gallagher said, "you've told me quite a story, you and the missing girl, but all I've got is a burned-out café that seems to have been arson. I've got a Jeep, and you, and I can't connect you to the café. Not yet, at least."

"Me? Why would I burn it?"

"That I ask myself. But I am asking myself a

117

lot of questions and none of the answers make sense. If the folks around here even guessed at some of what I've been thinking they'd run me out of office.

"Hokart is missing. Now the girl is missing, too. Two missing people and a fire." He paused. "How do we know this isn't aimed at you?"

Astonished, Raglan stared at Gallagher. "At *me?* How? And for what reason?"

"I don't know. I just don't know anything and I'm reaching. Hokart have any reason to want to get rid of you?"

"No. Of course not."

"He invited you out here. Asked for your help, you say. Then he doesn't show up and there's some cock-an'-bull story about other dimensions, parallel worlds, and all that. There's a building burned and Hokart disappears, leaving nothing behind but a Jeep and what you see here. Then that Kawasi disappears when you are alone with her. Something about this smells to high heaven."

He walked back to the ruin and stopped in front of the blueprints. "I'm fishing," he said irritably. "I just don't have anything that makes sense. For all I know, you could have murdered both of them."

"I'd no reason to kill Erik and nothing to gain by it, and if I was going to start killing, it wouldn't be a beautiful woman. There's never enough of them around."

"I grant you that." Gallagher was studying the circle where the kiva would have been added to the house Erik had planned. "Fits, all right. Suppose he could have dreamed it? I've heard stories of men going to sleep and waking up with answers. Maybe this was like that."

"He didn't know the kiva was there—nobody did."

"Any other ruins around?"

"In the canyon over there. He told me there were a couple of rock shelters for storing grain. And, of course, back up the canyon there are two or three ruins, one of them near a spring."

"I know about them. Been there a time or two." Gallagher walked out and looked down the mesa. "Odd. It does look like it had been cultivated at one time."

"The Anasazi planted crops on the mesas but I've never seen one like this. It's different, somehow."

Gallagher took off his hat and ran his fingers through his hair. "I've got to look at this every which way," he said, almost as if thinking aloud. "I'm going to run a check on Hokart. I want to know who he was and where he came from." He stared at Raglan. "That goes for you, too."

"Fine with me. As for Hokart, I doubt if you will find much."

"Maybe, maybe not. Can't leave anything to chance. Everything a man does is rooted in his past somehow. If we check him out, something may turn up."

"Let's take a look at the kiva."

Gallagher shook his head. "Wait. I want to

think this out before I start going any further. First, I'd like to find that girl. I need to question her. Should have done it before but you snowed me with all that talk about other dimensions or whatever it was."

"I think she went back to the Other Side."

"You implied that. What about your dog? Could he find her?"

"He could, I expect, but they don't like dogs over there. They don't understand them. But what about the cliffs? She could have fallen over. It must be five hundred feet down to the river."

"No tracks I noticed." He glanced at Raglan. "It was the first thing I thought of, and the tracks would have been plain enough, leading toward the edge."

He ran his fingers through his hair again. "All right, let's look at the kiva."

XIII

MIKE RAGLAN DID not move. "Gallagher? You said the Paiutes had a sheet-metal garage? How large?"

Gallagher turned squarely around. "Big. Big enough for four cars, but they have sort of a workshop in one corner."

"A place like that costs money. I wonder what they needed it for? Seems to me a four-car garage is quite a lot for a couple of old Indians who raise a little stock and collect junk for resale."

"So?"

"Could be more than meets the eye. Did you check the mileage on the van?"

"I did." He flipped the pages on his notebook. "Fifty-one thousand, two hundred eighty-eight miles."

Raglan's eyes went toward his car. Suddenly he wanted to be seated in it, driving back to the condo. "A lot of mileage for an old couple, even with that other man around."

"I thought of that."

"Think about it some more. Are you driving back to town? I'm spooky about this place. I want to get back where there are people."

"All right. Let's stop by Eden Foster's place. She's not far off your route if you're driving back to Durango. She heard you were around and asked if you'd drop by."

"Who is Eden Foster?"

"Somebody to know if you live around here. She's interested and she's active, if you know what I mean. Used to teach in some eastern university. Moved out to Santa Fe, and then she decided she liked it better here, so she bought out a dealer over on the highway and she sells Indian art, paintings, jewelry, and rugs. Only the best."

They had reached the cars. Gallagher paused, looking back toward the mesa. "Raglan? I wouldn't mention those tracks if I were you. No need to get a lot of crazy rumors started."

"You're right, of course."

"And that white van? It may not have been the same one. I'd bet there's two dozen white vans

121

between here and Tamarron, and we've no evidence the man who entered your place has any connection with the one outside the café.

"If folks started putting this together we'd have all sorts of rumors going around, just when all that was sort of quieting down."

"What do you mean by 'all that'?"

Gallagher hesitated. "There's been talk, over the years. It's easy for somebody to disappear out yonder. When it happens, it always revives every old story they've ever heard. There's talk of witchcraft, too. Most of the Indians won't talk about it, but the belief is there. Most of them can point out a witch or two, but don't think it is just the Indians. Most of the whites who've lived here any length of time hesitate when you ask, and then just shrug it off. They won't admit they believe, and maybe they don't, but they don't disbelieve, either."

Chief was standing off a little, his head up, nose in the wind. "What is it, Chief? Something wrong?"

The dog came closer, but looked back again toward Erik's shelter. "I think it's Kawasi," Mike said. "He's worried."

"You lead off," Gallagher said, "I'll follow."

Mike Raglan motioned Chief into the car, then got in himself. As he drove off he said, "I'm wondering, too, Chief. Why did she go off like that? Why did she run away?"

When they reached the highway, Gallagher

pulled alongside. "We'll go to Eden's. Make it by lunch," he said. "She sets a good table."

Gallagher pulled on by and Mike followed, the big dog filling the seat beside him.

"Looks like we're in trouble, Chief. Gallagher's a good man but he's got a job to do, and right now he has two missing people and a burned-out café, and I'm the only connecting link. All I have to offer is a cock-and-bull story that in his place I wouldn't buy for a minute."

Chief offered no comment, not a growl, a whine, or a yawn. He simply kept his eyes on the road.

"Just the same, Chief, I'd like to know more about that garage. No reason why they shouldn't have it if they want it, but what do they use it for? Does somebody find it convenient as a place to leave cars when they are not being used?"

Up ahead, Gallagher slowed, then turned right off the highway onto a gravel road that led around a small hill, pulling up in a gravel parking area before a two-story house built of native stone. There was a wide veranda, and to the right of the house a wide green lawn, several beautiful old trees, and a lot of flowers. Before Mike had a chance to do more than notice them, Gallagher was going up the steps. Raglan followed as the door opened.

Eden Foster was a stunning woman. She was slender and dark with large gray eyes. She was wearing a beige blouse and slacks, and a turquoise necklace.

"Gallagher! You're just in time for lunch!"

"Don't you think I know it?" He turned slightly. "Mike Raglan, this is Eden Foster."

Their eyes met and he was suddenly wary. He could not have said why. She was beautiful, with a lovely smile, and a warm handshake to greet him. "Come in, won't you?"

Inside, it was dark and cool, Navajo rugs on the floor and a couple of very fine ones on the walls. There were many shelves of books. Mike noticed three of his own, and near them two books by Evans-Wentz and one by Eliade.

The breakfast room to which they were shown was cool, fronted by glass with a fine view of the garden he had glimpsed.

She glanced over her shoulder. "You'll forgive me, I hope? I asked Gallagher to bring you if he could. I did not want to miss a chance to meet one of my favorite authors."

"Thanks, but I am not really a writer. It just happens that I've written a couple of books."

"Nevertheless, you're an interesting man and most of them just pass through. Good company is hard to find when one lives so far from everything."

She turned toward what was evidently a kitchen door. "Mary? You may serve now, if you will.

"You're younger than I expected. From your books I would have thought you older."

"It's the light in here," Raglan said. "It's deceiving."

Mary was a Navajo girl with large dark eyes. She brought a tray with sandwiches, and a bowl of celery stalks, olives, and spears of cucumber. For a moment, as she turned to go, she was standing behind Eden Foster, and Mary looked directly at him, her face expressionless.

Eden turned her attention to Gallagher, asking about his wife, his children, and his garden, in that order. Mike listened, ate a celery stick, and looked out the window, but he was thinking.

What was it about her? She was beautiful, and had a figure a man could dream about, so why had he become suddenly suspicious? What was it about her that bothered him?

She turned to him then. "And you, Mr. Raglan? Will you be with us long?"

"Call me Mike. When you call me Mr. Raglan, I start to look around to see if my father is here." He paused. "No, I shan't be around long."

"A new book?"

He shrugged. "Visiting." He glanced at her. "The books are incidental, written when I have leisure, but this is just a visit to a friend."

"A friend," Gallagher said, "who is building a house over in the desert."

Raglan looked at the garden. He had not come to talk, but to listen. Had Gallagher brought him here simply to meet a neighbor or was there more involved?

Eden Foster sat opposite him, and poured coffee. She looked up at him. "That would be Erik Hokart, I expect? I know of no one else building over that way."

It was a large desert, he thought, and there

must be others who were building. "He's a friend of mine," he said.

"I wonder if his wife would want a home out there. Women usually like to be close to other women."

"He's a single man," Gallagher said. "Likes to be alone. Isn't that right, Mike?"

"He has a lot to think about." But then, so they would not think Erik too alone, Mike added, "He's a very important man to a lot of people. You can bet the government knows where he is."

Eden's large gray eyes met his. "Is he so important, then?"

"To them, he is." Did Mike notice a little frown around her eyes, he wondered, or was he being overly suspicious? "There are people in the Pentagon who would consider him a national treasure."

That might be stretching it a bit but not very much. He took a sandwich from the tray. "Beautiful flowers," he commented. "They add so much to a place. And I like to see the marigolds there."

Eden Foster glanced toward the garden. "Marigolds?"

"They help to keep insects away," Raglan said.

"I wouldn't know. Mary takes care of the garden." She turned her attention to Gallagher. "You must invite Mr. Hokart to come over. I should like to meet him."

"He's not around," Gallagher said. "We'd like to talk to him, too."

126

She looked at Mike. "But you're his friend. You must know where he is."

"Of course." He picked up another sandwich and smiled at her. "I do know. I know just about where he is and we'll be in touch. I'll tell him you want to meet him."

The smile had gone from her eyes. They were cool now. Or was he imagining things? He had been doing a lot of imagining lately, so he was probably seeing ghosts where they did not exist.

He sipped the coffee. It was very good, with a slight flavor he could not quite place. He started to mention it, then decided not to. "You've a lovely place here," he said. "This was a nice thought, Gallagher."

"It comes with the territory," Gallagher said. "What kind of an investigating officer would I be if I didn't know where there was a free lunch? And in good company?"

"I'll agree on the company." Raglan smiled at Eden and her eyes warmed, lingering on his. He was glad then that he had known a lot of women. This one knew what she was doing, all of the time.

The conversation turned to local topics and people and he enjoyed his coffee and another of the tiny sandwiches. In the distance he heard voices: Mary talking to someone, but who?

Of the people and conditions about which they talked he knew nothing, although Eden seemed well informed, until she commented, "There was a fire over your way. We could see the smoke. Anything serious?"

"Only to people who eat there. Benny's Café burned. Grease fire, I expect. They happen every once in a while." He got to his feet. "We'd better run, Mike. Time I checked in with the office. Be seeing you, Eden."

Mike got up, picked up his hat, and followed Gallagher to the door. As he passed the book-shelves, he glanced again at the titles. "You've some interesting books. I'm flattered to see mine among them."

He stopped at one bookcase and took down one of his books, idly riffling the pages. "The next time I come over I'll sign one for you, if you like."

"Would you? That would be wonderful!"

He paused on the steps. "If you should see Erik before I do, tell him not to worry. Everything will be all right."

Her expression was wary. He glanced quickly at the table near them as she took his hand. "Do come again, and there's no need to wait for Gallagher to bring you. He's always so busy with that awful police work."

"Can't be helped, Eden. There's too much going on. That fire in town, and then we can't seem to find Erik." Gallagher paused. "Or that girl, either."

Eden Foster had started to turn away. Now she stopped and turned around.

"Girl?" Her tone was a little shrill.

"Pretty girl. Young. Big dark eyes. She was

around town and then suddenly she disappeared. If we don't find her soon, we'll have the feds down here, nosing around."

"What sort of a girl?" Eden asked. "A Navajo?"

"No, but she looked like an Indian." Gallagher's eyes were innocent. "You talked to her, Mike. Was she an Indian?"

"Not from around here. At least that was my impression."

Eden's eyes were on Raglan's. "You *talked* to her? And she disappeared?"

Mike Raglan chuckled. "Not while I was talking to her. She was too polite for that. Seemed like a nice girl." He paused. "She left that café just in time. It burst into flame not a moment later. She was lucky to get out."

He got into his car and pulled away, Gallagher following. When he drove into town he pulled up in front of the café where he had talked to Kawasi. Gallagher parked alongside him.

"Pretty woman," Gallagher said. "Food's good, too."

"You're a devious man, Gallagher."

Gallagher's eyes were innocent. "Thought as long as you were going to be around you should meet people. Eden's one of the brightest and damned good-looking along with it."

He paused looking up the street. "Smart woman. Hasn't been here all that long but she's made friends. Been a guest at the governor's mansion two or three times, has money in the bank, good credit rating. Keeps to herself, but goes out to dinner at the homes of the best folks, supports local charities. Not in a big way. Modest support. No talk about her. Respected woman. Nobody would say a word against her."

Mike Raglan rested his arms on the wheel. "Mary seems a nice girl."

"Navajo. I know her folks. They live over toward Navajo Mountain, where they run some sheep. Mary did well in school."

He paused. "Indians don't make much show of what they know, and I'm betting Eden Foster thinks she hired what we back in Oklahoma used to call a blanket Indian, meaning no disrespect. What I mean is that Mary not only has considerable education but she's bright.

"Her father's gettin' along in years, so when Eden offered her good money, she took the job. That way she can stay close to home and her father."

"Those books of mine? The ones Eden has? She just bought them. That book I had in my hands hadn't been read, and it was the third printing, which came out only last month. I think Eden Foster wants to know what I am and how I think."

"Maybe so."

Neither man moved, just sitting where they could talk without raising their voices. Mike Raglan spoke after a minute or two. "Eden Foster should read some detective fiction if she plans to play games around here. She needs to get used to our ways."

"What d'you mean by that?"

"She's careless. Remember that Eric Ambler espionage story I mentioned? The one the prowler took?"

"I remember your story."

"It was lying there on the table near the bookshelves."

"Hell, a lot of people read his books. I do myself. Doesn't mean a thing."

"No? Gallagher, I get a lot of books, so when I finish one that I intend to pass on to somebody else I make a check on the cover with a marking pen so I won't get it mixed up and keep it around. That book had my mark on it."

——— XIV ———

BACK AT TAMARRON, Mike Raglan went down to the San Juan Room and his usual table near the window. With a cup of coffee before him he took out his notebook and opened it to a blank page.

What did he actually *know?*

Aside from Erik's daybook, he knew only what Gallagher knew: Two people had disappeared and a café had been burned to the ground under what seemed peculiar circumstances. The information in the daybook gave him an advantage which he was not yet prepared to share with Gallagher.

The police officer would immediately seize it as evidence and he wished to review the material himself. Moreover, there was small chance it would be accepted at face value.

Had Erik not written down his day-to-day experiences he would simply have vanished without a clue, and after a few days it would have been taken for granted that he had fallen off a cliff into the river, and no further questions would have been asked.

If what the daybook implied was true, considered with what Kawasi had told him, those who had been called the Anasazi existed on the other side of a curtain, carrying on their own civilization and wanting no communication with anyone from this side. Apparently there had been a way through that was occasionally used until blocked off by the dam that created Lake Powell. However, there seemed to be an area, in the vicinity Erik wished to build in, that was an anomaly, a region of occasional erratic openings caused by some local instability. The window in the kiva appeared to be outside that instability and to offer a permanent way into the world beyond the veil. Undoubtedly that was the reason it had been closed off by filling in the kiva. That, of course, was supposition. Somebody already on this side had wanted it open—hence the glowing red line on Erik's blueprint.

Raglan was irritated with himself. Why had he not checked the kiva? Had he deliberately avoided it? Was he afraid of what he might find? Did he fear to look beyond, because of what he might discover?

We accept the familiar and the usual. We are comfortable with it. We do not want our nice three-dimensional world shattered. We enjoy our certainty, and even Einstein shied from the erratic world of the quantum theory. It suggested a chaos with which he was not prepared to deal.

Each of us enjoys the familiar and the usual. No matter how miserable it may be, one's own home is a haven. To step through the door, drop into a familiar chair, and sleep in one's own bed is vastly comfortable. It is an escape from the world outside. It represents safety, security. Once inside the door, one can lay down the burdens of the world and relax. In a larger sense, our three-dimensional world is such a place. We are used to it, and the suggestion that it may be only a part of a much greater reality is disturbing.

On the notepad Mike Raglan wrote: *Erik.* What did he know of Erik, after all? A cool, quiet, reserved man, a scientist with a considerable aptitude for business, not one likely to go off on a tangent, nor to give much credence to the fantastic.

Either Erik's notebook was an elaborate fiction, something completely out of character, or it was something Erik believed to be true. Knowing the man, Raglan decided the daybook had been written in good faith, written actually for Erik himself alone. Sending it to Raglan had been an afterthought, conceived in a mood of sheer desperation.

The material in the daybook fitted no pattern of

hallucination with which Raglan was familiar, especially given the man and the circumstances.

Suddenly a memory of the old cowboy and his gold intruded. His gold, and the warning. The area the cowboy talked about had not been sharply designated but was probably now on the bottom of Lake Powell. There had been no lake when the story was told.

Below Erik's name Raglan wrote the name of Kawasi.

She could be an actress hired for a part. It could be a plot to extort money from Erik, but no such request had been made, and nothing in this sequence of events fit the pattern.

What could he expect from Gallagher? The man was a sober, serious police officer of considerable experience as such. Moreover, he had lived in the area, knew the people, and understood a good deal about the Indians and their beliefs. Enough to consider what was happening with an open mind.

What did he know about Eden Foster? Raglan was positive Gallagher had taken him there for more than a cup of coffee and a sandwich, yet he could scarcely have expected to discover anything as positive as the paperback book.

The man who had entered his condo had either been there, in Eden Foster's home, or he had met with her somewhere. So there had to be a connection.

The man who had come to the condo had known where to find him. Eden Foster must also have known; hence, others would as well. That they were willing to kill had been demonstrated at the café, so he must move with care. There might even be somebody in this room right now, watching, waiting.

Obviously, with Erik out of the way he himself represented their biggest problem. Therefore he must be captured or eliminated.

Mike Raglan let the waiter refill his cup, his eyes wandering over the room. Several of the people he knew. They were regulars. The tourists were obvious enough, often with children, or discussing plans for the day. Two tables were occupied by men who sat alone, which could mean nothing at all.

One of their people might be a regular employee here, or on the housekeeping staff.

Eden Foster did not, of course, know he had seen the book, and even if she did, she could not believe he had known it for his own. She was well established here and would not believe herself suspected, something that was in his favor. Yet he must be careful.

Putting down his pen, he considered the situation, going over in his mind the little he knew. He had first come into this country on a very poor wagon road that ran east of Navajo Mountain. He remembered how he had been struck by the stark beauty of the land, and he had himself thought of building a home atop one of the mesas, just as Erik had.

All that country had been known and traveled

over by the people the Navajos called the Anasazi, studied by latecomers as the cliff dwellers.

At first they lived in pit-houses atop the mesas. From the beginning they had begun learning how to use every drop of available water. Later they had moved down from the tops of the mesas into the great open caves in the cliff faces, building houses of native stone with doors wider at the top than the bottom. Various reasons have been offered for this but it was probably a simple one: A person carrying a water jar, a bundle of firewood, or the carcass of a game animal needs more space for the upper part of his body.

Occasionally the caves had springs, but usually both water and food had to be brought to them, carried down precarious paths or up from the canyon below. The expenditure of effort must have been enormous, only reasonable if some threat demanded defensible positions.

In the latter half of the thirteenth century there had come a long drought and with it attacks by nomadic, raiding Indians coming down from the North. No doubt these were advance parties of the invading Navajo, Apache, and Ute peoples who were to populate the region in later years.

Whatever the cause, their cliff palaces were deserted, their fields abandoned. The Anasazi disappeared.

They were there, and then they were gone.

Some evidence indicated that a few Anasazi had merged with other groups to become the Hopis. Others might have joined other Pueblo groups, but the greater part seemed simply to have vanished.

Suppose, when the drought persisted and the attacks increased, that some of the Anasazi elected to return to that Third World from which they came?

Fleeing from our world, they had returned to that which had grown evil, preferring to face an evil they knew rather than starvation and death. Once there, they would have wanted to close off the way to deny any pursuers a chance to follow. Over the centuries, an almost paranoid fear had built up of what lay on the other side.

It was possible, as Kawasi seemed to imply, that only a few of the elite knew how or where to cross over, and that they had occasionally done so to obtain things not otherwise available on the Other Side.

Mike Raglan finished his coffee, staring at the two names on the otherwise blank page.

Erik. Kawasi.

She knew him. Had met him. Yet there must be another involved, for when Erik had pleaded for help, he had spoken in the plural. Who was this other person?

Erik seemed to have become a prisoner, yet Erik was an intelligent man with a vast store of knowledge that might help him to escape.

Evil? What evil? Had those who returned to the Other Side taken up the ways of some of their relatives from Mexico and Central America? The Aztecs had engaged in bloody sacrifices of many thousands of people each year, most of them prisoners taken in war. Recently it had been discovered that the Maya did likewise. Was that the evil from which the Anasazi originally fled? Or was it something else? Something less tangible, something insidious?

He sat very quietly, trying to consider every aspect of his problem, but the unavoidable fact remained: Erik was a prisoner, probably on the Other Side, and he must be freed.

Moreover, Mike could think of nobody who might help. Gallagher had his own concerns and more than enough to keep him occupied, but suppose Mike could contact that old cowboy of whom Kawasi had spoken? Suppose in freeing Erik Hokart he could also free that old man?

Certainly, in his years on the Other Side Johnny must have learned a great deal just in order to survive. The more Mike considered that possibility, the more he liked it. Yet first his base must be secure.

He must know more about the Paiutes, if such they were, and more about Eden Foster.

Above all, he must remember they would be attempting to kill or capture him.

His eyes swept the room. One of the men who sat alone was gone. The other remained: a stocky man with a bullet head and short-cropped hair, wearing a neat gray windbreaker and slacks, and under the windbreaker a navy-blue T-shirt. He was facing the other way but in such a position as to catch Mike's slightest move from the corner of his eye. It was probably chance, no more. The man might be a guest, might be attending a convention, or just be out for the golf or fishing.

Mike must be prepared. On the stairs, when walking, driving, or just at home. They would not wish to attract attention, so they would probably make a try for him when it could be done unobtrusively.

Once he had been good at both karate and judo. How good was he now, after the years had passed?

His thoughts returned to the problem before him.

What manner of people would he find on the Other Side? What conditions?

Judging by Kawasi and the unknown visitor at Tamarron, they were people much like himself. That was what the evidence indicated. But he must not make the mistake the white man did in judging the Indian, and vice versa. Each came from a certain cultural background, and assumed that certain attributes were typical of all men when such was not the case.

There was no such thing as human nature, if by that one believed that certain reactions and responses were typical of all men.

Our patterns of behavior develop from what we have been taught and from the responses of those about us with similar origins. The people on the Other Side would have an altogether different background and, hence, different responses.

Obviously they had no desire to reveal their presence to those on this side of the curtain. If his

139

assumptions were correct, there were several living on this side for one reason or another. Eden Foster might well be one of them, and if she was she had learned to fit in. She belonged. She had made friends.

She had located the sources of power and had associated herself with them. She had friends at the Statehouse and, no doubt, others in business as well as politics. She had met and become friendly with Gallagher.

Did Gallagher know or suspect who or what she was? Apparently he did, but what had given her away? Why did he suspect her of being something other than she seemed? The fact that he had taken Mike to meet her was an indication of something. Had something caused suspicion that she was not all she pretended to be? Or had something Mike said started him thinking?

He glanced around again. Several people had left the room. The waiters were used to him, knowing he often sat long over his coffee. Often they paused by his table with bits of comment, questions about his work, or gossip about some of the more transient visitors at the lodge. They were a bright, interested lot and some were students at the nearby college.

The man with the gray jacket remained where he was, seemingly uninterested in what took place around him. Positioned as he was, he could see from the corner of his eye when Mike got up to leave, if he got up. He could also see people who stopped by the table, but he was too far away to overhear.

"How's the place doing?" Mike asked the waiter who served him frequently. "Is the lodge full?"

"No. The biggest convention just left. We're about half full. I'd guess."

"Many strangers around?"

"Very few. A few singles. People passing through."

"Know that fellow in the gray jacket?"

"Him? He's not staying in the lodge. He's some kind of a foreigner."

The truth of the matter was, Mike Raglan was scared.

Certainly not of the man with the bullet head, nor of anybody else. He was afraid of that other world, of venturing into someplace where nothing would be as he knew it. Above all, he did not want his world to be different. He could deal with three dimensions, and with three-dimensional people.

In his study there was an atlas, and he could open it to maps of any land on earth. He could put a finger on Afghanistan, or point out where the Mitanni had lived, or to the site of Babylon, and even to Three Dragon Pass. All that was real. What he did not wish to discover was that between any two numbered pages, 357 and 358 for instance, there were an infinite number of worlds of which he knew nothing.

Here in this room was stability. He could walk down those steps each morning, be given a table, and go to the buffet for breakfast. Of that he was sure.

If he went through that window in the kiva, all bets were off. Yet that was where he must go.

He did not want to go. He wanted to walk away and never look back. He wanted to go to Los Angeles, meet friends for dinner, or just sit down with a good book.

But he had to go.

XV

HE WAS WATCHING for his chance. The glass doors behind him opened onto the terrace, where the tables were unoccupied and the umbrellas furled. The only activity was from squirrels prospecting for crumbs.

Suddenly there was a scuffle near the entrance, two teenaged tourists having fun. Startled, the man in the gray jacket looked up, and Mike Raglan moved.

He had already signed his check, so he got up quickly, slipped out the glass door and down the steps to the lower level.

His car was parked against the curb and close by, with Chief patiently waiting in the back seat. He swung around, skirted the pond, and was on the highway in a matter of minutes.

He watched in the rearview mirror until the entrance was lost from sight. Nobody had appeared. He might have been mistaken in his man, but he did not believe it.

Why were they watching him? To find an opportunity to kill or capture him, without a doubt. They had no idea how much he knew, but that he knew more than was good for them was undoubted. He had some communication from Erik. He had talked with Kawasi, which they probably knew, and he was in touch with the police.

Obviously they had established a base of operations on this side of the curtain, yet how familiar they were with life in his world Mike could not guess. Eden Foster, if she was one of them, obviously knew a good deal. The man in the gray jacket might never have suspected there was a door in what to him must have seemed a glass wall.

What had happened after he left? Had the man tried to follow him? Or had he been completely puzzled by his disappearance?

Trying to remember, Mike did not recall seeing the man pay his check, so he must have been stopped before he could leave.

It was a long drive ahead. Moving his pistol into a good position on the seat beside him, Mike headed west, driving fast but within the speed limit. He had no desire to be stopped now.

As he drove he turned over the situation in his mind. Unless Erik somehow escaped, Mike had no choice. He would have to go through the curtain and find him. "And that won't be easy, Chief," he commented.

The big dog's head lay across his thigh, and only an ear twitched. "You're like me, boy. You'd sooner stay on this side."

Nothing showed in his rearview mirror except occasional cars or pickups going about their usual business, but he trusted none of them. His thoughts ranged over the problem.

The kiva entrance to the other world, if such it was, apparently opened into some kind of a controlled area. Kawasi had feared it, and so must he. There were said to be other, erratic openings and it was through such a one that Johnny had gotten through. One or more of these openings lay in the vicinity, if the stories were to be believed. Yet the opening through which Johnny rode when chasing that errant steer might now lie beneath the waters of Lake Powell.

The legends of the Hopi told of a long migration with occasional stops until they found the particular place they sought. And when they found the place it was close to no running water, nor was it in a rich and fertile area. Why had they chosen such a place?

Undoubtedly, people from the cliff dwellings had merged with the Hopi and shared legends, but why that particular area? Because it was close to the place of emergence?

The legends themselves were confusing, because other peoples had joined what became the Hopi and brought with them their own stories. The kiva, now a ceremonial center, was constructed much like the dwellings of the Koryak of Siberia.

The ventilation system was the same, too similar to be a matter of chance.

Another legend had the Hopi crossing a great sea to get where they now were.

It was said that a sorceress had come with them from the other world, and brought evil with her.

He glanced into the rearview mirror. Nothing in sight, yet he must not assume the man in the gray jacket, even if he was one of them, was the only one. The man in the white van must be somewhere about, and there might be others.

Where, he wondered, was Kawasi? How had she disappeared so suddenly? She would not have ventured into the kiva, of that he was sure. Was there another opening close by? Had she deliberately left him without so much as a word? Or had she been seized by her enemies?

He swore bitterly. What the hell was going on? And what could he do about it?

Supposing Erik had been seized and was being held on the Other Side? What would he do if he crossed over? How could he find him? How would he even know where to begin? Obviously their clothing would be different from his, and he would immediately be seen as someone different. The trouble was, he had no information. He did not know his enemies, if they were enemies, and he did not have any means of passing among them unnoticed. He had no idea where a prisoner would be held or under what circumstances, or how he was guarded. To cross over blind would be foolhardy in the extreme.

Why had he not asked more pertinent questions when Kawasi was with him?

Judging by the few he had seen, they looked not too different from people on this side, yet what if that was not the case? What if the people he had seen had been deliberately chosen because of their resemblance to people on this side? Certainly their customs would be different, and he would be walking into a trap if he crossed over with no more knowledge than he now had.

Crossed over? Was he actually buying that story? Did he believe in such a thing?

Suppose it was an elaborate fraud? A kidnapping not for ransom but for what Erik *knew?* It had happened before, and Erik Hokart was a man of international reputation in his field.

So what could be done? He simply did not know. None of his tried investigative methods seemed to help in this situation. He would return to the mesa, camp there, and await developments. They might move against him, or Kawasi might return.

What of the Poison Woman, so-called? She had appeared suddenly on the mesa, miles from anywhere, and had, according to Erik, disappeared into the kiva. If there was not another side of the curtain, where had she been hiding in the desert?

He swore softly. "Raglan," he said aloud, "you're getting in over your head."

The small town of Dove Creek lay just ahead. This was one of the places where Zane Grey had lived briefly and where the local citizens claimed much of *Riders of the Purple Sage* had been written. He slowed down, thinking of stopping for coffee, then decided to drive on. As he drove out of town he glanced back and saw a pickup carrying two men pull out on the highway.

He stepped on the gas. It was a long way to the next town, and the road was often empty. He dropped his hand to his pistol, shaking it free of its scabbard. He was a good driver and had qualified in a defensive-driving course given for the Secret Service. He knew something of evasive action. The trouble was that the highway offered almost no place to go except itself and a few roads turning off into the desert, any of which could turn into a trap.

The pickup was behind him, a good half mile back and maintaining its distance. He stepped up his speed but noticed that he did not pull away.

Despite his suspicions it might be nothing at all. They were more than likely simply some ranchers heading home.

His thoughts returned to the problem. If there was another world parallel to this, in some other dimension, perhaps, what would it be like? How would it differ from this?

He had read science fiction about such things but remembered none of it.

They would be what we call Indians, of course, but they must have progressed beyond what the cliff dwellers were when they abandoned their cliff houses and returned to that other world. Yet "progressed" in what way? What were they like now?

Those he had seen, if not accomplished actors, seemed little different from the people on this side, yet that *seemed* was a large word. Actually, he knew nothing about them.

If he saw Kawasi again he must remember to ask these questions. Apparently, access to this world was strictly controlled and perhaps had been nonexistent for many years, perhaps even centuries. Kawasi had suggested they wanted much from this side but did not wish to make themselves known.

The car behind him was gaining. The road was empty now and they were closing in.

The highway dropped into a hollow, rose out of it, then dropped into another. To the right he suddenly saw a small turn off into the brush, apparently something used by highway work vehicles. Instantly he turned into it, pulled behind a couple of cedar trees, ready to drive back onto the pavement when he could. He took the gun from the seat and held it in his lap.

Only an instant, and their car went by, driving fast. Apparently they were not expecting evasive action and probably were not accustomed to car chases. He counted a slow ten, then pulled out onto the highway, letting them get well ahead. He was still in the hollow and out of sight if they looked back, so he climbed slowly, topping out on a rise to see them far ahead, driving fast.

He returned the gun to the seat beside him and slowed his pace. Evidently they believed he had increased his speed and they were doing likewise.

Monticello was not far ahead, and if they did not realize what had happened before then, they would probably stop there to try and find him.

Long ago he'd had friends in Monticello but he doubted if any remained whom he knew. Entering the town, he turned off and, avoiding the main street, drove down back streets until he emerged on the highway headed south.

It was after midnight when he finally got to sleep in a motel room, and he awakened as usual in the cold light of dawn. For a moment he lay still, listening.

Down the street somebody started a car. Somebody else passed his room, walking along the parkway. A moment of silence and then a door opened and closed, and he heard boots walking across gravel.

He lay perfectly still, listening. Seven hundred years ago all this country around, but mostly to the south, had been inhabited by those whom the Navajo called the Anasazi. This had been their land, its true length and breadth not yet established, nor the limits of its culture. Yet much was known of them.

Father Escalante had come this way seeking a route from Santa Fe to Monterey, California, in 1776. Father Garces, that intrepid adventurer in a cassock, had come up from the south, exploring a wild and lonely land, only to turn back. Who first had seen the cliff dwellings was without doubt one of those unknown hunters or prospectors who

149

found almost everything before the official discoverers came on the scene.

W. H. Jackson, photographer for the U.S. Geological and Geographical Survey, was guided into the area by John Moss, who told him of the ruins and, when asked, indicated where they were to be found. Moss is sometimes represented as a mere miner. He was much more than that. He was a man who, leading a party of prospectors into Indian country, had no trouble with Indians. He met them, smoked with them, ate with them, and established a relationship that endured. No matter that others had trouble with the Utes, Moss did not. He had welded a friendship that was to last. In subsequent years he founded Parrott City and operated mines in several states, including Colorado and Arizona. Undoubtedly the Utes had told him of ghost cities high in the cliffs, and he was a man who would have been interested. Jackson, following the directions of Moss, visited at least one of the ruins. At the time no one had any appreciation of their size or extent. It remained for the explorations of the Wetherills to demonstrate that.

Jackson had gone into the ruins in 1874, and others followed, guided by the Wetherills.

The cliff dwellings had been strongholds, but the people were vulnerable when working in their fields. Invading Indians from the North, perhaps the Ute and the Navajo, had stolen their grain and killed many of their people. Nor had the cliff dwellings themselves been secure. The first white

150

men to visit found the bones of the dead scattered about, pitiful evidence of what had taken place.

It is often forgotten that the Indian the white man encountered had himself been an invader, sometimes preceding the white man by but a few years.

The Anasazi themselves had come to the country from elsewhere and settled first on the mesa tops, where the ruins still remained, many of them hidden, however, by brush, trees, and grass. No matter what other reasons have been given, it seems obvious they would not have abandoned their mesa-top homes for the great caves without reason. Only a few of the cliff dwellings had springs, and water as well as food and fuel had to be carried into the cliff dwellings at great expenditure of labor.

Mike Raglan swung his feet to the floor. For a moment longer, he listened to movements from outside. A traveler was loading a car, and there were voices of children, then a woman's admonishing them to be quiet, that people were still sleeping.

He shaved and showered, thinking of what he must do. Gallagher would be around, and would have questions for which Raglan had no answers. Yet he might have information, too.

Two men were looking at his car when he emerged. They were, he was sure, those who had followed him the previous day.

"Something I can do for you?" he demanded. "You lost something?"

Deliberately, he was belligerent. If they wanted trouble they could have it, and nothing was to be gained by seeming to be afraid.

"No. It is nothing. I look at car."

"Help yourself." He gestured widely. "There's a lot of them to look at." He pointed toward a police car in front of the café. "If you have any questions the police will be glad to answer them."

"Police? Who speaks of police?" As he spoke, the man was glancing around; then, hurriedly, they turned and left.

The tourist with the children commented, "They've been hanging around all morning. Obviously they want nothing to do with the police."

Raglan glanced toward the café. Gallagher would be waiting.

"See you!" he said, and waved a hand.

XVI

GALLAGHER WAS SEATED at a table in a corner eating breakfast. "Figured you'd be along," he said. He gestured at the food. "Been up since four A.M. and didn't want to wake the folks."

Raglan seated himself where he could watch the street. Gallagher smiled. "Careful man. Now I like that."

He added butter to the toast. "You make trouble for a man. I had things about wrapped up around here until you showed up. Everything quiet, no problems except for a few Saturday night drunks and the usual pot-hunters. I haven't had a decent night's sleep since you got here."

"Sorry."

"Don't be. I need the exercise." He glanced at Raglan over his coffee cup. "What's happened?"

Raglan shrugged. "There was a man at Tamarron who might have been tailing me. There was a car tailing me on the road yesterday and two men looking over my car when I came out this morning. When I pointed out your car, they skipped."

Gallagher sized Raglan up carefully. "You think they were some of your friends from over the line?"

"I couldn't swear to it, but I know."

Gallagher chuckled. "Yeah, I know how that is. I know a half-dozen thieves around here, and they know I know them, but I haven't a thing that would stand up in court and they know that, too."

Raglan ordered his breakfast and stared out the window. Neither of them spoke for several minutes. Raglan reminded himself that he liked Gallagher. He was a good man, a tough man, and one with imagination. At least he had an open mind.

"The world's gettin' too damn complicated," Gallagher said. "Used to be a man knew who his enemies were and where to find them. If you made a deal with a man, you shook hands on it and nothing more was needed. Now you got lawyers, you got the government, you got everything

153

tangled in red tape, and then things like this come up. Who knows about fourth dimensions and parallel worlds?"

"That isn't really new. Einstein started it all back in 1919, I think it was. From all I hear, he didn't like it much, either. Most people are still living in that nice, comfortable world that Newton accepted."

"I don't know anything about that." Gallagher filled their cups from the pot the waitress had left. "Supposing what you suggest is fact. Supposing that when the Anasazi left here they went back to that world that was evil. What do you think it would be like now?"

Raglan shrugged. "Hard to tell. It would depend so much on what influences there were that affected their culture. They were planting on mesa tops, learning to use all the water they had. I suspect they'd become pretty good dry farmers but they were into irrigation, too.

"Off to the south, where Phoenix is, there was the Hohokam culture who understood irrigation very well. Some of the ditches they dug couldn't be improved upon.

"There was a connection with the Hohokam. I don't know how much of a connection but there was probably some trade and exchange of ideas, so if the culture they had persisted on the Other Side, I would guess that by now they would have a very advanced system of irrigation, one that was strictly regulated."

"When you need water," Gallagher agreed,

154

"somebody has to control its use or there'd be fighting all the while."

"Exactly. And there seems to have been, for a long time at least, an effort to close off any communication with this side. To develop a civilization needs input from other peoples. Europe had a lot of useful rivers, lots of coves, harbors, and the like, so it was easy for people to come and go and each one brought new ideas, new blood.

"Nobody knows how old seafaring was in Europe. For years everything was based on what we knew about the Mediterranean, but there were ships in the Persian Gulf, the Indian Ocean, and the Pacific just as early, if not earlier than the Mediterranean. There was seafaring in the Baltic and Atlantic, too. All of it enabled ideas to spread, introducing new weapons, new tools, new crops." Raglan paused to sip his coffee.

"What are you going to do now?" Gallagher asked.

Raglan shrugged again. "Go back to Hokart's mesa. Hang around out there and see what I can learn." He paused. "I've got to find Erik. He asked for me to come, he almost begged me to come, there at the end. That wasn't like him. He was scared."

"Aren't you?"

"To be frank, yes. I don't know what's over there. If I go, I don't know that I can ever get back. Johnny never could make it and from what I gather he was a pretty canny old cowboy."

"You be careful."

"I'll do that." Raglan paused. "Seen any more of Eden Foster?"

Gallagher shook his head. "I'm not liable to. Not for a while. The missus like to flew off the handle when she heard I'd been over there. She doesn't know Eden but she suspects the worst."

Raglan was silent, and then he said. "The way I see it, judging from what I might call contacts with them, they don't know much about how we function over here.

"Eden knows, but she's only one and for reasons of her own she may not be sharing what she knows. Maybe it's because she just doesn't think of it that way. Little things, about how to spend money, getting change, paying checks in restaurants, and even the structure of our buildings.

"At Tamarron, I don't believe that fellow even suspected there was a door behind me. He saw a glass wall and took it for granted. He was sitting so he could watch me and the entrance, so when some confusion distracted him, I slipped out that door."

Raglan watched the movements outside, There was nothing going on beyond the casual, everyday life of the town. Where was Kawasi? Was she safe? Or had she, too, been taken?

"Postmistress spoke to me this morning," Gallagher commented. "Said Mr. Hokart had not been in to pick up his mail. I told her to hold it. He might be out of town."

"She buy it?"

"I don't believe so. She didn't say anything but

she looked doubtful, said Mr. Hokart was always very particular about his mail." Gallagher pushed back in his chair. "That's the beginning of it, Mike. Folks are going to start asking questions. This is a small town and they don't miss very much. Hokart was never what you'd call neighborly, but he was always friendly in passing and one way or another he did quite a bit of business here in town.

"He bought groceries now and again, ate in the café, and he bought hardware—nails, tools and such. . . ."

"Ammunition?"

"Uh-huh. He bought quite a lot. Aroused some curiosity, as it was pistol ammo. Said he was shooting at targets, trying to perfect his shooting."

"Reasonable enough."

"Sure, anybody will buy that. None of us shoot well enough. No matter how good you are, you can always get better." He paused, staring out the window. "Anyway, folks are asking questions, wondering why he hasn't been in. But they've just begun to wonder where he is. Soon they will be asking questions about that, and then they will begin to wonder just who you are and what you're doing here."

"I expect that."

"Yeah? But are you ready for the next thing? They will be wondering how come you are around and Hokart's vanished. They will be asking about the connection. They'll be suspicious.

"When they start asking questions they will be

wanting answers, and I don't have any answers. Do you?"

"I am a friend of Erik's. It is as simple as that."

"If you're such a good friend, why don't you know where Erik is?" Gallagher stared at him. "You see what I mean? This is a small town. Everybody knows everybody else, but they don't know you. Erik wasn't one of them but they accepted him. He was doing something they thought foolish but he was doing it on his own land and he was willing to pay for it, so they are on his side."

Gallagher was silent for a few minutes, then he added, "It's already begun. Over at Mexican Hat. Woman in a store over there asked about Erik Hokart. Wondered where he was, and then added that he was probably out on the mesa with you. She added that if anybody knew where he was it would be you."

"A woman said that?"

"Uh-huh. Nice-lookin' woman whom they didn't know but they said she'd been in before. Looked like a city woman."

"Eden Foster?"

"Sounded like her. Looks to me like some folks may not wait for suspicion to grow. They'd just help it along a bit."

Mike Raglan thought about it. The question Eden Foster asked would be repeated, and of course, that was as planned. When Erik did not appear, suspicion would grow. She did not need to

158

accuse, only to ask a few questions and start people wondering.

"See what I mean? If I give them your answers they'd put me in a booby hatch, and I wouldn't blame them." He looked across the corner of the table at Raglan. "Seems to me you're in trouble, my friend. If you're coming up with any answers it had better be quick."

Raglan knew he should leave here now. He should check out of the motel, drive back to Tamarron, check out there, and catch a plane for Denver and then New York.

After all, what was Erik to him? Hokart was just a man whom he knew, like many others. Of course, the thing he could not escape was the fact that Erik had called on him for help. The man was alone, faced by God knew what in the way of enemies. Of course, if Mike went on, he would have the same enemies.

He got up. "See you, Gallagher." He turned toward the door.

"You going out there?"

"What else can I do? Cut and run? He trusted me to get him out of this, and there isn't anybody else."

"There's me," Gallagher replied.

"You're an officer, with a duty to a community, and no telling what will come of this. Besides, I'd rather have you on the outside. I may need help."

"What did you mean when you said there's 'no telling what will come of this'?"

Raglan walked back to the table and spoke more

159

quietly. "Gallagher, think about it. Supposing a lot of them come through some night? Without warning? You've got a small town here. They know how many you are and what your communications are. Supposing they decided to come over?"

Gallagher stared at him. "Now you're really going off the deep end. Why would they do a thing like that?"

"I don't for a minute believe they will. It was just an idea, but how many would it take to descend on a sleeping town?"

"More than they are likely to have," Gallagher said. "Everybody in this town has a gun, most of them two or three. These folks do a lot of hunting in season, so they not only have weapons but they know how to use them and when."

Raglan walked to the cash register and paid the bill, then walked out into the sunlight. Gallagher followed him.

"Damn it, man, why'd you have to bring up an idea like that? Now you've got me worried."

"Look, I doubt if you believe any of this, and I don't know what to believe myself. It was just one idea following another. The legend is that the Anasazi left the Third World because it became evil.

"Evil in what way? What did they think of as evil? The Aztecs, the Mayas, and some other Indians from south of here believed in human sacrifice. According to the best reports they sacrificed literally thousands of people. Is that what they meant by evil? Did they think of human sacrifice as evil? Probably not, as it was a religious rite."

They stood on the curb near Raglan's car. "Gallagher, I don't know what to believe. I'm a confirmed skeptic, but that doesn't blind me to the fact there's a lot we don't know. We're only beginning to learn about this world, and believe me, the ideas of our grandchildren will be altogether different from our own. They will take things for granted of which we know nothing now.

"The world is changing fast. When I was a youngster there were still a hundred jobs a man could do who had no education. Most of them have vanished. It's not even a machine world as we knew it. Now it's a computer world, and if you don't have education and the ability to adapt you're out of it. You either get an education or find a place on skid row."

"Maybe."

"You've seen Mesa Verde, Gallagher. That culture lasted a thousand years at least. Do you think they doubted it would last forever? When someone looks at Mesa Verde and the ruins left by the Anasazi, he should not just wonder at them but he should think of what they must have thought. What did they believe? We can reconstruct their world from the artifacts that have been found, and we know how they lived, but what did they *think?* How much did they know about other Indians? Probably there was interchange of trade goods and ideas with the Hohokam or the Mogollon cultures. There seems to have been some trade as far away

161

as Central America. They've found mummified parrots in the ruins and other evidences of trade.

"Did they know anything about the Mound Builders? What did they know of eastern Indians? And were any of the eastern Indians actually living where the white man first found them?"

"So you going back down there?"

"Leaving now. Soon as I can pick up a few supplies at the store."

"Be careful, Raglan, and for God's sake, don't you disappear! I'll have trouble enough explaining Hokart!"

He was still standing on the curb as Raglan drove away, and in the rearview mirror Mike saw him take off his cap and run his fingers through his hair, then walk back inside.

A half hour later, with Chief sitting beside him, Raglan was headed back for the mesa.

And he did not want to go. He just didn't want to go at all.

XVII

THE ROAD WAS empty, and he stepped on the gas. He wanted to get off the highway and into the desert as quickly as possible. So far there was no indication that he was followed or observed, but there was always a chance that somebody was already down the road or out in the desert awaiting him.

The day was hot and still. Heat waves shimmered in the near distance. He turned on the air conditioning, and Chief made a try at curling up in the seat beside him but it proved impossible. There was simply too much of him and he lopped over, resting his big head on Mike's thigh again. Raglan did not like that very much, as it made it more difficult to get at his gun. He picked it up and put it between his legs where it would be quicker to grasp.

At first there was much cedar alongside the road, but it thinned out and then disappeared, giving way to sparse brush and cactus.

A car appeared in the road ahead of him, a camper with a man and a woman in the front seat. The woman was driving. Moments later he saw them disappear to the left over a low hill.

The turnoff, a scarcely visible set of tire tracks, lay right ahead. Slowing down, he made the turn. The highway was empty and the trail on which he now drove seemed to show no fresh signs of travel. He slowed down still more, for the road had many dips and bends.

Chief sat up, watching the road, suddenly alert. With the windows closed and the air conditioning on, there was small chance he had smelled anything, yet he seemed to know where they were going.

Raglan's thoughts returned to the problem. If there was more than one opening to the Other Side, as there seemed to be, where were they?

Kawasi had implied there were occasional, erratic openings that permitted passage.

What was it like over there, and what rules, if any, governed the openings? The window in the kiva seemed to be an opening that was or had been stabilized. But what of the others? And where were they?

Johnny had gotten through by accident but in all the years since had not been able to discover a way to return.

Mike pulled up on the crest of a hill and slowly checked the area around him, examining every clump of brush, every cedar, every rock formation. By coming here alone he was walking right into their hands, yet there was no other place that held a clue to Erik and his whereabouts.

It was very still. Turning, he looked back the way he had come. The road was empty, just a narrow, winding way among boulders, brush, and outcroppings of sandstone. Uneasily, he looked around. He had always loved the desert, its vast distances, the silence, the creatures that knew how to survive, for if nothing else, the desert was a place of survival. Everything that lived in the desert had found some pattern for survival, some means of adapting to the heat, the cold, and the lack of water. Each in its own way had found a means to conserve moisture.

He got back in the car and started the motor. Easing forward, he tooled the car around bends in the road, up small slopes and down steep declivities.

Off to the south he glimpsed the abrupt shoulder of Monitor Mesa. Erik's mesa lay on the near side of the San Juan River, a tributary of the Colorado. The canyon was deep, and not far from there a ford had once existed called The Crossing of the Fathers. It was there that Escalante had crossed in 1776 when trying to find a route to Monterey, in California. Due to the backup of water from Glen Canyon Dam, the Crossing was no longer of use.

This had all been Anasazi country until their disappearance seven hundred years before, yet their presence had left little evidence behind. Had they not liked this area any better than he? There were the remains of two cliff houses up the canyon, but they were several miles away.

Arriving at his former stopping place, he studied the terrain and found he could drive a half mile closer to Erik's ruin. Swinging the car around, he pointed it toward a clump of cedar. When he reached it, he turned the car to face in the direction from which he had come and then backed into partial hiding behind the cedar. For a moment then, after he switched off the engine, he sat listening. Then he opened the door and stepped out, Chief bounding past him.

Again he listened, then carefully closed the door, making as little noise as possible. He locked the car and pocketed the key.

"Let's go, boy," he said softly, taking up the few packages he had momentarily placed on the hood. With another look around he started for the mesa. It was only a short walk now.

They had gone no more than a dozen yards

when Chief stopped short, head up. Raglan's eyes went to the mesa. Beyond the bulge of red rock that was to be a part of Erik's house something moved.

Moved, and was gone. He stopped, studying the area with care. Had he really seen something? Or was it a figment of the imagination? Apprehensively, he looked around. He was in the enemy's country now.

The trail was uneven and littered with rock. He could not keep his attention on the ruin without risk of tripping.

His thoughts went back to his Paiute miner friend with whom he had first come into this country, and to the old cowboy who'd told him about the gold he had found. Had that place been below Lake Powell? Or was it nearer here? Suddenly he realized, as his thoughts came together, that it had been close by. He would have to look at the old map again. "Get in and get out," the old cowboy had said. And the map had indicated a place.

Excited, he began to hurry. Chief was trotting along, just ahead of him, but alert.

The ruin was deserted and showed no evidence of anyone's having been there since he had last visited the place. He set down his groceries, putting those that needed refrigeration in the small icebox. With Chief beside him, he went over to the kiva, stopping at its edge to look down into it.

It appeared unchanged. The "window" seemed the same, but Chief shied away from it, growling a little. Mike could see no fresh tracks, so he walked back to the ruin and gathered materials for a fire.

The map the old cowboy had given him was of a way through the veil, but also to a place where gold had been stored.

Stored by whom? And when? He had too many questions and not enough answers. But the old cowboy had warned him that the people on the Other Side knew when the veil had been penetrated. He had barely escaped.

That had been many years ago, but would the situation have changed? Suppose he could find how that cowboy had gone through? Would they still know? And where? And how did it happen that the gold was there, unguarded?

If it was there, unguarded, it was because the powers that were did not know it was there.

Therefore it must have been a deposit left by some previous generation of which this one knew nothing.

It also was likely that it was in an area rarely visited. If that was true he might manage it himself. Yet if he was in a remote area when he reached the Other Side, he might be too far from Erik to be of any use.

Mike Raglan slowly put the materials for a fire in place but did not light it. That would come later. For the present it was light and he needed to think.

How much did they know? How much did they understand of this world and how it functioned? How much did they understand of equipment?

Obviously, the man who'd driven the van had known how to drive. Eden Foster, too, knew how at least some parts of this world functioned, but did she know enough? And how much had she communicated to them? Might she not, to preserve her own power, have kept something back? How much did she prefer that culture over this?

Could she be turned? Could she be made an ally instead of an enemy?

He doubted the possibility but it must be considered. Another thought occurred. Was she herself a Poison Woman?

He walked outside. The sun was setting as he stood looking across at the sun-bathed walls of No Man's Mesa.

He told himself it was no different from any other such formation, yet the strange flare he had seen would not leave his mind. And who or what were the strange creatures he had heard on that night? Indians, out for some ceremony of which he knew nothing?

It was near that mesa that the old cowboy had found his entrance to the other world. Near, but where? Mike tried to recall the old map the cowboy had given him. The San Juan River had been on that map, but on which side had the opening been?

From among Erik's papers he found a sheet of drawing paper and began slowly to reconstruct the map as he remembered it. The map itself was in his condo at Tamarron. He had not believed he would need it.

The river, Navajo Mountain, the Moonlit Water—these places he remembered. He studied the items placed on the map and added another mesa to the west of No Man's, a much bigger one. Putting down his pencil he walked outside to look around again. Chief stayed close beside him.

"We've got to watch 'em, boy," he said softly. "We don't know what we're getting into."

Twilight lay upon the desert, and No Man's had gathered its blanket of shadows around it. Navajo Mountain still had a crown of gold and crimson, the gold fading, the crimson lingering. Raglan turned quickly, hearing no sound, seeing nothing. "You're getting jumpy," he said aloud.

After walking back to the ruin, he lit his fire. Chief was scenting the breeze, head up.

The night was cool, as desert nights are inclined to be, and the planet Venus hung its lantern in the sky. He studied his crude map, adding Mike's Mesa.

He added fuel to his fire, then broke out a box of crackers and took a handful. He tossed one to Chief, who caught it deftly and looked grateful.

Trees. The old cowboy had mentioned trees. Raglan shook his head. In this country? There was a good bit of cedar but he had seen nothing else. On that first night, riding to his expected meeting with Erik, he had seen cottonwoods along the wash. But the old cowboy had mentioned a large number of trees and much shade. There was water in the canyon, too, and a couple of Anasazi grain-storage caves, walled for the purpose. He would have to do some scouting.

He unrolled his sleeping bag in the corner of the ruined wall. Nothing could come at him there—nothing human, at least.

What did he mean by that? Nothing *human?* What was he expecting?

Sourly, he stared off across the desert toward Navajo Mountain. That was just the trouble. He did not know what to expect. He did not want to go, yet Erik was expecting him, hoping for him, and there was no one else. Without Mike Raglan it was all up to Erik himself. And what could Erik do?

That would depend on the situation and Erik's ingenuity, of which he should have a plenty. He was a man who had come far on his intelligence, his reasoning power, and imagination. Much would also depend on the kind of people with whom he must deal.

What was their background? What was their education? What language did they speak? And what was their culture like? Even when people spoke the same language they did not always mean the same things.

His thoughts returned to Eden Foster and the Navajo girl who worked for her. He remembered how the girl had looked directly into his eyes, but in no flirtatious manner. Had she been trying to warn him? Or had she been measuring him against them? A bright girl, Gallagher had said. He must talk with her, somewhere alone when Eden Foster was not around.

Raglan made coffee and ate a few more crackers while waiting for it, adding fuel to his fire meanwhile.

In their heyday the Anasazi occupied more than 40,000 square miles in Arizona, New Mexico, Utah, and Colorado. Their ruins were everywhere, some mere heaps of debris, some broken walls of carefully laid masonry, indicating a growing skill in architectural construction.

The study of such ruins was comparatively new, and the science of archaeology itself was scarcely one hundred years old, much of that time a learning process. First it had been necessary to learn how to conduct a dig, how to determine the ages of the sites and objects discovered, and how to preserve what they had found.

The science had suffered and still suffered from preconceived ideas, and attempts to make discoveries fit preconceived patterns. One such idea was that the introduction of agriculture had given birth to other dramatic changes. Discoveries at Bat Cave, for one instance, showed that the introduction of planting long preceded the production of pottery.

The fact was that in the beginning, agriculture had demanded longer hours of disciplined labor than food-gathering and hunting. To a settled community a crop failure could be a disaster.

Supposedly, planting had caused hunting to fade into the background, but the Cheyennes had given up agriculture and returned to hunting. Without a doubt this had been due in part to a population explosion among the buffalo, providing a stable diet to a people to whom hunting was a sport as well as subsistence.

He poured his coffee and looked over his shoulder. It was dark. In the distance beyond No Man's there were stars, but were they the same stars?

He shook his head to shake off the disturbing thoughts. He was creating ghosts where none existed. Kawasi had said the mesa looked familiar, like something from the Other Side. Could something exist in two worlds at the same time?

Suddenly he realized he was hearing footsteps, approaching footsteps.

A figure loomed at the edge of the firelight. It was Gallagher.

"I figured you needed company," he said.

And what, Raglan asked himself, did he know about Gallagher?

XVIII

GALLAGHER TOOK A campstool and sat down. "Got worried about you," he said, pushing his cap back on his head, "and I figured we should talk some more.

"I'm not much on talk, usually, but sometimes something comes of just bringing out all aspects of a problem and just mulling over it."

Raglan offered no comment. He was thinking about Gallagher and how he had arrived. Had

172

Mike been so preoccupied that he had not heard the sound of a car arriving? Or had Gallagher's car simply not made that much noise? Or could he have used some other means of arrival?

Despite his suspicions he trusted Gallagher. He liked the man, believed he wanted to cope with the situation, but understood that, although he acted friendly, he was on the whole impersonal in his attitude—as he should be.

"We've got two ways to look at this," Gallagher said. "We can look at it logically like it was a kidnapping or murder, and investigate it from that standpoint. Or we can accept this idea of another world and see where that leaves us."

"Which we've both been doing."

"Right."

Gallagher poked a stick into the fire. "Had a couple of queries about Hokart. From back east. Seems he usually calls his office and they've not heard from him."

They sat listening, and Raglan looked at Chief. The big dog had not lifted his head from his paws but his ears were up.

"If he doesn't show up soon we'll have a lot of inquiries. Hokart's a mighty important man, seems like, and yesterday, while I was gone, somebody from the governor's office called. He said the governor wished to consult with Erik Hokart and would he call back as soon as possible?

"We've got to find him, Mike, and right away. This is going to blow the lid off."

"Does Eden Foster know?"

"I made a point of talking about it. I was over there today, just sort of dropped in. She always wants to know what I am doing, so I told her I was hunting a missing man, and that if I didn't find him there'd be people all over the country around here, looking into everything.

"I also mentioned that one of the places they would immediately check would be Hokart's camp, and the kiva."

"What did she say to that?"

"Not much, but I could see she was bothered. She was kind of impatient, wanted to know what was so important about him, and I just told her any citizen was important, as she should know, but Erik had worked with some important people and was considered very special by many of them. Then I told her they'd never stop looking until every possibility was exhausted."

"Did she say anything about me?"

"I was coming to that." He chuckled. "First time I ever saw Eden pay much mind to anybody in other than a business or social way. She asked me if you were married."

"Probably wondering if anybody would miss me if I disappeared."

"Oh, no. Not this time. Sounded like she had a personal interest."

Raglan was skeptical. Eden Foster was an attractive woman who might be expected to have an interest in men, but he doubted if she had anything other than a business interest in him. He said as much.

Gallagher refused to accept it. "If I know anything at all about women, she's interested in you."

Raglan looked out of the door and across the mesa toward No Man's. "If I know anything about women," he said, "Eden Foster is nobody to mess with. She's got a mind, but she also has a will and she doesn't like being thwarted. I could see that in her. I have a hunch that intellectually and personally she's a defector."

"A defector?"

"Suppose what we surmise is true? That she's an agent, a lookout station for the Other Side? My hunch is that she has come to like it over here, and although she could never be one of us, she likes the life here better than where she comes from.

"I don't mean she'd betray them. She's like some of the Soviets sent here or to Europe. They begin to enjoy the life and they don't want to go back. Here they have access to things they cannot get over there, and they are free of many of the pressures."

Gallagher was silent, mulling it over. The air was cool and the night was still. Chief arose and walked outside, stretching.

"What worries me," Raglan said, "is that we don't know their capabilities, nor do they know ours."

"They know a damned sight more about us than we do of them," Gallagher said. "Eden Foster is here. She's been making contacts, listening, reading, learning. We don't have any communication with her side of things, nor do we actually know there is another side. I still can't escape the feeling we're being had."

Raglan was uneasy. The kiva was there and its opening into another world, or whatever it was, an unpleasant fact. Erik Hokart was over there somewhere, and it was a fact that those who held him must know something of this world.

Yet how much did they know? How accurately had Eden Foster judged this world, and how accurately had they read her messages, if such there were?

It was never easy for one people to understand another when their cultural backgrounds differed drastically. If he only knew more of how the Anasazi had lived and thought. Many of the outward evidences of their living were obvious. Their buildings, from pit houses to cliff apartments, were easily seen. Some of their pottery, their tools and weapons remained. Yet as they ground their corn with mano and metate, what were they thinking? What was it that ordered their existence?

"Have you got a knife?" Gallagher asked. "Sometimes one can be mighty handy."

"I have one."

Gallagher glanced at Raglan, a wry look on his face. "Sometimes I think I should pull you in just to see what you're carrying."

"You'd make me mighty unhappy," Raglan commented. "I might just move out and leave you with your friends from over the line. Then you could handle it all by your lonesome."

176

Chief had returned and was lying across the doorway, his head on his paws.

"Anything you're carrying," Gallagher said, "you're likely to need. You might have a chance if you could tie up with that old cowboy you told me about. The one called Johnny.

"The trouble is a man wouldn't know how to act over yonder. In this country there's so many foreigners and strangers we don't pay them much attention, but in a place like that . . .

"How would you get food, for instance? Do they have eating places? Or do they eat at home? What would you ask for? If you went over there you wouldn't even know the names for things or where to go to find out anything."

Raglan agreed, then added, "The cliff dwellers lived by farming. The Hopi are very skillful dry farmers, and the Hohokam had extensive irrigation projects. So, unless there was some drastic change, the Anasazi probably continued to develop as an irrigation civilization, and most such develop very rigid governments. Somebody has to control the water so it can be evenly distributed, and that calls for authority."

"What about this evil they talk about? They say the Third World was evil."

"Your guess is as good as mine. What is evil? Our conceptions of evil are a result of Judeo-Christian ethic, but their conceptions of evil may be entirely different. The Maya and the Aztec, who were probably kin to these people, indulged in human sacrifice on a grand scale. If you go over there you might find yourself stretched out on an altar."

"That's for you, Raglan, not me. I've my own work to do."

Long after they slipped into their sleeping bags, Mike Raglan lay awake, listening.

Listening and thinking. The night was very still and cold, and although he heard nothing outside, he heard Chief growl deep in his chest. Yet the big dog did not rise, so the danger, if anywhere except in his dreams, was not close.

At dawn he was out of his sleeping bag and making coffee when Gallagher came in from outside. "Been looking around," he commented. "Took a look at that kiva."

"It's more than I've done. I've been shying away from it."

"Can't see anything through that window," Gallagher said. "Might be anything in there, and it's right on the edge of the cliff thataway—"

"The dog went through. I suppose Erik did, too, but I don't know." Raglan paused. "Gallagher? Do you know this country right close around here? A canyon with a lot of trees?"

"Are you kidding? This isn't tree country except for some cedar and an occasional cottonwood in the bottom of a wash."

"If that kiva offers an opening to the Other Side, it is an opening right into their hands, but according to what I've heard there are other openings, and one of them is a canyon with trees. I'm going to have a look."

"I got to get back to town." Gallagher reached for the pot. "For heaven's sake, take care of yourself. All I need is another guy disappearing around here."

They drank coffee and talked; then Gallagher got up and started back to his Jeep. When he reached it he turned and looked back, hesitating as if reluctant to drive away. Then he got in, swung his car around and headed back toward the highway.

Raglan stood listening to the sound of the motor until it died away, then turned back to the ruin. He put together a small pack, checked his gun, and called Chief. "Come on, boy, we're going for a walk."

On the old canvas map, No Man's had pointed like a gigantic finger. Pointing at what?

The way was rough, but he took his time, glad he had hiking boots rather than the western boots he usually wore. He walked around one of the red rock domes and then down into the gully beyond. He had to pick his way with care, for there was much loose rock and the solid rock was uneven. A "hole" in western lingo might be any basin, hollow, or even a canyon, and over here somewhere was something of the kind. Several times he paused to look around, to choose his way but also to see if there was anyone following him.

He saw nothing—only an eagle high against the sky, only a lizard that darted into the shade of some brush. It was a world of silence, with no sound but those made by his own passage.

Across the river and stretching off to the south was No Man's Mesa, huge, ominous, mysterious. He worked his way down a precarious sandstone slope. Any misstep might send him pitching down a hundred feet or more. A broken leg out here alone could be the end of him. He paused near a juniper and crushed a leaf in his fingers, liking the faintly pungent smell, listening to the song of a canyon wren. There was no other sound.

He worked his way, Chief sometimes following, often leading, down a steep canyon wall. He glimpsed the bright-green of foliage that indicated the presence of water, but it needed another hour of hard clambering and climbing before he was within sight of the trees.

They were there, all right. At first only a clump was visible, but when he reached the edge of the canyon he could find no way down. The canyon wall bulged outward and there was no edge. To walk farther out was to fall off. For an hour he worked his way along, seeking for some break in the wall down which he might work his way. There was none.

Occasionally he glimpsed trees down below, and once he thought he caught the gleam of water. Finally, he made camp under a rocky overhang, gathered wood for his fire, and prepared a camp for the night. A good-sized cedar shielded his fire from observation, although the reflection against the back wall might be seen.

There was considerable deadwood lying about

and he gathered enough for the night, most of it cedar washed down the canyon from higher up.

As the crow flies, he doubted he was more than two miles from the ruin and its kiva, but even with the flashlight he carried he had no desire to try to cross that rough country in the dark.

A coyote spoke inquiringly into the night, and somewhere out in the darkness, a rock loosened by one of the many natural causes, fell into the canyon, bounding from ledge to ledge. Only a small rock, but one more item in the continual change wrought by frost, rain, sun, and wind.

He had only a small fire, and he did not lie down but leaned against the backwall, a blanket around his shoulders. He dozed, added fuel to the fire, and dozed again.

The night waned, the moon arose, flooding the canyon with ghostly radiance. The towering spires above the canyon wall took on shadows, and he let the fire die down to red coals, adding just enough fuel to keep them alive, with an occasional bright-yellow flame as the new fuel was attacked. The wood from the cedar smoke smelled good, and he thought how often cedar had been used, in many countries, for sacred ceremonies. He himself had watched a medicine man waft smoke over tribal elders with an eagle's wing to purify them before an important conference.

He took cedar bark and added it to the fire, and then, suddenly, as his hand reached out to the fire, it stopped, arrested in movement by some small sound, a sound not normal to the night. Chief also sensed its presence.

Something, far up the narrow canyon, had moved in the night.

Something that was not a rock falling or a wind stirring the junipers. It was something alive.

Alive? At least something that moved, alive or not. Something that came nearer in the night, something carefully moving, something approaching, something that tried to make no sound.

He was seated well back in a corner of the rock, not easily visible, his fire a few feet away, the shadow of the cedar looming large before the cave, but with openings on either side. He could see a star over the rim of the rocks opposite.

The coyotes had ceased their chatter. The night was still, waiting, and now he heard no sound.

Under his blanket his fist gripped a gun butt, but what use was a gun against a ghost? Yet, did ghosts make small whispers in the night? Something brushed against brush; something ceased to move, something that was looking, peering, trying to make him out, the small light from the fire making the finding of him more difficult.

His shoulders were against the rock. One hand held the blanket edge, the other the gun.

XIX

"MAY I SPEAK?" The voice was low, not unpleasant.

Raglan waited for several seconds, then said, "Come forward, into the firelight. Come very carefully."

The man was tall, with high, thin shoulders and a scholar's face. He wore a turban, small and tight-fitting, and a sort of robe gathered at the waist by a broad leather belt. On his feet he wore hard-soled moccasins. He carried no weapon that Raglan could see.

"Be seated," Raglan said, and when the man looked puzzled, he repeated, "Sit!" and gestured at a place near the fire but directly in front of Raglan.

The man seated himself, cross-legged, and looked over at him. His costume did not surprise Mike Raglan, who had lived through the hippie period of the sixties and was astonished by nothing.

"Speak, then," Raglan suggested.

"You look for something?"

"Aren't we all?"

The man smiled suddenly, revealing white, marvelously even teeth. "I think yes. It is our way, to seek." His smile vanished. "It is the way for some of us, but a dangerous way."

He paused a minute and then, speaking slowly as if groping for words, he said, "I think somewhere you live in a nice place. I think it is better you go there."

Raglan still held the pistol, but it was hidden by the blanket and he did not know whether the man guessed that he held a weapon.

183

"I have lost a friend. I search for him."

"He is gone. You will not find him, and if you try to look you will go where he has gone." The man paused. "I try be friend to you."

"If you are a friend, bring Erik Hokart to me and then I shall know you are a friend." He spoke slowly, seeing that the stranger had difficulty with the words. "If he does not come, I shall continue to search. If I do not find him soon, many will come. They will find him and they will also find whatever else can be found. There will be no secrets then."

"It must not be."

"Sorry, friend, it will be. They will come first to the kiva on the mesa. They will go through the window. They will find Erik Hokart."

"There will be fight then."

Raglan shrugged. "They will expect it. Many will come. First, there will be policemen, and after that, the army. Many, many men, with weapons and machines. Nothing will stop them."

The man shook his head and smiled again. This time he smiled less warmly. "Do not say untrue thing. You are few. You are not strong."

"Who told you that? If that is what you have been told, you cannot trust those who speak. We are many, and we are strong, and where my people come, nothing is ever the same again, which is often a mistake they do not recognize."

Raglan was puzzled. The man's speech was slow, somewhat halting, the words carefully enunciated. He looked to be an intelligent man, and he did not appear to be seeking trouble. Yet who else might wait out there in the darkness? Even as they talked, Raglan strained his ears to listen.

There was something interesting here. The man seemed to be warning him, yet trying to avert danger. He offered no threats.

"Long ago," Raglan said, "when my people first came to this country, only a few came west to trade for fur. The Indians they met despised them for their weakness. They saw only a few men, or often one alone, and they traded for skins. To the Indians they met this was foolish and weak. If they were men, why did they not trap their own fur? The Indian had no idea of the millions of people in the eastern lands. It is the same with you. You have seen a few of us and do not know how many of us there are.

"You do not know our insatiable curiosity, our drive to investigate, to explore, to learn. No barrier will stop my people, even if some should wish it. No doubt your land has minerals we could exploit. It may have timber. It may have much we need or believe we need. There is no barrier to stop the mind of man, nor the feet that follow, nor the hands that will do what is to be done.

"You have but one choice. Return Erik Hokart to us and we will close up the opening in the kiva and bother you no more."

"It is not possible. It is not I who say he can be free. I am but one man and have no authority. Go," he added, "and do not come back. If the window in the kiva was a mistake, the mistake was mine. It was I who wished to open the way."

"You?"

"An ancient tablet told of the kiva and the opening to your world. I am he who is Keeper of the Archives. Into my hands all such things come. In the Halls of Shibalba there are many Tablets, lying long-untouched. They are writ in the ancient characters which cannot be spoken. I have writ them in your tongue."

"In English? Why?"

"It is read by few, but known by several of my kind, and such knowledge as I have discovered is not for the people." He hesitated. "Nor even for the Masters."

"I thought The Hand was your ruler?"

He stared at Raglan. "You know of The Hand? How could you know such things?"

Not wishing to betray Kawasi, Mike said, "We, too, have our archives."

"It cannot be! You know nothing of us! No one from your world has ever entered ours and returned!"

"You are sure? Not even many years ago?"

He hesitated, then said, "It is not in the Archives."

"You have examined them all?"

"Years would be needed, and I have but begun."

"Then you do not know. You know only what is commonly said. What is agreed upon. A scholar does not accept. He questions, examines, then suggests a possibility."

The man was silent, and Raglan added fuel to his small fire. Then the man spoke.

"What I say is true. You must go. The man you seek has been taken before The Hand. The Hand will dispose of him as he sees fit. No one opposes The Hand."

"No? What of the followers of He Who Had Magic?"

The man stared at Raglan, then shook his head. "That is a legend. There was no such person. There are no such people."

The flames flickered under a touch of wind. The two men sat silent, staring into the fire. "It would have been well to have left the kiva closed," Raglan said mildly. "You have begun something that cannot be stopped." He paused. "Our legend is that your world is evil. How is it evil?"

The man's eyes avoided Raglan's. He gestured about him. "What is this place?"

"It is a place in the desert. The river out there is the San Juan. It is a Spanish name, as the Spanish once came to this country and left their names upon the land."

"You have cities?"

"Very large ones, far from here. The nearest is over one hundred miles away, but there are towns, and people. There are roads that lead to the cities. Most of them are far away."

Chief had been lying quietly. Now he stirred, and the man started to rise, obviously frightened.

"It is all right," Raglan said. "It is my dog."

Uneasily, the man looked at Chief, whom he could scarcely make out, lying deep in the shadow of the cedar.

"We can talk of our cultures later," Raglan said. "Now we must speak of Erik Hokart. You say he is a prisoner of The Hand, so we must speak with The Hand."

"You do not know what you say. It cannot be done."

"You can take me to him."

"It is impossible. You do not comprehend. Nobody can go to The Hand. My hair is touched with gray, yet I have never been in his presence.

"My life is spent among the Tablets. I am their protector, and of our people few even know of their existence. Long ago our rulers came there to study, but it has been many generations since one of them has come. Once we who were Keepers of the Word were called in council, but it is so no longer. The Hand may not even remember that we exist."

As they talked, Raglan began to understand a little. The Archives had been accumulated in ancient times, beginning long before the Escape, when some of the people fled the growing evil and took shelter beyond the veil. For over one thousand years they had lived in the new world they found, until drought and invading savages drove them to return. In the intervening time they had forgotten the horrors from which they had fled.

188

Some did remember and refused to return. They had merged with other tribes.

When originally they fled they had been workers in the fields and only a few of the wise men had gone with them, so they had known little of their own world.

Raglan asked about The Hand. Was it one man or several? Where did he live? Where would Erik be held prisoner?

The man shook his head. "I do not know. There is a part of our city where none may go. He will have been taken there, I presume. Only by command of The Hand may anyone enter, and those who go do not often return." He looked into Raglan's eyes. "So you see? Not many wish to go."

Raglan nudged a piece of wood deeper into the fire. "Why do you come to me?"

"I have said. You must not come. It is of no purpose."

"And I have said that if I do not find him, many will come, and they will come with anger and determination and nothing will stand against them. Erik Hokart must be freed. If you wish your way preserved, you must help me."

"I?" The idea astonished him. "What can I do? I am but a Keeper of Archives."

"Are there in your Archives no tales of warriors? Of men who accomplished great things?"

The man's eyes sparkled. "Many are the tales of glory and of bravery! Yet no one reads them now. No one but me and a very few others. The tablets

189

gather dust. The halls are swept to no purpose. No one wishes to learn, for now they believe they know all things. I doubt The Hand knows of my existence, and the Varanel, his guards, pass me by without notice."

His face was suddenly gloomy. "You spoke of my wishing to preserve our way. It is sacrilege, but I do not know if I wish it preserved.

"The lessons in the school are said by rote. No one thinks of what they mean. When tests are given there is much cheating and none seem to realize it is themselves they cheat."

"You speak of your Archives. They are on stone tablets?"

"How else? Of the Tablets there are countless thousands, all neatly stacked, some tied in bundles when they are upon one theme."

"All upon stone?"

"Some are upon baked clay. In those days our people were learning, and the Varanel were their servants. Now we no longer care to learn and the Varanel are our masters."

There was a silence then, and the fire flickered, and then he said, "It is good to talk. It is good that someone listens. I am much alone, and that is why I wanted a way into your world. Our people have closed their minds. They do not look for knowledge, for they believe they now possess it all."

"Yet they fear what our world can bring to them?"

"They do. I do not. Not really. I do fear, for I

do not know what it is you are or what you have. You seem so secure, so sure in yourself."

"Few of us are, my friend. It only appears so, but we do learn, and many of us love learning. Oh, we do have those who would stop learning where it is. Indeed, there are some who would have stopped it years ago, because what we learn endangers ideas they have long possessed. But there are men and women who want answers and they seek them in laboratories and libraries the world over. Our libraries," Raglan added, "are like your Archives, but ours are used, day and night, and their contents are put into books to be sold so that those may study who cannot come to the libraries."

"There are books about our people?"

"Many, and yet we know so very little. What we know has been pieced together from broken pots, ruins of cliff or pit houses, bits of moccasins, and remains of burials. Men and women work very hard to make sense from what we have discovered, but often greedy ones dig into the ruins and remove valuable evidence to sell it on the market, destroying forever our chance to learn.

"You see, we do not have your knowledge and we must try to date each fragment by where it is found, how deep in the earth, and in conjunction with what other materials. It is a slow, painstaking process but we are learning."

"Our history is important to you?"

"All history is important to us. From each we learn a little about survival, a little about what causes peoples to decay and nations to die. We try to learn from others so we shall not make the same mistakes, but many of us learn simply for the love of knowing. One of the greatest lines in literature was from a Russian writer who said, 'I do not want millions, but an answer to my questions.' "

"Ah, yes. I like that." Then gloomily he said, "We no longer ask questions. Except," he added, "a little bit about your world. We want some things you have but we fear what may come with it."

"You have a name?"

"It is Tazzoc."

"I am Raglan, Mike Raglan." He hesitated, then asked, "Have you ever heard the name Eden Foster?"

Tazzoc shook his head. "It is a name of you. Of one of your people?"

"Not exactly. The name is ours. The woman, I think, is one of yours, but she lives among us."

"Among you? I did not know there were such."

Raglan described her, but Tazzoc shook his head. "I know no one like that."

"What of Poison Women?"

Tazzoc smiled. "It is a fable, a legend. Yet, in the long ago it was said there were such. If any exist today, only The Hand would know."

"Could you enter the place where The Hand lives?"

"I? You jest. It is unthinkable. Only the Varanel may go there, and those who do not return. Oh,

192

there are some who come and go. They are the servants of The Hand or the Lords of Shibalba."

"Then it is possible?"

Tazzoc shook his head. "It is not. It is a Forbidden Place. This much I know. He who goes in goes directly to his place, and to no other. Even if you got in, you would be discovered at once."

Raglan waited a slow minute, and then said, "In your Archives? Is there not a map, a drawing of your Forbidden City?"

Tazzoc did not answer.

XX

THE CANYON, WHEN he reached it, appeared to be about two miles long, perhaps a bit longer. The east side was rugged and steep; on the west the wall slanted steeply, broken in places by cracks down which a man might make his way. Otherwise the rocks looked slippery and difficult. With much experience at climbing, Mike Raglan knew such areas were more difficult than they appeared.

In the bottom of the canyon there was a small forest of trees, none of which looked old. Here and there was a gleam of water, and he glimpsed what seemed to be Navajo sweathouses.

There were a few patches of open ground covered with what appeared to be bunch grass or other desert growth. He squatted on his heels and looked along the canyon, his eyes searching.

He did not know what he was looking for, or how to find what he sought.

He doubted it would be anything as obvious as the kiva, for the openings were transient, indefinite. For some reason at this point there was an anomaly, perhaps a break in the fabric of time and space. He knew little of such things and had no evidence that they could be, except for the occasional stories of mysterious disappearances.

Was there such a place as Shibalba? Or was it—and Kawasi and Tazzoc as well—part of an elaborate hoax?

He found a way among the rocks and handed himself down with care. It was part sliding, part climbing, and he descended with the awareness that getting in would be far easier than getting out. At one place he slid all of sixty feet down a steep rock face. When at last his feet reached the sandy floor of the canyon, his heart was beating heavily and he glanced around quickly.

Nothing. Just trees, sparse grass, and what might once have been a path, or more likely a game trail of some kind, although he saw no tracks of deer.

It was very still. Listening, he heard nothing, not even the stirring of cottonwood leaves. He walked in among the trees where it was shaded and cool, alert for any sound of movement. His hand moved to touch his pistol; then he walked on, aware again that he saw no tracks of any kind.

He considered what to do. Supposedly this was one of the places where occasional openings occurred, and if he found such an opening he must somehow mark it within and without so he could find it again. Yet if it was only an occasional opening it might never open again. He felt cold and he shivered.

What the devil was he getting into, anyway? He was a fool. He should climb out of this canyon, get into his car, and drive back to Tamarron and then fly home. To hell with it! Erik had gotten himself into this—let him get himself out as well.

He paused and looked carefully around. It was quiet, too damned quiet! Yet everything looked normal. If only there were some tracks! He couldn't see a chipmunk or even a lizard.

Then, looking through the trees, he saw the stone walls and opening of what was apparently one of the Anasazi shelters for storing corn. It was high up in the rocks and he had no intention of climbing up there, but it served to indicate that men had once lived here at least. He walked on, then paused, seeing the ashes of an old campfire.

Not much in the way of ashes. Whoever built the fire had not kept it burning long, judging by what remained. No longer than a man might need to boil water for coffee. Or to send up a signal.

He poked at the ashes with a stick, scratching them away. Only a thin film on the earth beneath. Odd, that. Hardly worth the trouble of building a fire.

He walked out of the trees and began skirting them, staying in the open, looking up at the cliffs. Something caught his attention and he looked down the canyon where it seemed to widen out. He frowned, shaking his head. Was something wrong with his eyes? The air was shimmering as though with heat, but it was not hot.

Raglan moved under the shade of a tree and peered from under his shading hand. Was it heat waves or some strange atmospheric effect?

He remembered one time on the shore near Puerto Montt when he had looked across at the isle of Chiloé, miles away. He had been able to distinguish separate leaves on the trees due to some telescopic effect of the atmosphere. He supposed there were other such places, but the only time he had experienced it was on that coast of Chile, and natives told him it was often the case.

Yet here he was not seeing with that startling clarity. This was a shimmering of the atmosphere that blurred his sight. He could see the shadows of rocks beyond but could make out no detail.

Within the shimmering there appeared to be movement, as of something coming, something approaching. He drew back deeper into the trees but stayed where he could still see.

Yes, something was coming—coming from the mists or the heat waves or whatever they were.

A man, and then another, another, and still another! Four men, walking in a staggered rank, each holding a weapon of some sort, each clad in pale blue.

Each wore a sort of helmet, each a sort of breastplate of dull blue, covering stomach and chest but not the arms. Below the waist each wore a skirt not unlike that of a Roman legionnaire with alternate panels of a thin metal.

Now they moved to the side until a good twenty feet separated them from one another.

Raglan moved back through the woods, turned and ran a short distance, then moved out of the trees into a jumble of rocks. He made no further effort to hide, sinking to one knee. He was wearing a beige jacket with several pockets, beige slacks, and a dark-green shirt. If he remained immovable there was not one chance in a hundred they would see him, as his clothing merged perfectly with the background. Nevertheless, he unbuttoned the strap across his gun butt.

They were searching, obviously. Searching for him or for Tazzoc? Or someone else?

For a moment he thought of opening fire, yet suppose they were only some outfit making a movie?

The nearest one was all of fifty yards away now, a man of about his own height but seemingly lighter in weight. These, he guessed, were the Varanel, the Night Guards of Shibalba.

One of them turned his head and looked right at him, but seemed to see nothing. Careful not even to blink an eye, although it could not be seen at the distance, Raglan watched the men walk past. Suddenly, as if on command they stopped, moved out in a half circle, and then moved forward.

They had seen the nearest sweathouse. Moving slowly, weapons lifted, they converged upon it.

They gathered around it, unable to decide what it was, no doubt thinking it some sort of a dwelling.

No, not that. They would know what it was if they had any memory of the past, for it was at least possible the Anasazi had used something of the kind.

They stood together, talking. From time to time they scanned the rock walls of the canyon. Suddenly, Raglan heard the distant mutter of a plane. Not many flew over here, but there were always a few. It was coming closer.

The Varanel had scattered, staring up at the sky. One saw the plane, and pointed.

Amazed, they scattered out a bit more, all staring at the distant plane. Then they drew together. Even at the distance he could hear the low mutter of their voices. Then, as one man, they darted for the shelter of the trees. Now he could no longer hear them, and could scarcely see one of them.

Where had they come from? Out of that shimmering haze? Was that the opening? How many of the Varanel were there? If they were to be the enemy he must know more about them, and it was obvious they had come here hunting for someone. Raglan suspected they had followed Tazzoc, but perhaps they had been sent for him.

They looked to be tough, capable men, and he was not inclined to underrate a possible enemy, particularly one of whom he knew so little. Feared men they obviously were, but for what reason he could not know or even guess at this point.

Mike Raglan considered himself no hero. He had no desire to risk his life for Erik Hokart but he was compelled by the realization that if he did not do what he could, he would be forever haunted by the man he had deserted when in dire need.

Assessing the situation, Raglan found nothing in it to please him. He had no allies. Gallagher could not be considered as such, for he was quite simply an officer doing his duty. He might seriously try to find Hokart, might even believe the story Raglan offered, but his help would only be here and upon this plane, when it fell within his jurisdiction. In Gallagher's place Mike would undoubtedly have done the same.

What of Eden Foster? Who or what she was he did not know. He believed her an enemy. He had seen in her house the book stolen from his condo, which indicated a connection. That she was intelligent was obvious. And she had somehow managed to establish connections with important people, none of whom would be inclined to believe anything against her, especially anything as preposterous as his story would be.

He heard no sound from the trees. The Varanel had either gone on down the canyon or were crouching there, waiting. Did they know about planes? Had they anything of the kind themselves? How different was their world?

Kawasi had told him little, but Tazzoc had talked readily enough and Mike had been reading between the lines as he talked. Yet, were his conclusions correct?

His best chance was to remain right where he was. Glancing back in the direction from which the Varanel had come, he could see nothing different. Either the shimmering in the air had ceased or he was positioned wrong to see it.

Where was Tazzoc? He had left some time before, as quickly as he had come, but where was he now? If he were discovered it would be the end of him.

A Keeper of the Archives! What a lot he might know! Yet he said there was little or no interest in them, and he was virtually a forgotten man, called upon for nothing, ignored in his forgotten little corner.

That implied a decadent civilization, a declining culture, yet there had been nothing decadent about the Varanel. They had moved with precision and with care, and when the plane appeared they had immediately taken cover.

Suddenly, he saw them again. They came from the trees, their weapons in their hands, moving forward, some fifty yards separating them now. One of them came abreast of him at not more than fifty yards, but although his head and eyes were continually moving, Raglan was not seen. He crouched, pistol in hand, waiting.

They went on by, neared a wall of rock, and closed ranks, then disappeared.

He waited several minutes, then moved into the trees. Once there, he stood against a tree trunk and waited, watching. He could see no movement, and he could hear nothing. He holstered his pistol and moved back into the woods. He must find a way out, and get back to the ruin on the mesa.

Raglan was discouraged. He had hoped in the canyon he believed was Johnny's Hole to find an opening into the Other Side that was unknown to them, but apparently there was no such place. No sooner had he appeared than the Varanel were there. Had they known of his coming?

Wherever he looked he found sheer cliffs of rocks difficult to climb, or places too visible from the valley floor. He needed a place where he could climb unseen, and unexposed to attack.

He found it at last, a narrow way to the top, yet it was almost dark when he sighted the ruin. Suddenly he had a bad feeling about it. Standing beside a juniper, he looked across the rocky waste and studied it with doubt. His decision was made on the instant. He was closer to his car. He would go there. In all this time Chief had stayed close and quiet, only at times voicing a deep rumbling growl in his chest, but usually pressing against him as if in warning.

Now Chief, sensing his objective, moved toward the car and, when he made sure no enemy waited, stood beside the door.

As quietly as possible, Raglan unlocked the door and got in, motioning Chief up beside him. He locked the doors, then started the car and moved out. A backward glance in the mirror showed nothing behind him, and in the gathering darkness the ruin was no longer visible.

He passed no other cars upon the highway,

once he reached it, and turned toward the town, wanting to return to Tamarron but giving up the idea in favor of the chance of seeing Gallagher again. He returned to the motel where he often stopped, left his car, and walked down to the café.

Gallagher was nowhere around and the place was almost empty. Two truckers sat at the counter and two other men, probably locals, were at a table.

He found a place in a corner out of the way, where he could watch the door, then ordered a meal and coffee.

He was tired, tired as a man could be, and worried. He rubbed his fingers over the stubble on his chin, trying to bring some order into his thinking. He had to get off the dime and do something, but it didn't make sense to go blindly into a place of which he knew nothing and where he would be immediately recognized as something alien.

The coffee came and it tasted good. He put the cup down, wondering where Gallagher was. He was somebody to whom he could talk, at least.

Suppose the Varanel had attacked him today and he had shot one of them? He would have likely found himself on trial for murder and nothing he could say would have been believed by anyone.

The waitress came with his meal. He sipped his coffee, then started to eat. He was chewing on his first bite when the thought came.

He would see Eden Foster. Maybe, just maybe,

she would intercede and arrange for Erik to be freed.

The waitress came to his table. "We're closing now. Would you mind paying your check?"

He fumbled in his pocket, found the money, and paid it. Suddenly he was hungry no longer. He ate a few bites, then put down his fork and walked outside.

It was very dark and he was alone. The street was empty. The light in the café behind him went out and he started back toward the motel.

He was almost at the car when he heard a rush of feet behind him.

XXI

RAGLAN SIDESTEPPED QUICKLY to the left, pivoted on the ball of his left foot, and swung a kick with his right toe at the nearest man—a Bando technique.

The kick caught the man behind the knee and he toppled into the path of the second man, who leaped his body and rushed at Raglan. Mike met the attack with a straight left to the face. He felt the nose crunch under his fist and moved quickly, swinging a kick to the groin. The man came down to hands and knees, and a kick to the head left him collapsed on the gravel.

The first man was up, and Raglan recognized the man he had suspected of watching him in the San Juan Room.

203

"All right," he said quietly. "Come on!"

Warily, his antagonist circled, then rushed suddenly. It was a clumsy technique and Raglan, who had served his apprenticeship in carnival brawls, stepped in quickly and threw a right to the belly.

The blow caught the man coming in and knocked the wind from him.

Backing off, Raglan went into his motel room and called the police. "Two men in the motel parking lot," he said. "They look like they've run into something in the dark. I think Gallagher might want to see them." He hung up without giving his name.

He had just taken off his shirt when he heard the screech of brakes and tires skidding on gravel. He did not lift the curtain but he saw the headlights and then heard someone say, "Get up from there! What's going on here?"

Raglan washed his face and hands to remove any blood that might have spattered. His knuckles were only slightly skinned. He was getting into his pajamas when he heard a light tap at the door.

"Open up! It's the police!" The officer did not speak loudly, and Raglan opened the door.

"Something wrong, Officer?"

"Somebody turned in a report and yours was the only light showing. Do you know these men?"

Bloody and in handcuffs, they stared at him, expressions surly. "That one"—he pointed—"I saw at Tamarron today. They told me he wasn't a guest. Looks to me like they tried to mug somebody who didn't want to be mugged."

"You didn't hear anything?"

"At the time I expect I was too busy to listen, Officer."

"Aren't you a friend of Gallagher's?"

"Gallagher? He's a fine man. Yes, I'd consider him a friend. If you need me for anything I'll be right here, or in the restaurant over there. I'll be glad to help in any way I can."

Later, thinking about it, he knew he had been lucky. His tactics had taken them by surprise, and in another conflict he might not be so fortunate. All species of men have some style of combat in which they are trained. Undoubtedly his attackers had not expected a fight but planned simply to overpower him with sheer strength; whatever skills they possessed had not been brought into use. There simply had been no time for them to adjust. The entire action had taken no more than a minute, so he must not become overconfident.

His own skills were limited. In his years of knocking about, from his early days with the carnivals to his travels abroad, he had picked up here and there some tricks of self-defense and had been trained in a half-dozen such skills. From China, Japan, and Tibet to Burma, Sumatra, and Java, he had learned what he could and had trained with some superb athletes. At the same time he had worked at none of them long enough to be truly proficient.

Naturally curious, he had acquired some understanding of each people's system of self-defense but had not practiced enough. He had an advantage over these people, he suspected, because he had been exposed to more different styles of fighting than they.

He awakened at daylight, shaved, showered, and dressed quickly. He had an idea Gallagher would be around, and after that he intended to see Eden Foster.

He had no idea that she would admit to any connection with these people or with Shibalba, but he intended to discuss the matter of Erik Hokart. There was always the chance that his release might be arranged by negotiation—certainly better than an attempt to go through the curtain and release him by force or by some stratagem. It was worth a try.

At the same time, he must be on his guard. By going to her home he was, in a sense, entering enemy territory. No doubt she had men on call who would like nothing better than to lay hands on him.

Gallagher was seated at a back table, his eyes quizzical, when Raglan came in. "Figured you'd be in about now. I didn't feel any need to wake you up."

"Things were lively around here last night. Sorry you missed it."

Gallagher glanced at the skinned knuckles. "Looks like you didn't. How was it?"

"I was lucky. I doubt if they believed I'd be trouble, so I got the jump on them. I didn't tell your boys much because I wanted to get some sleep, and to be frank, what could I tell them?"

"What was it? Attempted kidnapping or killing?"

"Damned if I know. They rushed me from behind and I simply went into action. Whatever they had in mind I didn't want any part of it, so I registered my objections. Have you talked to them?"

"*Talked* to them? I haven't even seen them! They disappeared from the jail sometime during the night. No sign of them. Just like they'd never been around!"

Mike Raglan told his story, briefly and to the point. The events in the canyon, his return to town, the rush from the darkness, his defense, the call to the police, and their appearance. "That's the gist of it. I'd know them if I saw them again. One was certainly the man I saw at Tamarron, and I suspect they are the two who followed me along the highway."

Gallagher stared out the window. "The heat's on. We've had two more calls about Hokart. An electronics outfit phoned, and a lawyer."

"I'm going to call on Eden Foster."

Gallagher nodded. "Business or pleasure?"

"Strictly business. I'm going to put my cards on the table and try to negotiate. She's an intelligent woman. We've agreed on that. We've got to get Hokart back or she will be on the carpet. I've got to make her understand the situation." He paused. "The trouble is, can she make *them* understand?"

Sunlight warmed the street outside. The truckers seated themselves nearby and ordered. Gallagher filled his cup from the pot left on the table. Mike Raglan sat thinking, wondering how he'd gotten himself into this situation, and what he could do.

Going to see Eden Foster might be just a stalling move. Was he really afraid to go through the window? Of course he was. Once on the Other Side, all bets were off. He had no idea how they lived, what he would need to do, or how he could find Erik.

There was, it seemed, some kind of an official area like the Forbidden City in Beijing or the Kremlin in Moscow, and only a few were permitted entry. Once inside, he would have to go directly to his destination, yet he had no idea what that destination would be. Information was what he needed.

What about Eden Foster? If she was working for them, was one of them, how much weight did she carry? How much influence? If he convinced her, would they listen? Apparently they knew scarcely more about this world than this world knew of them.

The Anasazi had been good people, seemingly a quiet, agricultural people who lived by hunting, food-gathering and planting. They planted corn, squash, and beans, and when the rains provided, their crops had been plentiful. In the good years piñon nuts had been a welcome addition to their diet.

Yet before their disappearance they had already become a regimented people. Their lives fell into definite patterns and there seemed to be little scope for invention or discovery. Pottery was introduced gradually and no doubt had an influence on the ready acceptance of beans as a supplement to their diet. The bow and arrow appeared among them, probably first used against them by enemies. For there were enemies. Fierce nomadic tribes were coming down from the North, regarding the settlements as their legitimate prey, as had always been the case.

The cliff dwellers could defend their dwellings, but to work their fields they had to go to the exposed mesa tops or perhaps a few fields in the bottoms of the canyons, and there they were exposed to attack. Their grain they stored in the most inaccessible places they could find, often in other caves above their villages, but the attacks continued.

Before their cliff dwellings were finally abandoned, there had been a gradual migration to the South. More and more of their people were leaving the cliff settlements in hopes of escaping the invading bands of Indians from the North. The first of these were undoubtedly the Paiute or Ute Indians, shortly to be followed by advance hunting parties of the Navajo-Apache.

"The American white man," Raglan suggested to Gallagher, "has never seen himself as part of a natural pattern. What happened here has happened in every land on earth. Men, animals, and plants tend to seek out a place where they can develop. Before the coming of the white man, who is the last of the invaders up to now, there were invading Indians from the North or South, attacking the settlements of those who preceded them.

"Several attempts were made to construct a more advanced way of living before the coming of the white man, each of which was destroyed by nomadic invaders. This obviously happened to the Anasazi, and a similar thing must have happened to the Mound Builders.

"Our Indians warred against each other, just as did the Mongol tribes before Genghis Khan welded them into a single fighting force. Tecumseh tried to do the same thing in America, and so did Quanah Parker, but any chance of uniting them against a common enemy was spoiled by old hatreds and old rivalries.

"In almost every war the white man fought against Indians, he was aided by other Indians who joined to fight against traditional enemies.

"When Crook fought the Sioux at the Battle of the Rosebud he had several hundred Shoshone allies fighting beside him. The Pawnee scouts led by Major Frank North were valuable allies against old enemies, and in the Southwest, Apaches scouted for the white armies against their cousins.

"What we must do is stop talking nonsense and understand that what happened here was the result of a natural historical development that no man could halt or change. If we were invaded by a superior race from outer space it would happen to us. Our dreamers imagine that contact with an advanced civilization would bring enormous benefits. On the contrary, it would destroy all we have of civilization, undermining our beliefs. We would become as other primitive cultures have become, a poor, benighted people hanging about the fringes waiting for a handout.

"Moreover, it would be our greatest scientists and scholars who would suffer the most, for their knowledge would be superseded, relegating their scholarship to an ash heap of discarded ideas.

"Any creature arriving from outer space would be as far ahead of us as we are ahead of the most primitive native of New Guinea, and what we refer to as science would be simply amusing to such creatures.

"Actually, if we wish to be happy on our green earth, the last thing we want is a visit from a superior people from outer space. Distant contact would be quite another thing, although the probability is we would have to learn a new language, a new math, and an entirely different way of looking at things. This would undoubtedly take generations and would be opposed bitterly by many factions.

"Men have never readily accepted new ideas. Our schools and general thinking are cluttered with beliefs long proved absurd by contemporary knowledge. Man has demonstrated over and over again that the last thing he wants are new ideas, even when they are desperately needed. Ideas are welcomed as long as they do not contradict theories on which scholarly reputations have been erected."

Gallagher was amused. "You're really wound up this morning. Supposing what we're talking about is true? What would it be like over there?"

"We can only guess. Judging by the little I've had from Kawasi and Tazzoc, it is a very regimented, locked-in society desperately afraid of ideas or strangers that might inject some discontent.

"I suspect a once-progressive society became locked into a pattern which they are struggling to preserve, and we constitute a threat. At the same time the powers that be are eager for some aspects of our knowledge, especially those aspects that can help them maintain the status quo."

"Do you think that's why they grabbed Hokart?"

"Not at all. They grabbed him because he knew of an opening into their world, but whatever they have learned since may make them wish to keep him. Right now I suspect they are experiencing severe intestinal discomfort from trying to digest even a small part of what he has to offer."

"Do you think he will help them?"

"If he's smart he will convince them he is too valuable to kill or torture, and I believe he will feed them just enough to whet their appetite until he can find a way to escape.

"He's no fool, and in time he will know that if he is to get away he must do something about it himself. What he does will depend on his own imagination and what materials he has access to that will be useful. He will also have to learn the limits of their knowledge so they will not suspect what he is doing. A man of his knowledge should be able to create explosives or gases that might help and, in time, broadcast facilities that would upset their carefully ordered world. It depends on how much freedom he can acquire, the state of their knowledge, and how much time he has."

Gallagher shook his head again. "Too much for me, but I'd like to talk to this Tazzoc guy. He could help us a lot."

"He could help us, but he could help Hokart even more. You see, Tazzoc will know what they know. He is a Keeper of the Archives and he will know more than anyone. That helps us."

"How do you mean?"

"The man's an historian and, after a fashion, a scholar. Such men are hungry for knowledge. To know a little arouses a hunger to know more. I've stirred his curiosity, and believe me, he'll be back to find me.

"There's my chance. Tazzoc can open the door for me. He is the key to everything."

"You think he will help you?"

"I'm betting on it. I'm betting my life."

XXII

USING THE TELEPHONE in his room, Mike Raglan dialed a friend in Denver, another in Washington, D.C. If they did not hear from him within two weeks, he told them, they had better investigate.

He directed them to contact Gallagher and referred them also to the daybook in a safe at Tamarron. Then he made one more call; if he was going to do this, he needed backup.

The moves he planned could lead to disaster, but no matter what happened to him, someone must know, for if there was life on the other side, and he had evidence of it, there was no telling what their intentions might be.

Volkmeer drove up to the motel at sundown. He was a tall man with narrow shoulders, somewhat stooped, with a weather-beaten face. He was fifty years old but looked ten years younger.

He wore a battered black hat, a blue shirt, gray vest, a pair of well-washed jeans, and boots with run-down heels. "Been years," he said, when seated. "Heard of you now and again. Never expected your call."

"I need help, Volk."

"Figured as much, but it's hard to imagine. Last I knew of you, you could do it all."

"Ever ride that No Man's Mesa country?"

Volkmeer took a cigar from his breast pocket, regarded it thoughtfully, then bit off the tip. "Time or two. It's a place to fight shy of."

He struck a match on the seat of his pants and lit the cigar. "Used to be Paiute country— Navajos never liked it much. I never liked it much, either."

"There's a mesa on this side of the river. Odd sort of place. Looks like the top was cultivated at one time or another."

"Witch plants."

"What?"

"Witch plants growed there. That's what an Injun boy told me. Forty-odd years ago when I rode in there with this boy, there was still a few volunteers comin' up.

"Mostly they died out over the years or been gathered and not replanted, but here and there some still lived. That kid an' me, we climbed up there one time to get a drink out of a natural tank in the sandstone. He knew about that mesa and when he seen the plants, he taken out. I mean we left."

"You never went back?"

"Some years later I was huntin' strays and hunted that tank for a drink. Rainfall collected there, thousands of gallons of it, and good to drink unless some animal fell into it. I remembered what that Injun kid tol' me—that the plants were planted by witches who wanted them for bad medicine."

"Ever camp up there?"

Volkmeer glanced at him, his hard old eyes cynical. "I did. Camped in an old ruin. Wall made a good windbreak and she was blowin' up cold. Eerie sort of place. I left out of there came daybreak. My horse didn't like it no better than I did."

Volkmeer put his hat on a chair. His hair was thin now, and gray, but he was still the man he had been, a grim, hard man with no nonsense about him. Years ago he had caught three rustlers

215

with some cattle of the brand he rode for. He brought them in, two of them over their saddles and the third with a knot on his skull.

"I remember when you rode for that outfit over in the Blues," Raglan commented.

"The Blues, the Henry, and the La Sals. I rode 'em all. There was still some bad ones hangin' out on the Swell back in them days. Cassidy was gone, and so was Matt Warner, but there were others around. Cassidy never bothered us, nor any of his crowd. Some of that later bunch, they didn't know no better, there at first. We had to dust a few of them with our Winchesters before they taken us serious."

He brushed ash from his cigar. "What you want of me? I was just settin' around goin' to seed up yonder, just wishin' something would happen."

"This may not be to your taste," Raglan said, and explained.

Volkmeer listened, then stubbed out his cigar in the ashtray. "You figure to go in there?"

"I am."

"I won't say you're crazy. I heard the like from old Injuns a time or two. Some of the young ones don't believe anymore. You got to talk to the old men and women, the kind I growed up with. Stories make your hair stand on end, believe me."

He paused. "What d' you want me for?"

"Backup. I want somebody who won't stampede. When I go through that window I want somebody standing by who will be there when I come back."

"You pulled me out of that mine, years ago. I owe you one. You came in an' got me when I figured myself a goner. There was nobody else around and you taken your life in hand when you come after me. You could have gone off an' left me and nobody would've known. Now, what do we do?"

"First, I've got to see a woman. Eden Foster."

Volkmeer gave him a bleak look. "Know her, do you? She come up to my place a few years ago."

Raglan was surprised. "Your place in the Blues? What did she want?"

"She'd heard I guided some parties back on the Ute reservation. Showed them a cliff dwelling called Eagle's Nest. You know it?"

"I do."

"Seemed like some kinfolk of hers lived there one time. She didn't actually say that, but I gathered it. She wanted to know what was around, any paintings on the rocks, and suchlike."

"What else?"

"She wanted to know if I ever got down to No Man's. I was sort of curious but I didn't let it show. I made no mention of No Man's or the Hole."

"Johnny's?"

"You know about Johnny?"

"No, not much. I do know about the Hole. I've been there and I'm going back."

"I never knew Johnny. He was before my time, but I heard talk. Johnny was a top hand, rode for several of the old outfits, and was a well-liked man. He was a rider. Broke the rough string for a half-dozen outfits, so they were all some cut up when he disappeared.

"Johnny usually rode alone. He'd come back a time or two tellin' about this Hole he found, with water, trees, and all. Folks didn't know whether to believe him or not but nobody wanted to ride forty mile just to prove him a liar. Johnny brung back some strays, mostly our stock that drifted south. Then he went back after some others and we never seen him again.

"It was common talk when I was a youngster. There'd been an Indian outbreak led by Old Polk and Posey, his son. That was about 1915. They killed a couple of Mexicans and when a posse went hunting them, they killed one of the posse. They'd been camped in Cow Canyon near Bluff when the posse came up on them, and there was a lot of shooting.

"Johnny had been riding over west of Bluff and when he didn't show up, folks just naturally figured he'd run into Posey and his bunch of renegade Indians. Anyway, he disappeared."

"He's still alive, Volk. Somehow he got over to the Other Side and couldn't find his way back."

"I find that hard to believe. Johnny was just a youngster but he was a good tracker." He paused. "Alive, you say? Why, he'd be over a hundred years old!"

"Not quite. But he'd be close to ninety, or maybe a year or two older."

"I'll be damned! Well, he was a tough man. If anybody could make it, Johnny could, from all I heard about him. You expect to find him?"

"I'll be looking, Volk. He's my key to what's over there, he and the two I mentioned; the girl named Kawasi and the man Tazzoc."

They talked the moon out of the sky and then Volk turned in on the twin bed. Mike Raglan sat awhile in the dark, just thinking. Then he went to bed himself, only to lie awake trying to consider all aspects of his problem.

What had happened to the Anasazi in the years following their return? They were far from a static culture when they vanished, and although changes were few, there were experiments with architecture brought about by the demands of the cliff caves in which they built their cities, if such they could be termed.

What would they have become had they remained here and been able to resist the attacks of the wild nomadic Indians who were coming in from the North and West? How would their civilizations have developed?

So much depended on water and the use of water that eventually their civilization, like those of Egypt, Babylon, the Indus Valley, and the Maya, would have had to agree to an overall control of water use by someone.

Lying in the darkness after he got into bed, Mike Raglan turned the problem over in his thoughts. There had been so much concentration on the native Americans found in possession when the white man came that little thought had been given to those who preceded them.

There had been excavations at Cahokia Mound, at Hopewell, and other places, as well as speculation about the Mound Builders, but much had been ignored that did not fit accepted theory. Too many workers in the field were inclined to ignore, as an intrusion, anything that did not fit previously conceived ideas. It was time for all such ideas to be set aside and for each bit of evidence to be examined with a completely open mind.

Nearly every state has had discoveries ignored or put aside as "fakes" because they do not conform. It would appear that several hundred people over a century of time had devoted much energy to planting evidence to confuse scholars whom they would never know, and from which they would never profit. If runes or other inscriptions were found that did not conform to scholarly standards, no allowance was ever made for the fact that there were few men in any country who could write, let alone write well. Whatever was found was simply that left by men often poorly educated but trying to leave a record.

Wanderers and seafarers were rarely scholars or even possessed of anything but rudimentary education. They would attempt to mark their progress with what signs they possessed.

It was time men abandoned the ridiculous assumption that two great continents dividing the great seas of the world, and surrounded by seafaring peoples, had remained isolated for thousands of years.

What was the percentage, Mike wondered, of people living in the Scandinavian countries who could write runes correctly?

Raglan rolled to his back, staring wide-eyed into the darkness. It was time white men understood that most of the Indians found in possession were latecomers, and all too little was known about who had preceded them.

It would be good to have Volkmeer with him. He knew the man, had worked with him long ago, and had been lucky to find his name in the telephone directory. He was a man who would stay with him when the going got rough, and from his brief experience with the Varanel, it could become very rough indeed.

First, though, he must see Eden Foster. If he could negotiate the return of Erik Hokart, all would be well.

How much authority, if any, did she have? Dared she take? And how much was she prepared to risk her own position to ensure the security of her people?

The picture he had been putting together might be mistaken, but his impression was of a small, tightly held civilization, strong in itself but desperately afraid of ideas penetrating from beyond the veil. No doubt they considered this world to be evil and wished to protect themselves from it.

Tazzoc . . .

Tazzoc was a man of knowledge, and no man of

knowledge was ever content with what he knew. He always wished to know more. No doubt Tazzoc had questions for which he wanted answers, and if so, he might be induced to trade.

Tazzoc did not believe, for example, in the existence of Kawasi's people. No doubt that information had been carefully kept. He believed, or seemed to believe, that He Who Had Magic was a fable. Yet no doubt in those stone and clay tablets there might be a clue, or even a history of the events that led to the exodus of He Who Had Magic and his people.

Somehow he must see Tazzoc again, must find some way of meeting Kawasi and, of course, Johnny.

It was daybreak when he opened his eyes. Volkmeer was already dressed and combing his gray hair.

"Let's have some breakfast," Raglan suggested. "Maybe Gallagher will come in."

As he was slipping into his boots he said, "I haven't talked about how to pay you, Volk, but I intend to."

Volkmeer glanced at him. "Did I ask? You need help. That's all that's important."

"But I have to pay you for your time," Raglan protested. "It isn't fair to take you from your work and not pay you."

Volkmeer shrugged. "I never like to talk about money until I've et. Let's get with it."

The air was cool, the sky overcast. Their boots

222

grated on the gravel as they crossed to the restaurant.

The place had just opened, and the girl at the cash register glanced around at them. "Hello, Mr. Volkmeer! It's been a long time!"

Volkmeer grunted and walked across to a table and sat down.

"I guess you get over here once in a while," Raglan suggested.

"Been a while, like the lady said. Mostly I'm over at Monticello or North from there."

They were drinking coffee when Gallagher came in. "Mr. Volkmeer!" he exclaimed. "I didn't know you two knew each other."

"Been years," Volkmeer said. "He found me in the directory." He excused himself and walked to the counter to buy a cigar.

Gallagher leaned closer and spoke in a low voice. "You sure do get around! Why didn't you say you knew Mr. Volkmeer?"

"Volk? I pulled him out of a collapsed mine tunnel once. Haven't seen him for years."

Gallagher stared at him. "Mr. Volkmeer," he said, "is one of the biggest ranchers and landowners anywhere around. He's got a home you just won't believe. He's one of the most respected men in the state!"

XXIII

MIKE RAGLAN CLOSED the car door and locked it, dropping the key into his pocket. Then he walked up the path to the door. It was shady and cool on the wide veranda and the flowers were as beautiful as he remembered them.

It was Mary, the Navajo girl, who answered the door. "I'd like to see Eden Foster," he said.

She stepped back, her large dark eyes on his. "I will tell her," she said. "Won't you be seated?"

She drew back a chair, brushed some invisible spot of dust from the cushion, and whispered, "Be careful!"

He did not sit down but stood glancing around the room. All seemed to be the same except that one of his books was on the table, his book on a visit to a long-lost monastery in the Taliangshan Mountains, near Tibet.

He heard a low murmur of voices from the direction in which Mary had gone, and looked around again. There were two doors leading to other parts of the house, another door into the garden, and a fourth that went out to an empty lawn bordered by trees.

Looking again, he thought he glimpsed a shadow on the grass, as of someone near the lawn door. Crossing the room, he turned a chair ever so slightly so that it blocked that door. Now the chair must be moved before the door could be opened completely.

Eden Foster came into the room, suddenly and silently, but with a smile of greeting. "Mr. Raglan! How nice! I was hoping you would call."

Today she was wearing sea-green, and it suited her. Her necklace was turquoise and coral, as were her bracelets. "May I get you a drink?"

"Coffee will do. It's a bit early for a drink."

"Of course." She gestured to the table. "I have been reading your book. What a strange place it must have been! Is it true that even the Chinese know little about the area?"

"It is true, but I doubt if they would agree. The people are related to the Khamba of Tibet, but have managed to maintain a sort of independence in their mountains."

"You visit many strange places, is it not so?"

He smiled. "And I am prepared to visit others. It has become a way of life for me."

Her smile vanished, and she took a cigarette from the box on the table. Oddly, she was nervous. Was she wondering why he was here? Or had his suggestion that he was prepared to visit other strange places alarmed her?

She seated herself and he did likewise. Mary brought coffee and they talked of the weather. When Mary had gone he said, "In going to strange places it is always a help if one knows someone who has been there, or someone who lives there who can be of help. One avoids so many mistakes."

"I suppose that is true."

"You heard about my friend? The missing man?"

"Miss—? Oh, you mean Erik Hokart? Yes, I have heard of him. But then, everyone has. This is a small world, after all."

"I have been hoping he would be found before the government becomes involved. It would be much easier for everyone if he could be found, and found quickly. The government can be very persistent indeed."

"And you?"

"As I have said, he is a friend." Raglan tasted the coffee. "I shall begin my search on the mesa where he planned to build. In that kiva, in fact."

"A kiva? It is just a round room, is it not? Were they not places of ceremony? What can be mysterious about them now?"

Raglan smiled. "This one has a window. My dog has been through that window, and Erik tells me there was a woman, a very beautiful woman who came through that same window."

"He spoke with this woman?"

"She wanted him to come with her, and according to Erik, even her walk was an invitation. He did not trust her."

"And you? You do not like beautiful women?"

"On the contrary, I like them very much. But there are times and places."

"She might have taken him to a very nice place."

"I am sure that was her intention. It would not have been mine, at the moment."

"You must be very strong. Are you?" Her eyes were lovely. She put down her cup and, bending her knees, put her feet up on the sofa.

"I was thinking of Erik Hokart," he said quietly, "and all the trouble there will be if he is not found."

"It concerns you, doesn't it?"

"Very much." He looked across at her. "And it should concern you." He waved a hand about. "All this is very nice, an easy, comfortable way of living. It would be a pity if you lost it."

She was silent, and angry, he thought. Yet when she looked up, her eyes were innocent. "I do not expect to lose it, Mr. Raglan, now or ever. I have friends, very important friends who will not wish for me to be disturbed."

"And when their reputations are at stake? When they are suddenly exposed to investigation because of their relationship with a very beautiful young woman?"

"Our relationships, as you call it, have been—"

"I know they have, Eden. I know it very well. I believe you, but who else will? You must have read the newspapers enough to know that a man's political life hangs by a very delicate thread. Scandal can be destructive, and few wish to risk scandal."

He sat back in his chair, but alert for any sound. Was anyone listening? Or would they await her signal? He doubted she would permit listening, yet what if someone had the power to overrule her wishes?

227

"Eden, we had better talk, and seriously. I want Erik Hokart back safely. I believe you have the power to bring him back. If you do not have that power, you must do all you can to convince those who do that Hokart must be freed, at once."

She rubbed out her cigarette and poured coffee from the pot. She looked at him, then looked quickly away. She was worried, that much was obvious.

"I do not see why—" she began.

"Stop it, Eden. You do know why. The night after my arrival from back east a man broke into my condo at Tamarron and carried off a book. It was not the book he thought it was. The last time I was here, with Gallagher, I saw that book here, on your table."

He put down his cup. "You have learned a great deal about how we live over here, but you have not learned enough. Nor do the men who come to help know enough, and they have blundered. For your own welfare, Eden, I suggest you intercede and get Erik back here."

"I cannot." Her eyes were bleak. "I have no power. I am told what must be done. I am not asked."

"You cannot speak to The Hand?"

Startled, she said, "You *know?* About him?"

"I know, and I know about the Varanel. But do you know about the dissidents? The people who escaped to the mountains with He Who Had Magic?"

"That's nonsense! It is a legend!"

"I know otherwise. You know only so much as The Hand wishes you to know, the Hand and the Lords of Shibalba."

She stared at him. "How do you know so much? Nobody—"

"If you do not help me, Eden, I shall go over there and bring him back."

She laughed, but it was contemptuous laughter. "You? Do not be foolish! In minutes they would have you! You would not know where to go, what to do! Within minutes you would be a prisoner, and when they had what they wished from you, you would be dead!"

"Suppose you helped me?"

"I? You are insane!" Yet she looked quickly, nervously around, as if she feared someone might be listening.

He lowered his voice. "Think about it, but think fast, because if he is not returned here within forty-eight hours, I am going over, and when I go, I won't be making it easy for anybody."

He got up. "You are my only chance to do this quietly, peacefully. You've got forty-eight hours, and not a minute more. I want Erik Hokart back here and in good shape, or I go get him."

"You? Alone?"

"I'd better do it that way. The next thing they may be sending the Delta Squad or the Marines." He was just talking now, but she could not know that, or how important Erik might be. For that matter, Raglan didn't know, himself.

"They will kill you now."

"They can try. But you know that daybook? That record you tried to get back from me? It is in a safe place, far from here, and if anything happens to me, it goes right to the top. I can't take the chance of letting something like this exist without their knowing."

"They will believe you? They will think you're crazy!"

"Perhaps. A few years ago they would have been sure of it, but too much has happened. We have put a man on the moon—"

"So you say. We do not believe it."

He shrugged. "Nevertheless, it is true, and our people are prepared to accept what would have been impossible a few years ago. The average man knows at least something about black holes, and our science fiction stories and films have introduced a lot of speculation and some understanding. And even your people used to study the stars."

She looked up at him. "Why do you say that? What do you know of our people? We cannot see stars. The heavens are misty. We do not see the moon or the sun."

"No *sun?*"

"Oh, it is there! But it is behind clouds or something—I do not know."

"There is no speculation?"

"Of course not. Why should there be? Our work is enough, and our families. Such speculation is idle, wasteful. We know everything we need to know."

"You believe that? After living here?" He

paused, then very casually, he asked, "What of your history? Are there no records?"

"Why keep records? Oh, I believe there were, but they no longer exist. Besides, who would need them? Who needs to know what is past?"

"You have artisans? Men who work with wood and metals?"

"Of course."

"How do they know what to do when they take up a bit of wood or iron?"

"They know what to do. They learn from their fathers."

"That is history, Eden. The skills men acquire are a part of history. If they did not pass on their knowledge, their history, each workman would have to learn everything all over again. That is why we have history in books, so that we can profit from the experience of those who have gone before."

"And yet you make the same errors again and again!"

"Too true. The records are there but too few are willing to learn. For example there's a lot of talk now about using cocaine. It was quite a big thing before the turn of the century, then almost died out in the time of World War One, but now it is back, all the lessons learned in those earlier years forgotten. The people of the drug culture act as if they have made an original discovery, and instead are sending their lives down the same drain as others did years ago."

He was silent, then held out his cup for more

coffee. She evidently knew nothing of the Hall of Archives, and probably very few did. Was that Hall in the Forbidden area? Was that how he could gain entry?

If she did not know of the Archives, how many did? Tazzoc had implied that he was left alone. No inquiries came; nobody used his records. If he had visitors at all, they were infrequent.

"You must help me, Eden, and help your people in so doing. If we can get Erik Hokart back, your world will be left to go on as it has. If not, I shall have to come after him."

She laughed bitterly. "You would be killed! You would have no chance!"

"If I go," he said quietly, "I will go armed and prepared for trouble. Even if they kill me, what I will do will change everything. If nothing else it will start people thinking, wondering, and once someone begins to think, there is no end to it. If one asks questions, one will want answers."

"We have weapons, too."

Of course they did, and he knew nothing about them. What of those the Varanel carried?

He needed to know so much more! So very much! He tasted his coffee, put down the cup. "You have lived among us," he said bluntly. "Do you wish to go back?"

"Do you think your world so superior, then?" She spoke with contempt. "Do you think I cannot leave it?"

"You can, of course, but do you want to? Our way of life is different, but you seem to find it not uncomfortable." He looked around, taking in the pleasant, casually easy living room. "I do not know your life. Is it better than this?"

She hesitated. "No, it is not. It is much worse. It is more . . . more barren."

"You need not go back."

Her eyes met his and shifted quickly away. So she had been thinking of that?

"How could I live?" she wondered aloud. "What would I do?"

"Your income is from them?"

"Of course. Anyway, I could not. I am watched. Everybody is watched. We are not trusted. If they knew of what we talk I would be taken back. I would be killed."

"There is somebody who watches you?"

She shrugged. "Of course. I do not know who. I do not know how."

"Is your house bugged? You know the expression?"

"Of course. I read your newspapers."

"You must have income. You live well. How are you paid?"

"It is not like that. We are given gold, sometimes gems to sell. Nobody is paid, as you say it, except that those who work with me are given gold or money by me."

"And how do you get yours?"

"It is brought to me from over there."

"And you have no superior here? You said you were watched?"

She shrugged. "By someone, I do not know

who. Sometimes messages come telling me to meet someone. I do not know how, but it is arranged. It was so I met the governor, several senators, and men in your army. Invitations came to me."

He stood up. "Remember: forty-eight hours. Erik must be returned or I go after him.

"Think about it, Eden. You have a chance. You could move away from here, go to Washington, to Paris, London! You could be far from anywhere they could reach you. Help me and I shall help you. You could find happiness here."

"I? I shall find happiness nowhere." Her tone was suddenly bitter. "There is no happiness for me. Long before I could think, my way was made for me." She looked at him suddenly, sharply. She was beautiful, really beautiful. "You have not guessed? I am a Poison Woman!"

XXIV

MIKE RAGLAN DROVE away from the house of Eden Foster, watching his back trail. He did not like what he was learning nor want to believe it. The Indian people he had known were not like this, and he had known many in his younger years. What he had to realize was that these were not like any people he had known, and their reactions would be different.

Forty-eight hours! What scared him was that he had laid down an ultimatum for himself as well. If Eden Foster could not arrange Erik's release within that time, he now had promised to go in after him.

Tazzoc was the man he must see, but how to find him? He had believed the man would come to him, stirred by his scholar's curiosity, but Tazzoc had no way of finding him when he was away from the mesa. Hence, he must return, make himself available. Tazzoc could not only tell him about the Forbidden area but could also tell him how to come to him once he was inside.

No one, he remembered, was permitted to wander about within those precincts. Once inside, one had to go directly to one's destination. After that . . .

He shivered. What the hell was he getting into, anyway? He loved this country. Being here again brought back all his old feelings for it. He knew exactly how Erik must feel.

He would live here himself, when he finally settled down. He loved this wide, beautiful land of desert, mountain, and canyon. In the old days, little time as he had spent here, he had made friends among both Navajo and Ute. An old Navajo medicine man had taught him about wild plants and their values as food or medicine. He had wandered the rough country with him, listened to his stories, and had developed a deep love for the country itself.

His thoughts suddenly returned to Volkmeer. Who would have dreamed that that tough old cowhand would become a wealthy man? It just proved one never knew. He was a tough old boy, and even in the days when Mike Raglan had known him, he owned a few head of cows wearing his own brand.

Well, that had been a start. He chuckled. What a fool he had been! He had believed he was enlisting the support of an old cowhand who would like to make an extra dollar helping a friend. And he was about to offer a deal for a few dollars to one of the wealthiest men in the state!

Fortunately, he had not embarrassed himself by making his offer. Nevertheless, Volkmeer was the man he needed.

He returned to the motel, gathered together what he would need, and put it in the car. Then he drove down to the café and parked the car where he could see it.

Gallagher was not around, so he ate alone, watching the street and thinking. He would drive to the mesa, look around, and hope for a meeting with Tazzoc. He would wait most of forty-eight hours and then he would drive out to meet Eden Foster.

When he left his car at the closest point to the ruin and let Chief out for a run, he saw nothing of Volkmeer. He had been hoping the man would be there, just for company. It was still bright and clear, not a cloud in the sky when he reached the ruin.

Nothing seemed to have been disturbed. He went to the kiva and looked in. It was like any other he had seen—just a little better preserved, that was all. He shied from the window, but looked at it anyway.

Just a window, looking no different than any other. The trouble was, it *was* different!

He went back, picking up wood as he went, although there was little around. He broke some dead branches from a piñon, picked up a couple of pieces of cedar lying among the rocks at the mesa's edge. Seeing several good pieces farther down, he climbed down to get them, and when he looked up, Tazzoc was there.

"I wait for you," Tazzoc said. His tone was wistful. "We know so little. Our world is isolate. To the west is desert."

"It has been explored?"

"Oh, no! It is forbidden. What lies beyond we do not know. The Hand says we are all. There is no more. To ask questions is not good, but we see old ruins, and some of us wonder.

"It is spoken that we live today, and we live tomorrow. What is past is finished and we do not look back." He paused. "I am Keeper of Archives, once important. Now forgotten. I fear to speak or they might be destroyed." His voice lowered and he looked from one side to the other as if fearing to be overheard. "I am forgotten, too, but I wish to *know!* I study our Archives, and so many questions arise! There is no one to whom I can talk, I—"

"You can talk to me, but are there no others? None like yourself, who wish to know? And to remember?"

237

"No doubt there are but they fear to speak. The Hand has listeners everywhere."

He sat down on a slab of rock. "When I am gone there will be no other." He looked up at Raglan. "Always there has been a son, but I have no son. The doors will be closed, the Archives forgotten."

"We should have them. Such a record is priceless."

The sun was warm on the rocks where they sat. "I think this is true, what you say. We who have been Keepers, we believe it is so."

Tazzoc closed his eyes for a moment. "It is wonderful, your sun. So bright, so warm."

"Yours is not so bright?"

"Oh, no! Not bright at all! Our sky is not what you say . . . clear?"

"About the Archives? Does no one come there? No one at all?"

"It is rare thing. Long ago many come—that was when The Voice spoke."

"The Voice?"

"It was what you call oracle. A voice that spoke what was to be, and we stood silent to hear. The Voice ruled, The Voice foretold, and The Hand did what The Voice said. Then The Voice became unclear, and The Hand would explain what The Voice intended. After a while The Voice ceased to speak and we had only The Hand."

"You say people used to come when The Voice spoke. Was there a connection between The Voice and the Archives?"

"The place of the Archives was what you call temple. A place in which to pray." Tazzoc paused, looking around at him. "All men need moments of silence. All men need to pray, if it is only to speak to themselves in the silence, to formulate their desires, and to say to themselves what they wish to be. Some of our people believed in the old gods, some did not, but all needed to pray."

That made sense. The earliest writing known had been in temples where an account was kept of tithes paid or gifts to the gods. It had been so in Ur of the Chaldees, in Babylon, Nineveh, and Tyre.

So in Tazzoc's world The Voice had been displaced by The Hand? A coup? Or had The Voice simply died out? Something of the same kind had happened to the Delphic Oracle in Ancient Greece, and there might be a pattern to such things.

"Those Archives of yours? Do you have any idea of their range? The number of years covered?"

"Oh, yes! I cannot claim to know them, but it is a part of our first training to know something of their origin. The first writing was on clay. These first tablets were lists of tenths paid to the temple. It continued after a number of years with added symbols, indicating that one who was behind in payments would pay later. Then there were lists of what belonged to the temple and where it was stored.

"Then a man made a plea of being assessed too much, and told of his land and his house and what he possessed and what he could pay. In this way the words increased. The language grew.

"The Archives are vast. Thousands of clay tablets and engravings on stone. Then there were many shelves of thin sheets of wood, used instead of clay, which was no longer practical.

"Long ago twelve were numbered to care for the Archives, of which my family were directors. One by one they died or were taken away until I am alone. I come and go, a shadow they scarcely see."

"Does anyone ever try to enter the Forbidden area?"

"Who would wish to? It is feared. Those who belong there go. No others consider it."

Yet if he could get in? Could he find Erik?

Suddenly he remembered the golden map the old man had copied, and he had that copy. Was the Forbidden area included?

"In your Archives," he said carefully, "is there a plan of the area?"

"Oh, yes. Our ancient leaders planned everything with great care. There is a shelf with nothing but plans, designs of each building, each room. Except for the Death Doors."

"The *what?*"

"You see, it is a Forbidden place. Each knows where he must go, but he knows nothing else. Only The Hand knows all. Hence, the door you might open could be a trap, and there are many such, throughout the area."

"A trap? How?"

"Each room is dark when the door is opened. Not until the door closes do the lights go on, so if you try to enter a place you do not belong, you are trapped.

"When the door closes, lights go on, but in the traps there are no lights, and there is no air. He who enters the wrong door is caught in a room with no chance of escape. Such rooms permit no sound to be heard outside."

Tazzoc's eyes held a sort of triumphant glow. "A mistake means death. No one comes to look. No one cares. There are dozens of such rooms, so few guards are needed, and even if you were suspected of being an interloper, rarely would anyone interfere. Soon you will enter a wrong door."

"How large are these cubicles? These rooms?"

"Who knows? No one has ever come out to tell of them."

"No one has ever escaped?"

"How is it possible? The walls are stone, many feet in thickness. When there is no air, one dies."

"Does no one ever make a mistake?"

"Who cares? And who would know?" Tazzoc smiled. "No one has ever complained."

"The area must be large?"

"Many of what you call acres. There may be ten such rooms. More likely there are fifty. Perhaps no one remembers."

"Are there such rooms in your place of the Archives?"

Tazzoc shrugged. "There are doors I do not open. Who knows? The Hand does not care for those who blunder, or who try to go where they are not wanted. From the earliest time we are told not to open doors that are strange to us."

How, in such a maze, was he to find Erik Hokart? Yet where he was held, others must have been kept before him, so someone would know.

The old man Mike had met in Flagstaff so many years ago had found gold—found it in some apparently abandoned place. "I would be interested"—he spoke slowly so that Tazzoc could follow—"in a history of your people. From what you say, yours is a small country, rigidly ruled. Apparently your people do not know of those who fled to another part of your country—"

"This could not be."

"I have met a girl from such a group. She is a descendant of He Who Had Magic."

Tazzoc shook his head doubtfully. "It is a wild tale. It would not be permitted. Besides"—he shrugged—"where would they go? How would they live?"

"There are no places in the mountains? Or the desert?"

"No one ever goes there. These are fearsome places."

"Have you no records in your Archives of travel to such places in the long ago?"

Tazzoc was uncomfortable. He peered uneasily around. "There were tales, wild tales told by irresponsible people. They are not believed. There is a section of the Archives . . . It was forbidden to look there."

242

"And you have not? Your father did not, nor your grandfather?"

Tazzoc was uneasy. "There was said to be another place of Archives, forbidden to us. Some said it was only a tale, that such a place did not exist. It was a place for The Voice when long ago people had to go to its temple, a journey of many days. Then The Voice came closer and lived in the Forbidden area. A pilgrimage was no longer needed."

A temple where The Voice had been, an ancient place for archives, now abandoned. Could that be the place? Certainly, such a place would not have been casually built. Might there not be another opening there? A permanent one?

The old cowboy from Flagstaff might have gotten through near such a place and found the gold, and a way he could use at certain times.

"Tazzoc, I must come to your world. I must help my friend escape. If he does not, others will come and your world will end. Men of great power desire his return, and if they do not find him soon, they will be searching these hills. I have told this to the woman, Eden Foster.

"If there is violence, your precious Archives may be destroyed. I do not wish that, nor do you. If you could help me, we could save them, possibly even bring them back to our world where they would not gather dust but would be studied."

Tazzoc was silent for a long time. Finally, he shook his head. "I do not know. I wish the Archives saved, but to free your friend? It is impossible. Nobody would dare such a thing, and you are but one man. . . ."

"One man can often succeed where many would fail. You see," Mike added, "our scholars would like to know what happened to what we call the Anasazi after their return to your world. They seemed a good people, a people who were progressing toward something important. In your Archives there would be records, perhaps, of what they did and what they thought. This is important to us. The Anasazi had learned much of building and were learning more. They had become skillful farmers within the bounds of what was possible for them. No doubt, had they not been attacked by nomadic Indians they would have survived the drought and expanded their irrigated areas. They would have expanded their trade, also, and exchanged ideas and farming methods with the Maya."

Tazzoc got to his feet. "I have been too long away. Much as I wish it, I cannot help. I know nothing, and I speak with few. If questions were asked I would be seized and questioned."

He paused. "This much I can do. I can bring a cloak such as this, and shoes such as mine. I can show you the portal through which I go, and the route I take. The rest is up to you."

When Tazzoc had gone, Raglan sat alone, thinking. So, then. He was going. It was no longer a vague idea, no longer something about which to think. It was up to him now.

But what of Erik? What was *he* doing? Mike

could not believe he was not thinking, contriving, planning. What materials could he find? What subterfuge could he employ? Would he try to escape? To communicate?

He'd told Mike that as a boy he had made a crystal wireless set. Could he do it now? Would radio waves cross the divide between the two worlds? What was he doing over there? Or was he doing anything? Was it possible for him to help Mike, or himself?

Above all, what did they *know*? What science did they have? What were the weapons the Varanel carried? What was their range?

His life depended on the answers to his questions. His life, and who knew how many others'? What were they thinking of, beyond that veil? What evil awaited him?

—————— XXV ——————

MIKE RAGLAN DECIDED that if he were Erik, and a prisoner of those who had no reason to keep him alive, his first thought would be escape. If immediate escape seemed out of the question, he would try to convince his captors he was worth more alive than dead.

The authority to whom he must appeal would be The Hand, but if he could not be reached, then the Varanel.

From what Kawasi and Tazzoc had said, a watch was kept on everyone. How this was done he did not know, but Erik's knowledge was electronics, so if he could convince them he could build equipment useful to them, he might be kept alive. He might also gain access to equipment useful in an attempt to escape or communicate. But what if they already possessed methods superior to any he knew?

After all, our world had progressed along certain welltrodden paths of inquiry, but were they the only ones? Our thinking had been channeled into courses assumed to be the only avenues of communication, but what if there were others of which we knew nothing?

Suppose their methodology was entirely different? The Newtonian conception of physics, for example, has been completely upset by Einstein, first, and then by the quantum theory. Nor will this be the end. Of one thing only can we be sure: What is today accepted as truth will tomorrow prove to be only amusing.

The Anasazi had returned to a world they had previously fled, but no doubt many had remained behind, and the two had combined to produce what now lay just beyond the window in the kiva.

Some, probably those who had returned, had abandoned the world they found and gone to the mountains, where they had carried on much as they might have in our world.

What was the evil they had fled? It would be simple to suggest something tangible such as a monster of some sort, a plague, or encroaching enemies, yet was that actually the fact?

Had the evil been religious practices such as those known to the Aztec and the Maya, where human sacrifices ran into the thousands and the stench of their blood-stained altars, like those of the Carthaginians, had to be overcome by incense?

Or was the evil something more subtle, such as religious bigotry and ignorance? For those who sacrificed the hearts of thousands to keep the sun in the sky no doubt believed themselves right and correct in what they were doing.

What he seemed to be facing was an autocratic government ruled by The Hand, and supported by the Varanel, a small military clique of superbly trained fighting men. These had succeeded in keeping control by restricting exploration, ideas, and the world in which they all lived, but such rulers were apt to be highly suspicious, paranoid, and fearful of strangers and the ideas they might import.

Erik was an intelligent, perceptive man. He would undoubtedly grasp the situation immediately and begin planning their escape. He had used the plural, had spoken of "us," which implied he was not alone. Although that did not necessarily mean a woman, it was a fairly safe bet it was.

Was she a prisoner also? Did they know about her? Or was she an outside ally upon whom he might count for assistance?

Erik would be a prisoner somewhere in the Forbidden area. This large block of structures was restricted, it seemed, to the use of The Hand, the

Lords of Shibalba, and the Varanel. Judging by the comments of Tazzoc, only a part of this block of structures was in use and many areas had been abandoned, such as the Hall of the Archives. Tazzoc was no doubt accepted as one of the servants who occupied themselves in maintaining the area.

So then, Mike must gain entry to the Forbidden area, examine one of the plans, locate the place where Erik was held, break him out, and escape.

Simple enough to frame in words—quite something else to accomplish.

First, Tazzoc must bring him the costume. Then he must study and rehearse walking like Tazzoc, with Tazzoc's stoop-shouldered carriage. Once inside the Hall of Archives he must go to the shelves of maps, find those needed, and study them. Once he knew where to go he must move quickly, careful to arouse no suspicion, and free Erik. Then they had to get away, and an escape route must be planned before that time.

No matter how much they might try to avoid being seen, they must expect pursuit. That was where Volkmeer would be useful. He could stand by the window and stop any pursuit.

If only Mike could communicate with Erik, get word to him somehow to let him know what was planned, or to discover what he himself was doing, if anything.

He tried to consider every possibility, yet even as he considered the situation coolly, he was frightened, appalled at what he was about to do.

248

He was going into an enemy area without adequate intelligence, no knowledge of their capabilities or weapons, and in a place where he would be quickly identified as a stranger. He would be one man against thousands, one man alone.

Of course, if possible, Erik would try to communicate with him. Suddenly he remembered the sunflower on the dog's collar, the sunflower on the sweater he wore.

Had that not been communication? But with whom? With Kawasi or someone else? Someone who was not only friendly but who had been able to pass through from the Other Side. Someone who had needed a pencil but had not known how to sharpen it.

Often before this, Mike had gone into dangerous country. There had been bandits in western China when he had been traveling there, and in other areas his motives had been suspected. He was investigating ancient mysteries but was often suspected of being a government agent or a spy for one faction or another.

More than once he had been in trouble, and in the process of knocking around he had picked up a variety of skills for protecting himself. He had a feeling he would need them all.

He checked his pistol, then his boot-knife. Another knife he slung down the back of his neck under his shirt.

The idea of the sunflower returned. These sunflowers were unlike those he had known in the Middle West, which were often as large as dinner plates. These were wild sunflowers and much smaller, but they grew everywhere. Obviously, they had some significance to the person who took the pencils and who had provided Erik with a sweater.

Raglan built a fire from the wood he had gathered, a small fire for coffee and comfort.

Where was Volkmeer? The old rancher no doubt had business to arrange before he could be gone for several days, but he should be along soon. The possibility that the old cowboy and miner he had known could have become well-off had never occurred to him. Yet why not? Volkmeer was a shrewd, patient man, who must have had ambitions, although he had never voiced them that Raglan could recall. Like many a western man, he had dabbled in mining, prospecting occasionally, and sometimes working a lease in some mine. Gold in the San Juan River Canyon had never appeared in paying quantities. Several mining ventures had been tried, only to fail because of the extremely small size of the flakes. Occasional pockets had been found, he supposed.

Chief was lying just inside the door of the ruin. Mike Raglan stepped around him and went into the night. It was very dark and very still.

The air was fresh and cool. The time was soon. If Tazzoc got back with the extra cloak, it would be time to move, yet he would see Eden Foster one more time. After all, he had given her forty-eight hours and she might accomplish something.

He looked off toward No Man's Mesa. It lay dark and ominous, a little south and west of where he stood. The Hole would be almost due west, and perhaps a shade north. Suddenly there was a light pressure against his knee.

It was Chief. He dropped a hand to the big dog's head and scratched back of his ear. "I'm going to leave you here when I go," he said. "If I don't show up, you go find Gallagher. He's a good man and he would treat you right."

Come to think of it, Chief was probably the only one who would miss him—Chief and perhaps his agent. Somehow in traveling about the world, writing, thinking, he had not made friends. Acquaintances, yes. Temporary friends whom he probably would not see again, but no friends as such. He had no family, and had never had, for that matter. He was a man alone.

"When this is over, Chief, we're going to change that. We're going to settle down, establish ourselves and have some friends."

He'd been busy, he told himself, and to have friends you had to stay someplace, put down roots. For a while back there, when he was a youngster working on the paper, he had been about to make friends. He hadn't, though. He was an outsider there, too. He didn't fit in. Wherever he'd gone, he had been a stranger. Conversations had a way of getting around to high school or college days, or to mutual associations in the town they were living in, and in all that he had no place.

"The truth of the matter is, Chief," he said softly, ruffling the hair on the big dog's neck, "if I didn't come back, nobody would care very much."

He walked back to the ruin, glancing around in the outer room, where the blueprints were gathering dust. He and Erik were two of a kind. If Erik had not thought to notify him, nobody would have known what happened to him. Although, apparently, that had changed for him over there, for when he had written of escaping he had said "us." Somebody would be coming back with him. He was no longer alone.

It would be easier to cope with what lay on the other side if he knew more of what they believed. Basic beliefs are important, even when they are largely ignored. In our world, with each religious system there is a code of ethics or something of the kind, a sort of behavior that is considered right and just. To understand any people, one must have some idea where they are coming from, and so far he had nothing beyond obedience to The Hand, the Lords of Shibalba, and enforcement by the Varanel.

The moon was rising and the canyons were gathering deeper shadows. The river caught the moon's reflection and gave it back to the sky. He built his fire up and listened, but there were no sounds in the night.

What could Erik do? Would he have access to materials? Could he construct some means of communication? Would anything of the kind work across the divide? Could he put together some kind of weapon? Had he been able to convince them that he could be important to them? Had he even tried? Was he given a chance even to talk?

Above all, what was The Hand like? A superbrain? An ignorant man? A paranoid?

Eden Foster was his representative here, but was she the only one? Who controlled his goon squad?

Above all, what did The Hand *want?* A better spy system with which to watch his own people, no doubt, but information from here as well, and some equipment. Above all, he wanted no suspicion of their existence.

His own people were severely restricted in their movements, and no hint of dissension or the possibility of it was allowed to exist. Yet some of his people must know of the existence of those who had been followers of He Who Had Magic, such as Kawasi.

Mike liked having the old stone wall behind him. Liked the protection it provided. Yet he was uneasy, always uneasy.

Where was Volkmeer? And Gallagher?

Suddenly, his skin prickled. Something—something moved out there in the darkness.

Every sense alert, he waited. He had heard no car, seen no reflected lights. He touched the butt of his gun, and the feel of it was reassuring. He waited, listening.

And he heard it again.

Something was out there, something coming closer.

Over in the kiva, a small stone fell, rattled among rocks, then fell again.

Of course, a car might come without his hearing it. What of Gallagher that time?

Who, he wondered, were his enemies? Did he have any allies whom he could trust?

Gallagher, probably, and Volkmeer.

The thought left him empty. How much could they help? How much did they actually believe? Did they believe what he said, or were they just humoring him?

Stark black towers against the sky, island mesas, bathed in white moonlight. Not far to the south a place called Oljeto, meaning Moonlit Water. How well the Indians had named it!

The night was chill. He shivered. From the cold? Or because of something else out there? What was it that lurked in the shadows, sometimes heard but never seen? Was it those creatures, the Hairy Ones?

He would talk again to Tazzoc. He would listen to his voice, he would learn to imitate his walk, he would take the cloak with him, belt it as Tazzoc did, and with luck he could get into the Hall of the Archives and from there to the place where Erik was held.

He would go into that other world and he would find Erik, and when they returned they would blast this kiva, or close it off somehow. They had to, because somehow he knew there was something wrong over there, something twisted and strange.

He remembered Tazzoc suddenly, and how the old scholar had seemed to revel in the knowledge

254

of the secret doors and of the trapped men. Was it the cleverness of it? Or was there something more? Something evil, even in him?

He unrolled the sleeping bag but did not get into it. Instead, he lay down on top of it and pulled his windbreaker over him. A sleeping bag was fine but he couldn't get out of it fast enough. And tonight he might have to.

Did the shadows move out there, or was it his imagination?

He got up again and added fuel to the fire, and then he lay down with a flashlight close to his hand, as well as the pistol.

What he needed was a good night's sleep, and he would not get it tonight. Something moved, or was it the dancing of the flames? Had there been a shadow, a . . .

XXVI

TRUSTING TO CHIEF, at last he fell asleep. Several times the big dog growled, low and deep in his chest, but Mike Raglan slept on, unaware.

He awakened in the cold clear light of dawn, and looked beyond the thin tendrils of smoke rising from the ashes of his fire to the distant blue bulk of Navajo Mountain.

He lay there, hands clasped behind his head, just resting. These last few moments before rising often offered the best rest of the night. Lying there, he reviewed his situation and the moves remaining to him.

Today he would return to Tamarron and he would drive into town and talk to a banker whom he knew. If he did not come back from this venture, he wanted his affairs in order.

He must check at Tamarron to see if any messages awaited him. On his return he would visit Eden. The time might not be up, but he had decided he would wait no longer.

Both Erik and Kawasi knew of his place at Tamarron, as did his enemies, if such they could be called. He got up, shook out his boots, and put them on. The morning was incredibly beautiful. There was no movement on the river but he expected none. Few boats came this far up and the river runners passed quickly by. Glancing over at No Man's, he saw its top bathed in sunlight, its base still deep in shadow. Ominous, but magnificent, too.

He stretched, feeling good. Well, he'd better. He would need all he had in strength, agility, and wit to face what lay before him. Over near the base of the red rock that Erik had planned to make one wall of his house, he saw some wild flowers, several of them sunflowers. He picked one, and returning inside the ruin to Erik's blueprints, he put down the flower and on a sketch pad wrote: *Erik—I will need your help. Any time now.*

It was a wild gamble. Somebody using a sunflower as an emblem had come from the other side, somebody who had been friendly. That somebody might know where Erik was, might be able to communicate. In any event, nothing would be lost.

It was a long drive to Tamarron. He stopped briefly at the motel and at the café.

No messages. No sign of either Gallagher or Volkmeer.

He told the waitress that if Gallagher came in, to tell him Mike Raglan had gone to Tamarron, and would be back the following day.

He saw no one on the road, and was not followed. It was like entering another world. He drove first to the lodge to pick up his mail, then to his condo. It was a beautiful sunlit day, and people in bright costumes were playing golf on what must be, he thought, one of the most beautiful courses in the world.

Once inside he glanced around but nothing had been disturbed. All appeared to be as he had left it. The mail needed only a matter of minutes. A check for an article recently completed, a note from a friend about a ruin recently discovered in Colombia, a letter about some mummies found near Arica, in Chile, that seemed to be five thousand years older than any discovered in Egypt. A couple of bills, and a brief note from a girl he had known in Rio, and when was he returning to Brazil?

He changed shirts and, while buttoning his shirt, looked out the window. The snow where he had seen the tracks was gone. It had been the last of

257

the season, and in just the few days that had passed, everything had changed. Of course, he was a thousand feet higher in altitude than on the mesa of the ruin. These were the San Juan Mountains; down there he had been in semi-desert.

The Navajo reservation had once lain just to the south of him, covering an area larger than the combined size of Belgium and the Netherlands, half the size of England.

Turning away from the window, he looked around again. This was real. This was *his*. His living quarters in his world. A comfortable, easy place to be, a world of pleasant reality with people coming and going, enjoying themselves or working, a place he understood and liked. And out there?

He shied from the thought. He would be going into something he neither knew nor understood, and there was a chance he might not return.

What if he opened one of those doors that could close behind him, lock him in forever? With nothing around him but blank stone walls, impossibly thick, and on the floor the bones of unfortunates who had preceded him?

He need not go. He could stay here, then catch a plane and fly back to New York or to Los Angeles. Erik might make it on his own.

Slipping into his coat, Mike Raglan knew he was arguing with himself to no purpose, for he was going back. He was not even sure if he was making a free choice. It might be that all his years of becoming what he was were dictating the issue.

How much choice did a man have, after all? Are we not all conditioned to certain expressions of life? Do we have a choice, whether we run or fight? He slipped a notepad into his pocket and went out to the car.

He was hungry. That was reality, and an issue he could confront here and now.

As he turned up the road, he drove over a spot where a couple of years ago he had seen a weasel cross the road with a gopher in his mouth.

Was he to be the weasel or the gopher? The predator or the prey?

What the hell, he told himself. They've grabbed Erik, they burned the café, they tried to get me. They laid out the course they wished to travel. If they wanted it that way, they could have it.

Magic. He had been a magician, but would that help? The chances were that they would be better at it than he. After all, most of the basic illusions were known to many people, including witch doctors in Central Africa or in the jungles of Brazil.

When he was seated at a table in the San Juan Room and had ordered, he glanced around the room. It was at least two-thirds full, a bright, interested looking bunch of people. As he considered it, a tall old man, quite heavy, got up from a nearby table and crossed over to him.

The man was well dressed in a casual, western fashion, had rumpled gray hair and a pleasant smile. "Mr. Raglan? May I join you?"

"Please do."

He ordered coffee and looked at Raglan. "Been

259

wanting to talk to you, Raglan. We know some of the same people, Gallagher, for instance."

"He's a good man."

"He is that. One of the best." The old man paused, his eyes wandering about the room. "My name's Weston, Artemus Weston. Used to be a banker, one time. Retired a few years back. Been a lot of things in my time. Punched cows when I was a youngster, mostly over Utah way. Had a head for figures, an' my boss seen it. Saw it. He took me into the office to handle his books. Done that for a few years an' then the boss went into bankin' and took me along. When he passed on, I kept on at the bank, settled his estate."

Weston took up his cup and sipped coffee thoughtfully. "S'pose you're wonderin' what I'm gettin' at. Just stay in the saddle an' listen.

"Man like me, doesn't talk a lot, listens mostly, he picks up things. Hears things. I done some surmisin', too. A body does, you know. Never had much book-learning but I could put two an' two together. There at the bank the boss moved me into the loan division. I had a head for business, did well with the loan part of it, but I handled property the bank owned, too.

"Don't get me wrong. This was a two-by-four western town bank where all the business we done in a month a city bank would do in a day, maybe. Thing we had to do to survive was to know the folks.

"People we did business with. We had to know them. Did they pay their bills? Did they put in

260

the hours or were they shiftless? Who was their family? Was somebody sponging off them? Did their ranches have good grass an' water? Things like that. We had to know, and mostly we did. We knew things about folks they'd have been embarrassed to tell. We never talked about it, but one way to be successful in the small-town bankin' business is just to know folks, to know what goes on in their heads.

"Few days ago I was talkin' to Gallagher. He speaks well of you, an' I've got a granddaughter back East who reads what you write. Swears by you.

"Gallagher says you got a friend missin' out thataway?"

"I have."

"Rough country. Easy for a man to get lost out there." He paused again to taste his coffee. "Easy to get lost but not easy to disappear. Dry country. Has a way of preserving whatever it gets. Dries 'em out, but keeps 'em. A body now? It doesn't fall apart like in wetter country, so if a man dies out there, they usually find his remains.

"Found a couple of them myself. Dead cows, too, an' horses. Takes years to do away with a body. So if you miss somebody there's got to be a reason.

"Now you take that country? Wide, beautiful, and mostly dry as all get-out. I love it. Could ride forever in it, only I don't ride anymore. Too old to break any bones, an' even the best of horses can fall. That's rough out there.

261

"Strange country. Looks all wide-open to the eyes, but you an' me, we know different. The Navajo knew different and the Hopis knew. So did the Paiutes.

"More of them around when I was punchin' cows, and some of them were a bad lot, like that bunch that run with Posey. Steal a horse right from under your saddle while you're sittin' on it. But there was places they wouldn't go. Other places they did go but they were careful."

He let the waiter refill his cup. "S'pose you wonder what I'm gettin' at?"

"No, I'm enjoying it."

Weston chuckled suddenly. "I'm an old fool! Buttinsky. Got no call to come worryin' you with my talk. No call at all, 'cept I like what Gallagher had to say an' I got to worryin' some.

"I rode that country quite a few years, as cowboy an' as a banker checkin' on things. Rode it a lot just for the pleasure. Some of it I fought shy of."

He waited awhile, looking around the room, and Raglan waited with him, his curiosity excited. "Mostly we had to know if a man was good for a loan, an' one time or another, most of them came to us. Most of 'em, but not Volkmeer."

Startled, Raglan looked up, but the old man's eyes were wandering—his eyes, but not his attention. "Volkmeer punched cows, branded a few heads here an' there. Don't recall he ever had any breeding stock, there at first, but he registered a brand and bought a few head, mostly steers.

262

"Those steers, now? Good stock. Never knowed any steers that were good for breedin'. Ain't in their nature, but nonetheless, here an' there one sees such a herd gatherin' size. Somebody with a wide loop, y' know? Well, first thing y' know, Volkmeer's runnin' a couple of hundred head. Then he rode off up into the Oregon country and bought several hundred head of white-faces."

"He was always a shrewd man, Weston." Raglan spoke carefully. "As for the wide loop, you and I both know that many a big rancher got his start with a running-iron. There were always cattle in those old days that ran wild in the breaks and folks got around to branding them when they had time. Unless somebody got there first."

"Sure. Man, the stories I could tell you! I've seen some herds grow mighty fast, like every cow-critter was havin' four or five calves a year!"

He paused again, running his fingers through his gray hair. "I rode some with Volkmeer. Knew him well. Cagey man. Never talked much. He taken a stab at minin', too, like most of us."

"I pulled him out of a cave-in once."

"Heard about that. Fact is, I heard the story when it happened.

"Volkmeer did pretty well. First thing you know he's buyin' himself property. Bought him a ranch, paid for it in cash money. Then he put in a bid on some land adjoining what he had. This was maybe a year later, and the folks that wanted to sell had to close a deal right away. I mean quick. Something tied up with a dead man's will. Several people wanted that ranch and we just told 'em the first man who could come in there with cash money could have it.

"Volkmeer got it."

"He paid cash?" Raglan asked.

"Sort of. He come into the bank, ridin' ahead of some others who wanted that land, too, and he paid for it in *gold*."

There was silence. The people in the room were disappearing, off to the mountains or to Durango. Slowly, Mike finished eating. Weston was trying to tell him something, but what was it?

Gold was not uncommon in those years. Men often cached gold coins until they had quite a stake. Many deals were made in which gold was the only money exchanged. After all, there were a lot of mines.

"I heard he had done well," Raglan commented. "I was surprised, as he didn't look it when he came to see me and I figured I was about to hire an old cowboy to stand by me. I had no idea he'd become so successful."

"He was in an almighty hurry. He wanted that property the worst way, so he paid in gold. Taken it right out of his saddlebags."

"So?"

"Seemed odd, to me. The shape of it, I mean. The gold he paid me was in *discs*. Round discs thicker in the center, tapering off to the edges."

Inside, Raglan was suddenly cold, chilled. He stared out of the window at the cliffs topped with forest. In his memory he was hearing a voice, the voice of another old man, that one in Flagstaff, long ago.

"Ree-fined gold, boy. Discs, like. Size of a saucer."

XXVII

MIKE RAGLAN LOOKED across the table at Artemus Weston. He looked more like a cattleman than a banker, but that was apt to be the case in these western towns.

"You're retired now?"

Weston nodded, without turning to face him. He was staring off across the room, but what he was seeing was probably in his memory. "Ain't got long now." He turned his eyes toward Raglan. "Too many years behind me and my health's not what it was. Figured a young man like you, you ought to know."

"Why did you think it important?"

"I'd guess you know why, or you'd surmise. That there was the only time I ever saw gold like that, but livin' in a place as long as I have, a man hears talk. Volkmeer got himself rich all of a sudden, seems like. Might have found himself a cache somewheres."

He took a cigar from his pocket and bit off the end. "A man in bankin', even an old cow-chaser like me, he thinks about money. Money's what he deals with, money an' people. Out here in the West it wasn't our way to ask questions, but that can't stop a man from wonderin', and I done some wonderin' about where that gold come from.

"Wasn't all this worry about income tax, those days. A man didn't have to explain where money come from. Volkmeer got rich mighty fast. Bought other property, here and there, and it seemed to me either he'd found a cache or somebody who had was paying him for something."

Weston got to his feet. "Talked enough. Time I was headed home. Get tired easy these days. Ain't like it was when I could ride forty hours at a stretch an' done it, many's the time, with cows or the like."

He looked down at Raglan. "Used to have a lot of friends among the Injuns. Spoke Navajo since I was a youngster. Some of the old men used to come in for loans now and again. Never had one welsh on me. Always paid up when they got around to it.

"Now and again we'd just set an' talk, an' I heard some tales make your hair curl. You be careful, boy. You just be careful. You're ridin' bareback into some rough country."

Raglan watched the old man walk away, weaving a path among the tables. Artemus Weston must indeed have been disturbed to have come here to see him. The old man must have made considerable effort just to get there.

Volkmeer? With gold such as the old cowboy in Flagstaff had found? How had he come by it? And whose side was he on, anyway?

Volkmeer, a hard, tough old man, and a rich

one now. Was he an ally or an enemy? Suppose it was the latter? Suppose the man he had selected to back him up could not be trusted? He dared not take the risk, but how to be rid of him now that he had enlisted his aid?

It was time he drove out to see Eden Foster, and then made his move. Of course, she might have been able to intercede for Erik, but Raglan doubted it. From the little he knew, The Hand was all-powerful.

He started to rise, then sat down abruptly. The Lords of Shibalba! Why had he not remembered before this? Several years before, investigating the discovery of a Jaguar-throne in Central America, he had occasion to read the *Popol Vuh*, a sacred book of the Quiché Maya, and if he was not mistaken there was a reference to the Lords of Shibalba!

A waiter came to the table. "Were you leaving?"

"No, bring me another cup of coffee. I'll be here for a while."

He got out his notebook and started to jot down what he remembered.

Shibalba . . . an underground world inhabited by evil people who were tormentors of men, a place of dread and horror.

The Cakchiquels had believed Shibalba to be a place of great power and magnificence, but a place well known to them.

Hence, in the past there must have been some

connection, some exchanges between the two worlds.

One thought prompted another, and he began to jot down every word he could recall, hoping each would stir some vagrant memory. He had used the method often and it always helped. Just seeing the words brought back other words seen in conjunction with them. For a half hour longer he worked, thinking, remembering.

So then, the connection between the Maya and the Anasazi extended to more than trade? Perhaps. In dealing with bygone peoples it was always *perhaps*. One had to learn, surmise, and then learn more, often proving the original theory mistaken.

Prevailing opinion often affected theory. In an age when peace was much to be desired, there was a reluctance to think of the Anasazi as warlike. The Maya had been deemed peaceful until the numbers of their human sacrifices became obvious. Many reasons other than defense were advanced for the retreat of the Anasazi from the mesa tops to cliff houses. It should have been immediately obvious that no sensible people, no matter how desirable cliff houses might seem in some respects, would endure the drudgery of climbing steep ladders day after day with food, water, and fuel for any reason but sheer necessity.

Memory can throw a golden aura over bygone years until only the pleasures are remembered. So it must have been for the Anasazi of the Four Corners region. Each day they must have had to go farther and farther afield to find fuel or building timbers, suffering from drought and stalked by fierce nomadic Indians. The world abandoned so long ago might suddenly become very inviting. Perhaps, also, the old evils might have vanished in the interim.

Mike Raglan signed his check, returning to his condo to write a few letters and pick up a few essentials, including emergency food packs he used when mountain-climbing.

Now to see Eden Foster! He glanced around, saw nothing suspicious, and got into his car. Deep within him he was hoping, desperately hoping, that Eden would tell him Erik was released, or about to be released.

No man goes willingly to his death; each believes he will survive somehow. Each of us is not only a participant but an observer. The world we see around us exists only for us and in our own mind, so when we die, that world dissolves, although it may exist in other minds in other forms.

Mike Raglan was thinking that as he drove westward. These mountains, forests, and deserts were his for the time in which he observed them, and it was hard to imagine a world in which he was not. He knew that now he went toward a destination he did not want, a way he had not chosen. Each of us, he reflected, is to some extent a child of our conditioning. We grow to believe certain things, to accept certain things as true and right. Loyalty and honesty, for example. Even a thief who steals, cheats, or defrauds is furious if he is robbed, cheated, or betrayed. And he, Mike Raglan, was

trapped by a sense of loyalty, of what was perceived as honor.

It was a pleasant, sunlit afternoon when he drew
up before the house of Eden Foster. He turned his
car around and parked facing back down the road.
From now on every step he took, every minute he
lived was tight with danger.

She answered the door herself. Her features
were tight and pale, her eyes large. As she stepped
back from the door, he took a quick look around.
There was no one else in the room.

He walked over and sat down with his back to a
wall. They seemed to be alone, but he was quite
sure they were not. Now, suddenly, now that the
moment was upon him he was ready. It was coming, all right. To hell with it, he was ready. If they
wanted trouble he was ready for it.

"Where is Erik?" he demanded. His tone was a
little harsh.

Her lips tightened, and he saw some anger come
into her eyes. He had started off wrong, damn it.
"After all," he said, more quietly, "he is my
friend."

"I know nothing about him. You have come to
the wrong place."

He shrugged. "If that is the way you want it."
He paused, then said, speaking calmly, "I have
drawn maps. I have written a complete report and
have had copies made. They will go to the United
States government, to the state capital, to the
Highway Patrol, to the FBI, and to various newspapers. If something happens to me, all will be

alerted. I have given them a time schedule within which I shall act and within which they should hear from me."

Her face grew whiter still. Her lips were stiff, and when she spoke she had a hard time framing the words. "You do not know what you do. Your own world will be destroyed."

"If anything is done it will not be settled by me. The problem is in other hands if anything goes wrong for me." He looked up at her. "I need your help."

"My help? You are joking. I cannot help you. Even if I were so minded I could not. I am watched. I do not know by whom." Her eyes held on his. Even now, in this moment when she was obviously frightened, she was beautiful. "I did not know how closely I was watched until now. They know you are here. And they know why you are here. I do not believe they intend for you to leave."

"They are fools. Instead of stopping things, that will only open it wide."

"The Hand rules. Nothing thwarts him." She got to her feet suddenly. "Oh, you're right! I would like to stay here! I would like to forget all that! I would like to be a part of your world forever, and not go back!

"I like it here. I like the way you live, the bright sunlight, the people. But I cannot! I am a slave! I am a tool used by The Hand."

She paused again and then spoke recklessly. "I

271

do not know if he hears. It may be that he does, but I must speak what I believe.

"I think The Hand is a man, simply a man, all-powerful in his world, but a man ignorant of your world, ignorant of anything and everything beyond his reach. He has never been thwarted. Nothing has ever been permitted to stand in his way and he cannot conceive of a power greater than his. And he has power, enormously great power. He has weapons which your science has not even dreamed of, and he will use them. Do not think he will not. And he can, if he so wishes, close all avenues to his world.

"Yes, I mean it. Long ago, when his world was younger and wiser, there were great advances in science, advances far beyond yours. Those advances ceased many years ago, but he has access to power such as you cannot believe, a power to destroy life. And he will do it. He has no fears of your world except of ideas. He knows little of you but despises you as weak and inefficient.

"You must understand. The Hand has never seen a newspaper or a book. He cannot read and can scarcely imagine it."

"You have seen him?"

"I? Nobody has seen him! Perhaps the Lords of Shibalba who are his supporters. I doubt if even the Varanel have seen him. So far as anyone knows, he has never moved from the Forbidden area, and no one is allowed to approach him, but his eyes and ears are everywhere. Even now he may be hearing what I say."

272

"How do you dare?"

She lifted her eyes to his. "I do not intend to go back."

"You know nothing of the others? Of the dissenters who live in the mountains?"

"I have never heard of such people. I do not believe they exist."

"However, they do exist and The Hand is aware, if you are not. They are descendants of people who returned from here—whom we call the Anasazi. They fled your world of evil and created their own world."

"I do not believe that."

He indicated a small sunflower he was wearing in his buttonhole, a practice he had started only a few days ago. "Do you know this flower?"

She shrugged. "I have seen it here. It is not permitted over there."

"Not permitted?"

"It is not grown, and where grown, must be eradicated."

"Why?"

She shrugged again. "It is a rule. We do not question rules."

"It is a symbol, I believe—perhaps a symbol of rebellion. It is used at least by some of those who fled to the mountains."

"So you say. How do you know this?"

He avoided the question. "You must have seen maps of our country? Of the state, at least? Have you not wondered that your land is so small? So limited in area? For so it must be. I believe much is kept from you."

She was silent and then she said, "I believe it, too. Since coming here I have changed, but your country disturbs me. It is too . . . too open. I am bothered by this. In my country everything is regulated, organized. Everyone knows exactly where he is, what is important, what he can do."

"And what he cannot do?"

"We do not think of that. We know where we live, where we work, where we go for amusement. It is enough."

"What of Erik Hokart?"

She hesitated. "Nothing. I informed the Lords of Shibalba that he was missing, that officials here were disturbed that he was missing, and there would be trouble."

"And?"

"Nothing. You see, they think so different from you. They cannot understand that one man disappearing would matter or be noticed. We think in another way than you. It is . . . it is like you and the Russians."

"How do you mean?"

"Their newspaper people serve the government, so they believe yours do, too. They cannot accept the idea that newspapers are free to publish what they want. In Russia every newspaperman writes what the government wishes. Newspapermen gather information. Therefore they are spies.

"In our world if somebody disappears, no questions are asked, and . . ."

She got suddenly to her feet. "You must go! Go now!" She glanced again at her watch. "I had not realized it was so late. Please! Go at once!"

Without another word he stood up and started for the door. Then he stopped abruptly. The door was opening, and two men stepped in. He recognized them both.

Eden Foster stepped quickly back and they came for him. Of their intentions he had no doubt.

He left them none about his.

XXVIII

INSTEAD OF RETREATING or trying to escape—which he knew would be futile in any event—he moved in and, with a flip of his foot, kicked a chair into their path. The nearest rushing man tripped over the chair, and as he hit the floor, Raglan kicked him in the head.

The second man skidded to a halt and whipped a knife from his belt. Without slowing down, Raglan dropped his right hand to the table, scooped up a dish of guacamole standing on Eden's sideboard, and slapped it into the man's face. Then he kicked him in the crotch. The first man was struggling to get up, so Raglan swung a backhand blow with a wine bottle that stretched him out on the floor with a smashed ear and a bleeding scalp.

"They're too confident," Raglan explained. "They need to spend some time on the streets.

I don't believe anybody ever resisted them before."

"Nobody would dare," Eden said.

The second man was pawing the guacamole from his eyes. Mike Raglan picked up the fallen knife. "Lie down," he said, "or I'll give you a new waistline with this."

He waved a hand at the mess the fight had created. "Sorry about this, Eden, but your boys need better manners."

She was staring at him, white-faced and shocked. "Just muscle won't handle it, Eden," he said. "These boys are playing in a rough league when they come here. Take my advice and cut loose from them. If you can't help me get Erik back, think of yourself. Cut your ties. Move away. Go east or something."

He walked outside to where their car was standing. Passing it, he used the knife to rip open a couple of tires, driving it deep and pulling back on it. The blade was razor-sharp and the damage considerable. He tossed the knife into the brush across the road and got into his own car.

He drove swiftly but carefully back to the motel, parked the car, and went to the café.

Gallagher was seated at a back table. He looked up with a wry smile. "Had an idea you'd be in. Have you seen Eden?"

"We visited some. Then there was an interruption."

Gallagher looked at him over his coffee. "Tell me about it."

"Two husky boys who thought they were tough," he said. "Not from around here. I read them from The Book."

He reached for the pot the waitress had left and filled his cup. "Whatever is done I must do myself. Eden can't help me."

"Can't, or won't?"

"Can't, I think. Apparently nobody will listen. She's ready to defect, I think. Likes it here."

"So, now what?"

"I'm going over. I've no choice now."

"You really believe that stuff, don't you?"

"I have to." He paused. "Seen Volkmeer around?"

"No, I haven't. I drove over to see him and he wasn't home. At least if he was, he wasn't receiving visitors."

Mike Raglan was tired. The brief difficulty at Eden's had been exhilarating if nothing else. For one brief moment he had confronted something tangible, something he could handle. The rest of it was all too elusive, too vague, nothing he knew how to cope with. Frauds and deception were something he understood, but this was a reality beyond anything he knew.

He thought about Volkmeer. Always a cold and quiet man, not given to talking, he now presented even more of an enigma. True, Raglan had once saved his life, but how far did that go? There was always that "yes, but what have you done for me lately?" idea.

Volkmeer had become suddenly wealthy, and

on at least one occasion that wealth had come from golden discs of the same kind that old cowboy had found on the Other Side. So what did that mean? That Volkmeer had found his way to the same cache? Unlikely, but possible. Or that he had found some other cache? Or that he was being paid that way by somebody he served?

Volkmeer was a dangerous man. A solid, dependable man in his own way, and that was just the reason Raglan had wanted him for a backup man. But where did he stand?

Gallagher spoke: "Told you I went to see Volkmeer? He wasn't to home, but I looked around there, just as a man might comin' an' goin'. No reason to do more. Got him a mighty fine place there, mighty fine. Makes a man wonder."

Raglan looked around at him. "Big house for a single man," Gallagher continued. "Three-car garage, an' Volkmeer drives a pickup, mostly. At least, whenever I've seen him.

"Makes a man curious, so I did a little nosing around. Seems like he's contributed to several political campaigns. Never goes to the big fund-raisers, but his name shows up on the lists big enough so's most office holders listen to him.

"Ranch house is tucked back in the hills, sort of out-of-the-way. Nobody can see who comes and goes. There's two or three back roads into his place, and one of them has seen a good deal of travel here lately. More than you would expect on an out-of-the-way road like that." Gallagher paused, taking his time. They were both watching the street. "One set of tire tracks matches tires on that van."

Gallagher put down his cup. "Figured you should have it to think about."

"You spoke about money contributed to campaigns. Where do you stand?"

"I'm appointed, not elected, but he spoke for me when my name came up." Gallagher wiped his mouth with the back of his hand. "I call 'em as I see 'em, Mike, an' don't you ever forget it. I was huntin' a job when I found this one."

He paused again. "This isn't the first time I've had ideas about Volkmeer. Whenever a man gets rich all of a sudden, I get curious, and the cattle business hasn't been all that good lately. I'd like to make some legitimate money myself, so I'm right curious as to how it's done. Volkmeer claimed income from mining operations where nobody was working."

They talked at random for a half hour, talking of football, old-time fighters, and bronc riders. Gallagher seemed to be watching for something and Raglan was in no hurry to get on with what he must do.

"Like that big dog you've got," Gallagher said suddenly.

"If he shows up without me, you can have him."

Gallagher glanced around. "You think that's likely?"

Raglan shrugged. "I'm going into enemy country, into a place I know nothing about, where every hand will be against me, to find a man who's carefully hidden away. I'd say I had one chance in a million."

"Why d'you do it?"

"He's depending on me. Just like folks depend on you. And he's got nobody else."

"How long d'you figure to be gone?"

"As long as it takes. I don't know what time is like over there. I don't know what anything is like. We're used to this world, but over there it can be completely different. I may be gone a matter of minutes, but more likely it will be a week or even a month. I hope to wind it up in what is a few hours of our time."

Slowly, he explained the little he knew. "This Forbidden area covers a lot of ground: big buildings, thick stone walls, built ages ago. Much of it no longer used. I get a picture of an autocratic power that has gone to seed, that's dying on the vine, so to speak. Of a people who have not only lost the will to resist but to whom the idea of resistance no longer even occurs. The dissident elements pulled out long ago and went to the mountains where some of the descendants of the old Anasazi still live.

"They want some of what we have but are afraid of contaminating ideas coming through. I don't think there's any superpower over there or any great guiding intelligence. It is a cramped little world filled with fear, hatred, and held together by fear of anything from the outside. I could be wrong as hell. I just don't know, Gallagher, except

280

that when Erik opened up that kiva, it was like opening Pandora's box, if you recall the old myth."

"I should be going with you."

"I don't want you, or anybody. If I can't take care of myself I'll be of no use, and I know more of what to expect than anybody I'd take. I don't want to have to think of anybody but myself, nor worry about what's happening with anybody. If I can't do it alone, nobody can. You've been conditioned for your work. A good cop can sense trouble before it begins, and in that kind of world, I know what to look for, up to a point."

He turned suddenly as a shadow loomed over the table. It was Volkmeer. "Been huntin' you," he said, and pulling back a chair, he straddled it, leaning his arms on the back. "Thought I'd look in here one more time before I started out to that mesa you talked about."

"Good to see you," Raglan said. He got up. "Gallagher? As soon as I get back I'll be in touch."

Gallagher turned to Volkmeer. "Raglan is a friend of mine, too. Take good care of him."

"I'll do that," Volkmeer said. "I'll do just that."

"If anything goes wrong," Raglan said, "you'll be hearing from back east. Help them all you can. And if you see my friend with the busted ear and cut scalp, throw him in jail on some pretext or other and hold him until I get back. He might even come up with answers if you ask the right questions."

Outside, Volkmeer said, "What was that about the man with a busted ear?"

Raglan shrugged. "Couple of muggers tried to use some muscle when I was visiting Eden Foster. They didn't understand their business well enough."

Volkmeer glanced at him. "I don't see any scars."

"I said they didn't know their business."

Volkmeer glanced at him again, but offered no comment. Only later, he said, "Two of them, was there?"

"They have the same trouble here I'll have over there. They don't understand how different things are. Whoever is their contact here is either lying to them or is ignorant. They can't seem to grasp the fact that a man or woman may be nobody, but if they disappear or are murdered they become important. Even if Erik wasn't who he is, questions would be asked."

"And who is he?"

"An electronics expert, and one who has worked with both the FBI and the CIA. He has testified before Senate committees and every newspaper in the country knows who he is. They are already beginning to ask questions."

Volkmeer ran his gnarled fingers through his sparse hair. "Never knew him, m'self. Heard about him."

"They'll be asking questions, Volk. And they will be wanting answers. That fire that burned the café will be first on the list, and they will go through those ashes like you wouldn't believe. I'll be questioned, and so will you."

"Me? I don't know anything."

"They won't assume that, Volk, and if anything happens to me, I've left a list of people and places."

Volkmeer swallowed, his Adam's apple bobbing. He looked off toward the mountains, blue in the distance. "Well, I hope they find him."

"It won't be quick, Volk. They will follow every lead, talk to everybody, demand explanations for everything. You see, Volk, they have *time*. If there's any discrepancy in a story, they will find it and follow it up. They will check the records on mining claims, tax returns, and everything you can imagine."

"I guess you're right. Never thought much about it." He paused. "A man gets on a trail sometimes, seems easy at the time."

"What are you suggesting?"

"Me? Nothin' at all. Just sort of thinking about all that out there, wondering what will come of it."

"Don't come out there, Volk, unless you are ready to go the route." He turned to look at the older man. "I am going in there after a friend, Volkmeer, and that's all. There's nothing in this for me but a lot of trouble, and if you come along, that's all I can promise you."

"Reckon I know that, Mike." His hard old eyes measured him. "You got any idea what you're gettin' into?"

Raglan did not answer. What was he doing, anyway? All he had to do was walk away or drive

283

away. Nobody would know the difference, or care. The hell of it was, he was going into this for a man who was not really a close friend. But the man had called on him for help.

After all, what did a fireman know about the person he dragged from the fire? Or the passing stranger who saved a drowning man? One did what one could. From the best motives in the world he was trapped into a situation where he might die a very unpleasant death, when he would rather be almost anywhere else, doing almost anything other than this.

He swore, and Volkmeer glanced at him. "Gettin' cold feet?"

"Hell, Volk, I've had 'em from the beginning! How the hell does a man get into such a situation? I'm no hero. I'm just a tough, self-centered guy who has been trying to make a life for himself."

"Like me," Volkmeer said. "I got tired of punchin' somebody else's cows, always makin' money for the other feller. Wanted some of my own."

"Well, you've got it, but is it yours? I expect it is if nobody has a claim on you."

Volkmeer removed his hat and wiped the hatband with a rough hand. "Watched 'em build that dam. Watched the water back up behind it, fillin' all those old canyons where I used to ride, covering ruins, filling up kivas. I tell you it was like a blessing, like a blessing.

"I never thought—"

Mike Raglan walked to his car. He was in no

mood to listen to more. His mind was made up and he could delay no longer. It might already be too late.

He glanced around at Volkmeer, standing undecided. "Get one thing straight, Volk. I'm going in there planning to come out, and I'm going to bring Erik Hokart with me. And anybody who gets in the way is in trouble, and I mean *anybody!*"

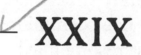

XXIX

WHEN MIKE RAGLAN walked into the ruin on the mesa, a robe was lying across his sleeping bag. Beside it was a worn turban of the kind Tazzoc wore. Mike sat down on a campstool and got out his old canvas map.

Maybe he was a coward. He knew he was scared. In his years of knocking about he had gone into some tight and dangerous places. He had walked the mean streets of the world, he had gone into ancient, supposedly haunted monasteries, he had explored catacombs where the dead were buried, but before he had always had a fairly clear idea of what he was facing, and here he had only the vaguest.

He studied the map given him so long ago by the old cowboy in Flagstaff, who had copied it from part of a map on a gold plaque.

The entrance the old man had used was now under water, but the other one he had known of was over to the west, in the place Johnny had found when rounding up strays.

Looming on the map, drawn with remarkable accuracy, was No Man's Mesa. In the old days one could cross the river easily, but now it was a long way around by car. The dam had backed water up the canyon and deepened it considerably.

He had to cross over and he could not safely use the window in the kiva. That led, he had been told, into a trap. Still, Chief had gotten through and had apparently not been injured.

Well . . . as a last resort, maybe.

He would try the Hole. There was an opening there and with luck he could find it.

What had become of Kawasi? More and more he found himself thinking of her. There had been a wistful loneliness about her that stayed with him. Large, beautiful eyes, soft lips . . .

What the hell was he thinking of? This was no time to be thinking about a girl. His job now was to cross to the Other Side and survive it, then to find where the Hall of the Archives was, and, once inside, try to find a way into other parts of the structure without getting himself trapped in one of those built-in tombs.

"You're a damned fool, Raglan," he told himself. "Go on into Durango and catch a plane out of here. To hell with it."

Yet he was not going to do it. Even as he thought of all the intelligent reasons not to do it, he knew he was going in. Yet he had to be honest with himself. Was it altogether because of Erik? Or was it the challenge of the unknown?

He had spent months exploring ruins of the Anasazi, he had slept in their kivas in far-out, lonely ruins. He had followed their trails, stood upon fields where they once planted maize and squash, fingered shards of their broken pottery, and in his heart he felt a kinship. Some had undoubtedly merged with the Hopi, others with the Mimbres, and many had died. Yet, if it was even remotely possible that some had gone back to that Third World, he wanted to know how they fared.

Sometimes, seated alone in one of their ruins, he had felt himself one of them. He had watched in his mind those small copper-skinned people grinding corn, carrying water up the steep trails, weaving cloth, going about the day-to-day business of being themselves.

What had happened to them? From the little he had learned, and if what they told him was true, some had fallen in with the Evil Ones who had remained behind, but some had fled that world, gone to the mountains or canyons, and there carried on as they might have, had they remained at Mesa Verde, Hovenweep, or Chaco Canyon.

He checked his gun again, then from his small pack he took another, a Heckler and Koch 9 millimeter, stowing it away in a special holster inside his belt at the small of his back. That was simply insurance. It was the Smith & Wesson .357 on which he intended to rely.

Where was Tazzoc? He needed to talk to him once more. He needed more guidance, more advice!

And where was Kawasi? Was she yet alive? Or had they taken her? Killed her or kept her a prisoner?

He went outside and walked to the kiva's edge, looking into it. Were those fresh tracks? Made by whom? For what reason?

He looked at the window and it stared back at him like an open mouth, with spots on the wall seeming like eyes. He shifted his feet uneasily, glancing over his shoulder.

Chief moved up beside him, growling a little, then sniffing the rocks that made up the circular wall of the kiva. Had something been there? Something that climbed out and prowled about the ruin?

The sky was a magnificent blue, with only a few scattered clouds. The river lay bright in the sunlight, and No Man's brooded in silence.

Was there a trail to the top? He could see no place for it, only the bare red walls rising sheer from the piles of talus. He had been told there was no trail, but an old Mormon had said there was. There were wild horses on the top, horses that must have found a way up and down, for the winters would be bitterly cold, with icy winds sweeping across the unprotected tableland.

A lone buzzard swung against the sky in solitary awareness that it had only to wait. All things came to it in the end.

Would there be buzzards over there? Or eagles? Were there gateways in the sky through which they could pass? Uneasily, he watched the buzzard, then shifted his eyes to the red rock land around him and searched it with care, knowing there could be eyes where none seemed to be.

He looked around, feeling himself observed, but saw nothing. He walked across the mesa and down the steep slope on the side away from the river, going back the way he had come and, after some time, finding his way down the steep cliffs to the bottom of the Hole.

The first thing he saw were mountain-lion tracks. A big lion, and one there not long before. The place seemed empty, and it was quiet. Leaves whispered their secrets into the stillness, then held still, listening for replies that never came. He walked along, his footsteps the only sound, slight as it was.

Indian painting on the walls. In places the desert varnish had slipped away, and what stories might have been written there, lost. He found his way along a narrow ancient path. Surely, in such a place where there was shade and water, there must have been Indians. But the trees were not old, perhaps no more than forty years in place, and what had it been like before? Had there been other trees? Burned perhaps, or their timbers used by Indians in building or for fuel? There were sand heaps. What lay beneath them?

Navajo sweathouses, only the cedar posts left, leaning together. And those other huts, built by someone other than Navajos, he believed. By Paiutes? He did not know, but the shape was different. They were not hogans.

Here was where he had seen the Varanel, but how had they come to be here? Pursuing someone? Or something?

He stopped, his back against a sandstone wall, to look carefully around. Somewhere here there was an opening into that other world.

Tracks! The Varanel must have left tracks.

His back to the red rock wall, he studied the canyon before and around him, searching the rocks for some variation, some anomaly, some indication. He found nothing.

He touched the butt of his gun for reassurance and it felt good under his hand. Again his eyes searched the terrain, and then he left the wall and went down into the trees. Over there, where he had first seen the Varanel, there was a vagueness, a shimmering. He could feel his heart beating heavily.

He moved forward through the trees; then, stopping against the trunk of one tree, he looked carefully around.

Someone was here. His every instinct told him something was here.

He moved across the open space to another tree, merging his body with the tree trunk. Again, warily, he looked around. If somebody watched him now, where could they be? Keeping his eyes straight ahead, using his peripheral vision, he waited for movement.

Where? And who? Or should it be *what?* There were strange creatures on this side, but what might lie over there? What kind of appalling monsters might there be?

Suppose they were invisible? There were sounds beyond the reach of the human ear. Dogs could hear them, insects possibly. What if there were colors beyond the range of the human eye? Colors no human could see? Suppose some such thing approached him now?

If men could pass through from one side to the other, what about animals. Chief had done it, going both ways. But what of their animals? Might they not have wild animals of some kind unsuspected?

Moving as a shadow moves, or as the wind, he went to another tree and still another. There he crouched, waiting and watching, alert for any breath of sound.

From where he now waited he could look across the open space where he had seen the Varanel.

Empty. Nothing.

He touched his tongue to dry lips, not liking the thought of moving away from the shelter of the trees. He would be exposed, vulnerable.

The worst of it was, he did not know what to look for, or exactly what he would do when he found it.

He shivered, although the day was not cold. He should get out of here, back to the camp in the ruin, back to something like security, back where he knew where he was and what must be done.

Yet he had found nothing. The day would be lost, and there was so little time.

What was Erik doing? Was he tied hand and foot? Was he imprisoned in a cell? Dying in one of those tombs? Or had he somehow won a reprieve? Convinced them he had more to offer by living?

He moved along the border of trees, looking across to where the Varanel had gone.

He could see nothing but a sweep of sand, some desert growth, and, beyond, a low ridge of sandstone.

Where had they come from? Where had they gone?

He watched; then his eyes went to the lone buzzard in the skies overhead. Suddenly, with a chill he wondered: What if that was not a real buzzard? Or was a trained bird? Trained to observe him?

That was nonsense. He was thinking foolish thoughts. He moved on to another tree, almost on the edge of the sweep of sand, and there he waited again, listening.

Did he hear a sound? A sound of singing? Of chanting? Somewhere a long way off? He glanced around again.

He would withdraw. It was growing late, and he must return to the ruin before he broke a leg scrambling over rocks in the darkness.

He heard the chanting again, many voices singing a monotonous song of few words. It was not his imagination, but where did it come from?

They must be close, very close, for he sensed

they were singing in low tones. Uneasily, he pressed closer to the bark of the tree, trying to locate the source of the sound. It seemed to come from somewhere out there before him.

If he was attacked, and he killed one of them on this side of the curtain, how would he explain the body? Who would believe such a fantastic story?

He had no evidence to present but the daybook, which could be considered a piece of pure fiction. After all, he was a writer with books to sell and it might be considered an elaborate publicity scheme. So to get help from the proper authorities was out of the question.

Nobody would accept the story for reality. Mike Raglan knew he must accept the fact that he lived in a world concerned with the deficit, with the arms race, with coming elections. People were thinking about paying rent, keeping up payments on a house or car, and planning for a vacation where at least some of them would come to Mesa Verde and wonder at its builders who lived so long ago. They would wander through the ruins while a park ranger explained them, and when they returned home to Vermont, Iowa, or wherever, they would repeat what they had heard and show the pictures they had taken.

What if he were killed out here, now? His body might not be found for years, for who came to this lonely, forgotten place?

Standing among the trees, looking up the sunlit canyon, Mike Raglan knew he was alone.

Alone as he had never been, alone with a reality

no one could share, facing a situation for which he had no answer and where he could expect no help. Whatever was done he must do himself.

What of Volkmeer? Well, what of him? Where did his loyalties lie? With a man who had helped him once, long ago? Or with a people who had given him wealth such as he had never expected to own, and which might, by some means, be withdrawn?

All he had expected of Volkmeer was somebody to cover his retreat, if pursued. Somebody to help him at that last minute when he might be at the end of his strength. He could forget that. He was on his own. Yet, when had it not been so?

He had never had any help from anybody. What he had done had been done by him and him alone.

Something moved in the trees behind him. He dropped his hand to his gun and turned sharply around.

XXX

It was Kawasi.

She stood alone under the trees, watching him. His eyes swept the trees and brush about her, finding nothing of which to be doubtfull.

"I have missed you." It was not what he intended to say, nor what he wanted to say or should have said, but it was the simple truth. He had missed her.

"I cannot be long away. They wait for my words."

She made a quick, inclusive gesture. "This place where we are? This is sacred place. This is special place for my people. Some say it was from here we first went into your world, but I do not know if this be true."

With one quick glance toward the way he had been going, he turned and walked back to where she stood. "What of Erik?"

"I know nothing. They have him, I believe."

"Somehow I must find and free him."

"It is impossible. Nobody ever escapes the Forbidden."

"I cannot believe your people—"

"It is not my people. Those who have him are the Lords of Shibalba, the evil ones. To escape them is impossible."

"What of your people, led by He Who Had Magic?"

"It was long ago and had never been tried before. In the dark all were present. By light all were gone. They tried to find us but we closed the ways and they could go no farther. There was much war, but finally they went away and bother us no longer."

"Come with me to the ruin. There's such a lot I should know."

They walked on, and she led the way, moving quickly and surely through the trees. She spoke over her shoulder. "This is place where nobody come, only sometimes a priest. All this"—she gestured again—"very uncertain place."

She left the trees to climb up to a bench that skirted the cliff. "We do not understand, but all this"—she swept a hand to take in the Hole, No Man's, and the mesa of the ruin—"all this is somehow . . . disturbed? Is it the word? It is uncertain place. Sometimes all like this, trees, water, cliffs . . . other times there is nothing solid, nothing we can be sure of. Sometimes an opening is here, sometimes there. It is like shimmering veil, like spray from a waterfall, and on the Other Side—"

"It is always this way?"

"No. It is a sometime way. Then something happens. . . . It is not earthquake, but something like, only it is in space. No, not space! It is in the essence of things, the overall! Something happens, makes dizzy. The eyes do not seem to see what is there. Then all is still, slowly everything settle, and after that, no openings! All is close! Close for long, long time!"

"But when are there openings again? When does it go back?"

She shrugged. "I do not know. The last time was before I am. Before I am born. Long time before. He Who Had Magic made marks on wall each time of which he knew. In his living time there were two."

Mike Raglan swore under his breath. So these so-called openings, even the "always" ones such as the kiva, might be closed at any time and remain closed for years. He shook his head irritably. The sooner he could get the hell out of all this, the better. He was perfectly happy with a normal, everyday world of three dimensions, and how did it happen that these Indians, of all people . . .

Still, the Maya or one of their predecessors had devised one of the most perfect calendars. They understood Time, in one sense at least.

What was reality, anyway? Might it be nothing but a certain atmosphere of recurring phenomena to which we have become accustomed? And how do we know it is the only such "reality"?

Our reality today is vastly different from the reality of 1900, for example. The reality of 1900 was of steam trains, horse-drawn drays, Saturday-night baths, and straight razors. If someone had suggested that soon a man might sit in his living room, flip a switch, and see what was taking place in South Africa or Australia, he'd have been thought to be off his rocker. Reality is what is generally accepted as such. Man alters it at his convenience.

Each of us has a vision of the world that belongs to him alone, and when he dies that world dies with him. Others may share in some parts of it, but none will see it exactly as he does, nor will all experience it in the same way, for they are living with their own vision of reality.

Each man's vision of reality is based upon his life experience, the influences of people, places, books, dreams, work, all the various aspects of his existence that go to make up him, or her.

He shook his head angrily. Forget all that. It was time he gripped what reality he was facing. What he had to believe was that it would be like getting on an elevator and getting off at another floor. He would have to deal with what came and get back on the elevator, with Erik, just as damned quick as he could.

He paused. "Kawasi? You said the Hole was a sacred place. I've looked around and there is no sign of any long residence there. There is water, lots of it in comparison with what's around here, and there are trees. Did nobody ever live here?"

She shrugged. "It is unreal place. All seems what is expected and then it is not. Look! Do you see animals here?"

"I saw the track of a mountain lion. A big one."

"Hah! It is no lion. Jaguar. A were-jaguar. There is spirit of evil man in him. He follows to kill, to destroy."

He knew the stories of werewolves and knew that in Africa there were leopard-men, so why not jaguar-men?

"There is a place down there where one can go through to your world. I think I even saw the Varanel disappear into it." He explained, telling the story of what he had seen.

"Maybe there." She shrugged. "But close upon us now is a place. It is said by some to be the place our people left the Third World and came into this. I do not know if this is true. It was there they returned to the Third World." She pointed into the canyon. "It is over there, a place like a stone funnel. What you call funnel.

"He Who Had Magic sketched a plan showing all the ways. It is very small area, after all. The funnel is hidden place but it will bring you through close to us.

"All this"—she gestured wide—"is place of no steadiness. I do not know your words, but it is place where nothing can be sure.

"There is opening where The Hand is. We hear speaking of it from those who knew, but the speaking was long ago."

They walked on in silence. It had grown quite dark, and although she seemed amazingly sure-footed, he was not. She paused, seemingly aware she was moving too fast for him. Athletic though he was, the altitude was higher here and his breath came harder in the thin air.

"Where you are?" He was thinking of the gold the old cowboy found, and particularly the map. "Do you know of any ruins there? I mean, very ancient ruins?"

"Oh, yes! There are stories. Some believe. Some do not. We do not go far from where we live. It is not our way. We hear speaking of old places where now no water is. No one goes there. How old? We do not know."

"But if there were ruins, there must be water?"

She shrugged. "Springs go dry. Rivers change course. All is desert."

They reached the mesa top. The ruin lay dark and silent under a sky of a million stars. He stopped her with a touch on her arm, for something moved in the darkness. It was Chief.

When he had a fire started and coffee on, he got out some cold cuts and fruit.

"I am afraid for you," she said. She glanced at the robe and turban. "This is what you will wear?"

"It is."

"This robe is that of a Jaguar priest. Do you know this?"

"No, I did not. Is it special?"

"Not many still live. He Who Had Magic was one. They were men of wisdom, of great knowledge."

"It will get me where I wish to go, into the Forbidden area after Erik."

"It is not possible! You do not know what you do! The Forbidden is . . . what you call it? A maze? Only The Hand knows all the ways. The Varanel know a little but not all. It is said The Hand preserves himself so, because only he knows the way to his chambers, his private rooms. It is said he appears to them on a balcony above a great hall, and speaks from there in a great voice."

"And if he dies?"

"There is always another. I do not know from where."

"You have seen The Forbidden?"

"Only from a distance. It is vast, a mountain-building of black stone, polished stone." She pointed across the river at No Man's. "It is like that! It stands alone above the city, not red like that, but all black!"

They were silent then. He made sandwiches and passed a paper plate to her, then filled their cups. It was very quiet now, very pleasant. The fire took the chill from the air, and outside the door they could see the stars against the black sky.

Kawasi began to talk, slowly and quietly but in a precise way, speaking as of something learned by rote. She described the outer appearance and size of the Forbidden. It was one gigantic construction, one building that was a city. Johnny had told her it was what was called a citadel. It was a fortress-city above the country below. The walls were sheer. The Lords of Shibalba and the Varanel each had their own apartments, yet each was restricted to an area and there were no areas in common.

"If same number exist as of old, there are twenty-four Lords, and five hundred of the Varanel. No man knows how many servants, and they not allowed to cross over from one area to another."

Slowly, trying to forget nothing, she told him what was known. It was little enough and all very general in content. Obviously the place was an intricate maze of passages, tunnels, and rooms, some of the rooms said to be all of glass reflecting one's own image a thousand times but also reflecting all the other mirrors, glass walls, and seeming openings, until one went mad searching for a way out. The description reminded him of the Glass House sideshows from his old carnival days, but obviously on a much vaster scale.

"And the prison area?"

"There is none. None we know of. All we know we piece together, little by little, from legends maybe wrong or out of date. Prisoners were just taken to a room and left to be questioned by the Varanel. But we know so little. And that little may not be right and true. When little is known, much is imagined."

The fire crackled cheerfully and he added a stick or two. It was, he admitted to himself, vastly comforting just to be with Kawasi, to sit quietly with her and not think too much about what was to come tomorrow.

"What is it like among your people? How are you governed? What is your role?"

"I am leader—what you call chief. Among us there is no name of position, no what you call title. One is because one *is*. One is not *born* to be leader—"

"Yet you said you were descended from He Who Had Magic?"

"That does not matter if I am not wise. Among my family there have been many who were wise. So, many leaders. But we cannot command. We can only advise. If we are often wrong, they no longer listen. It is very simple.

"Much was settled long ago. There are things done and not done, and if something new comes, a council is chosen to decide what is to be done. Often, I sit in council. Now, by their choice, I speak for them. How long this will be, I do not know."

She paused. "There are some among us who

302

believe we should follow The Hand, that we should abandon our mountains and go to live among the others. I do not believe this.

"They look down from the mountains and see green fields that lie below. They see orchards and water. Often for us there is small water, and our fields grow dry and crops wither. Then the numbers grow who would go down to The Hand.

"The Hand has people among us who talk trouble, who speak against me and those who are with me. I do not know what is to happen."

"Don't they know how rigid is the control by The Hand?"

"They do not believe, or they shrug and say what does it matter if we eat well? Some shrink from decision. The Hand means power to them. They hope to have some of that power for themselves. In truth, they have been promised so."

Mike Raglan leaned against the old wall. He tilted his head back and closed his eyes. It was a relief just to relax. Yet his mind would not rest. It prowled the edges and corners of the problem like a hound on a scent.

The Forbidden was apparently a maze, a labyrinthine system of rooms, corridors, and halls, connecting and interconnecting, and built over a space of centuries. If what Tazzoc told him was true, it was possible that no one person now knew the entire area. The organization within the system had been set in motion ages before and proceeded to function from sheer inertia. No children were allowed within those sacred precincts, for children

303

have curiosity which could only be stifled with time and continual conditioning.

Undoubtedly, even as the Hall of Archives was no longer visited, there were other areas abandoned or forgotten.

He knew much of mazes. It had begun with the Glass Houses in the carnivals with which he traveled as a magician's assistant. His Lebanese friend had told him the story of King Minos and the Minotaur. Ariadne had given Theseus a ball of thread, and, fastening one end of the thread, he had unwound it as he found his way through the maze en route to his fight with the Minotaur, half-man, half-beast. He had used Ariadne's thread to find his way back.

Undoubtedly that was the most famous labyrinth, yet the largest by far was one, long destroyed now, that existed in ancient Egypt. A vaster work by far than the pyramids. Herodotus and Strabo had both written of it: a place of more than three thousand rooms, vast colonnades, enormous halls covering an area estimated to be one thousand feet long by eight hundred broad, and on at least two levels, one of these below ground. The Forbidden, he gathered, was at least twice that size, judging by all he heard, yet even that might be a gross underestimate.

"Kawasi? I am going over tomorrow. Will you show me the way?"

She got up and walked outside and he followed, fearful that she would leave him once more. "Kawasi? I must go."

"I know, but how can I send you to death? For there is no way—no way he can be freed."

"Will you show me? Or must I chance the kiva?"

"Oh, no!" She hesitated again and then replied, "So be it. You are stubborn. Nothing I can say—"

"Nothing."

"I will show you. I will take you over with me, but then I go to my people. What you shall do, I do not know. One thing: There is one whom you must fear.

"He is tall, taller than you, and very strong. He has great power also. He enters the Forbidden as he wishes, and we fear he knows much of us. We think he controls the spies among us and influences those who talk of leaving to join the Lords of Shibalba. You will know him if you see him. He has presence, a commanding presence. No one disobey him." She paused. "He sent for me by one of his people. I refused, but he sent word he was coming for me and to destroy us."

"He has a name?"

"Zipacna. Whatever you do, beware of Zipacna!"

XXXI

TOMORROW!

There was no more to be said. He was committed. Leaving Kawasi in the inner room, he bedded down near the drafting table with Chief at the opening, near him. There he could look out at the stars, perhaps for the last time.

What kind of thinking was that? Nonsense! He would make it. He would find Erik, and they would come back, and so would whoever Erik had with him, no matter how many.

Yet this might be his last night on earth as he had known it, for when he returned, if he returned, would it ever seem the same again?

He smiled grimly into the darkness, and said, half-aloud, "You've been a damned fool before, Mike, but this one takes the cake!"

Looking across the river at the vast bulk of No Man's, he shuddered. The shudder was involuntary, brought on by what unknown presentiment of fear he knew not. No Man's, black, ominous, mysterious. The time was now.

Nothing, not even the wild windswept vastness of the Chang-Tang would be like this, nor even those strange trails he had followed to the hidden monasteries of the Bon-po, nor his visit to the lost castle of Kesar of Ling. Nothing could be like this.

There had been magic there, too, and he had not known then what to expect, yet it somehow had seemed fated from his first meeting with the wizened little man in the streets of what was then called Suchow, east of the Jade Gate.

He had walked knife-edge ridges, followed trails that skirted a gorge three thousand feet deep, with nothing but death promised at the journey's end.

He had survived, and he would survive now.

But this was a story he would never write, as he had not written those others. There were some things a man kept to himself, always. Some stories had to remain buried inside you. Before that trip into the Kunluns, he had not believed that, but now he knew it was true.

Lying awake, his dreams lit by the candles of the stars, he thought it out carefully. Every sense must be alert. He must make no misstep. He must enter the Forbidden and walk slowly and quietly across the outer court to the Hall of Archives. Once inside the Hall, he must find the area of maps at once and seek out the chart of the Forbidden.

He must be ever wary of those Death Doors. He must find Erik and free him, and then they must escape by the quickest possible route.

What of Kawasi?

He sat up suddenly. *What of Kawasi?* She was returning with him, going to her people, but what then? What of him? What of them together? Did she know how he felt? He had not spoken. Well, after a fashion he had. After he had freed Erik, would she come with him? Could she come? Dared she leave her people, whose welfare was in her hands?

Something seemed to stir in the night, a vast, weird sensation such as he had never felt. It was as if the whole earth gave a slow sigh, and then subsided.

For a moment he thought he felt an earthquake, but the earth did not tremble. No rocks fell.

He lunged to his feet, somehow shocked and frightened. Frightened of what?

Kawasi was beside him. "Oh, Mike! It is happening!"

"What's happening?" He was irritated because he did not know. He could not explain. It was unlike anything he had experienced.

"It is what I spoke of! Do you remember? How I said sometimes the openings are all closed? And it lasts for many years? Thirty, forty years or more?"

"I remember your mentioning it, of course, but—"

"I have been told of it. This . . . what just happened, this happens before. When it happens again, it is for a long time, maybe forever. I do not know what it is. Perhaps time itself shudders, perhaps space. Perhaps what happens here is in time with something else. Just as there are earthquakes, may there not be—"

"How much time do we have?" Suddenly he was very cool, very alert.

"I do not know. It is quick. Twenty-four of your hours, perhaps forty-eight. No more, I am sure. Whatever you would do, you must do before then. You must find Erik and get him out, or stay the rest of your life on the Other Side."

"I'd be with you."

Even as he said it he knew he was selfish. He wanted to be with her, but he wanted her on his side of the curtain. He wanted her with him, in his world.

He wanted to take care of her, to make a place for her, and over here he could do it. Over there he would know nothing, he would be out of the picture, at least for a long time.

"We can't wait, then. We've got to go now."

"All right," she said.

Even as she spoke he told himself he was a fool. This was the perfect alibi. If the curtain was drawn, if the ways were closed off for thirty years, what could he do?

If he could stall, just delay a little, he could keep her over here and he would not be duty-bound to go after Erik. He would have Kawasi and they would be frcc to build a life here, in his world.

"Mike? If we are going . . . ?"

"All right," he said, and they went down the mountain in the darkness, down the canyon into the place that Johnny found.

His mouth was dry and his throat tight. He was scared.

Yet at the same time something was swelling within him, some strange eagerness, some anticipation for what was to come.

Now! he told himself. Now you'll find out! Now for the ultimate, the final adventure!

Adventure? The word had always irritated him. It was so cheaply used, a cheap, romantic word on the lips of those who had never experienced anything like it. Being adrift in an open boat at sea was an "adventure," but who wanted it?

Kawasi went quickly down the canyon and he

followed. It was not quite as dark as it had been, or was it just that his eyes were growing accustomed to the night? No, the moon must be rising beyond the mountains.

He had always believed he was good in the mountains, but Kawasi was better. She moved like a ghost over the broken rock, scattered pebbles, and among the low-growing brush, moved almost without a sound.

She was of that world, if it existed, and there must be a simple, logical explanation. We are a people, he reflected, who thrive on explanations. No matter what happens someone comes forward with a simple explanation and the mystery vanishes or is thrust into its respective pigeonhole and conveniently forgotten. Of course, if there are a dozen people present, there will be not one but several explanations, and the one presented by the person with the most authority will be accepted.

Kawasi stopped suddenly, lifting a hand, listening. He heard nothing. What *was* he getting into? All his life he had heard of time warps, had known that our seemingly orderly world was actually far from orderly.

Standing slightly behind her, aware of little more than vague darkness, Mike Raglan tried to bring himself back to reality. He was a young man, with a beautiful girl, alone in a desert, and supposedly she was about to lead him into another world, a world that existed parallel with his own.

"It is here," she whispered. "Take my hand."

She stepped forward quickly and he had a quick,

310

flashing vision of a tunnellike opening at his feet, and then he fell.

There was a moment of gasping horror as he seemed to be falling into a pit, and then he struck the ground, face down.

A moment he lay still; then, lifting his head, he spat dust from his mouth and tried to sit up.

A hand pressed down, and someone hissed, "Ssh!" warningly.

He lay still, swearing to himself, but in the midst of the swearing he heard movement and was suddenly alert. Someone was near them. Someone was approaching.

He felt movement beside him on the ground. It was Kawasi. Her fingers gripped his, warning him again. He lay perfectly still, wanting to reach for his gun, yet dreading the thought of what a pistol shot would do to the night. It would certainly bring enemies, if any were about. He would be rid of one, perhaps, only to have a dozen or a hundred come down upon them.

His chest felt tight and uncomfortable and he was suddenly conscious of his breathing. His breath was coming in gasps as if he had been running. He fought to stifle the sound.

He was immediately aware of something else. He was lying upon *grass!*

Not rock, but grass. Above all, he could smell it. He could smell the dampness of nearby water, too. And there was a vague smell of something burning.

He could feel Kawasi beside him, her hand

clutching his, warning him. Who was approaching? And where did this grass come from? There was some in the bottom of the Hole, but a coarser grass than this.

A voice spoke, but he could not understand the words, and then there was a reply from a greater distance. The footsteps ceased to move, and mentally Raglan gathered himself, preparing to leap to his feet.

Footsteps again, retreating now, and then again the voices, speaking in some foreign tongue. He had a smattering of languages, never staying long enough in one place to be proficient, but this was unlike anything he knew. It was, he decided, more like Castilian Spanish than anything he could remember. Like, he reflected, but unlike.

A stick cracked as if being broken for a fire. Almost without a sound, Kawasi got to her feet and he followed. Still holding his hand she started off, keeping to the darkness. Suddenly he could see the fire, a low blaze with several men lying about, wearing blue.

The *Varanel!*

A border guard, or something of the kind. But why here? Why— He paused so suddenly that his grip stopped her. It hit him so hard he caught his breath.

They were on the Other Side!

Impossible! It was . . . ! "Come!" she whispered, and he followed, careful not to stumble. They were still walking on grass, moving toward what appeared to be trees. Once among the trees she stopped. "Something is *wrong!*" she whispered. "Something is very wrong! What are they doing here?"

There was something close to panic in her tone. He looked around, and dark though it was he could see what must be the sky, although he saw no stars. Towering above the forest on the edge of which they stood was a cliff that must rise a thousand feet sheer from the ground. There was nothing like that near the mesa of the ruin.

"Where are we?" he asked.

"My village is near. Only a few miles. And these—these people have never come so close!"

"Kawasi, I do not know your situation, nor that of your people, but that is an army patrol encamped for the night or on guard here. Any soldier would recognize the signs at once. Either the approaches to your village are being guarded or they are preparing an attack."

"Attack? Oh, no! They must not!" Her voice was anguished. "Oh, Mike! I've been too long away! I fear! I fear greatly!"

He put his arm around her. "Take it easy, honey. Now let's get down to business. How do we get to your place from here?"

Her momentary fear and doubt seemed to ebb away. The need for action dispelled her anxiety for the moment. Taking his hand again, she went swiftly along the edge of the woods. At a pause, he whispered, "Careful! There may be scouts out, or other parties."

"I do not think so. Nobody ever fights them. Nobody has resisted them for many years."

And that, he told himself, might be their only advantage. He had noticed that in the strong-arm men he had encountered in the parking lot at the motel. They had not expected resistance, at least not the resistance offered by a fighting man who knew his business.

"It is far?"

"Only a few miles."

"Will there be a guard?"

"A guard? Oh, no! There has never been need for one. Not for a long, long time."

So what started the ball rolling, he wondered. Was it Erik? Or had Erik escaped somehow? Was this part of a searching party? Or had they—he caught his breath—decided to do what he had suggested to Gallagher, come through to the other side, in force?

The idea did not greatly worry him. They might overcome a few outlying ranches or take over one of the marinas on Lake Powell, but once the word was out, there were too many homes with weapons, too many citizens who were prepared to defend themselves.

Gallagher, for example, could have a hundred armed men deputized to help within a half hour after realization of the necessity. There was almost no place in the West, and in many parts of the East, where this was not true. No enemy paratroop attack had ever been made into a country where the citizens were armed. And of course, they had the advantage of knowing the country.

With Kawasi leading, almost running now, they wove their way among boulders, up a dry wash, then a narrow path up the face of the cliff. Obviously, she was accustomed to this, but he was not and the altitude was high. It was growing lighter. Daybreak, perhaps? But it was too soon. He glanced at his wristwatch.

Three A.M.?

He swore suddenly, and Kawasi looked around. "What is it?"

"When I came through," he said, "I was going to mark the place so I could get back. Now I don't know where I am."

He was in a world he had never wanted, facing enemies he did not know, and he had no means of escape.

Above all, there was little time. Only a matter of hours until the openings were closed forever, or for more years than he cared to contemplate.

Buster, he told himself, this time you've done it! This time you've bought the packet!

XXXII

AT THEIR FEET was a vast black gulf, and around them great wind-scoured cliffs and jagged spires, an unbelievable chaos bathed in deep shadows and misty gold light. Awed, he stood transfixed by the dark grandeur of the sight. Kawasi tugged at his sleeve. "Come!" she whispered.

Leading him, she plunged down an unseen path into that bowl of blackness, switching back and forth across the face of the cliff into the cool darkness below. Once, during a momentary pause, he glanced back up to see a leaning tower of rock like a great warning finger, a warning of he knew not what danger.

When they reached level ground, she was almost running. Nearby he heard water.

"A stream?" he whispered.

"Irrigation ditch," she replied. "There are miles of them. This is our land, all down this canyon and on the mesas around us. That is why I am frighten. We did not believe they knew where to find us. For a long time we are undisturbed. Now that is over."

They reached a well-trodden path, and before them loomed the dark bulk of some kind of a structure. His eyes could dimly find its outlines. A pueblo not unlike those near Taos but vastly larger.

Kawasi walked to what appeared to be a blank wall, moved something with her fingers, and spoke into what must have been a speaking tube.

There was a muffled response and a moment later a ladder was lowered from the roof above. Kawasi climbed swiftly and he followed. The ladder was withdrawn by a man to whom Kawasi spoke swiftly and sharply. Turning, the man ran into the door of his sleeping quarters. Mike could

316

hear the man talking to someone else, apparently spreading the alarm.

Kawasi did not linger. She led him swiftly along the roof to another ladder, fixed in position. On this second level several men awaited her and she spoke rapidly, evidently explaining the situation and the necessities of the moment. He could see them peering at him; then they moved away, scattering out.

"Do you expect an attack?"

"We must be prepared. This might be only a scouting party."

"Do you think they know where you are?"

"How can we know? We must act as if they did, and act promptly."

"It was not a large party. Maybe you shouldn't let them get away."

She turned sharply. "What do you mean?"

"If they are the only ones who know where you are, and they could not return with the information . . . ?"

"You mean . . . *kill* them?" She was shocked. "They are Varanel. Nobody has ever killed a Varanel!"

"Not even Johnny?"

"Well . . . perhaps, but it does not seem possible. They are invulnerable!"

"Nobody is invulnerable," he said, "and if they are a danger to you, why not?"

"We do not attack. We only defend."

Mike Raglan walked on beside her for several steps. "Often it is better to attack first. Destroy

317

them before they can attack, and before they can return with the news of what they have found."

"We never attack first," she insisted.

She opened a door in a wall and they entered to a subdued light. She closed the door carefully and they mounted three flights of stairs. At each landing there was a door which she ignored. At the top, another door opened upon a terrace. Here there were trees, a fountain with running water, and a pool. There were many flowers, and the terrace extended off into the darkness, where he could dimly make out rows of planted crops.

She opened still another door and they stood in a wide and spacious room. At the far side there was a fireplace, and there were several divans covered with what appeared to be Indian blankets. "It is my house," she said.

The stone walls were hung with tapestries and the floor beneath was carpeted.

"Sit you," she suggested. "We will have food, and men will come to talk. We must decide what is to be done."

"My advice is to get that patrol before they can tell what they have seen, if they have actually seen this place."

"To kill a Varanel? It is not done. To kill a Varanel is the greatest evil."

"Why?"

"It is not done. It has never been done. It is the greatest evil—"

"Who told you that?" he asked, irritated. "The Varanel?"

"No, but it is so. It has always been so."

"Do they not sometimes kill others?"

"Oh, yes! They kill or enslave. It is their way."

"But you do not kill them? Somebody, honey, has sold you a bill of goods. They can kill you, but to kill them is a sin. I believe you should think about that," he said, "and just where that idea came from."

A voice spoke from outside the door. She crossed the room and opened it. Six men came in, four of them older men, judging by the whiteness of their hair. They all wore belted cloaks of some thin material.

Swiftly, she explained. Then she turned to him. "Mike? I did not see. How many were there?"

"Seven, in sight. I believe that is all there were. If we were to move swiftly, we might get them all."

She explained and there were exclamations of astonishment, almost anger. Only one of the younger men kept silent, glancing over at Mike with appraising eyes.

"They say as I have said. Nobody kills a Varanel. If they attack, we will defend."

"And if you kill one then? In defending yourselves?"

She looked uneasy. "We have never killed one. I do not think we can."

One of the older men spoke, relating some incident. The others nodded. Kawasi explained. "Long ago a madman tried to kill one. He struck him three times with a blade. Nothing happened."

319

"They wear armor," Mike explained, "under those blue jerkins or whatever you call them. Those whom I saw were wearing some kind of armored vest or shirt. I am sure of it." He paused a moment. "Has anybody ever tried hitting them on the legs? Or in the throat?"

"We do not attack the Varanel," she insisted.

He shrugged, irritated. "Then you might as well surrender and become slaves. It seems to me you have no choice."

"Nobody has ever struck a Varanel!" Kawasi said.

"I struck a couple of their boys and it worked very well. I'll admit they seemed surprised. From what you say, it must have been quite a shock to them."

Raglan glanced from face to face. These people seemed no different from others he knew, yet different they must be, for this was a world he had never known. Were they a softer, gentler people than his own? Or had they lived so long in isolation that they no longer remembered what the real world was like? These were descendants of the cliff dwellers, a people who had chosen to retreat from drought and attackers, to return here and take shelter. Were they hiding from danger? Or were they afraid of their own instincts?

They had evolved, but how much and in what ways? This apartment of Kawasi's was a lovely place, but so far he had only glanced at it. How far had it developed from the simple structures at Mesa Verde or Chaco Canyon? Was it only the single-line development from then until now without any input from the outside? And how far apart were the two worlds, this one of Kawasi's and that other, darker world ruled by The Hand?

His own world had developed in constant strife—struggle against the elements and the greed of other men. Was war a natural thing among men? Was it a part of their development? Or their path to extinction?

"You have no contact with the world of the Varanel?" he asked.

"None, and we wish none. Here"—she gestured about her—"we live in peace. We run water upon our plants. We grow fruit on trees and bushes. We have found many sources of water, and each has been improved. We have learned each place where there is dampness, and we have planted there. If there is space for but one plant, we have that one plant. Each bit of ground is used. We have learned to gather the rain from off the mountains, letting it run into our pools or our ditches. Nothing is wasted. The food left over, the leaves that fall, all is returned to the soil. We gather the droppings of animals and we crush the hulls of nuts. Each of us works in the fields or forest."

"You have animals?"

She nodded. "We raise what you call cattle, and sheep as well. No goats. They are too destructive and will eat every growing thing, given the chance, even the bark from the trees. Long ago we decided there would be no goats, for wherever there are goats there is desert. If there is no desert, in time goats will create it."

"There are forests in your mountains?"

"We cut down only trees that are dead or dying, and we gather every fallen branch for fuel." She lifted her eyes to his. "It is not easy, our life. Each has a plot to cultivate. Some have several plots. Each year we try to put by some grain for the bad years when no rain comes."

"You must make a choice," Raglan suggested, "to fight the Varanel or to lose all you have."

"We cannot fight them. It is impossible."

The young man who had been standing aside spoke then. "I will fight them," he said.

They turned on him, astonished. "You, Hunahpu? You would dare fight the Varanel?"

Kawasi translated as he spoke: "I have talk to John-nee. He has fought them. He has beaten them. They come no more to seek him.

"We do not wish to die. They do not wish to die. If some are killed, they will go away and come no more."

They talked excitedly, angrily, among themselves, and Raglan turned away. Whatever they decided to do was none of his affair. He had come for the purpose of finding a way to free Erik, and that was just what he must do. Yet one thing came to mind.

"Kawasi? Is there any other way for the Varanel to enter your valley?"

"Yes, but it is far from here."

322

"To guard this path would be easy, but it must be guarded at once. You have weapons?"

"Bows and arrows, spears, and blowguns."

"And the Varanel?"

"They have other weapons. I do not understand them. Something penetrates and does something to your inside. After a time you sicken and die. It can be within minutes, sometimes days. It is not a poison."

"I would suggest you guard the path. Is there a place where you could roll stones upon them? Look, it is none of my business but you need someone willing to fight, someone who can think in terms of combat."

He paused. "That young man? Hunahpu? Why not put him in charge? He at least is ready to fight. If you do not have the weapons, use what you have, think, contrive! There is always a way!"

This was not his fight. He wanted to get Erik and get out of here, get back to his own world and forget all this. Even—

No, not Kawasi. He did not want to forget her.

Ignoring them, he crossed to a divan and got out his old canvas map. It made no sense. If he just had a landmark, something to indicate a location.

Suddenly, he found it. That leaning tower of rock, like a gigantic finger? It was there, on the very edge of his map! It might be different, but . . .

No, there was the trail down the mountainside, that dotted line! Beyond was a maze of mountains, cliffs, peaks, canyons, and in the midst of them a small red cross. What did that mean?

To the south was open country with lines marking what must be irrigation ditches, and then a cluster of black squares that must be buildings; then, at the end of the valley, a massive black structure—that had to be the Forbidden! He studied it with care, the wide avenue leading up to it, the great gates, and the smaller door beside the gates.

Suddenly he was aware the others had gathered about and were studying his map. Excitedly, one put a finger on the Forbidden, and then to something he had not yet seen, a path leading from the mountains and coming up to the Forbidden from the side, a path that seemed to end in a blank wall.

"What is it?" he asked Kawasi.

"There is no such trail," she said. "But such a trail might lead to an entrance nobody knows."

"This map," Raglan explained, "was copied from an ancient map found in a ruin. It may be there was such a trail and it has been forgotten, perhaps even by The Hand, and the Varanel."

Kawasi looked at him, startled. Then she shrugged. "Who would go there? It is a place of death. A place from which no man returns."

"I am going there," he replied, "and through the door beside the gate. That is where Erik is, and I am going after him."

Raglan got to his feet and rolled his map. "And

when he is free I am coming for you. I want you to go back with me."

"And leave my people? They need me."

"There is Hunahpu," he replied.

Startled, she looked from him to the young man who stood aside, waiting.

"Put him in charge of defense," Raglan suggested. "He at least is ready to fight. I think he will do well."

Day was breaking and the sky was faintly yellow. He went to the window and looked out across the terrace at the looming black mountains beyond. It was a starkly beautiful land and reminded him of Machu Picchu in the Peruvian Andes, the hidden city of the Incas.

All about were towering cliffs, and below were green fields of maize, squash, beans, and other crops he could not distinguish at the distance.

The pueblos were like those seen in New Mexico, except these were much larger, the work more finished, and there were roof gardens everywhere, some of them carved out of cliffsides. Water had been brought from the mountains and piped into the buildings and the ditches.

"Is this your only city?"

"Oh, no. Others are larger than this, and farther up the canyons. Some are in caves, as at Mesa Verde."

"*You* have seen Mesa Verde?"

"Oh, yes! I go with tour-ist. A park ranger explained it all very nicely."

"Was he right?"

"He did not speak of the always watching for enemies. At first they did not find us. They killed people in the flat lands and took their grain. We watch, and make no sound, but finally they find and attack my people. Some enemies were killed and some fell from cliffs when they try to come down toeholds cut from the rock. They did not know the steps were keyed."

"Keyed?"

"Coming down the cliff you must begin with the correct foot or you would come to a place where you could not go down or back up. Our enemies hung there until they tired and fell. It is very far to fall."

XXXIII

THE OLD MEN clustered about the map, brows furrowed, intent upon its every line. "We do not have things such as this," Kawasi said. "Although some tell that He Who Had Magic knew of such."

"It is a design," Raglan said, "showing how the land lies. I study it to see how I must approach the Forbidden and how to escape when I am free of it."

"Nobody has ever escaped," an old man said.

Raglan was irritated. "You have been telling yourself that for years, and somewhere, sometime they told you that. I shall go in, and God willing, I shall come out, but do not tell me again that it cannot be done. Do not tell yourselves that."

Raglan got to his feet. "Tell Hunahpu," he said to Kawasi, "that he must find men who believe as he does, men who will fight the Varanel. Then he must think of how to defeat them. Use the country against them. Destroy the trail if need be. Stop them, or you will all be slaves."

"And you?"

"I shall do what I have come for. I shall find Erik and free him." His eyes turned to hers. "Then I shall come for you."

Their eyes held. "I do not know if I can go," she protested. "My people need me."

"Not unless you can lead them. Do you not see what is happening? The same thing that happened before when your people fled to this side. They fled because they were afraid, and they had no organized leadership. To defeat such an enemy you cannot have each person deciding what he or she will do. When nomadic Indians attacked your people, they drifted away, family by family, until nobody remained who could or would resist. It was the same when you abandoned your homes and fled back to this world.

"To protect yourselves you must have organization. You must work together. If you are to follow the old ways, Kawasi, your people are doomed."

He waved a hand. "Are you prepared to lose all this? To have someone else reap where you have sown? You have no choice, Kawasi. You must fight or be enslaved. Some of you will undoubtedly be killed—certainly you will be, for you are a leader and a possible focal point of resistance."

"You could help us."

"I could do nothing for you that you cannot do for yourselves if you but wish to. It is far better you are led by one of your own. I am not a hero. I shall try to help my friend escape because he relies upon me.

"You are a great people or you could not have built all this, but if you will not save yourselves I cannot save you. Hunahpu will fight. Help him."

"What of us?"

"If I get Erik safely home, I shall come for you, unless you can escape and come to me. We are equal, you and I, but you have your duties and I mine. Let us be about them."

No, he told himself, he was no hero. If he was, he would stay here, lead them to victory, and then save his friend. Or die trying.

Well, he did not want to die. He did not want to be where he was. He would have liked to be safely out of it with Kawasi beside him.

He shouldered his pack. Hunahpu was watching him, and Raglan turned again to Kawasi. "Tell him to ambush them. To aim for their throats, their legs, their faces. Get on the cliffs above them. Roll rocks down. Kill them any way you can, but kill them." He stared into Hunahpu's eyes. "You must show them that a Varanel can be killed."

He turned to Kawasi. "Where is the other way out? I must be going."

From the terrace she pointed the way. He turned again to her. "I can do nothing for your people they cannot do for themselves, but if you are to exist, you must fight. You must defeat the Varanel. There are but five hundred of them, and you will have more men than that."

"Where will you go?"

He gestured toward the wild and broken country. "I go there. I am going to find the ruin left by He Who Had Magic or whoever was before him. There is a map there, and I wish to see it. Then I shall enter the Forbidden and find Erik."

"It is—"

"Don't tell me it is impossible. I shall do it because I must.

For a moment he took her by the arms, looking into her eyes. "Do not doubt that I love you. Do not doubt that I shall return."

When he was on the trail up the canyon he looked back. She stood on the terrace looking after him, and he lifted a hand. "You're a damn fool," he said aloud. "If you were even half smart you'd take that girl and run. You'd get out of here before the roof falls in."

That quake or whatever it was? How much time did he have? He no longer remembered how much time had passed. Five hours? Six, perhaps? He would have to hurry.

When he left the canyon of the green fields, he entered upon a trail where no tracks appeared. If any had come this way, it had been long ago, indeed. He went along the trail, climbing steeply up, working his way around boulders and into a forest. Needles lay soft beneath his feet. Bears were here, and mountain lions, too. He saw their claw marks on trees, and droppings beneath his feet.

He walked on, aware of all around him, yet moving swiftly. He was, he knew, cutting across the wild country and actually drawing closer to the valley of the Forbidden. Nowhere did he see any tracks of men or any sign of hunting, trapping, or woodcutting. The forest here seemed not to be used. What he was seeing was a society that had drawn more and more into itself, a tight, narrow little world fearful of all that lay outside and controlling all that lay within. Centuries of domination had left the people with no belief in resistance. He doubted if the idea even occurred to them, and if it did, it was quickly stifled by the same defeatist comments he had heard among Kawasi's people.

Yet the Anasazi had evolved. Their architecture was better, their fields better cultivated, their irrigation system advanced. Given outside stimulation there was no guessing what heights they might have achieved.

He paused to catch his breath. This air was not the same, for the altitude, judging by the plants and flowers, was not great. He was in a forest region which in his own world would be aspen country, with spruce above and around him.

From a break in the forest he looked for his finger of rock, found it, and took a bearing. Not far now.

Suddenly he stopped. He looked carefully

around, unbuttoning his coat to get quicker access to his pistol. He had seen a track, the track of a fairly tall man, but not heavy.

His eyes found nothing. Ahead of him he could hear a waterfall. Not a large one, but a fall nonetheless. He let his ears become accustomed to its sound and then began to sort other sounds from it, distinguishing one after another.

Somebody had been here, somebody who wore moccasins and was over six feet tall. The Indians he had seen were mostly not over five feet eight inches.

Zipacna was tall, they had said. And he might be the most dangerous of all.

Who was he? What was his relationship to The Hand? Was he a minor captain? An important one? A deputy leader? An adviser? Just *what* was he? Kawasi had feared him, so he would be wary.

Raglan went down a steep aisle among the trees. Below him there was bright sunlight, leading to an open place, out from among the trees.

Pausing beside a tree, Mike Raglan surveyed the area before him. Down through the trees lay a small meadow; beyond it, a stream. His eyes had not yet become accustomed to the odd light, but there was no glare. It was a vague, yellow light, like that sometimes seen in the plains country of the Midwest before a storm. Here no storm impended, nor any change in the weather he could detect.

He waited, watching, unwilling to go down into that open meadow, yet knowing he must. Beyond it some of the rocks seemed to have a formation that did not look natural, as if they had been shaped by hand.

When that old cowboy whom he met in Flagstaff had broken through to the other side, it had been near a ruin, a ruin where he had found a map on a gold plate. The old man had copied only part of that map, showing how to return to where he found the gold. It was the rest of that map Raglan wished to see.

The Forbidden was a huge building, several times larger than the Pentagon, and it was a maze of rooms and passages. If there was a map, it would make it much easier. Of course there were other maps in the Hall of Archives, but this one, scratched on a gold surface, might be much the best.

Moving forward a few feet, he stopped behind another tree. He had found no more tracks, and the meadow before him was empty. He went swiftly down, crossed the meadow, and went up into the trees and the forest of rocks beyond. Almost at once he came upon a corner of the ruin.

He studied the path. No tracks, yet much of it was bare rock, and tracks might not show. He rounded the corner and stood at the upper edge of a shallow valley of ruins, a valley not of meadow and grass but of bare red rock created by what he could not guess. At a glance he realized the ruins were ancient, older than anything he had ever seen, anywhere.

Mike Raglan had looked upon many ruins, but

his first impression of this was one of extreme age. His second was a creeping sense of horror—why, he could not say. The area he overlooked must cover more than fifty acres of ruined walls, toppled columns, a surprising number of intact roofs. He sat down on a flat rock, fallen off a wall, and studied the situation. He didn't like it.

Carefully, inch by inch, he studied the ruin before him, taking his time to fix the layout in his mind. This might be where his old friend had come through; this might be where he had found the gold.

How many men could have taken enough and never returned? Few men were content with just enough. Few could resist the lure of just a little bit more. A comfortable life was rarely sufficient. Most men and women wanted wealth, and that old cowboy had known where it was and how to get it. Had there been something else, something he had not told?

Nothing moved. The valley of the ruin was high on a ridge of some sort, and the broken edges that surrounded it seemed to be the edges of a flat surface, like a mesa top.

Still he did not move. Yet time was nudging him to act.

He shuddered. What was wrong with him? Why was he apprehensive? He had explored many ruins in Egypt, Tibet, the Takla Makan, and in India. He ran his eyes over these ruins again. There was little time, and he must get on with it, yet still he did not move. Occasionally there came to his nostrils a vaguely unpleasant odor that was somehow familiar, but he could not place it.

Did anything live down there? Had animals moved into the old temples? If there were temples.

Raglan got to his feet, glancing around him once more. He saw nothing. Then he started down the path into the ruin.

He saw no birds, no chipmunks, not even a lizard. Did nothing live here? He paused again, wary of the ruins. No flies, no bees, not even a whisper of movement. He walked on, his feet making small sounds in the grass.

It must have been an imposing city in its day, if such it had been. The ruins bore no resemblance to any pueblo he had seen. He walked down a space between buildings. It was not a street or even an alleyway, simply a space, now overgrown with grass. Before him was a stone basin at least ten feet in diameter, but it was dry. On the far side was an opening as of a good-sized pipe through which water must have come into the basin.

He walked around it and saw opposite him a door, a very tall, narrow opening and beyond it, only darkness. He stepped closer, and peered within. He could see nothing. He started forward, then stopped.

It could wait. First he must see what lay outside. He stepped back from the entrance and looked quickly around, then walked away, suddenly relieved. Twice he glanced back over his shoulder.

What *was* the matter with him? Why had he

not gone inside? After all, he suddenly recalled, he had a flashlight. Scarcely more than an inch in diameter and ten inches long, but extremely powerful, the light would have pierced that blackness like a sword blade.

He walked on, stepping over fallen columns, skirting great blocks of masonry. Several buildings had caved in, and many were intact. Nevertheless the columns and the decorative stonework showed signs of aging such as he had never seen in Greece, Egypt, or the Hittite ruins in Turkey. Whatever this had been, it must be older than anything known on earth, yet the architecture, although different, showed evidence of considerable development. This had been no beginning civilization, but one that had grown, developed, and matured.

He looked around him again. All was still. Nothing moved now, not even the wind.

He walked down another opening between buildings and suddenly another opened before him. The pillar at the side of the door had fallen across it, one end still partly in place. The door was not blocked, however; he could easily go either over or under the pillar. It was a good-sized building but this was some sort of a side entrance. Within, as in the other building, all was black and his eyes would not penetrate that darkness. He started forward. This time he would see what, if anything, was inside.

He stepped up to the door and peered inside. Directly before him was a screen, placed so one had to turn either right or left to go around it. He

335

had seen the same effect several times in Asia. The idea was that evil spirits have to travel in straight lines and so could not follow beyond the screen. Smiling at the idea, he started to duck down under the pillar.

"I wouldn't go in there, if I was you."

—— XXXIV ——

THE VOICE CAME from behind him. Only a moment before, he had looked all around, seeing nothing. Slowly, he straightened up and turned.

About twenty feet away stood a tall old man with long white hair. He had a narrow, saturnine face with amused blue eyes, a carefully trimmed beard and mustache. He was dressed in carefully fitted buckskins and moccasins.

"Johnny?" he asked.

"Know me, do you? Well, there surely ain't many of me to confuse nobody. I'm Johnny. Who're you?"

"Raglan, Mike Raglan. I came over to find a friend and take him back."

"Come of your own free will?" Johnny shook his head. "You must be some kind of damn fool. This friend of yours? You know where he is?"

"In the Forbidden area. He was brought over from the other side by some strong-arm guys."

"Brought over? They must have wanted him bad. They don't bring anybody over, and there's no way back. I been lookin' for more years than I can count."

"I'll find him and take him back. You, too, if you'll help."

"You know a way back?"

"Not right now, but I know where several should be. We've got to work fast. There isn't much time." Raglan explained what Kawasi had told him.

"Know all about it. That's what stuck me at first. Same thing happened right after I come through. I kep' tryin'. Done me no good." He cocked his head to one side. "Know Kawasi, do you?"

"I do, and I want to take her back with me."

"Don't blame you for that. She's a fair lass, that one. Bright, too. She's got gumption."

Raglan gestured toward the door he had been about to enter. "I'm looking for a place where gold is stored. Where there's a map scratched on a gold plate."

The old man sat down on a flat rock. "How'd you know about that? I surely never told nobody, and those folks"—he jerked his head back toward the pueblo—"they never come over here. Never come at all."

Raglan explained about the old cowboy in Flagstaff and his gold. Johnny chuckled. "Smart, that's what he was! Smart enough to take enough an' stay away."

He gestured around. "The way I figure it, this here was settled by somebody thousands of years

337

back. No kin to them. No kin to anybody around now, the way I see it. They had gold and lots of it. There's several tons of it, near as I can calc'late. I seen that map you speak of—never saw it as a map. Figured it to be the plan of something."

Raglan was puzzled. "That outfit you got on? Looks like it had been tailored for you."

"Was. Tailored by me. By my ownself for me. Back when I was a youngster, Pa put me to work with a tailor. Wishful of me learnin' a trade. I stuck it for three year, from time I was twelve to 'most sixteen. Then I taken out for the West.

"Here a man's got nothin' but time, so I tailored myself some fancy duds." He brushed his whiskers with a hand. "Keep trimmed up, too. I remember hearin' of Englishmen stationed in the jungle somewhere an' how they always dressed for dinner, even when all alone out there. 'Morale factor,' they called it.

"Well, I done the same. Figured I'd go to pieces if I didn't. Wear tailored clothes, trim my beard, keep my places revved up an' neat."

"Places?"

Johnny chuckled. "I got a bunch of them. Hideouts. Scattered around, so's I don't make the same trail all the time. A man always goes the same way an' somebody smartens to where he lives. I got smoked an' dried meat in all of them. Dried fruit, too, nuts an' seeds I c'lect. Nobody knows where those places are but me, so's nobody can tell nobody else. Sure as you tell somethin' to one person, they will tell somebody else, an' warn them not to tell. Of course, they do."

"The man I'm looking for is called Erik Hokart. They've had him several days. Do you know anything about the Forbidden?"

"No, an' nobody else does. Maybe The Hand knows, an' maybe Zipacna."

"You're wearing a pistol?"

"Black powder. Make my own. Been doin' it for years, an' right now I'd say I make as good a black powder as can be made."

"You've tangled with the Varanel?"

Johnny spat into the sand. "That I have! Three, four times. They leave me alone now, but don't you take them light. They've got some sort of gun—makes no sound but a sort of *thwat*, but it shoots an arrow into you.

"All it needs is a scratch an' it does you in, starts something happening inside you. I seen a wolf killed thataway and its insides was all wrong, somehow. Whatever it is, it upsets the way things work inside you.

"I seen that wolf shot an' they didn't know I was anywhere about. I laid there a-watchin' it. Wolf went down. Struggled a mite, then lay still. Tongue hangin' out, pantin' like. Several times it tried to get up an' couldn't.

"Looks like whatever it is sort of takes their strength so's they can't move nor fight. Then they die."

"Something that affects the metabolism? The cell structure, maybe?"

"I wouldn't know about that. I only know what I seen. Believe you me, I stay clear of those fellers, an' you best do the same. If you run into them, don't waste your time. Kill them quick or they'll nail you."

"You have a rifle?"

"A Sharps Big Fifty. Brass ca'tridges. Load 'em myself. Make my own powder and shot. Back up yonder I've got me a lead mine that's almost half-silver. Somethin' else in there, too. Zinc, I reckon."

"Why did you advise me not to go in there?"

"Lizards! Damn big ones! Get to be eight, ten feet long an' they can run down a deer in fifty yards. Don't seem to try if its further. They'll weigh three to five hundred pounds, I reckon."

"Like the Komodo lizards," Mike suggested. Then, as the old man looked blank, he added, "Komodo is an island in the East Indies. Indonesia, they call it now. They find lizards of that size on Komodo and the island of Flores, across the strait. They are meat eaters and they'll run down a horse in a short distance."

"Sounds like 'em. Set up on their hind ends an' look around. Make almost no sound in the brush." He gestured. "Some of 'em live in these ruins."

The old man stood up. "Come along. I'll show you where the gold is. Got no use for it, m'self. Cached some here an' there in case I got a chance to get back. Figured I'd need it over yonder."

He looked suddenly wistful. "Like to go back.

Kinda would. Doubt if there's anybody knows me back yonder now, with all the years between.

"Healthy here. Never had a cold since I come over. I don't see many folks, an' maybe that's the reason, but I'm more'n ninety year old now, I reckon. Ain't been sick a day since I come over.

"Hoss died. That was a pity. Lived to be almost forty, then just died on me. Old age, I reckon." He peered at Raglan. "Them automobiles now? Did they ever catch on?"

"They're all over the place now. They paved the roads for them."

"Paved? That's kinda hard on the hosses, aint it?"

"You don't see many horses except on ranches. Even there they use pickups and Jeeps more than horses."

"I'll be damned. What's them 'pickups'?"

"A kind of car with a place behind the driver to carry supplies, bales of hay, whatever."

Johnny led the way down among the ruins, and then at last to another tall, narrow door. Stopping, the old man got out a stub of candle. "We'll need some light. Dark in there."

"Keep it. I've got a flashlight." He flashed the beam into the dark opening, and gasped.

The gold was there, half-covered by the accumulated dust of years, but gleaming bright beneath the powdery film. The room was a sort of vault, its sides honeycombed with openings, each one stacked with discs of gold such as the old cowboy had mentioned. In the very center of the room, above a heap of the discs, was a pillar. On it was the gold plaque. He stepped closer, studying it.

The Forbidden was, literally, a maze. It was a labyrinthine tangle of rooms, passages, and columned halls, and at the center a court, a group of larger rooms. For a moment he studied the design. It was a challenge, but a challenge to which he would not have the time to respond. Somewhere, in all that insane spider web of rooms and passages was Erik, and he must be found. There were also the rooms of death, which must be avoided. Suddenly, something about the shape and design began to seem familiar. There was something about it. . . .

He shook his head. Whatever it was would not come to mind now. He indicated the diagram of the maze. "Johnny, I've got to get in there and get out, with Erik."

"You ain't got a prayer. That place is guarded by the Varanel an' the Lords of Shibalba. Even if you could figure a way in and a way to get out."

Raglan continued to study the maze. In his wandering about, solving mysteries and puzzles, he had often walked mazes, including those in England at Hampton Court and Longleat, but there were dozens of others, some only in patterns on the floors of cathedrals such as Chartres, Amiens, and Ely.

"It ain't only that," Johnny warned. "This here country is right deceivin'. Have to get used to it. Distances ain't what they seem, nor heights, either. You got to develop a new set of senses to handle it."

"I won't have time, Johnny. Whatever is done must be done in the next few hours." Then he added, "I've got a way in. I've got a friend inside there."

"That's another thing. You just think you got a friend, if he's one of them. Kawasi's folks, they're different. They are good folks, mostly. But them down there? Don't you trust any of them. Lyin' comes natural to them. So does deceit. Do it for the fun of it. Lead you right into a trap if they can. They would rather see you fail than succeed, no matter what you're doin'. I've had truck with 'em. Know what I'm talkin' about. Most of 'em would risk their own necks just to betray some-body. They thrive on betrayal an' deceit.

"When the Anasazi fled this place they fled that sort of thing, leaving a world that was evil. Don't you think there's exceptions. Any one of them down there would go out of his way just to trick you into injury or death, and then set by and watch you suffer."

Raglan continued to study the plaque, but he was wondering now about Tazzoc. He remem-bered the peculiar gleam in Tazzoc's eyes when he spoke of the rooms that were traps. Tazzoc had seemed to relish the idea.

"They'll even do it to each other. Only thing I can't figure is how they've lasted this long, mean as they are."

Tazzoc had seemed sincere, but was he? Was

the cloak only a trick to get him inside? To have him captured? Or would Tazzoc wait and let him be trapped in one of the death rooms? But he had promised to help. Tazzoc had wanted his Archives appreciated and, if possible, saved.

Mike had no choice. It was his only way inside and he must take it, then play it by ear, and handle each emergency as it arose. Well, he had experience at that, and he had been warned.

"I'm going in, Johnny, and I'm going to bring Erik out, no matter what happens." He turned to Johnny. "How long will it take to get down there?"

"Couple of hours. Only the last few minutes will worry you."

Raglan studied the trail that seemed to end in a blank wall. That made no sense unless it was some kind of an entrance. Because this path was shown on the design did not mean it was visible on the ground, only that it was there, and it led to something.

Johnny glanced around, then said, "Does a body good, talkin' to somebody speaks his language. I taught Kawasi an' some others. Convinced 'em they'd need to know it, but part was pure selfishness. I was lonely, like. That Kawasi now, hungry to know. Ever since she was a little tyke, always askin' questions about how we live, think, work, all that kind of stuff. Zipacna was the same."

"Zipacna?"

"Oh, sure! He lived amongst them! Acted like he was one of them but he was against 'em from the start. I'd not take any of them to my places.

Met 'em in the woods, like. Zipacna, he was always after me to take him to where I lived. Finally I got suspicious. Seemed unnatural he'd persist. All the time he was a traitor. His mother was a witchwoman. So he speaks English better'n anybody, better even than Kawasi, because he's been over to the other side."

"You're sure?"

"Been over several times. Brought back some doodads, too. Some folks think he hisself is The Hand."

As the old man rambled on, Raglan listened with only half his attention. He was concentrating on the diagram on the gold plaque.

Most of it represented the Forbidden area, yet there were other diagrams in the corners of the plaque, and one seemed to be this ruin where he stood.

Suppose there was a way to the other side from here? After all, that old cowboy could not have carried his gold very far. It had to be very heavy. Suppose somewhere among these ruins there was an opening he could use?

"Johnny? What about this place? Was there ever an opening from here?"

"Never heard of it. But then, those folks over at the pueblo, they never come here. They turn their heads away from this place. Even Kawasi."

He swept a hand. "All this here is *old!* Older than them pyramids you got back yonder. There's a place over there"—he pointed—"a hall, sort of, lined with figures of animals, deer, buffalo, lla-

345

mas, all sorts of animals, an' at the head of the hall the biggest statue of a jaguar anybody ever did see. Ever' one of them is carved an' polished until they shine.

"Beautiful, that's what they are! But no figures of man or woman!"

"Men did not think of themselves or their women as beautiful. They could see the symmetry and the beautiful movements of animals, but their own bodies seemed clumsy by comparison. Possibly that's why so many primitive peoples worshipped animals, because of their beauty, either sitting still or in movement.

"Early man was awkward by comparison, and ill-formed, too. It needed years of breeding and the desire for beauty before man began to achieve it."

Johnny stood up again. "You figure to do all you say, you better have at it. You ain't got much time." He paused, looking around. "Maybe I better come with you. Maybe I better."

XXXV

DOWN THE MOUNTAINSIDE lay the collapsed ruins of what had been a mighty city, a fortress, or whatever it was. Only a chaotic mass of tumbled stone remained. Fallen columns, broken statues, ruined walls, and cavernous black openings that gaped threateningly on every side. Mike Raglan led the way, threading a path through the tangle, wary always of enemies.

Below them and far off he could see the vast black bulk of the Forbidden.

"Basalt," Johnny said. "Volcanic rock like you see in lava-flows out west. Shaped and polished like glass. God only knows who built it, but I doubt any human did. No windows, no doors— only that gate and the small door beside it."

"There might be one where that path ends."

"Don't count on it."

"Johnny? If you want in this, get back up that trail somewhere with that Sharps and be ready. When I come, I'll likely come fast."

"How you goin' to find him? Take an army a month to search out all those passages and rooms, if what we saw back yonder was a map."

"I've already got an idea." Mike paused, studying the ruins scattered along the slope before him. He wondered what had destroyed the original structures. The passing of ages had done their work, but there must have been some cataclysm, some frightful disaster that brought doom to all who lived here.

"Do the people of the pueblos never come here?"

"Them? No, they don't. They pay strict mind to their own affairs. If they are curious they surely don't show it. Mostly they won't even talk of this place, but they've not seen it, either. There's nothing lives here they want, and those big lizards have killed all that lived here. Now they go afield to hunt theirselves."

347

"Did you say you've killed them?"

"Time or two. They don't die easy, Raglan. They surely don't. You fight shy of them."

Mike eased his pack on his shoulders, shifting the straps. They walked on, and Johnny explained what he had learned about what lay below, with occasional references to Kawasi's people. "Like they lived on two islands, miles apart. There's no trading going on, no traffic back and forth. Folks down below there refuse to admit there's anybody around but themselves, whilst Kawasi's people just tend to their knitting. There have been a few clashes in the past, but The Hand never lets his people know about them, and the folks on our side usually come out losers, although The Hand has never made a direct attack on the settlements. Always on small parties out cutting timber."

From atop the pack Mike took the folded robe Tazzoc had given him and donned it; then he switched his rubber-soled shoes for moccasins like Tazzoc's. Several times during their walk he had paused to pick up bits of stone. Some he discarded, but he had been alert for what he wanted.

He found it at last, an outcropping of white chalk. At the base of the cliff he picked up a dozen fragments and put them in his pockets. Johnny watched but offered no comment.

"When I was a youngster, schools taught us mighty little, but the times were such a man just had to learn to think. There was nobody we could call on, so we just naturally solved our own problems our own way. When a different set of circumstances showed up, we just figured out how to cope. My folks made most everything they used with materials out of the woods or from hunting.

"These folks who came back over from our side, they made out. They fitted themselves into the world they found, and learned more all the time.

"If you get the idea they are like us, you'll be wrong. They are different an' they think different. Folks back to home used to talk about 'human nature.' Ain't no such thing. What they called human nature was the way they'd been taught, and they figured everybody had the same feelin's, same reactions. Well, it ain't so. Injuns had been raised different from us an' they reacted different. Over here, folks are different.

"You take them down there, for example. I think they all hate one another. Everyone seems to be secretly tryin' to figure ways to outwit his neighbor or even his brother. Lord knows there's meanness enough in our world, but to these people meanness is a way of life.

"Not Kawasi's folks. Different as day an' night. But those down yonder—don't you trust anybody. You may think this Tazzoc is on your side. Don't you believe it. He's on his own side an' nobody else's."

"He wants to save his Archives. He wants them to be used."

"Maybe. I think prob'ly he does, but that won't change him none. If he can do you in, he'll do it.

He will do it even if it hurts him. I seen it happen."

What was that Erik had said? To trust nobody? Did he know, then? Had he already discovered or perceived what people he was dealing with?

"How could such a people exist?"

"You call that existence? They are dying of their own hatred, killing themselves off with their own poison."

Johnny stopped behind a shoulder of rock where the dim trail took a sharp turn to skirt the valley below. From here the streets and alleys were plainly seen. Only a few people moved about. There seemed to be no wheeled transportation within view.

"Kawasi's folks now, they're *different*. Different from us, too. Started as a farming people and kept to it. They spend a lot of time selectin' seed. More'n we do. They see things in seed I never saw an' they discard all they don't want.

"They've learned how to use water. We waste most of the water we use on plants in the field, or did in my time. They use more plants than we do. Lots of stuff we pulled up as weeds when I was a youngster, they cultivate. All up an' down these canyons and on the mesa tops as well—they've used every bit of space. Miles of the canyon walls have been terraced for crops, an' some of them you can't even see how they got to them to plant.

"Here I am, talkin' up a storm when you got other things to think about. Trouble is, I've had nobody to talk to in a long time. I learned a bit of Kawasi's lingo but not enough.

"You be careful down there, d'you hear? I'll be yonder with my Big Fifty and ready to use it if you get out o' there."

"I'll get out."

Mike Raglan adjusted the turban and, without a glance backward, started down the path behind the brush. Right below was a place where he could walk into one of the narrower streets that would take him toward the Forbidden.

His heart was pounding and a feeling of uneasiness crept over him. He was a damned fool. He should go back up there and find a way out and get out. He was a fool to go into that maze, where every other door might be a trap.

The streets were empty. If anyone observed him, he did not see them. He walked steadily, adopting the gait of Tazzoc as well as he could. At the end of the street the enormous walls of the Forbidden loomed massive and black. Again his hand touched his pistol. If he went out, he would go fighting.

From long practice his was a photographic mind. He had begun when an apprentice magician in his boyhood, memorizing cards and where they fell, and he had used every device for improving his memory. Before him now was that map, and the inner rooms of the Forbidden were a maze through which he must find a way.

Were they watching him? Had he been betrayed? Before him loomed the giant wall, soaring high, then sloping back into a rounded roof. A massive gate to his left, and beside it the smaller door. He walked up to it and put his hand on the latch.

As he touched it he felt a chill. He was still a free man. He need go no farther. He could turn around and walk back and lie to them. He could say the door was locked and that he dare not demand its opening. He could say . . .

He would not, and he would not lie. He had come this far and he would go on, to whatever lay ahead. After all, he had never expected to live forever.

He glanced to his right. Dimly, he thought he could see the path Johnny would be watching. It led down through some wild brush and then faintly along the mountainside among the rocks. That was the way he would go if he had to escape. Not through the town, which would be a trap, but along that path.

He lifted the latch and stepped in, closing the door behind him. He was in a wide, stone-paved court, empty but for two of the Varanel who stood together some hundred and fifty feet away, near another wall. They were talking together, paying no attention to him.

Ahead of him he could see a dozen doors, and to the extreme left a narrow passage leading along one side of the main building. It was the way Tazzoc had said he should come.

Holding himself to a slow, methodical walk, he started for that place, but watched the Varanel from the corners of his eyes. They were still deep in conversation.

He walked on. It was there, not sixty feet away. He counted his steps, mouth dry. He was scared. Apprehensive, at least. Now they had stopped talking and both were looking at him.

Watching him? No, just looking—probably so used to that robe that they scarcely saw it. He was a part of the surroundings, and he must act accordingly. The slightest wrong move and he was finished.

How could he find Erik? Capture somebody and force him to tell him? But who would know? Probably less than a dozen even knew there was a prisoner, and fewer would know where he was held.

One more step and he was past the corner and into the narrow passage. The guards had gone back to talking, and he took that step, then moved from the corner into the deeper shadow of the black wall.

He was in an arcade, a row of slender pillars on his left, a blank black wall on his right. His footsteps made faint sounds as he walked. There were doors on his right, a row of them. He ignored them and walked ahead. There was the door to the Hall of the Archives.

Tazzoc had said nobody came there. Or rarely. In the past they had come, but most had forgotten there even were any archives. And they cared less. After all, they might ask themselves, what was there to learn about such a closed society?

He glanced back. No one. He took the last step and reached the faded green door. His hand went out for the latch.

A sound behind him, a word of objection, or so it sounded.

He turned sharply around. It was a small man with thick gray hair and a thin, scrawny neck. The man shook his head, gesturing him away. Then slowly, he spoke, as if feeling for words long unfamiliar. "Do not. They know you come."

"Thank you, but I must go. A friend is a prisoner."

The small man furrowed his brow, trying to understand, then shook his head but added, " 'Thank you' is good. Once . . . long time back, we speak so. No more. Nothing is *thank you* now."

Raglan wanted him to understand. He held his wrists together as if bound. "My friend is a prisoner within. He must be freed."

The man seemed to grasp the idea but shook his head. "No. Tohil will have him. He will be thrown upon the Tongue."

What he meant Raglan could not imagine, yet the old man sounded friendly and he was in no position to doubt. "You speak my language?" he asked.

"I am Camha. When young I was one who learned. The Varanel had seized a man to question, a man from your side, and he gave answers to our talking. It was decided some should learn your speak to cross over. We wished things you possessed and we did not. Five were trained. Then a decision was made. No go. Stay."

He paused, blinking his eyes slowly. "Amongst us we speak often to keep alive our learning. We have books. We read, and your land is good. We think maybe better than here. Then our books are seized and we are forbidden to speak of your world." He looked off down the long arcade. "Once to read of great books is to taste what is never forgotten."

"And do you not have books?"

"Only the word of The Hand. Only what is told us to read."

"Do you know what this place is? The Hall of Archives?"

"It is forbidden. We who know of it do not speak of it. We only wish to look, to see."

"Do you know Tazzoc?"

"I know, but do not speak. We walk afar from each other for fear."

"The Hand has great power."

Camha bobbed his head. "It is true."

"We have a saying that power corrupts."

"It does. Power not only corrupts he who wields the power but those who submit to it. Those who grovel at the feet of power betray their fellows to hide themselves behind the cloak of submission. It is an evil thing."

"You wish to go in with me? To the Hall of Archives?"

Camha shivered. "I have fear. I am an old man. My bones are weak. I have an old wife whom I love and children whom I love, although they ignore me. They fear I am tainted and I am notseen. Yet I love them still. I understand, and forgive.

"To enter there? Ah, if I could go and come! I cannot. My old woman would be alone then, and it is too late for us to be alone. I must forget the love of learning and remember she who has walked beside me this long time."

Camha looked into Raglan's eyes. "They would destroy that, also, but love is with us still, here and there. The Hand wishes no loyalty but to him. Such rulers begin by demanding a little and end by demanding all.

"Go in, and if you escape, bring something out to share. To share with anybody, but to share. Knowledge was not meant to be locked behind doors. It breathes best in the open air where all men can inhale its essence."

He turned away, then stopped again. "You know what is a maze? It is a maze in there, and if the way is not known, you will surely die. It has been said, by someone, that one should keep to the left. I do not know this to be true. That, too, could be a trick, a device to lure one on in confidence, only to betray.

"We are betrayers all. Perhaps even I. I am no longer sure. Go, find your way. We have talked this little time, one to another. It has been good, very good! I go."

Who was Camha? He had entry to the Forbidden. He knew where the Hall of Archives was, and he had spoken well.

Again Raglan was alone beside the green door. What awaited him within? Would he find Tazzoc there? Or would the Varanel be waiting? Or the Lords of Shibalba?

Erik would be guarded. Or would they believe guards essential in such a place? If he was guarded, the guards themselves might indicate his place of imprisonment.

This Hall of Archives had once been a temple, and that needed thinking about. A place of worship? Or simply the place from which an oracle had spoken? From which The Voice used to speak?

That would imply there must be a secret place where The Voice might be, and from which it might speak. In his travels he had visited other such places and there had been a hidden place from which the oracle spoke.

This Voice, too, had faded out. Its clear message became mere gibberish, like that of the Delphic Oracle and others. But the priests of gods or oracles do not willingly relinquish the power The Voice provides. There had been cases where the priests usurped the power and spoke for The Voice, pretending to be it.

Hence there had to be a place from which they could speak. If he could find that place, he might reactivate The Voice.

The Hand did not come to the Hall of Archives, and according to Tazzoc, no others came.

Hence, the place of the oracle might have, over many years, been forgotten.

Surely, The Voice must not only have had a secret compartment from which it spoke, but also a way to reach that compartment unseen.

A passage that might go right to the apartments of The Hand? A way to discover where Erik was kept?

Someone had said—perhaps it had been Kawasi—that The Hand knew what people thought and said. Even her people knew of speaking tubes, so certainly the older people would know of them as well.

First, to enter the Hall of Archives. He dropped his hand again to the latch. He opened the door and stepped inside. The heavy door closed behind him.

It was a harsh, cold, definite sound. The door shut hard, and something clicked in its lock.

He was inside. Would he ever get out?

XXXVI

THE DOOR BY which he entered opened on the left of the main hall, a vast space beneath a vaulted ceiling. The floor of the central hall lay some fifty feet lower than the level at which he entered, and on a dais approximately a hundred feet away was a massive table in front of three high-backed chairs. The space in the hall before them was empty.

On either side of that space and sloping back to

358

the wall was a series of tiers, resembling bleachers. These were banks of shelves of books, each one bound top and bottom with slabs of thin wood, like Tibetan books. Before each line of shelves was a walk, and at intervals steps leading to the tiers above and below.

Raglan's eyes searched the room. He saw no one. Behind the three chairs was a concave latticed wall.

On his right a stair led down to the main hall, with a line of massive columns, one to every other tier, each at least four feet in diameter at bottom, tapering as they rose.

At some time in the distant past ceremonies must have been held here, and the great doors would have been thrown open for processions to enter and approach the dais.

Once more his eyes swept, then searched, the vast hall. Of course, something or someone might be hiding down there among the shelves of books, or might be watching from behind the lattice of that concave wall.

Somewhere here were the maps he wished to see, perhaps to find some clue to the place where Erik was held.

This hall, vast as it was, could be no more than a mere corner of the huge building that was the Forbidden, and the maze, if it was truly such, lay outside this room. Yet the place where he now stood gave him a sense of great age.

Tilting his head back, he looked up at the vast space above him. Around the hall, above the tiers of shelves, there were balconies. No doubt it would have been from those balconies that the Lords of Shibalba looked down upon the processions below.

He was not afraid, he told himself. What he felt was awe, but there was something else, too—some uneasiness such as he had never felt before.

"The Archives of my people." The voice came from behind him and he almost jumped, he was so startled. He fought down the urge to turn quickly. It was Tazzoc.

"They are impressive." Raglan nodded toward them. "Those I see seem to be on some sort of paper. I expected clay or stone."

"Those are stored below, in another room even larger than this." Tazzoc paused. "Do you have anything to compare?"

"Oh, yes! We have the Library of Congress, and many university and public libraries in my country, but other countries have vast libraries, too."

"On *stone?* Or *clay?*"

"Actually, no. Most of those are in museums where scholars may have access to them, but many have been copied and are available in easily held books or on tape."

"Tape?"

"A mechanical means of recording books and oral transcriptions. It enables a library such as this to be stored in a much smaller space."

Tazzoc nodded. "There is a tale—I cannot speak for its truth—that we had such devices many years ago, and that The Hand has them now. It is also said that fresh ones are constantly made to enable him to see whatever he wishes of our activities without leaving the Forbidden."

"And you do not know where he lives?"

Tazzoc gestured. "Somewhere in there, at the center of what you call a maze. It is in there your friend will be. Somewhere near the center."

"You spoke of maps? Of plans?"

Tazzoc led the way, walking quickly along the face of one tier of shelves. Raglan could see that each shelf held stacks of books tied with string. The wooden backs were inscribed with characters.

Turning suddenly, Tazzoc climbed a steep stair, passing several tiers of shelves, and then in a back corner he indicated a row of shelves. "It is here."

"Tazzoc? If we come out of this, there will be a place for you in our world if you wish to go. If not, I believe meetings could be arranged with our scholars. They would be fascinated by your Archives, and you would have a place of honor among them. Above all, copies of your Archives could be made so they would last forever."

"I would like that." There was pathos in his voice. "Often I am lonely. There is a need to talk, to share thoughts, to learn what others think. Here, I have only the Archives."

Raglan lifted a book from the shelf and carefully took off the wooden slab that covered it. The thick paper, not unlike papyrus, was covered with characters. He put it aside and opened out the chart that followed.

The making of maps and plans must have long preceded what man conceived of as civilization, for the finding of places, the returning to them, or the giving of directions to springs or rivers must have begun shortly after man first began to wander the land. The Egyptians had made a god of Khonsa, the maker of plans, and Raglan had once been permitted to examine the Turin Papyrus, dating from 1320 B.C. which located an Egyptian gold mine. The Romans had drawn careful road maps for the use of their legions or the couriers who followed them.

The first map was a remarkably clear rendition of the area around the Forbidden. The mountains from which he had come and where the Anasazi had rebuilt their world were indicated only by some jagged lines, although at one point there was a crowded area of squares, rectangles, and small circles that must indicate the ruin he had visited. Near this place was a remarkably well drawn picture of a giant lizard. Tazzoc disappeared into the lower areas and Raglan turned to the shelves. Swiftly, he checked book after book, searching for the plan of the Forbidden. Tazzoc had assured him it was here, although he had not seen it in years. When he reached the very lowest shelf he found it, a larger, flatter book.

Dusty and old, it had probably not been examined in many years. The top of the tier of shelves on the level below was over waist-high and formed a convenient desk for opening the books. With extreme care he undid the knots that held the pages together, then lifted off the thin slab of wood that was its top. Unfolding the crackling paper, he spread out the plan.

Remember, he warned himself, you are dealing with an alien mind. Yet the plan before him had been carefully drawn, possibly by the very architect, if such there had been, who designed the building.

There was a maze, and, a little back of center, a rectangle that indicated what was probably the focal point, the dwelling and executive mansion of The Hand. Nearby was another area of six rooms of equal size which might be cells for prisoners, and beside them a larger space that might be a guardroom.

The Hand's area, if such it was, was not diagrammed. No rooms were indicated. Deliberately, no doubt, his area remained a mystery.

Accustomed to study, Raglan had given the map a quick once-over, and now he began to check details. In the left-hand lower corner was an area that had to be the Hall of Archives; in the right-hand corner opposite, an area not quite so large that seemed to be the quarters of the Varanel. Between the two the great gates opened into a court and, beyond it was the entrance to the maze.

The maze was not simply a winding passage but halls, between long lines of rooms. Some of these would be the death traps, but which ones?

Was there any indication on the plans? Here and there were minute notations, but in characters he did not comprehend. Surely, the trapped rooms would be indicated on this plan, and even though he did not know the language, each trap must be indicated by a similar character. Within a few minutes he had noted twenty-six rooms marked by the same figure. Two were even side by side.

A quick scanning on the design showed no other figure that marked more than two rooms, and that only in one case. Yet how to remember which rooms were the ones marked? He ran his eyes along the hallways, noting the number of rooms. He glanced again at the map, then looked more carefully. This was a plan, not necessarily the one from which the structure had been built, but a plan as it must have been on completion. Of course, it would have been altered since, in which case all bets were off.

But . . . Puzzled, he studied the map again. In those rooms marked by the figure he suspected to indicate the traps, there was something else. Something just inside the door. . . .

Time was passing, and he had no time. Worried, he studied the plans anew. It seemed that the floor inside the trap rooms fell steeply away in a sort of ramp. Anyone stepping in would step down. . . ?

No steps, just a short, steep ramp by the looks of it. A slippery ramp, perhaps? And the heavy door closing behind him? No chance to turn quickly and get out, nothing against which to brace himself to push against the door.

Simple, but effective. If one glimpsed the fact that he was entering a trap, there was no effective way to escape it. Raglan felt a chill. What was he getting into, anyway?

Getting into? He was already in. Now to get Erik and get out.

And who was it he must avoid?

Zipacna, a man he had not seen, a tall man, a strong man, a man to be avoided at all costs.

Folding the map, he returned it and retied the strings, replacing the book upon its shelf.

But what was *that*?

A smaller map had fallen to the floor. He stooped to pick it up, then heard someone coming. Those footsteps were not Tazzoc's. He dropped to his knees and, still gripping the map, flattened himself out on an almost empty lower shelf.

Someone was coming. Somebody who paused, maybe looking around, then came on. Coming his way. His hand went to his waistband, and he stayed, listening.

The footsteps came on, paused. Sandaled feet, a robe of fine material. Then the feet moved on. There was a rustling. After a moment there was a voice, a commanding voice.

"Tazzoc!" Words followed, but he could understand nothing. From a distance Tazzoc was replying, quietly, submissively. There were moments of conversation and then, after a few minutes, a door opened and closed.

Raglan lay perfectly still. Who had gone? Was it Tazzoc or the other?

Minutes passed until he heard footsteps again.

This time he recognized the step. It was Tazzoc. Raglan slid out of his hiding place.

"You are here! I was afraid, terribly afraid!"

"Who was it?"

"It was Zipacna. He never comes here, so why did he come today?" Tazzoc was frightened. His hands shook, and he kept looking around. "You must go! Now! I cannot risk it! If you should be found here I would be ruined! Destroyed! Please, please, go now! At once!"

"I am going, but you know nothing, have seen nothing." Turning, Raglan walked swiftly away, then ran up the stairs to another level, then still another. Light fell from a narrow window behind a balcony. Pausing, he looked at the map that had fallen from the book.

It was very old. Undoubtedly it had some connection with the map of the Forbidden or it would not have been tucked away in that book. Staring at it, he recognized nothing. Then realization came to him.

It was this room! It was the Hall of the Archives when it had been a temple, before the great structure of the Forbidden had been added. It was this room that had been the Holy of Holies.

No archives then, but rows of seats looking down on the flat rectangle below, which must have been a ceremonial center or an arena.

He must get out of here. Suppose Zipacna had seen him, and simply gone to call the Varanel? If he was to find Erik he must be moving. Yet the map in his hands gripped his attention.

There was the table with the three chairs over-looking the arena, and that latticed screen, all of stone, that stood behind it.

At a corner of the stone screen there was a part of the screen that could open, allowing passage into the area behind it, but at the back there appeared to be a passage opening into the maze, and a way through the maze to the apartments of The Hand!

Below him, in the wall, there was another opening. He went swiftly down, working his way through the shelves. Here and there were piled stacks of books, and some flat stones covered with writing. He found a door and stepped in front of it to feel for a handle or latch. Instead, the door began to swing away from him, and beyond lay a lighted passage.

Behind him, among the shelves, he heard a scurrying movement, then a sharp command. Tucking the map into his shirt front, he ducked through the door, turning left into the maze.

Quickly, he ducked into the first opening and waited, flattened against the wall, listening. His hand went to his gun, but even as it did so, he withdrew it. This was no place for a gun. The report of a heavy-caliber pistol would reverberate through all these corridors, alerting everyone. What he needed here was a knife, or simply his bare hands.

The light was vague, but there was light, al-though he could not determine the source. This had been true in the Hall of Archives as well, he now remembered, but he had given no thought to it.

He waited, listening.

Yet as he listened his mind was searching out the maze about him. He had turned left and suddenly. From here on, every turn must be carefully chosen. In such a labyrinth as this a man could lose himself forever. Even at Hampton Court in England, a much smaller maze, people often had to be escorted out.

He glanced at his watch and his stomach went sick and empty.

So much to do, and so little time!

He started forward, then shrank back. Someone was coming! Along the hall before him, someone was walking, drawing nearer with each step.

He backed into the shadows of the alcove. He had no friends here, and death lay all about him.

Yet if death was to come now, it must be a silent death, quick, with no warning. By now the Varanel would be searching. By now they would expect an interloper.

He waited, poised and ready.

———— XXXVII ————

A FAINT PERFUME, an essence he could not identify, a light step, and a rustle of garments.

She was slender, graceful, rather taller than he expected. In the vague light her features could not be clearly seen, but she stopped suddenly, turning her face toward the dark alcove in which he stood.

"If you will come with me?"

His left hand went into his pocket, feeling for the chalk he had put there. "At some other time," he suggested, listening to see if others followed her, but hearing no sound.

"But I can take you where you wish to go." Her tone was persuasive. "It will be easier if you are guided." She put out a hand toward him. "I wish to help."

"No doubt, but I shall do better alone."

She shook her head. "Alone, you can do nothing. There are people here who would like to help."

He had stepped closer. A quick glance showed him she could be carrying no other weapons than those she was born with, which were potent indeed.

"Where would you take me?"

"To Erik. That is what you want, is it not? He is not far from here, and waiting."

"I'd be delighted to see him." With the chalk held behind him he made a scratch on the corner of the recess. "With such a lovely guide, it would be a pleasure."

She started off, and he spoke again, lying to her. "You must not walk too fast. I have a foot that is hurt."

"Oh? I am sorry."

At each turn he made a mark upon the wall until she stopped suddenly before a door. She pressed a wooden block set into the rock wall, and a door swung slowly outward. Stepping back, she smiled and gestured for him to proceed.

He smiled. "You do not know our ways. In our country the lady always goes first." He stepped back and indicated that she should precede him.

The door gaped open. She gestured toward it. He bowed, smiling. "Please?" She started toward the opening, and as her foot touched the threshold the door started to close behind her. Raglan caught her sleeve and pulled her quickly back.

She turned on him sharply, pulling her arm free. "Why? Why you do that?"

"I feared you would be crushed in the door." Should he have let her die? It was one of the trapped rooms, he was sure. "If you can take me to him, do so. If you cannot, return to those who sent you and tell them I am coming. Tell them also, if they wish people to believe the Varanel are invulnerable, not to send them against me."

"You are a fool!" she said contemptuously. "A poor fool!"

"But one who saved you from death. Do you think they would open that door for you? Have they ever opened one for anyone?"

She stared at him. "Why you do this?"

"It is a custom of my people, often called 'chivalry.' Perhaps it is a foolish custom, but it is ours. I would not like to think of you slowly dying in there, beating upon the walls with those small fists, then adding your bones to those already there."

"You are a fool." She said it but her tone was no longer so positive.

"Of course," he added, "I expect you planned on escaping after I was safely inside. I would be trapped. You would slip out before the door closed. Maybe they suggested that, but you see, they know. It cannot be done. That huge door is too heavy and there is no foothold, and no time. They were prepared for you to die with me."

She drew back from him. "It is not true."

"You know your people better than I. Possibly I am mistaken, but the impression I have is that everyone is expendable in your society. That is why it is dying."

"Dying?" Her contempt was obvious.

"Walking through your city I passed many empty buildings, many unused. Obviously the population was once greater than it is today.

"I have seen no signs of recent building. Your structures are all very old. Your world is static, and when a culture ceases to grow, it begins to decay. You could learn from the people in the mountains."

"There are no people in the mountains."

"You have been there to see?"

She shrugged. "Who wishes to go there? It is nothing but a place of barren hills."

"You are not curious?"

"What is 'curious'? I do not know it. The mountains are a bore."

"And beyond them? Beyond the desert out there?"

371

She shrugged again. "Why you speak of nothing? It is nothing out there."

"And the ruins?"

"Ruins? I know of no ruins. This where we are is Shibalba. Shibalba is all."

"And what of me? Where do I come from?"

She stared at him, disturbed and irritated. "It does not matter. You are wrong. You must not be. You do not belong among us. You do not belong anywhere."

He chuckled. "No doubt there are a lot of people who would agree with you." He was wasting time. "I am going now. Follow, if you wish. If you doubt that your people care nothing for you, enter that room again. I promise you will never come out. Or go back and tell them you have failed. That I would not follow you.'"

Leaving her, he walked swiftly away. He would try the left-hand rule. It worked in many mazes. If it worked here, well and good. If not, he must begin over again. Regardless, he must beware of a loop that would bring him back where he began.

Once, before making the next turn, he glanced back. She was still standing there, looking after him.

Keeping his left hand on the wall, he followed it into a niche and out again. As he emerged, he made a chalk mark, then hurried on, keeping in mind the map taken from the Archives. He had but one wish now: to find Erik and get out of here, to get back to his own world—preferably with Kawasi beside him.

What was it about her? Why should she, more than any girl he could remember, capture his attention? So little had passed between them; almost nothing had been said, and he had spent so little time in her company. Yet he could think of no one else. He wanted to think of no one else.

The long halls were empty. At intervals there were closed doors, opening to what he could not guess. To traps? To living quarters? To storage rooms? Shrines? Each turn he marked with chalk so he would know where he had been.

Unless someone realized what he was doing and followed, wiping out his marks.

The place had a dank, musty odor that he did not like. The light, powered by some means he could not guess, was dim, so that objects could be seen but few details were visible.

He slowed his pace. After leaving the girl who had tried to entrap him, he had seen no one. How far had he traveled, and how many turns? A dozen? Twenty? He had forgotten. His hand felt for his weapons. All were in place, and he had a feeling he would need them. His left hand on the wall, he turned again. The passage grew suddenly lighter, but here the reason was obvious. Near the top of the wall there were long, narrow windows. This then, must be an outside wall.

Those openings to the outside were at least twelve feet above his head, impossible to reach because of the sheer wall, and what lay outside one could only guess.

Pausing suddenly, he looked at the floor. Hurrying as he was, he had scarcely noticed the change in the footing, but he walked now on native rock, a dull, red rock not unlike that near the place he had come to think of as the Haunted Mesa.

Suppose, in his own world, that this was actually Erik's mesa, or close to it? Suppose there was an opening from inside here? Was that not one of the stories he had heard? That such an opening existed?

If such there was, and he could find it, what a shortcut to escape when he had found Erik! No retracing his steps, but simply to plunge through, perhaps into the kiva itself!

He paused to listen. Had he heard something? Some distant sound? Some still far-off pursuit?

He hurried on, following every twisting turn of the labyrinth, always keeping his hand on the left wall. He turned suddenly to find himself in a hall of glass! Everywhere his eyes turned there was glass. There were glass walls, mirrors, walls he could see through to other glass walls beyond them. Now he must remember not to think he saw an opening, but always to keep his hand on that glass wall.

His sense of direction, if he possessed such a thing, was completely gone. The convoluted twistings and turnings of the maze had taken care of that, and now all he had about him was glass. He remembered that when he was a boy working with the carnivals, there had often been sideshows with glass houses, and he had had to learn the way of getting in and out. Was this the same?

He moved on, keeping his hand on the glass wall. He started forward and immediately smashed hard into glass. Keeping his hand on the glass, he turned more to the right. Again he smashed into glass.

How could that be? He stood still and let his left hand follow the glass around. Finally, he found the opening and moved cautiously forward. He managed only a few feet and came up against glass again. Frustrated, he started to turn sharply away and for a moment lifted his left hand.

Quickly, he put it back. In the same place? How could he know? And supposing some of these glass walls revolved? Suppose it was so arranged that the pressure of his step would make a sheet of plate glass swing around to cut him off?

Cautiously, he moved on, slowly feeling his way along. At times he closed his eyes, and it was easier that way, for whatever he saw was deceptive.

Was he going in a circle? There was nothing with which to mark his progress, as the chalk did not seem to work on the glass. Whether it was something to do with the chalk itself or the way the glass had been treated, the chalk would leave no mark.

He turned and turned again, his fingers following the wall, and suddenly it came to an edge. He felt around it. There was a mirror opposite him in which he could see himself and all the glass behind him, but on his left there was an opening back into the maze.

Pausing in the shadows of the door he consulted the old map. The blank wall before him should be the place of The Hand. To his right and some thirty feet away was another passage, and the doors to the six cells, if they were such, opened off that passage. There, too, was the guardroom.

He had until now been impossibly lucky. His quick study of the map and some slight knowledge of mazes had helped. The maze, after all, seemed quite simple. Yet what if he had not seen the map beforehand, and had not held to the left-hand rule?

He could easily have spent days wandering in the glass maze alone, to say nothing of what had gone before. There were, he recalled, several trapped rooms in this area, and although there had been no such indications on any one of the cells, a trap might exist there, also.

Suddenly, he tilted the old map, squinting his eyes to see. There, just around the corner and inside The Hand's quarters, there was something. The drawing had grown almost illegible in places and he could not quite make out what was indicated. Some sort of passage or tunnel, or at least a door.

He folded the map, touched his tongue to dry lips, and stepped into the open.

Nothing . . .

He glanced both ways again, then turned to the right and walked to the corner.

He turned, and found himself facing a Varanel! The guard saw him at the same instant and opened his mouth to shout. Mike Raglan had no time to think, to plan, to consider. He lowered the boom.

He struck, straight from the shoulder with his weight behind it. The Varanel had automatically stepped toward him and caught the punch coming in. It landed right on the side of his chin, with his mouth open, and the jaw crumpled under Raglan's fist.

The Varanel went down hard, dropping his wand or whatever it was. Raglan stepped over him, his foot coming down hard on the tube, for such it seemed to be. Something in it broke and crumpled under his foot, and then Raglan was crossing the space to the doors of the cells. He was running when he reached the door. He grasped the handle to open the door but nothing happened. He spoke Erik's name, listening for a response.

There was none. He turned and jerked open the next door and was staring into the eyes of four Varanel grouped around a table.

One of them, obviously an officer, reacted quickly. His command, whatever it meant, was directed at Raglan. He spoke quickly, sharply. It was obvious the idea that Raglan might not obey was completely beyond his comprehension.

Raglan realized this at the same instant that he saw, hanging on a hook just inside the guardroom door, a ring with several large keys. Reaching up, he took the keys, then stepped back and pulled the door shut.

There was a shout from within but he had already turned away.

There was a narrow passage alongside the guard-room and he stepped into it, running lightly until he faced two doors, one on either side. He moved quickly to the one on his left, thrust the key home, and turned it.

The door came open under his hand but he did not enter. He reached for his flashlight and shot the straight golden beam into the darkness.

On the floor, apparently unconscious, lay Erik Hokart.

At Raglan's feet there was a small ramp. Behind him the door was swinging slowly shut.

———— XXXVIII ————

RAGLAN STEPPED BACK quickly, but in the moment the heavy door swung shut, Erik's eyes opened and looked straight into his. Then the door closed and Raglan stood alone in the passage.

There was a rush of feet behind him and Raglan turned swiftly, drawing his pistol as he turned.

The nearest man was not ten feet away. Lifting his left arm as if to ward off a blow, Raglan fired from under the elbow.

In the rock-walled passage the gun boomed like a cannon, and the bullet caught the charging Varanel in the chest. Whatever armor he might be wearing under that blue jerkin was no defense against the .357.

Raglan fired again, and a second man clutched his stomach and plunged face downward on the floor.

Shocked, the others halted, then scrambled to run, horrified by this unexpected resistance. For so long they had believed themselves invincible and invulnerable, and now two men had been struck down in seconds. The first was dead, the other screaming. Brave though they might be, nothing in their life experience had prepared them for this, but Raglan knew that once the shock was over they would return.

Swiftly, Raglan stooped and caught the dead man by the collar. Again he opened the massive door, but this time he dragged the Varanel's body into the opening to prevent the closing of the door. Stepping over the body, Raglan ran down to where Erik was struggling to rise.

Grasping his arm, Raglan wheeled toward the door, half-dragging Erik behind him. Somebody was outside, trying to pull the dead Varanel from the opening. Letting go of Erik, Raglan leaped over the body, and as the man outside dropped the dead man's foot and reached for a weapon, Raglan drove the muzzle of the heavy gun into the man's face.

The Varanel fell backward, rolled over, and lunged to escape. Raglan reached back, caught Erik's hand, and pulled him through the door.

"Can you walk?"

Erik nodded, but his weakness was obvious.

His face was ghastly, and there were bruises as from a beating.

For an instant Mike glanced left to right. On the left lay the maze from which he had emerged, a death trap for a man in a hurry pursued by men who knew the maze. To the right the passage went straight for some fifty feet and then curved away out of sight. What lay beyond he had no idea.

Directly opposite was a door to what he believed was the quarters of The Hand. Gun in hand, he pressed the wooden block imbedded in the stone, and surprisingly, this door, too, swung open. Beyond was a lighted entrance and a screen before a door that looked to be carved from ivory. Raglan stepped through the door, Erik following. Behind them the door swung shut.

Almost instantly a voice boomed out, shouting harsh commands in a language neither understood.

Ducking around the screen they found themselves in a sort of foyer, facing a concave wall in which there were four tall, narrow doors, two on each side of a gigantic figure of a leaping jaguar carved from black basalt.

Frozen in its leap, jaws agape, revealing very real teeth and claws distended. Raglan was appalled and amazed by as frightening a piece of sculpture as he had ever seen. It was awesome, and splendid as well.

Again the voice boomed out, obviously commanding them to leave.

Raglan glanced at Erik. "Are you all right? Can you make it?"

"Go ahead. I'll try."

Four doors? He tried to remember his map but did not recall anything such as this. In fact, there had been no details of these apartments, if such they could be called. Were these doors traps as well? Obviously at least one of them was not, but which one?

Raglan dropped to his heels to examine the doors as well as the floor. One door had to be used more than the others—perhaps even two doors. If there was a trap here, that door would show the least use.

The building was very ancient and here, as in some of the castles and cathedrals of Europe, the stone itself was worn by the passage of feet. Raglan stood up and pressed the block beside a door. It swung slowly open.

Beyond was light, and they walked through, Mike Raglan, gun in hand. What lay beyond he did not know, but what he wanted now was a way out.

An angry voice boomed at them again, but this time there was a tinge of hysteria.

"What is it?" Erik whispered. "Can that be a man's voice?"

"Speaking through some kind of a tube or trumpet," Raglan suggested. "I doubt if anyone has ever refused to obey its commands before."

Then, surprised, Raglan looked at Erik. "You

381

mean you have not seen The Hand? I thought you would have been interviewed by him?"

"It was the one called Zipacna. From what I heard, The Hand appears to no one."

They stood now in a vast domed room. Facing them was a stone wall, not quite waist-high. Beyond it was a vast gulf of emptiness, and beyond that the gigantic head of what must be an idol with bulging eyes, fat cheeks, and a gaping mouth. A tongue was thrust from that mouth, and the tongue was hinged.

"It's like Baal, the god the Carthaginians worshipped. They sacrificed children to him—often as many as five hundred at a time.

"Fires burned in the belly of the monster and the sacrifices were thrown on the tongue, which they tilted back on hinges and dropped the children into the fires."

This was a nightmare from which Raglan dearly wished to awaken. There were doors to the right and left of the idol, and they took the one on the left, hurrying now.

The door opened onto a passage leading toward the back of the building, not where he had hoped to go. He led the way along the passage, watching for a turn. It came suddenly, and they went to the right. Now he slowed their pace. Erik, his strength weakened by who knew what privations, was making hard going of it.

Erik stopped, leaning against the wall. He shook his head. "Better go without me," he panted. "No strength."

"Take your time. We're going out, and we're going together."

From somewhere deep within the building there was a low rumble. Then the voice spoke, this time in English: "You will *die!* Now there is no escape!"

The Varanel did not seem to have followed. Were they denied entry, even in an emergency? Or was this the precinct of some other force? The Lords of Shibalba, for example?

There was no sound from around them. Raglan thought back to the map on the gold plaque, then to the other from the Archives. There seemed to have been a passage that led from this area back to the old temple that had become the Hall of Archives.

Those maps were very old. How many now knew of that tunnel? He closed his eyes, trying to recall every detail of the maps.

"Starved," Erik muttered. "Starved me."

They had to get out of here. Raglan took Erik's arm. "Come on! We've got to keep moving!"

Twice he tried doors, but each time they did not respond to the pressure of his hand upon the wooden blocks. Were these always closed? Or had they some means of locking all doors from some center of control?

Worried, he hurried on, occasionally slowing to allow Erik to catch up. They had to get out of here, and there was so little time!

Yet he saw no one, saw no sign that these passages were even in use. Suppose he encountered another maze? Or was turned back into the one from which he had so recently escaped?

On his left, he was sure, were the apartments of The Hand, but he had no business with him. The sooner they could get out, the better.

Another door on his right, and he pressed the wooden block. The door swung slowly outward. Before him were three steps down, and then a tunnel. Should he chance it?

He hesitated, not liking it. He never liked closed-in feelings, anyway, but this should lead back to the hall. The direction was right.

"Let's go!" he said and, snapping on his flashlight, led the way. No sooner did the door close behind them than he wished he hadn't. The tunnel was walled and roofed in stone, some it cut from natural rock, some fitted stones.

The air was dank, musty. Erik stumbled after him.

Red rock around him now, the tunnel hewn from solid rock. There was dust on the floor, occasional cobwebs. There was no evidence that the passage had been used in a long, long time.

Fear welled up, choking him. He stopped, fighting for control. What if there was no way out? What if this, too, was a trap? He pushed on. The air was bad and it was hot. Sweat poured down his cheeks and neck.

How far had he traveled from the Hall of Archives to where he had found Erik? He had worked through only the edge of the maze until he reached the mirrors and the glass walls, and it was hard to estimate the distance.

Erik stumbled and fell. Helping him to his feet, Mike Raglan could sense that the man was all in. His strength was gone.

"A little farther, Erik? We've got to get out of here."

"All right. Just . . . just a minute. This damned air . . ."

He straightened himself away from the wall, braced himself. "All right," he said. "I'll make it."

They started on. The narrow beam of the powerful flashlight pierced the darkness of the tunnel. He should have counted the steps. Should have made some kind of an estimate of distance.

Water dripped from the rocks overhead. They seemed to be climbing. Erik paused again, and Mike stopped, only too ready to rest. His own breath was struggling. It was the air. In this closed-in space . . . His head was aching.

Suppose the tunnel was closed at the other end? Could they ever make it back? And could they escape from the tunnel if they did? The foul air . . . They had to get out.

He started on, stumbling a little, and heard Erik coming behind him.

He fell.

For a moment, on his hands and knees, Mike stared at the damp sandstone floor. His breath was coming in great gasps; his head was heavy with a dull ache. He struggled to his feet.

Erik was leaning against the wall. His face was deathly white and he was struggling to breathe through lips turned blue.

They started on, staggering a little. Raglan's chest felt tight, constricted. He breathed with difficulty.

The tunnel curved slightly and they confronted a door. There was the wooden square. Desperately, Raglan pressed it.

Nothing happened.

Filled with panic, he pressed again and again. Nothing.

"My God!" Erik breathed.

"You'd better pray," Raglan said. "There's nothing else will get us out of here now."

He stabbed at the square again, pushing against the door with his shoulder.

It moved. Something moved! Only slightly, but still a movement. He kept a continual pressure on the wooden block while beating against the door with his shoulder. Slowly, the door opened.

"You press it," he told Erik, and lunged against the door. The crack widened, and there was light—light and air.

Leaning against the door he gasped at the fresh air, breathing deeply, then coughing.

The door opened slowly, stiffly, reluctantly. Erik stumbled past him into the space beyond.

XXXIX

THE ROOM IN which they found themselves was circular. On their right was a sort of divan about eight feet long, on the left, shelves holding a number of books of the sort seen in the Archives. Covered with dust, they showed no sign of having been disturbed for many years.

Directly before them was a rounded cubicle and, about five feet from the floor, a tube like the small end of a megaphone. Curving away on each side of the cubicle, a latticework.

They were behind the lattice screen in the Hall of Archives. This must be the place from which The Voice had once spoken.

On the left and right were steps leading down to a lower level. In the center of the room a fountain bubbled with water. Warily, Mike Raglan tasted it. The water was fresh and cold. He drank deeply, suddenly aware of how desperately thirsty he had become.

Would they guess the route he had used for escape? Did they even remember that the passage existed?

All about were evidences of a dying civilization. Suspicion and hatred, as well as denial of any existence but their own, had sapped their strength and narrowed their intellects. Certainly, the builders of this vast structure had been creative men of great power, and in control of an extensive labor force. Yet he had seen no signs of recent building or even of repair. Confined to routine tasks, the people obviously did what was necessary and no more. There had been no time to study the wide acreages of irrigation surrounding, except to note that they were green and lovely, obviously producing what was needed.

The early civilizations of the Nile, Tigris-Euphrates, and Indus Valley had all been based on irrigation. The same seemed true of the early cultures in Peru.

The descendants of the Anasazi had not only irrigated but had terraced their mountainsides, utilizing every foot of possible soil. Here in their secluded world they had hoped to remain aloof from those who followed The Hand.

"We've got to get out of here," Raglan said. "Our time's running out."

Erik straightened up. "Let's go!"

Raglan started, then stopped abruptly. From the great hall below he heard a sharp command. Glancing down through the lattice, he saw a dozen Varanel led by a tall man wearing what appeared to be a coat of mail, but a brand-new one of shimmering metallic links. One glance was all Raglan needed. This was no decadent remnant of a dying civilization. Whatever else he was, this was a man!

This had to be Zipacna.

What is there that lies within the male beast that makes him, sometimes, lust for combat? Raglan looked upon Zipacna then and saw clear his

388

destiny. All his life long, though there had been times when it was impossible, he had tried to avoid trouble, had walked wide around the possibility of it, and taken the alleys to avoid the streets where danger was. The climbing of mountains and the walking of narrow trails, or sailing rough, reef-strewn seas, had taught judgment. Growing in strength and fighting skills, he had also grown in caution and the hesitation to use the skills he knew, yet there was something in the man called Zipacna that raised his hackles.

Good sense told him to get away as fast as he could. To save himself and Erik, to find his way back and quickly, before his chance to escape was gone and his life lost here in this place. Yet his every urge drove him to shout through the megaphone, if such it was—to shout a challenge to Zipacna. He started for it, bristling, then stopped.

Stifling the urge, he said, "Let's get out of here, *fast!*"

They ran down the steps, taking the stairs on the left, closer to the wall where the old trail had been glimpsed. Perhaps there was a trail, perhaps not, but it must be tried. Pausing on the steps, he remembered he had fired two shots and shucked the empty shells, reloading the chambers.

Erik had gone before him, and suddenly he halted. Hurrying, Raglan almost ran him down. Erik was pointing.

In their path, in the dank tunnel, was one of the giant lizards.

Obviously, the beast had found some way into

the passage, and how many years it had inhabited the place was anybody's guess.

It was there, directly before them, and there was no way past it.

A moment Raglan stared, shocked and unbelieving. The creatures were amazingly quick, and its tongue was flicking, testing the air, catching the scent. The lizard knew they were fresh meat, and it indicated no sense of fear. Without doubt it had eaten men before, and had found no reason to avoid them.

"Step back, Erik." Raglan was suddenly calm. This was something he could not avoid. It must be faced here and now. As the beast stared at him, he saw its muscles gather and he fired.

The report of the .357 in the narrow passage was thunderous, but the beast was not ten feet away and its head was the obvious target. It lunged, and he fired.

Its skull burst like a dropped melon, and they rushed past it just as it exploded into death throes and raked the walls with its talons. Appalled, Erik turned to look back. "Keep going!" Raglan urged. "They're right behind us!"

His light bobbing as he ran, he now led the way up the slanting tunnel.

The floor was muddy, and there were signs that the monsters came often to this place. It was cool and dark, and no doubt it had been long since anything living was discovered here. Before them, light showed.

Mike slowed his pace. Erik caught up and said, "We don't know what's out there."

"If we're lucky, Johnny is."

"Johnny?"

Mike explained, moving forward cautiously. So far they had been lucky, very lucky, indeed. But there was little time left.

What about Kawasi?

Dared he try to return to the pueblos of the Anasazi? How far was it? And what lay between?

He flipped the switch on his flash and thrust it into his pocket.

"Somebody's coming!" Erik warned.

They had emerged on a hillside, with the black, towering bulk of the Forbidden behind them like an enormous wall of black glass. At their feet lay the merest vestige of a trail, long unused.

Below them and on their right lay the town, its even streets empty as always, its green parks, trees, and occasional pools all bright in the veiled sunlight.

Mike Raglan led the way down the path. First, to get Erik away. After all, that was why he was here, where he had never wanted to be. His thoughts returned to Zipacna. What was it about the man? Some domineering quality, quality against which he had always rebelled? What was it in him that resisted any idea of tyranny? As a boy he had always bristled when larger boys had tried to bully him or anyone near him. He had believed that the feeling had disappeared with maturity, but it had not.

Erik had paused on the low ground. The Forbidden loomed behind them, some distance off now. "I'm sorry, Raglan. I'm about done in."

Raglan turned his back on him. "Reach into my pack. There's some trail mix in there. You know— seeds, nuts, and raisins. Grab a pack, but keep going. Our time's running out."

Erik fumbled with the pack and Mike's eyes went back to the Forbidden. Men were emerging from the tunnel, men in blue: the Varanel.

He did not know their weapons' range but had no desire to risk it. From what he had seen, the range was limited, but how could he be sure? Maybe there was a different setting that would offer greater range. He started on, Erik stumbling behind him, trying to eat and run at the same time.

Now they were winding across a boulder-strewn hillside, and the blue-clad men behind them were gaining. Before them was a crest of crags, looming along the edge of what would have been called rimrock back in his country.

Erik stopped. "Go ahead, Raglan. I'm not going to make it."

Mike Raglan stopped. "You think I've come all this way for nothing? Go ahead of me, and just follow the path."

He shook several loose rounds into his side pocket, for easy access.

The clouded sunlight left no shadows on the hillside. The town lay shimmering in its vague light, and above it in the distance, at least a mile away now and probably farther, was the black awesome presence of the Forbidden.

All was green and lovely in the distance, yet the grass here was yellow and faded. Did it ever rain here? It must, yet the grass was dying, and the brush around was desert brush, not unlike that on the Haunted Mesa.

Was he close there? Was there a veil through which he might step? And what of her whom he loved? Would he see her again?

The Varanel were closing in now. Soon they would be within range of his pistol, and it had a good range. He had often done distance shooting with the magnum. It called for steadiness of hand, a good eye, but the gun was a powerful one. He stopped, waiting.

Suddenly, from up on the rimrock and some distance off there was a dull boom.

The jacket of the nearest Varanel suddenly blossomed with red. He took two forward steps and then fell, all of a piece, and face down. The big gun boomed again, and Mike saw a rock near the next man spatter broken chips under the bullet's impact.

He turned his back and walked on, following Erik. Behind him the pursuit had stopped. The rimrock was a good six hundred yards off, but at the Battle of Adobe Walls, Billy Dixon had knocked an Indian off his horse at just under a mile, with the same kind of rifle. A Mexican had done likewise during the Lincoln County War.

They were climbing steeply now. The Varanel

started again, and again the big rifle boomed. A second man fell, his neck bloody.

"We're going to make it, Erik. Johnny's up there with his buffalo gun."

"I can't leave her." Erik stopped. "Raglan, I just can't."

"Where is she? Who is she?" Mike asked, but Erik was too out of breath to answer.

Overhead a buzzard soared. One of theirs? Or one of ours? Or was there always a way for them? Mike topped a rise, looking down upon what was apparently a dried watercourse. Once there had been a river here; even the fallen trunks of great old trees were there, an occasional one still standing. It was a weird, desolate scene.

He paused beside Erik. He was looking at what lay before him, standing on the very edge of a vast desolation. What lay beyond? Were there other people? Perhaps a real civilization? Or was this all? This dreary waste stretching away to the end of time, to the end of everything?

And this was so close, so close to his world, his rich, green, wonderful world! He had never valued it so much as now.

Johnny, carrying his rifle, was coming down the mountain toward them.

How far away were they? Had they traveled in distance? In Time? He did not know. He had never known about such things. His world had been one of illusion, and the solving of easy mysteries. Of course, there had been times . . .

394

Johnny came down to them. "Raglan? Can you take us back? You said you could."

"Maybe," Mike said. "I'll try."

In the distance a finger of rock pointed at the sky. Was it the same?

He was tired, very tired. Somewhere among those distant crags was the opening to his world, and he wanted nothing so much as to be there, crawling into his own bed, to sleep, to rest. Time was short, and they had far to go.

Yet what was Time? Was it the same here as over there? Did they even measure time there? Could Time be measured?

He started on down the hill toward the long-dead forest, its bare arms entangled with other bare arms, no life, no birds, no animals, not even an insect. Nothing. What he saw was a blighted place, something struck by forces of which he knew nothing.

Now they were in the forest, only skeleton trees, twisted, agonized branches like arms writhing in a nameless torture. The only bark lay on the ground in great, ragged strips, threads trailing from it. In the dead silence, even their steps seemed to make no sound. A dead forest in a land too dry for them to rot, a place where decay seemed unknown.

Before them was the bed of a wide river, and suddenly Mike stopped. "Johnny," he whispered. "Look!"

A white stone, standing on edge, then another and another.

"A graveyard," Johnny said, awed. "Somebody was here!"

They walked nearer, and paused. Scratched on the stone was a name, below it the simple words:

BORN: 1840
DIED: 1874

On gentle feet they walked among the stones. They counted forty-one stones, all the dates in the same range of years, none earlier than 1810. The latest recorded death was 1886.

"Can't figure it," Johnny said. "These folks all in one passel, all the gravestones written in English!"

Mike Raglan pointed. "There's your answer!"

Along the bank of the dry riverbed was what remained of a steamboat.

"That will be the *Iron Mountain*. Disappeared in 1872, fifty-five people aboard."

XL

TOGETHER THEY WENT down to the bank of the dry river, following along the shore to the gangplank, its boards gray with age. The name of the steamboat was still there: *Iron Mountain*.

It was not a wreck, but had come to rest on the bottom of what must have been a flowing stream. One stack had fallen forward at some much later time, and the end of it rested on the smashed railing. Here and there a door hung on its hinges. Its almost flat bottom rested comfortably. The door to the main cabin was closed. Boats still hung from the davits.

Erik sat down on a timberhead. "I've got to rest. Sorry, Mike, but I'm all in."

"Take your time. I'm going to look around."

There was no time, but Erik could have a moment's rest while he looked about.

He opened the door to the main cabin. All was in order, yet it was obvious people had lived here. They must have stayed with the riverboat, hoping that whatever force had brought them here would take them back. One after another they must have died and been buried on the hill.

Not all of them. Forty-one graves had been counted, and if he recalled correctly there had been fifty-five passengers and crew. Such, at least, was the story. He could vouch for none of it except that the steamboat was here, as it must have remained for over one hundred years.

At first they must have suffered from shock; obviously then they had wondered what had happened, where they now were, and how to get back. No doubt there was discussion, argument, and some local exploration, limited by fear that the steamboat might be transferred back while the explorers were gone. After a while, no doubt, that possibility must have become improbable.

Slowly they adjusted, although no doubt hope remained. Some would have loved ones awaiting their arrival in St. Louis or whatever river port might have been their destination. Some were on business, some going to stations upriver, others just adventuring.

Hope must have lasted long, while they clung to the one thing familiar: the steamboat.

The main cabin had obviously become a community hall where all gathered. There were tables there, and in one corner the few books aboard had been gathered and a sort of library organized. In another corner a store had been set up for the purpose of passing out what clothing was available as what they possessed wore out. There had been cases of clothing, boots, shoes, and other articles destined for some place upstream. From a tablet on a table, Raglan could see an effort had been made to keep a list from which to compensate the owner if they ever returned.

There was no evidence of turmoil or confusion. All seemed to have proceeded in an orderly fashion and with decorum.

Yet there had been trouble, but not from among themselves. Obviously, they needed one another and reacted accordingly. The trouble had come from something outside.

Bales of cotton had been arranged around the rails, and behind one he found a dozen brass cartridge shells and a Henry rifle. Kneeling down where the marksman must have knelt, he sighted toward shore. Up there in those rocks . . .

There were dishes on the tables in the main

cabin, and there was still chopped wood alongside the fireplace.

In the pilot house he found the one skeleton, still wearing dried-out leather boots, clothing in rags.

The skeleton bore no evidence of violent death. He must have been one of the last to die, as his body remained unburied.

Johnny came up from the Texas, the officers' quarters. "Found some powder," he said. "I don't know about it."

"Probably no good any longer," Raglan waved a hand. "Pilot, I expect."

He looked around again. How must the man have felt? Yet he had stayed with his steamboat. Obviously, he or someone had maintained discipline. Some of the people had gone off exploring, trying to find where they were or some way to return.

Did they know what had happened?

"We'd better get going." Raglan gathered up a small stack of account books and one that might have been a log. "Put these in my pack. I'd like to go over them when there's time."

Erik got to his feet as they came down from the boiler deck. "Sorry. I'm played out. They didn't pay much attention to feeding me."

Mike Raglan studied the distant hills. He knew only approximately where they must go. He started off, crossing the dry riverbed on a diagonal, heading for what seemed to be a dim path as observed from the upper deck of the steamboat. Paths usually led somewhere and were always a time-saver if the direction was right. In cutting across country, a man never knew what he might encounter.

From time to time he stopped to study their back trail. There would be pursuit, of that he was sure. How soon it would begin and what form it would take he had no idea. There were Varanel ahead of them—at least the patrol he had seen near the Anasazi pueblos. Had they some means of communication? If they knew he was coming, they could set up an ambush.

Where was Kawasi? And what had happened at the pueblos?

Several times he sighted vestiges of ruins not unlike the ruins found in Arizona and New Mexico, but there was no time to stop or to collect even the simplest of artifacts for future study.

The air was very still. Uneasily, Raglan looked around. Nothing, so far as he could see, moved upon the landscape, yet he had a haunted feeling, a sense of imminent disaster. There were no clouds, only that veiled yellow sky from which he could read nothing.

Mike glanced at Johnny. "Do you feel it, too? What is it?"

Johnny shrugged. "No idea, but we better get where we're goin'."

Raglan started off again, walking swiftly. He was scared and he did not know why. There was a chill along his spine that worried him. What did his body know that he did not?

Before they reached the cliffs there was a vast

400

city of tumbled rocks. Huge boulders and slabs that had evidently fallen here in the past, unlike anything he had seen.

He led the way, following the dim, long-unused path that wound among the rocks, climbing higher and higher. Somewhere up here was where they had come through. He thought he could find the place. He hoped he could.

The trail went up steeply into the rocks and he hesitated, glancing back down the trail just covered. Somehow the air was no longer clear, and he could make out objects only as far as a few hundred yards away. From here he should have been able to see clear to the dry riverbed, but it was lost in distance. He climbed on, moving faster as he climbed farther, driven by an urgency he did not recognize. When he topped out on the ridge he waited for Erik, who was making slow time of it.

Johnny walked over to Raglan. The shrewd old eyes studied him warily. "Are we goin' to make it? I'd surely like to be among my own kind one more time. I'd like to get me a little cabin somewhere, just live out my days."

Raglan looked off to his left. She was over there somewhere, among her own people. If he took her away from all that, would she be happy? Was he vain enough to believe he could make it up to her? What right did he have to assume he could?

Erik's face was strained and pale when he came off the climb. He looked at Raglan with haunted eyes. "I'd no business getting you into this. I'd no claim on you."

"You spoke as if there was somebody with you," Raglan said.

Erik shrugged. "It was a dream. She got away, or they let her go." He sat down on a flat rock. "It was she who left me the sunflowers."

Raglan started to speak, then hesitated. Could it be that Kawasi was the one? It was Kawasi who had brought the daybook to him.

He turned abruptly. "We'll be getting on."

The path led into the rocks, up a steep trail through a narrow crack wide enough for them to move in single file. He looked back. Erik was behind him, Johnny following. He turned back, using his hands to help pull himself up. Here and there a projecting root offered a handhold, yet a subtle change had taken place.

The rocks now were weirdly shaped, looking like thick molasses frozen in movement. Once they had been molten lava. The climbers emerged suddenly on a small plateau covered with ruins, incredibly ancient. Fallen arches, tumbled columns, and long, unroofed halls, the walls covered with paintings.

The painted figures resembled some of the kachinas he had seen, but with a difference. The kachinas he had seen in the Hopi and Zuni villages, no matter how grotesque, had always seemed beneficent, but these conveyed a subtle feeling of horror, of fear. These were malevolent beings. "I'll be glad when I'm out of here," he said over his shoulder.

"Know what you mean. I lived with it for years."

Johnny paused, looking around. "Never seen anything like this. Not in all my born days. Figured I'd seen everything over here, but this here's different. This is all wrong."

Mike's eyes sought the rocks, the alleyways between the ruins. How did one get out of here? Where were they exactly? They were, he was sure, close to the point at which he had come through from the other side, but where was it? Had it been among these ruins? He remembered nothing of the kind.

"Raglan? Better decide what's next. They're comin'." Johnny pointed back down the trail. Not a half mile away the Varanel, a dozen of them, were coming out of the rocks.

Slowly Raglan looked around, trying to clear his mind of all but the immediate necessity. It was so much easier to be a follower than a leader. The responsibility could be left to another, and one had only to go along. Yet he was the leader and they trusted in him. He was the one who thought he knew the way back, but now he was near and he had no idea which way to turn. His eyes searched the rocks, trying to find some vestige of a way. The ruins invited them with numerous openings that might have been streets or passages, yet where did they lead? Were they traps? Were they to end in blind alleys? There was no time to try each one. His first decision had to be the right one.

"Johnny? Can you slow them up for me? I need some time."

Johnny walked to the rocks, looking back down the trail. "This light's deceivin', but I'll try."

He paused then and said, "Raglan? There's some of the Lords of Shibalba among them. They don't mean for us to get away."

Somewhere ahead of them, unless they had been destroyed by the people of the pueblo, was that other patrol of the Varanel. The worst of it was, he had lost track of time. There seemed nothing on which he could depend to count the hours or the days. The light varied so little. Raglan walked away among the ruins, trying to think, to find a way out. It had to be quick.

Kawasi—what of her? Could he find her again? He paused on the edge of a kiva. Here, too, the roof had fallen in like so many of those he had seen in his own world. He stared into it. No sipapu, of course, but the ventilation was the same, the construction the same. Around the inside were moving figures, or figures that seemed to move, for there was a series of them in different positions.

His thoughts were suddenly cut sharply by the boom of Johnny's Sharps Fifty. Standing on tiptoe he looked over a wall and could see a blue-clad figure lying in a deserted path. The man was obviously dead.

He looked into the kiva again. There was a window there, like the one on the Haunted Mesa, but not a window, exactly. More like one of the T-shaped doors so familiar from the ruins at Mesa

Verde. Only this door seemed to open on nothing. Or was it open? He walked closer.

This was not the way he had come. This certainly could not be the way the Poison Woman or others, including Tazzoc, had crossed to his world.

Where was Tazzoc?

He prowled among the ruins. There had to be a way, but how? Where?

If he could find the way he could send Johnny over with Erik and then he could go for Kawasi.

The Sharps boomed again.

He glanced over at Johnny. The old man looked at him, their eyes meeting. "Raglan? I can't hold 'em long. They're creepin' up on us, gettin' closer. We don't have much time."

Raglan dropped into the kiva, approaching the window. He could not see through it. Open it undoubtedly was, but here, too, what lay beyond was masked by that weird curtain of what appeared to be a thick smoke, or something akin to it.

Did he dare take a chance? He moved closer, and then, within, he saw the edge of the door slope steeply down, a smooth rock surface.

Another trap?

"Mike?" Johnny's voice was pleading. "For God's sake!"

He turned quickly. The old man was struggling to reload, and Raglan could see spots of blue darting among the rocks. He reached for his own gun, and then from behind him a voice spoke. An amused, contemptuous voice.

"I would not do that if I were you. It is too late, Mr. Raglan, much too late."

Mike turned slowly, his hair crawling at the base of his skull.

It was Zipacna.

Behind him were a half-dozen Varanel, and among them, Kawasi, obviously a prisoner.

XLI

TOO LATE?

Kawasi was a captive. If Johnny was taken he would be immediately killed, and as for Erik and himself, they would either be starving in cells or dead.

Even as Zipacna spoke, Mike Raglan knew it was too late only if he did nothing. If he was to resist, the time was now, not when he was a prisoner. He drew his pistol and fired.

Again their confidence worked for him. The great Zipacna was speaking, he who was never disobeyed. For men unaccustomed to resistance, believing themselves invulnerable, Mike's reaction was too swift. Before their minds could adjust and react, a man was down and dead, another dying, the rest scattering like sheep.

Zipacna's reaction had been swift and immediate. Even as he spoke he must have realized Raglan would resist, and his move was to save himself. Poised for instinctive reaction, Zipacna threw himself to the side and leaped for cover.

Almost as quick was Kawasi's reaction. She stepped aside and swung a hard fist to the throat of her guard. As she ducked away, Johnny was among them, swinging his clubbed rifle.

"Run!" Johnny yelled. "There's others a-comin'!"

There was an opening among the twisted, malformed lava rocks before them and Mike led the way. Down a steep chute over broken rock, and then a green terrace and a ruin, a few stunted trees. Beyond them a huge mass of rock, weirdly shaped.

The ruin offered shelter, cover of a sort. A few ruined walls, a kiva, and a roofless corridor ending in a T-shaped doorway.

It was a semicircular ruin with all the houses facing broken canyon country, somewhat like that between Navajo Mountain and the Colorado.

"Can we stop?" Erik asked. "I'd like to rest."

Once inside the ruin, Raglan paused to listen. "Take it easy," he suggested. "Johnny? Would you keep a lookout?"

Somewhere near he could hear the sound of running water. It proved to be a small stream running from under the slide-rock, a stream that had been guided away from its old bed and into a ditch. The water looked clear and fresh.

"Kawasi? Was it near here?"

She came to him. "You will go back now?"

"I must get Erik back, and Johnny." He turned to look at her. "And you, if you will come with me."

Her eyes searched his face. "You are sure? I do not know your world."

"You did not like what you saw?"

"Oh, yes! I like very much some things. Others I not—*do* not—understand."

He looked around. "Kawasi? We're near, aren't we? How do we get back?"

"It is a sometime place," she said. "I do not know all. He Who Had Magic was the one who knew, and he marked the ways he knew. I think only the door from the kiva is an always place."

"We haven't much time, Kawasi."

She led the way through the fallen walls, skirting a kiva and a round tower. She paused some distance from a T-shaped door. "It is there. Or it has been. I do not know." She looked up at him. "All this is uncertain. We are different from you, for we know our world is a sometime place, and all this where our two worlds come together and cross—all this changes. Now only the Saqua know. The People of the Fire. They come and go as they will, and sometimes people on your side believe them ghosts, or the walking dead. But they will not bother where fire is."

"I saw them once, down on Copper Canyon road. There was a bright fire on No Man's Mesa and they went toward it."

"I have seen this, too. The fire calls them back. I do not know why."

Raglan glanced toward the door. "That is where we came through? It does not seem the same."

"You will see. It is the same. You fell through the door, and got up. You came down here."

Turning, he called out. "Erik! Johnny! Come on!"

He saw them rise, saw them start toward him. Uneasily, he glanced around. The yellow sky remained the same, the green grass, the old, moss-grown stones of the ruined walls, yet something was wrong, very wrong.

Following Kawasi, he started up the narrow, grassy lane toward the T-shaped door. Behind him were Johnny and Erik.

Glancing back he saw Zipacna come from the ruins, the other Varanel coming one by one from hiding. He ran, in a stumbling run, following Kawasi. She came to the door and stopped, abruptly.

"Mike! Mike, it is not here! The opening is gone!"

He stopped beside her. If ever there had been an opening here it was gone now. Desperately, he glanced around. "Kawasi! Kawasi, there's got to be a way!"

"It is gone! We are caught!"

Johnny was loading his rifle. "If we could get to one of my places—"

"There's no chance now." He indicated more of the Varanel coming up from the trees.

"Be dark soon," Johnny said.

The Varanel were down there now, not three hundred yards away, and from where they stood there was no escape. Their little patch of ruins was all there was for them. Through a rift in the rocks he could see the valley of the Forbidden, not so far off as he had imagined. Or was it this deceiving light?

Vast, black, and ominous. At this distance it seemed much larger than he had believed. It no longer seemed so black. Was that the strange light that preceded darkness? What passed here for a setting sun? Only, no sun was visible.

"Ain't like them to attack at night," Johnny said. "We got until daybreak, if we're lucky."

"There's not that much time," Raglan said, "not if what Kawasi said was true."

"I don't know," Kawasi protested. "Only He Who Had Magic knew. Somehow he worked out the rhythm of the changes. He left writings that explained it, but I have not seen them. He said it was natural law, and only seemed unnatural because we did not understand. He said there were other such places, but they were few, and far apart. This one was all in an area of scarcely more than five of your miles. He said there were occasional openings, and they might happen just anywhere. He said our ideas of dimension and space would have to change before we understood. He said our three-dimensional world was fantasy, something we had become accustomed to and accepted as the all."

"We don't have to understand it," Erik commented. "We just have to make it work. I've an apartment in New York and that's where I'd like to be."

"We followed you, Raglan," Johnny said. "Up to you, ain't it?"

The light had grown dim. "Better gather any wood you see," Mike suggested. "We'll want a fire."

"There at the edge of the trees? Where they come down to the ruin? I saw some dead stuff over there."

As Erik and Johnny went to gather wood, Mike turned to Kawasi. "Is there any other place? I mean, it's our only chance."

"I do not know. I thought this place . . ."

"We have water and we have walls around us. If we have to make a stand, we can do it here."

Johnny and Eric returned with wood, dumping it on the ground. "There's plenty of firewood and we might be able to get away into the woods, come daylight."

Johnny glanced at Mike. "Nobody goes into the woods at night. Ain't safe. Them big lizards hunt at night, mostly."

Mike gathered twigs and bits of shredded bark. Then, powdering some of the shredded bark in his fingers, he put it in a hollow in a slab of wood. Making a bow of a curved branch and some rawhide looped about a stick, he put the end of the stick in the hollow and worked the bow back and forth to twirl the stick. Soon smoke was rising, and then a tiny flame. He brushed the burning material into the gathered bark and twigs. His fire blazed up and he added fuel.

He had an eerie sense of being watched. He turned his head suddenly.

The creature stood in the shadows beyond the ruins. It appeared to be naked, but covered with hair. It stared, and he stared back. Deliberately, he extended his hands to the fire. When he looked around, the creature was gone.

It resembled those seen that night in Copper Canyon. Like the creature who bumped into his car when answering the call of the light from No Man's Mesa.

There had been no animosity in the stare, only a kind of wonder. Or was it awe?

"Kawasi? Did you see it?"

"Yes. It was a Saqua, the hairy ones." She added, "We believe they worship fire, but do not know. Yet something about the fire attracts them."

"They know the ways to pass through to our side?"

"It is believed."

"Would they show us?"

She was aghast. "Oh, no! They are fearful things! My people fear very much! Anyway, they have no speech. Or we think they have none."

"But if they know the way?"

"You would trust them?"

He shrugged. Would he trust them? In any event, how to communicate? They certainly would not know English, if they had intelligence enough to understand anything. Were they animals or men? Even that he did not know, for, while seem-

412

ing like men, they acted like animals—and smelled like them.

"Have they ever attacked you?"

"No, but—"

"Maybe they just want to be left alone?"

Or maybe there was something else. He had extended his hands to the fire, held them there. Was there something in that? He had been doing nothing else that might attract attention.

"Johnny? Erik?"

They appeared from the darkness. "Johnny, I'm not going to waste your time with explanations, but I've a hunch. Let's all of us stand around the fire and stretch our hands to it. Just warm your hands, palm down."

Erik stared at him. "What the hell's the idea? My hands aren't cold."

"Maybe not, and probably we're wasting time, but I'm playing a hunch. It's just for a minute or two."

Johnny reached his hands to the fire. "If you say so."

"We're being watched, I think. The Saqua are out there, and they have some affinity for fire. I thought maybe if we showed something of the kind, it might help."

"With them?" Johnny asked skeptically. "They're animals. They ain't even human."

"They know the way through."

"Well, that's what's said. Seems like they come an' go as they like. I've heard talk of that."

They stepped back from the fire and Mike went

413

again to the forest's edge for fuel. It would be a long night, and fires were insatiable in their demands. Yet he needed time to think. If it was true the Varanel would not attack in the night, he had time in which to think, to plan. How many times had he told others that it was only the mind of man that distinguished him from animals? That a human being should take the time to think. All right, he told himself grimly, think, damn you! *Think!*

Telling himself to think brought no flood of ideas. He tried examining his situation from every view and could find no ready answer. Somewhere near, there would be an opening, if, indeed, it was not already too late.

Despite all the hiking about he had done, he had at no time been more than ten miles from where he now stood, and he doubted if it were much more than half that. Yet that long-dead river on which they had found the remains of the *Iron Mountain* must have begun far away, and the ill-fated steamer must have steamed north, hoping to find St. Louis or some such river port, only to find nothing and to tie up at last to a deserted riverbank, to move no more.

He, at least, knew what had happened. He did not understand the circumstances, yet he had heard of such things many times. At least, the idea was familiar to him but he doubted whether anyone on the *Iron Mountain* had ever heard of such a thing as happened to them.

Somewhere near was No Man's, Johnny's Hole,

414

and what he couldn't help but think of as the Haunted Mesa. Somewhere, just across that thin line dividing them from his world.

The Anasazi had known how to leave this world and go to his, and they had known how to return when their decision was made. Was Kawasi keeping something from him? Did she not wish them to return?

He stood at the edge of the forest, thinking, then began to gather wood. Something moved in the forest close by.

"For the fire," he said aloud, not hoping to be understood.

There was no sound, no movement. He filled his arms, resolving that if attacked, he would throw the wood into the face of the attacker and then draw his gun. Nothing happened, yet he could distinctly sense the presence of something living. And that odd smell? Yes, it was there.

"We want to go back," he said aloud, hoping somehow to communicate his need.

He withdrew one arm from under the wood, touched himself on the chest, and made a gesture outward, then repeated it with the one hand. "We want to go back," he repeated, and then walked back to the fire.

Johnny had gone to keep watch. Erik was seated, eating some of the trail mix from Raglan's pack. "Sorry," he said, "but I'm starved."

"I don't wonder. Take what you need."

Raglan dumped his wood and stood staring into

415

the flames, then sat down abruptly. "Whatever we do," he said, "we should do before daylight."

Erik wiped his hands on his pants. "Mike," he began, "I—"

Zipacna loomed suddenly, across the fire. He was smiling, obviously pleased that they were startled. "Don't worry about it," he said. "Tomorrow at noon I will show you the way. You can go, all of you."

—— XLII ——

NOBODY MOVED OR spoke, startled by his sudden appearance. Raglan was angered by the man's manner as well as his own carelessness, and at the same moment he knew he must not allow his animosity to affect his judgment.

"Show us the way, Zipacna? To one of your trapped rooms, perhaps? I think not."

"Soon you have no chance."

Raglan shrugged, assuming a nonchalance he did not feel. "So? If we stay, we will simply take over. Your country is ripe for it and we have already demonstrated that the Varanel are not invulnerable.

"The Hand has been wise to exclude outsiders. Over on our side we have a compulsive drive to move into any area that offers opportunity, and your country is dying. It is ripe for a takeover, as you yourself have decided.

"There is opportunity here. There are undoubtedly minerals to be exploited. Conditions would be different but ours are an adaptable people. We have taken to working in many countries, to deep-sea drilling and space travel.

"In fact, Zipacna, I have been thinking about approaching The Hand. He might welcome some controlled innovation."

Raglan had no such idea. He was stalling for time, talking off the top of his head while seeking a way out. What he wanted was to be back on his own side and to forget the whole affair.

Had The Hand a method of listening? Such devices were available in his own world and he already had been told The Hand sought such devices. Suppose he already possessed them and was listening now?

Zipacna was angry and restless. Obviously, he too wished to be free of the situation into which his boldness and his ego had projected him.

There was something else, too. Raglan had been feeling a growing sense of urgency. Was it some change in the atmosphere? Something caused by the approaching spacequake or whatever it was? From their attitudes he knew the others felt it, too.

Johnny put wood on the fire. "You had better go, Zipacna. There's nothing for you here. When we go, we will go our own way."

"You have until daylight," Zipacna said stiffly. "Only until then."

"I think you speak for yourself only," Kawasi said suddenly. "It is you who speaks, not The

417

Hand. You are of the Varanel, not the Lords of Shibalba. I think you reach for power."

"You? What are you? Only a woman!"

"Among my people, I speak and am heard." Her manner was cool, imperious. "You were nothing until somehow you crept through to the other side and learned a little, making yourself useful to The Hand. And then you found out about *her!*"

"Melisande," Erik said. He glanced at Raglan. "The girl of the sunflowers."

Mike Raglan looked from one to the other. What the hell was going on? Who was the girl of the sunflowers? Of course, there had been the missing pencil and the sunflower on the dog's collar, even the sunflower stitched inside the collar of the sweater. Could this be the girl Erik had meant when he spoke of "us."

If so, where was she? Where had she been? And who was she?

"Look," he said impatiently, "if we're going to get out of here, it's got to be now. We haven't the time to hunt up some other girl—"

"I won't go without her," Erik said.

Zipacna was ignored, except by Johnny, who, seated back at the shadow's edge, held his pistol in his hand, his rifle beside him. Johnny was watching Zipacna with sullen, angry eyes, waiting for a wrong move, and Zipacna was aware of it.

Some of the man's arrogant confidence seemed to have deserted him. Nevertheless, he was poised and watchful.

"Where is she?" Raglan demanded. "Whatever is done must be done now."

"She's close by," Kawasi replied.

So suddenly that it caught even Johnny by surprise, Zipacna dropped a hand to a wall and vaulted over into the darkness below. Johnny leaped for the wall but Raglan spoke sharply. "Don't waste the bullet. He's gone and we're well rid of him."

"He'll be back," Johnny said.

Raglan agreed but did not say so. His only thought now was to get out. If that prophecy was true, they had almost no time left, but of course it was an estimate based on a rumor, nothing substantial to it at all. Nonetheless, he was uneasy, with that unsettling sense of impending doom.

"All right, Kawasi," he said, "let's get her and get out. Zipacna will be back, and so will others." He turned to Johnny. "Keep watch. I've got to look around."

Kawasi disappeared, to where he did not know, but she knew this country better than he. He felt for his gun, then went back to what had been an opening.

The door was there but it seemed to have been walled shut with stone. He put his hand out to touch it, then hastily withdrew it. He didn't like the look of it, and glanced over his shoulder again.

Damn it, he had gotten Erik loose and now all they had to do was get back. But how?

He began slowly to turn over in his mind, as he prowled among the ruins, just what he knew or thought he knew. Mentally he drew a map, starting with the window in the kiva where there was an opening—an "always" opening, it was said. Possibly two miles west was the opening through which he had come with Kawasi, an opening also used by Tazzoc. The Saqua had disappeared at No Man's Mesa across the river and about equidistant from the kiva or Tazzoc's opening. This seemed to be the focal point, if such there was, of the anomalous area. It was too dark to make a search, even if he had had more to work with. Disappointed, he returned to the fire and got out his old canvas map. It had been copied from the map on gold, yet there were differences, added by the old man himself.

The one thing that disturbed him was the unexplained red cross marked on the map.

Obviously important, yet he could not at the moment recall anything the old man had said about it. For that matter, he had never explained the map itself.

"Johnny? You've prowled around this country. What do you make of that?"

After a quick glance around, Johnny leaned over his shoulder. "Ain't far from here, not as far as a body might figure," he muttered. "Can't say I've ever been yonder." He stepped back and looked around at the sky-lined ridges. "Used to have a time with cows," he said. "Come wintertime, they'd try to find a place out of the wind. With snow all over everything they'd sometimes halfslide down into some canyon, and come summer, with the snow gone, they couldn't get out.

420

"I've found beef cattle ten, twelve year old that never seen a man, seemed like. Holed up in those canyons with no way out. If lucky they got into one where, come spring, there'd be grass as well as water.

"Left to theirselves, cows can wander a far piece, an' that's how come I found the Hole. I was huntin' strays and here an' yonder I'd rounded up a good many. I rode up to the north end of the Hole and seen all that green. I just knowed cows would find a way down. When I rode back to the outfit I told them what I'd found an' they laughed at me.

" 'Trees, grass, an' water? You're havin' a pipe dream, Johnny.' That's what they said. We boys was always yarnin', o' course, so's there was some reason for them to be doubtful."

He took another long look at the map. He put a finger on a spot near the red cross. "Now that there. Looks like somethin'—"

"What I can't understand is that we were told the opening was controlled. That it wasn't safe, yet when Chief—that's my dog—when he went through, he seemed to be running off into the distance, barking after something. So how could it be so controlled?"

"The Hand has ways, maybe some electronic contrivance, that lets him know when anybody comes through. Or maybe it's some natural effect they've come to understand. Anyway, he does know."

They fell silent, studying the canvas map. Erik

got up and came over to them. "Sorry I've been so much trouble. I was weak as a cat."

"Shouldn't wonder," Johnny said. "Don't give it a thought. When that there Kawasi gets back, we got to make our try."

Mike Raglan looked away, then back at the map, narrowing his vision in hopes something would take shape that he had not seen. He was frightened, and admitted it to himself. He wanted to get out, and he had promised he would lead them. Vaguely, there seemed to be a trail of sorts to that red cross. Why had the old cowboy put it there? Or had he? Perhaps . . .

No, it had to have been the cowboy. There was some significance to that cross, nothing else like it on the map.

Where *was* Kawasi?

"This Melisande, Erik? You've actually seen her? Do you know her?"

"I'm in love with her. First time in my life, Mike, if you can picture that. We met and . . . Well, I don't know what to say. We started to talk. She's the last of them, Mike, the last of that crowd on the steamboat."

"Erik, the *Iron Mountain* vanished in 1872!"

"Her grandfather was aboard, carrying a lot of trade goods to establish a post in Montana, on the Upper Missouri. When the transfer came, nobody knew what to do, but after a few days he accepted it as something he did not comprehend but must live with. He and six others left the boat. The others were clinging to the one thing they understood, to their one grasp of reality.

"Her grandfather scouted the country, found a little valley watered by springs, built a cabin, and moved in with all that belonged to him. There was another couple with some youngsters who came with them. Her grandfather had a son, who became the father of Melisande. Simple as that. Now she's the only one left and she can't handle the gardening as well as the guarding.

"Her grandfather, when he had time to think, began sorting it out." Erik paused. "He must have been a remarkable man, with imagination beyond the ordinary. In his youth his father had kept an inn and he had grown up hearing much speculation by intelligent travelers who stopped by.

"One man who stayed for several weeks was a doctor who had formerly had charge of a hospital for the insane, and one man brought to him had been found wandering in the woods by a farmer.

"The man was dressed oddly and seemed to speak no known language, and had been put down as mildly insane. After a few conversations the doctor thought otherwise and began to spend time with the man. Then he discovered the man possessed a remarkable skill at drawing.

"Supplied with materials, the man drew an accurate pen-and-ink sketch of the farm where he had been found. Then he drew a vertical line, and on the other side drew a picture of a totally different world. In that world he drew a figure of a man. He touched that figure with his finger, then

423

himself, indicating the man in the drawing was himself.

"Then he had drawn a second figure of himself showing him passing through the line, and then a third picture showing him standing where he was found by the farmer.

"It was obviously an attempt by the man to explain what had happened, but others ridiculed the whole idea. However, nobody objected when the doctor had the man placed in his custody. He then learned English, adapted himself to life in his new country, patented a few minor inventions (or were they memories?) and settled easily into the life.

"Stories of the supernatural had been much in vogue during Melisande's grandfather's time. It was the period when Mary Shelley wrote *Franken-stein*. There was Irving's *Legend of Sleepy Hollow*, and the many stories by Poe and others of the kind.

"Melisande grew up with such tales and others told by her grandfather. He, as a matter of fact, outlived his son, her father. Realizing she would soon be alone, he explained what she must do.

"There was, he assured her, most certainly a way back. She had only to discover it and return to her own people. He had come upon some evidence to help her.

"He explained that while he did not pretend to understand the phenomena that caused the inter-changes, he had learned something of the conditions surrounding them. From the instant of the arrival of the *Iron Mountain* in this world, he had, because of the tales he had heard, understood what must have happened. Instead of bemoaning his ill fortune he began to ask himself how it happened and how it could be reversed.

"From her earliest childhood he had instructed Melisande in what life on the Other Side was like and what she must do. She must watch for the unexpected, for unnatural phenomena, and he had found three places which he suspected were important.

"Each day he set aside time for observation or exploration, and during the periods of observation he began to notice a reflection from one spot in the rugged country that did not appear to be from a rock or from water. When he went into the desert he found the reflection came from a mesa, a mesa that proved to be the secret hideout of He Who Had Magic. The reflection was from a piece of metallic equipment."

"Melisande told you this?"

"We were prisoners together, and I promised if I escaped I would take her back with me. But she escaped first. I do not know how." He paused. "I think Zipacna freed her."

"*Zipacna?*"

"He's an opportunist, and she was his opportunity. The Varanel had her, but he wanted credit for the capture. He wanted to deliver her himself to The Hand. I believe he felt sure he could take her again, when he wished, and when it would serve his purpose."

425

There was a scurry of movement and Johnny came around sharply, his pistol lifting.

Mike stepped into the shadows, his own gun drawn.

It was Kawasi, and with her another girl, a tall, blond girl, lithe and lovely.

"Now!" Kawasi said. "We have far to go before it is light. *Quickly!*"

XLIII

MIKE BUILT UP the fire, adding fuel and clearing debris from around it so the flames could not spread, and then they went away into the night.

They went away along the side of the ridge by a trail almost too narrow to see. Only their feet found the way, and they went into the hills.

The night was cool and there was no wind, nor were there stars or any light at all but a vague, somewhere moon.

Melisande took the lead and Mike followed third behind Kawasi, then Erik and Johnny, his rifle reloaded and ready.

It was so dark, Mike could not see Kawasi only a few feet ahead of him. Sandhills rose around them and, in the distance, the sheer walls of a mesa, and there were scattered towers of rock like fingers upheld in warning.

It was a fit night for ghosts, too dark for shadows, too black for anything but thought to penetrate. Like ghosts they moved, with only a whispering as their feet touched the ground and lifted. They wove among rocks, their moving bodies like needles in a tapestry of darkness. Melisande led the way and they followed on faith, trusting to her and to their feeling feet, searching out the way with each step along the ground.

They were mounting higher—this their legs told them, and their breathing, for Melisande moved swiftly, wasting no time. Finally, topping out on a ledge, she stopped and they gathered about her.

Mike had a bad feeling about the night. Something within him warned of trouble coming and he peered about, irritated that he could not see and that he must trust to another, not knowing where they went.

Johnny was beside him. "I think we're headed for that red cross on the map," he said. "I know some of this country."

"It's more than I do. I've no idea where we're going."

"Don't worry about it. That girl's lived her life here, knows it all better than me or any of them out there. She'd be a real catch for The Hand. I suspect he's had wind o' them for years, knowing they were somewhere out there.

"Her grandpa must have been some shakes of a man, carryin' on like he done, always figurin' to find a way out for her."

"What I'm worried about is that spacequake or whatever it is. We're overdue."

"Nobody ever said those things was on schedule. They happen when they happen. All a body can do is hope. An', Mister, I'm hopin'—an' doin' a little prayin' on the side."

Kawasi came back to them. "We will go on now, but stay close to the wall. On your right it drops away for several hundred feet."

"Should be daylight soon."

Mike moved over to Johnny. "Want me to bring up the rear? I can handle it."

"No doubt you could, but you ain't carryin' a long rifle. I don't want to be proddin' anybody on a cliff trail."

"Do you know where we are?"

"Guessin' is all I can do. She's been windin' around some." He paused. "Raglan? You get set for a scrap. There's somebody comin' up behind us."

It was no more than he had expected. Mike Raglan turned in behind Kawasi. Erik had moved up behind Melisande, so Mike was now fourth in line.

There were flakes of fallen rock under their feet now and once in a while one would get pushed off into the vast depths on their right. They could hear a rock falling, striking something below, then falling again.

They were climbing now. Starting out, they had gone down for several hundred yards. Then the trail became steep and they were climbing up. He kept his shoulder against the wall, and occasionally had to use handholds. Yet it was growing lighter, only vaguely but enough so he could now see the path on which they climbed.

Again they paused. Erik or Melisande was moving a rock from their path. He heard it fall, a small cascade of rocks following it. "Where are we going?" Mike asked Kawasi.

"It is said to be an opening. An always place. He Who Had Magic had a look-through glass pointed at it. He was watching to see who came and went, or maybe how it happened—I do not know."

They went on again, climbing more steeply. Mike was an agile and athletic man, but the climbing was not easy. He turned to look back. Johnny was very old, yet he seemed to be making out all right.

They emerged suddenly into daylight, or what passed for it in this strange, yellow world.

The plateau about them was scattered with juniper, none over a dozen feet tall, most much shorter. There were a few scattered rock formations, a little grass, some scattered pools of water caught from recent rains or melted snow, none more than two inches deep.

On their right was a huge red scar, scoured out from the top of the mesa. In the distance he could see a vast spread of canyons, mesas, and volcanic necks, all blue with morning light.

"Come," Melisande said. "It is only a little way now."

"You've been here before?"

She looked at him. "You are Mike? It is you he hoped would come. He said if anyone could get him out, you could."

"Without you we'd be nowhere."

She shrugged. "There are other places. This is the only one of which we can be sure."

She started away and he caught her arm. "Wait!" he whispered. "And look!"

About fifty yards away, Volkmeer was standing, a rifle in his hands.

"Who is he?" Kawasi asked. "Is it—"

"Volkmeer. He's supposed to be a friend of mine but he's taken money from them."

"Melisande? Where is the opening? I don't see—"

"You can't see. It is near that rock. The big one that looks like a dinosaur? Keep to the left and keep your eyes on the horizon. Look at the rounded mountain. Do not take your eyes from it. The opening is small, almost a window. When you are there you will see."

"Don't look like they're goin' to let us," Johnny said. "Do I start shootin'?"

"Wait," Erik said. "It is only one man."

Mike moved ahead. "Hi, Volk! Didn't know you ever came over to this side."

"Time or two." His rifle tilted. "Can't let you go no further, Mike."

"So you've turned against us, Volk? I didn't expect it of you."

"Didn't expect it of me neither. Then I got to thinkin'. I ain't a young man no more an' I been livin' soft on their money. You done me a turn one time, an' I'm obliged, but that don't cut no ice now."

430

"You've still got a chance, Volk. Remember? You said once that one time I could do it all. I still can, Volk, and I've learned a lot since then."

"Maybe, but I ain't alone."

"Kawasi? Melisande? When the shooting starts, *run!* Get through that opening, no matter how! Take Erik with you, even if you have to drag him. He's not armed, and we are."

Melisande hesitated. "The tubes they have are weapons. They must be within sixty feet to be effective."

"Get going," he said.

Volkmeer moved to stop them and Mike called out: "The last time, Volk! Get out of this!"

"Like hell! I—"

He swung his rifle as Raglan moved, and fired. He saw Volk's knees buckle and the man collapsed into a sitting position, his rifle falling across his ankles.

Behind him Mike heard Johnny's gun boom, and turned in time to see a row of Varanel rising from the ground, already nearly within range.

Johnny dropped his rifle and drew his six-shooter and fired rapidly. Mike joined in, and the line fell back. The girls were almost at the rock and he yelled at Johnny, "Let's go, John! Back off and run!"

Johnny started backing toward them. Then, glancing around, he yelled, "Mike! Look *out!*"

Raglan turned swiftly, but not swiftly enough. A blow struck his gun hand and he dropped his pistol.

Zipacna was facing him, smiling. "Now, you will begin to learn! And when we have put you away we shall teach you more!"

His right wrist was numb with pain, and Zipacna was closing in, his stick lifted to strike. He struck and Mike ducked under the blow and in close, not as Zipacna expected. Stooping low to avoid the blow, Mike swung a kick with his left foot, catching Zipacna on the knee. The larger man's leg folded and he fell forward. Mike hit him as he was falling.

Yet Zipacna rolled over and came up swiftly, favoring his leg but able to move. Now he was wary, but moving in, sure of himself.

Johnny was firing again. The Varanel were circling, holding back, but surrounding them on all sides. A quick glance showed Mike the girls and Erik were gone.

There was no time now. Zipacna was closing in, wary, but smiling and confident. Every people had some system of self-defense. What was his?

Johnny had found a place in the rocks and was reloading his rifle and replacing the empty cylinder of his pistol with another. That was the old way, for when loading took time, a man who needed a gun often carried fully loaded cylinders that could be quickly put in place.

"Johnny." Mike spoke loudly but he was watching Zipacna. "Get through the hole. You've no time."

"I ain't leavin' you."

432

"You've got to. When I get a chance I'll make my break."

"You have no chance," Zipacna said. "Now I kill you!"

He took a quick, fencer's lunge with his left fingers stiffly extended, stabbing for Mike's eye. Mike ducked in time and the stabbing hand skidded around his skull. But those extended fingers were like steel.

Mike feinted, then smashed a left to the body and missed a crossing right to the chin. Zipacna stepped back, then another of those stabbing lunges. The stiff fingers hit Mike just above the eye and cut deep, showering him with blood. Zipacna sprang close and tried to throw him with a rolling hip lock.

Mike stabbed his own fingers down into a spot just above the hipbone, and Zipacna's knees buckled. He fell and Mike fell with him. They both lunged to their feet, and Mike took a quick glance toward the place of the opening.

Zipacna struck again with the stabbing fingers, and again they cut deep. Blood streaming down his face, Mike dodged another stabbing blow and slipped inside, smashing both fists to the body, then whipping a right hook over Zipacna's shoulder that split his cheekbone.

Zipacna staggered and Mike moved in, smashing another hook to the body, and then a left that crunched Zipacna's nose. Zipacna staggered, then fell. Scrambling to his feet, he fought like a madman, clawing at Mike's face with steellike fingers.

Mike slammed another blow to the body, but it was corded with muscle. Nevertheless, Zipacna winced at the blow, and Mike put everything he had into a right uppercut, turning his body with the weight behind it.

The fist collided with Zipacna's chin. His feet left the ground and he came down hard.

Turning swiftly, Mike lunged for the opening he hoped was there.

In that flashing instant he saw that Johnny was gone, but just as he reached the spot, something thrown hard from behind struck him behind the ear.

He felt himself falling, and in that last instant of consciousness he lunged forward, then fell, face down. Something seized him violently by the collar and he was jerked along the ground. Desperately, only half-conscious, he tried to struggle, but the vicious grip on his collar would not yield. He was dragged roughly along the ground, and in that instant his last grip on consciousness failed.

Blood.

There was blood on the ground where he lay. The side of his face was against the earth and his eyes were open and he was staring at blood on the grass, blood on the sand.

It was his blood. His mind told him that, although he could not have explained how he knew. He moved a hand, wanting to touch his face.

"Hey! He's comin' out of it! He isn't dead yet."

"Hard man to kill," somebody said.

434

Somebody knelt beside him and gentle fingers touched his face. "He's cut on the forehead," somebody said, and then a woman's voice said, "It was Zipacna."

The voice was that of Kawasi.

"I'm all right." He spoke aloud. "Somebody threw something, hit me on the back of the head."

"You were hit, all right." That was Gallagher speaking. "You've got a welt back there as big as both my fists."

Struggling, Mike sat up. "I'm all right," he repeated. "Something grabbed me back there."

"It was Chief," Gallagher said. "He pulled you through."

"He what?"

"Grabbed you by the collar and pulled you through—just in time."

Carefully, Raglan got to his feet. He swayed for an instant, then steadied himself. "Did anything else come through?" He looked at Kawasi. "I mean, except our crowd?"

"Nobody. Nothing."

"Mike?" It was Erik Hokart. "Thanks. Thanks for both of us."

"It was nothing," he lied, "simply nothing at all."

He looked around. "Where are we?"

Gallagher hooked his thumbs behind his belt. "On top of No Man's, waiting for a helicopter to take us off."

"Isn't there a trail? There was supposed to be a trail."

"There is one," Gallagher said, "but we haven't found it yet. You come over with me next week and I'll hike it with you."

His head throbbed with a dull, heavy ache. Tentatively, he touched his brow. It was caked with dried blood now. He had been cut to the bone at least twice.

He wanted to get cleaned up, and then he wanted to lie down. He just wanted to rest, to sleep. He wanted to sleep for a week. He said as much.

"Not yet," Gallagher said, "I've got something to show you."

He would not explain.

The helicopter took them back to the Haunted Mesa.

At the ruin, Erik began gathering his belongings, and Mike picked up his backpack. He could see his car, not too far away. "We'll go back to Tamarron," he said to Kawasi. "Erik, you'd better bring Melisande and come with me. You, too, Johnny. There's plenty of room."

"Mike?" Gallagher said. "Got something you should see. That there spacequake or whatever it was happened last night. Happened just after Chief pulled you through the hole. Seems like ever'body wasn't so lucky."

"What do you mean?"

Gallagher had been leading him toward the kiva. Now he lifted a hand and pointed.

Where the window had been there were some fallen stones, and behind them an intact stone wall. Intact but for one thing.

A human body cannot pass through a solid. Or can it? The brick wall was there, and in the middle of it was Volkmeer's head, a shoulder, and one arm with a grasping hand.

The stones of the ancient wall, apparently undisturbed for centuries, were built around him, perhaps even through him. Somewhere on the other side was the rest of him, the part that did not make it through.

Volkmeer was dead. To all intents and purposes he might have been dead, almost mummified, for centuries.

"Try explaining that," Gallagher said. "Just try."

"You explain it," Raglan said. "I'm a stranger here myself."

They stood silent for a minute, and then Gallagher said, "Eden's gone. Deeded the place to Mary and just pulled out."

At the helicopter Gallagher said, "Want me to fly you back?"

"We'll drive," Raglan said, "But thanks." He paused a minute, then said, "Gallagher? Did you ever make fire with a bow and blunt arrow?"

"Sure. Lots of times when I was a youngster. An old Paiute showed me how."

Mike Raglan walked out away from the ruin, and thrust a stick in the ground, tying a red bandana to the end. "They should be able to see that," he said.

At the base of it he placed a crude bow, fashioned from a somewhat bent stick and a piece of rawhide, which he looped around a blunt arrow. Taking a short board from the ruin he gouged out a hole to receive the end of the arrow, then cut a notch from the hole to the edge of the board. In the hole he placed a few shavings; at the notch, the tinder for a small fire.

From his backpack he took a small magnifying glass and placed it on the top of a rock nearby.

Gallagher shook his head. "What's all that about? I don't get it."

"For the Saqua," Raglan said. "They need fire, they worship fire, but I don't believe they know how to make fire."

Kawasi was waiting for him at the car. Melisande and Erik were in the back seat.

Gallagher had walked over with him. "You're leaving, then?" He waved a hand. "What about all this?"

"All of what?" Mike Raglan looked at him wide-eyed. "I don't know what you are talking about, Gallagher. Erik thought about building a house out here but changed his mind. We came out to get him. That's all there is."

"Are you crazy? You've got the greatest story ever. You could write a book, you could—"

Mike Raglan started the car. He looked over at Gallagher, extending his hand.

"I could," he said, "but who'd believe it?"

The End

Author's Note

XIBALBA: also written as Shibalba, is frequently referred to in the *Popol Vuh,* the sacred book of the Quiché Maya, as the lower regions where lived tormentors of men, and a home of all things evil. It is mentioned in *The Annals of the Cakchiquels* as an underground place of great power and splendor.

HOUSE OF GLOOM: in Xibalba, a place of darkness and shadows, known to few, feared by all.

LORDS OF XIBALBA: referred to in the *Popol Vuh* as promoters of evil and destruction.

VARANEL: the Night Guards, soldiers of the Lords of Xibalba.

ZIPACNA: a mythological figure of great power, finally destroyed, or at least defeated, by Hunahpu.

ANASAZI: We do not know what the cliff dwellers called themselves or what they were called by their neighbors. The name is of Navajo origin and was given to the ancient ones who preceded the Navajo in the Four Corners area. That there was trade and communication between the Anasazi and the Maya is well established. Mummified parrots from Central America have been found in Anasazi graves. Archaeologists have been slowly piecing together the story of the cliff dwellers from fragments of pottery, weaving, sandals, and such, but they are hampered by the thoughtless vandalism of pot-hunters, who by removing a pot from its place of discovery make it impossible to place it properly in history. Often it is similar to removing several key pieces from a jigsaw puzzle, then expecting the puzzle to be completed.

Much fine, painstaking work has been done, yet we have only begun to learn what the Anasazi have to teach us. I, for one, believe man's life on this continent and our neighbor continent to the south is much, much longer than has been surmised.

A note on the text
Large print edition designed by
Kipling West.
Composed in 16 pt Plantin
on a Xyvision 300/Linotron 202N
by Genevieve Connell
of G.K. Hall & Co.